"JEFF GREENFIELD DOES D.C.—TO A TURN."
—*PEOPLE*

"Funny, savvy, savage, entertaining. . . ." —Mike Wallace

"A political thriller with wit and truth." —*Hartford Courant*

"A scarily plausible scenario . . . provides many ripe targets for satire." —*Los Angeles Times*

"A delightful novel . . . you'll laugh till you cry." —*Atlanta Journal*

"Jeff Greenfield sorts through the sordid truths and falsehoods about who really runs the country . . . includes a wonderful cast of characters." —*New York Daily News*

"Smart, sharp, funny, wicked." —*Entertainment Weekly*

"Riotous . . . wonderfully funny political satire . . . a civics lesson wrapped up as comedy." —*USA Today*

"The meanest, funniest, liveliest, most provocative smart-mouthed political novel . . . well researched and fast paced." —*San Antonio Express-News*

JEFF GREENFIELD is an Emmy Award-winning political and media analyst for ABC News. He appears regularly on *Nightline* and *World News Tonight*, has a weekly column on *World News Sunday*, and writes for the Universal Press Syndicate. The author of several nonfiction books, he lives in New York City and Salisbury, Connecticut.

ALSO BY JEFF GREENFIELD

THE ADVANCE MAN (*with Jerry Bruno*)

A POPULIST MANIFESTO (*with Jack Newfield*)

NO PEACE, NO PLACE: EXCAVATIONS ALONG THE GENERATIONAL FAULT

THE WORLD'S GREATEST TEAM

TELEVISION: THE FIRST FIFTY YEARS

NATIONAL LAMPOON'S BOOK OF BOOKS

PLAYING TO WIN: AN INSIDER'S GUIDE TO POLITICS

THE REAL CAMPAIGN

THE PEOPLE'S CHOICE

★ ★ ★

JEFF GREENFIELD

A PLUME BOOK

PLUME
Published by the Penguin Group
Penguin Books USA Inc., 375 Hudson Street, New York, New York 10014, U.S.A.
Penguin Books Ltd, 27 Wrights Lane, London W8 5TZ, England
Penguin Books Australia Ltd, Ringwood, Victoria, Australia
Penguin Books Canada Ltd, 10 Alcorn Avenue, Toronto, Ontario, Canada M4V 3B2
Penguin Books (N.Z.) Ltd, 182–190 Wairau Road, Auckland 10, New Zealand

Penguin Books Ltd, Registered Offices: Harmondsworth, Middlesex, England

Published by Plume, an imprint of Dutton Signet,
a division of Penguin Books USA Inc.
This is an authorized reprint of a hardcover edition published by G. P. Putnam's Sons.
For information address: G. P. Putnam's Sons, 200 Madison Avenue, New York, New York 10016.

First Plume Printing, September, 1996
10 9 8 7 6 5 4 3 2

LIBRARY OF CONGRESS CATALOGING-IN-PUBLICATION DATA
Greenfield, Jeff.
The people's choice : a cautionary tale / Jeff Greenfield.
p. cm.
ISBN 0-452-27705-1
1. Presidents—United States—Election—Fiction. I. Title.
PS3557.R39423P46 1996
813'.54—dc20 96–16389
CIP

Printed in the United States of America

PUBLISHER'S NOTE
This is a work of fiction. Names, characters, places, and incidents either are the product of the author's imagination or are used fictitiously, and any resemblance to actual persons, living or dead, events, or locales is entirely coincidental.

To my father, Ben Greenfield, who taught me to love baseball,
the Marx Brothers, punctuality, W. C. Fields,
and who was always, always there.

ACKNOWLEDGMENTS

When I first imagined this book some fifteen years ago, I needed someone to find real, live presidential electors. A young researcher, Sarah Turner, proved to be invaluable in conducting interviews with a wide variety of electors.

In 1987, I spent six months at what is now known as the Freedom Forum Media Studies Center in New York, researching this subject. Ev Dennis, who ran the place then and now, was remarkably supportive in permitting me to work on a project that would turn into a work of fiction rather than scholarship.

While at the center, I was lucky enough to be assigned a researcher named Jeffrey Trout, then a Columbia Law School student. He unearthed a treasure trove of legal and political material, without which this book could not have been done.

My long-suffering literary agent, Sterling Lord, has waited roughly a quarter century for me to turn out a work of fiction. My thanks for his patience and faith.

Speaking of patience, Neil Nyren, my editor, suffered through endless periods of silence without resorting to violence. His encouragement and advice kept me going.

So did a group known as "The Palmenis," five friends with whom I lunch just about every week. They are (in alphabetical order) Andrew Bergman, Jerry Della Femina, Dr. Gerald Imber, Michael Kramer, and Joel Siegel. Without their constant, incessant sarcastic and belittling comments, I would not have been inspired to finish.

More constructive encouragement came from a book by Anne Lamont, *Bird by Bird.* I commend this to anyone who needs a wise, witty voice.

To my parents, Ben and Helen; to my children, Casey and Dave; to my wife, Karen Gannett, my thanks for all they have taught me, and all that they mean to me.

"The Electoral College is the most dangerous blot on our Constitution, and one which some unlucky chance will one day hit."

—Thomas Jefferson, 1823.

"On Election Day … the United States once again played a reckless game with its destiny. This time, we were lucky. Next time, we might not be. Next time, we might wreck our country."

—James Michener, 1969.

PART ONE

THINGS FALL APART....

ONE

★ ★ ★

The walls were coming down all around him.

Panels of tinted Plexiglas, strips of chrome, sheets of steel were piled up in corners of the cavernous room. Dozens of workmen, dressed in the grimy overalls and sweat-stained work shirts of the laboring classes, paid by wage scales that were once the dreams of kings, pounded and pulled and wrenched the slabs of Formica and the computer consoles loose from their moorings.

Thirty-six hours ago, this huge hall had been lit by a hundred lights, packed with a hundred bodies, some of them instantly recognizable in twenty million homes, most as obscure as the lean, sandy-haired man of early middle age who sat happily at the keyboard of the room's last working computer. From across the continent, reams of print and countless bits of electronic data had flowed into the room, had been digested, massaged, reshaped, oversimplified, and flung back out again to tell a nation what it had done and why.

Now the room was being returned to its traditional purpose; from the costly, increasingly unattended business of covering the election of a President of the United States, it was going back to its regular, infinitely more lucrative purpose: the weekly professional football highlights show. The wall-sized map of the United States, with each state lit in red or blue to signify the victorious party, lay dismantled in a far corner; a wall-sized football, with computerized color-codes signifying victor and vanquished, was being hauled back into place by two oversized forklifts bearing six oversized stagehands.

Al DeRossa saw none of this, heard none of the chaos. The embodiment of the last two years of his life was being demolished—"teardown," they called it—but as he sat in front of the oversized monitor, Al DeRossa was a blissfully happy man. Maybe his prominent forehead was extending up toward the crown of his head, maybe his bank balance was in near perfect equipoise with his next support payment, maybe he had heard the word *politics* used as a sneer by the research crowd on the thirty-seventh floor once too often, but none of that mattered now.

In front of him was an IKXS 27000 Series computer, with a hard disk big enough to store the contents of a midsize city's main library. Telephone wires linked the IKXS to 6,200 miles of magnetic tape, and 475 laser discs, stored in temperature-controlled office suites in Rutherford, New Jersey; Oak Brook, Illinois; Vinings, Georgia; and Long Beach, California. Every five days for two years, hundreds of part-time workers had sat at computer consoles, dialing randomly selected phone numbers, persuading the wary, suspicious voices at the other end of the line to share their lives with a total stranger.

Forty-eight hours ago, on Election Day morning, more than ten thousand workers had positioned themselves outside schools, courthouses, town halls, apartment lobbies, general stores, and VFW headquarters, where the country went to vote. They asked those leaving the polls the questions Al DeRossa and his colleagues wanted asked. Astonishingly, almost no one told the inquisitors to leave them alone, to mind their own business, or to perform a complicated anatomical act. Instead, they told "Al's Army," as his friends called it, whom they had voted for, and why, and when they had made up their mind, and how much education they had, and roughly how much money they made, and what their favorite television programs were, and what they wanted the next President to do.

By noon on Election Day, Al DeRossa and his counterparts at the other major television networks, and at half a dozen of the nation's biggest newspapers, had a fairly clear idea of what would happen; information that they rigorously withheld from the public, on the ground that it might persuade them to stay home, but information that was the eager lunch talk of the political-journalistic community at expense-account restaurants from New York to Washington to Chicago to Los Angeles.

"What have you got?" the Anchor muttered into a pay phone outside the men's room of Le Mot Juste, whose headwaiter, Dominique, took reservations on an unlisted phone only.

"Whaddya hear?" rasped Chicago's most celebrated columnist, whose man-of-the-neighborhoods style and bearing earned him a six-figure income and five-figure speaking fees.

"So?" drawled the L.A. radio talk-show king, whose easygoing interview style had led a dozen celebroids into headline-making revelations, and who had named his boat *Enough Rope*.

Al DeRossa had taken these calls and dozens more, because twenty years in the news business had taught him the virtues of being an honest broker in the coin of the realm. He felt the buzz that came with knowing he was at the center of a really good story: a close election for the presidency, one where it was genuinely impossible to say who would win until some votes were actually counted.

And later, when the network's Election Night coverage began, he had the sense that he was in command on the bridge of a great ship in the middle of uncertain seas. It was his job to sift and winnow the data, to look at the computer simulations that told him New Jersey was eighty percent certain for Foyle and Block, to check the sample precincts one more time, and then to make the call, signal the technician to light up the blue light, press the key that linked him directly to the Anchor to let him know, "We're calling New Jersey for Foyle." No one had to tell DeRossa that if one of his troops, wired on three hours' sleep in three nights, had tapped the wrong numbers into the computer, if one of his $4.50-an-hour pulse takers had decided to duck into an air-conditioned fast-food joint, and had filled in those questionnaires on his own, then his New Jersey call might rest on quicksand. Then the Anchor would have to tell his millions that, no, "we were a bit premature in calling New Jersey for the Republicans," and in a hundred newspapers the next day, the army of media monitors would point to this moment as the network's prize blunder of the evening, and a hundred graduate students in media studies would wonder if this might make a fine master's thesis ("Al DeRossa and the New Jersey Projection: A Case Study in Media Arrogance").

It had not happened; the calls that Al DeRossa made had held up, and it was his California projection—California would decide it, they had known that since about two-thirty in the afternoon—that had enabled the Network to beat the competition by two and a half minutes, allowing the Anchor to declare: "We can in fact now project that MacArthur Foyle has been elected President of the United States."

All through that evening, DeRossa and company had coaxed the numbers out of the web of wires and screens, packaging the insights into one-sentence epiphanies for the Anchor and the Distinguished Commentator. Was it a soft economy that had almost done in Foyle? Yes, that had put the Rust Belt back in play, had swung Illinois and Ohio back to the Democrats, had almost cost the Republicans Alabama and Georgia.

Had Bill Mueller helped himself by going back to the old Democratic hymnbook, the tub-thumping "us against themism," the dire warnings that "our economic birthright has been put in jeopardy by a little band of malicious malefactors"? Apparently so; in the last two weeks of the campaign, the once-safe lead of Mack Foyle had eroded just enough to turn a comfortable victory into a nail-biter. Along with the steelworkers of Pennsylvania, the rubber workers of Ohio, the furniture makers of North Carolina, a good-sized chunk of the new white working class—the airline reservations agents, the real estate saleswomen in suburban Portland, the clerks in the video rental outlet in Arizona—had come home to the party of their parents.

And what about Ted Block? How close had the new Vice President come to derailing Foyle's bid for the White House? DeRossa had been adamant about this issue from the moment the choice was announced to a stunned Republican convention, through the conservative movement's halfhearted attempt to organize a protest vote against him, through the stumbling campaign that had inspired a thousand handmade signs ("Hello, Blockhead!"), and that had led an increasingly nervous Foyle campaign to dispatch Block to Alaska for the last four days of the election. ("Whatsa matter?" snarled a top aide to a handful of sarcastic reporters. "You guys got something against Eskimos?")

No, DeRossa argued, vice-presidential candidates don't decide elections. But for this election, the polls told a different story: the combination of Block's suspect loyalty and suspect intellect had helped push the undecided voters back to the Democrats; the resurrection of one of the most venerable political ads—the steady, ominous sound of a heartbeat playing under a photo of a slightly cockeyed Ted Block—had done its job. By Election Day, sixty percent of those polled said they regarded Block as unqualified to be President of the United States.

These exit poll results were reported to the viewers throughout Election Night by a radiantly confident, impeccably dressed, splendidly muscle-toned, dewy-lipped, thirty-two-year-old network correspondent who earned $450,000 a year, and who believed that Beirut was a province of El Salvador. Now, for almost every American, all this was old news; now it was time for the press to begin investing the newly chosen President with attributes they had never seemed to find in the stories and profiles and backgrounds and interviews of the dozen years when Mack Foyle was in the public eye.

Now Foyle's love of lascivious jokes had become "earthy humor." Now his warped view of American history—he once said that the internment of Japanese-Americans during World War II "was really for their own good"—had become "a bedrock faith in his country's nobility." Now Mrs. Greta Foyle, a relentless social climber whose affection for her friends was in direct proportion to their net worth, had become "the symbol of the New Glamour."

No one cared about Al DeRossa's facts and figures now. And that was just fine with him. He had been sitting at his computer for the better part of fifteen hours, with only an occasional break for caffeine, cholesterol, and a bathroom. He chewed on an unlit Montecristo #3, a concession to the Health Police, and to the benighted tastes of a younger generation that had never been taught the pleasures of a good cigar, and gulped down an endless succession of cups of Earl Grey tea. Once in a while the phone would ring, with another invitation to another symposium on "How the Media Covered the Election," invitations Al routinely refused unless they were taking place in Florida, California, or the Caribbean between Election Day and Easter. Otherwise, he tuned out the hammering and drilling, the crash of metal and plastic, the laughter and the cursing. Al DeRossa was in "the Zone."

He wasn't seeing images on a computer screen. He was seeing faces, families, neighborhoods, villages, and towns. He was looking at men and women filing into a warehouse in Nashua, New Hampshire, store owners staring out of their windows looking at a dying Main Street in Tama, Iowa. He was seeing old people, spry and comfortable, batting tennis balls back and forth at a Fort Lauderdale condo, and cadaverous, long-haired men standing outside the 7-Eleven in Amenia, New York, waiting for their wives and children, the wives two years younger and thirty pounds heavier than their mates.

Al had spent his working life talking with these people from one end of the country to the other. He was a born listener, the kind of man who could walk into a firehouse in Chicago at 3:00 P.M., face a dozen faces looking suspiciously at this stranger, and be invited to stay for dinner by nightfall. He could wander into a bar in Miami's Little Havana, and be swapping stories within an hour. He could ring a doorbell in Compton, California, and find himself drinking tea and eating homemade brownies that were cooked by the lady of the house, who'd tell Al about her son the computer programmer and her daughter the army officer.

Yet, unlike so many of his contemporaries who saw in high technology the death of real reporting, Al DeRossa had fallen in love with it at once. When the Network had come courting seven years ago, when they had first tried to beckon him away from his job at *America's Finest Newspaper,* they had sat him down with Richard Wilkins, the twenty-two-year-old high-school dropout who had helped develop the IKXS Retrieval System.

"You ever get to deal with real live people?" Al asked Wilkins, as he sat among the reams of computer printouts, the shelves of tapes and disks. Wilkins looked at Al like a patient father dealing with a slow seven-year-old.

"What do you think all this is, Al?" Wilkins asked him. "This is simply what you'd do if you could travel, read, and write with the speed of light. You want to know what single-parent baby-boomer housewives in the Southwest worry about? Go ahead; catch a plane to Phoenix and spend a month knocking on doors. Or"—Wilkins paused and hit three keys on his computer—"or you could find out right here. You think you'd like to know why college kids don't vote? Sure, take a nice, three-week tour of the Big Ten. But"—*click click*—"I can tell you right now if you'd like. It isn't a hunk of machinery, Al," Wilkins said, "it's simply the best reporter that never lived."

Two hours later, Al DeRossa walked into the offices of the managing editor of *America's Finest Newspaper* and quit. The next day, he was sitting by Richard Wilkins's side as the young man began his tour of the massive information retrieval system. Now, seven years later, Al had become Wilkins's best pupil, able to program IKXS so that it would tell him everything he needed to know about what was on the mind of America. At times, he almost felt as if he could hear the voices behind the statistics and percentages arrayed before him:

- The third-generation welder at Ford's River Rouge plant outside Detroit: "If I'm making more than my dad ever did, how come he bought a four-bedroom home for us while Mom stayed home, and I'm stuck in a garden apartment while my wife's working a thirty-five-hour week at a Piggly Wiggly checkout line?";
- The young lawyer at a high-toned law firm in Manhattan: "So I'm pulling down $78,000 one year out of school, and I paid more for dinner last night than I paid for a month's rent in New Haven; and how come I listen to my uncle talk about his days in the Peace Corps and I want to cry?";
- The housewife in Greeley, Colorado: "My kids come home from school and they want T-shirts with filthy words on them; we can't watch a TV show without somebody making some nasty joke about sex; I've got a nine-year-old boy who wants to dress in black and wear an earring, and somebody tell me how I raise the kids when I'm surrounded by a moral septic tank?"

They were all there speaking to you if you just knew how to listen, Al DeRossa believed, and so he sat at his terminal, pulling together the pieces of a giant puzzle that would sooner or later fall into place. Above him stretched a bank of monitors with the midday offerings of the miracle that was television. From a hundred different sources, signals were speeding along coaxial cables and microwave relays, were being flung

22,000 miles in space, where geosynchronous satellites, orbiting in a fixed position in the skies, instantly beamed these signals 22,000 miles down to receiving stations across the North American continent, bringing to anyone who wished to see, comedies that were driven from the commercial networks thirty-five years ago, earnest talk among cross-dressing gym teachers, daytime dramas of lubricious desires among the professional classes, and an all-news channel that was broadcasting, live, the newly elected President's first public appearance, at a massive rodeo celebration in Cheyenne, Wyoming.

Al DeRossa never even looked at this cornucopia. Like the captain of a giant airliner, he stared ahead at his computer console, flying slow and low across the country, mapping the contours of its soul. There was nothing about the choosing of the next President that could not be found here, Al thought.

That's what he thought.

TWO

★ ★ ★

Dead meat.

The smell of dead meat, from the uneaten portions of half a dozen hamburgers, three steak sandwiches, four sirloins, permeated the room.

It wasn't just dead meat, of course. Empty beer bottles, aluminum pots half filled with last night's coffee, this morning's coffee, three dozen cigarette butts, a hundred or more french fries covered with congealed ketchup on a dozen plates all helped give the room the distinct aroma of a lunch counter at a bus terminal in Newark, And since the Golden Lasso Motor Court's executive suite was nothing more than two rooms linked by a connecting door, the remnants of the meals were scattered across the two double beds where a roomful of the best political operatives were gathered for several hours of a frank and open exchange of views.

"You're dead meat!" Marsh had screamed at the press secretary, the pollster, the speechwriter, the senior adviser, the advance man, the room-service waiter, and the woman from the phone company. Marsh was the campaign manager for MacArthur Foyle, President-elect of the United States. He had spent six years working toward this day. Even now, dozens of corporate executives were poring over address books and Rolodexes, searching for a friend or client or associate who might have some line into Marsh. Five-hundred-dollar-an-hour lawyers were calling long-forgotten clients who might know Marsh, while visions of black robes and gavels danced in their heads. Washington journalists winced at the tough-minded gibes they had written when Foyle's prospects had seemed dim ("Dense Marsh," "Marsh Swamped"), and hoped Marsh would remember the more reverent judgments they had bestowed upon him when the polls looked better ("Forward Marsh!", "Marsh in Like a Lion!").

Marsh was now, for perhaps a hundred thousand of the most important, and the most self-important people in this country, the center of the universe. The pudgy, pale-faced, thirty-eight-year-old self-described wonk had even become a sexual object in the minds of innumerable women who had lived and played by Henry Kissinger's aphorism that "power is the ultimate aphrodisiac." And had he been any more beside himself last evening, he would have had to pay a double rate for his room.

"Dead meat!" Marsh bellowed, pounding his fist on the faux mahogany end table, which promptly shattered into pieces. "The men who"—he glanced at the pollster and the media coordinator—"ex*cuse* me, the men or women who brought us to this anal sphincter of our blessed land had better have impressive employment prospects in the private sector. Barely thirty-six hours ago, Mack Foyle was pronounced the next President of the United States; twenty-four hours ago he was in earnest telephone conversation with the President of Russia, the Queen of England, and the Pope. And where is the next leader of the mightiest nation on earth as of ten or fifteen minutes from now? I'll tell you, ladies and gentlemen. He'll be putting on a pair of boots, he'll be picking out a cowboy hat, he'll be saddling up a horse, and *he'll be pissing in his pants!* A rodeo in Cheyenne, Wyoming? Jesus Christ on a Popsicle stick!"

"Idathkheaddajoyce. . . ."

The mumble came from one of huddled masses yearning to breathe free of Marsh.

"I'm sorry; I didn't quite catch that."

Marsh spoke in a voice that was suddenly dead calm, a voice that, to those who knew him, was far more ominous than his high-decibel rages.

"I said I don't think he had much of a choice."

It was Alan Veigle, the deputy press secretary, the link between the Foyle campaign and the electronic media, the man who told the cameras where they could go, and who therefore helped tell America what Mack Foyle looked like, moved like, felt like. He was twenty-nine, razor thin, with eyes that darted about like a mouse measuring the distance from the cheese to the cat, and he knew more about the way an image would play on television screens than any five experts in the country. He could tell, with one look, whether the leaves on the trees behind the Candidate were warm enough, green enough. He knew how to change the location of a camera angle so that the Candidate's slightly squinty left eye would appear open, and he could take two inches off the Candidate's waistline by positioning the cameras on an imperceptible rise on the ground. He was a genius, and if he was the kind of genius who thought F. Scott and Ella Fitzgerald were John F. Kennedy's aunt and uncle, that had not proved much of an impediment to his career, now worth about thirty thousand dollars a month during high-level campaigns.

"Perhaps," Marsh said, his voice dropping to a near whisper, "perhaps you would like to explain that notion." The room had assumed the stillness of a summer afternoon at those moments before a violent storm explodes.

"Sure," Alan Veigle said. "October twenty-ninth. Great noon video-op set for the Tetons. Sunlight off the snowcaps. Two hundred crippled—"

"Watch it."

"Right. Two hundred handicapped—"

"Watch it."

"Right. Two hundred disabled—"

"Watch it."

"What? What?"

" 'Physically challenged.' "

"Sweet Jesus. All right, two hundred physically challenged kids on horseback behind him, ready to ride in formation behind the man who's promised to lead a Crusade into the Mainstream. What happens?" He shot a look at Marsh.

"What happens is that the campaign decides that the candidate needs another six hours of briefing before the last debate. The campaign decides that the candidate cannot skip the cocktail party for the Platinum Eagles, because they have each given fifty thousand dollars in legally exempt money to the party. So the campaign decides to eighty-six the two hundred kids, the one hundred wheelchairs, the four hundred crutches, the twenty-four Seeing Eye dogs, the three hundred twenty-five parents, and the assembled multitudes.

"So we announce that the candidate has a twenty-four-hour bug, and we put the candidate on a satellite hookup—remember how good he looked in the pajamas and bathrobe?—to these kids, promising that, win or lose, he will personally lead all two hundred of them down the main street of Cheyenne, Wyoming, to open Rodeo Days. Now you tell me how he backs out of that particular commitment as his first act as President-elect?"

"Pittsburgh," said the speechwriter.

Heads turned, lips pursed.

"When FDR was in Pittsburgh for a campaign stop one time, he made a flat promise that he later realized he'd have to break. When he asked one of his advisers what to do, the adviser said, 'Deny you were ever in Pittsburgh.' "

"Thank you for sharing that with us," Marsh said. He turned back to Veigle.

"I'm not sure you grasp the dilemma we have here," he said. "Two weeks ago, Foyle was going to ride on a float with a dozen or so kids. But this is Rodeo Days, Alan. Rodeo. As in 'horses.' As in 'Foyle on a horse.' He doesn't like horses, Alan. He doesn't like them at all. He told me once he greatly admires the French because they eat horses. But now we are in a situation where Foyle is going to have to ride a horse. And there will be several hundred cameras, all with a nice, clear shot at Foyle, and if he so much as twitches—if he screws up his face with that expression he sometimes gets if his chicken is undercooked—that picture is going to be flashed all the way around the world."

"That's a lock," said Alan Veigle. "He's saddling up at a staging area completely sanitized by the Secret Service. There won't be a press camera within a quarter mile. Look," Veigle said, "you tell me what's worse: the chance the candidate might look a little silly, or the sight of two hundred crip—two hundred kids on *Donahue* talking about how much they wanted to meet the new President."

Marsh was silent for a moment.

"Well, this is turning out to be the day I always imagined it would be.

In a few minutes, I have to return a phone call from Jack Petitcon, who will probably explain to me how, despite his Democratic Party ties, he got Foyle elected and how he wouldn't mind if his law firm's phone number were painted on the Washington Monument. Then I have to return a call from the Very Reverend W. Dixon Mason, who will explain the historic opportunity for racial reconciliation, and who can't be looking for more than, oh, I don't know, a seat on the Supreme Court and fifty Burger King franchises."

He jumped to his feet and began motioning the people out of the room.

"And now, I get to turn on the TV and watch the incoming President of the United States make a damn fool of himself."

He should have been so lucky.

THREE

★ ★ ★

God, it was so easy.

"No, my Lord, no, nothing like that, you poor sumbitch. Who been telling you such nonsense?"

He could almost sense the delight on the other end of the line at the hint of the patois, as though he were dropping his guard in the face of such daunting journalistic intensity. He wheeled away from the speaker phone on his custom-built oak desk and gazed at the commanding view of the Washington skyline. Most visitors gasped at the Jefferson Memorial. He was rather partial to the Bureau of Printing and Engraving.

"Come on, Jack," the high-priced columnist said. "This story's all over town; did you send in a memo that might have turned it around for Mueller?"

"Listen here, you remember what Kennedy said after the Bay of Pigs?"

Quoting familiar lines was a Jack Petitcon trademark; more than once he had seen attributed to him words that had come from Wilson, both Roosevelts, and de Tocqueville.

"You mean how victory has a thousand fathers and defeat is an orphan?"

It actually helped when they knew just enough.

"Hoah, boy, that Ivy League education rubbed off on you after all. Well, lemme tell you, defeat also has a thousand coroners. It's real easy to tell everyone how you'd'a locked the barn door tight after Nellie got away. So I want to be on the record that the Mueller campaign did a superb, and I mean su-*perb* job. Just 'cause you roll snake eyes don't mean you don't know how to shoot craps."

Now the high-priced columnist knew he had a story. Here was Jack Petitcon trying to wave him off a hot tip he'd gotten an hour earlier, from someone who'd had a good friend inside the Mueller camp, about Jack's brilliant, tragically ignored advice about turning the campaign around in the last days.

(If the high-priced columnist had had a little less self-assurance and a little more curiosity, he might have known that his tip came from a lawyer who was one phone call away from a Federal Communications Commission decision worth $3.6 million to his firm—provided Jack Petitcon made that phone call. But on such lack of curiosity Jack had built a tidy little empire.)

"Jack, this isn't coming from you; I'm on deep background now, and this ticktock has to be wrapped up in an hour."

"Hoo, buddy, you are one per*sis*tent sumbitch. Well, listen here, you tell me what you *think* you know, and I'll tell you what I *do* know, and maybe you can put something together that won't make you look like a complete fool."

And when the high-priced columnist hung up the phone, Jack knew what he had wrought. The "ticktock"—those now-it-can-be-told, minute-by-minute accounts of how Great Events Really Happened, those Teddy White knockoffs that filled the newspapers with what The Men Inside the room were wearing, eating, drinking, and smoking as they plotted the events that were to alter and illuminate our time—this particular ticktock would suggest, obliquely but unmistakably, that if only the fools in the Mueller campaign had heeded the street smarts of Jack Petitcon, the Hebrew from the Bayou, the Democrats might have recaptured the White House.

All of Jack's denials, all of his gracious words would be quoted in full, accompanied by the knowing asides of the high-priced columnist ("Privately, some inside the Mueller camp blame campaign strategist Joe Featherstone for shielding Mueller from Petitcon; he was, sources say, so determined to protect his access to the candidate that he just may have lost his man the presidency"). Let the punk who wouldn't take his phone calls choke on *that*.

This was what Jack Petitcon did best. It has been said that in Washington, the perception of power was power. Jack operated by a different lodestar: in Washington, the perception of character is character. Neither the fawning profiles nor the faux-tough pieces in *Parade, Vanity Fair,* and the *New York Times Magazine* had come close to cracking Jack's reflector shield.

He was the child of a well-to-do Baton Rouge lawyer-lobbyist who had spent his life plying the legislators of Louisiana with whiskey and women, but from the day Jack arrived in Washington with a House Committee staff job and a draft deferment, Petitcon had sensed the magnetic appeal of the exotic, and had been at pains to paint himself as the child of down-home, up-country romantic Bayou upbringing. The food in the Petitcon home had been roast beef, steak, chicken, and mashed potatoes; the music had ranged from Sinatra to the Dorseys to Glenn Miller. But to those who came with pencils and tape recorders and camera crews, Jack sketched a childhood of shrimp boils, clambakes, crawfish pulled from the waters outside his home, while tapping his feet to Clifton Chenier, the Zydeco Queens, and Fats Domino.

His mother had been a determinedly indifferent Jew, but Jack Petitcon's résumé listed his first name—falsely—as "Jacob." The mix of Jew and Cajun had proved completely irresistible to the Washington world. He good-naturedly accepted the "Hebrew from the Bayou" tag—a fair enough response, since he had coined it—and even printed mock recipes for blackened gefilte fish and jambalaya with kugel. The mix was a brew potent enough to intoxicate Washington: the man imbued with simple, country wisdom, gifted with a shrewd sense of political realities gleaned from his Louisiana boyhood, blessed with that learning and wisdom so typical of the People of the Book.

He was somewhere in his sixties, sleek, and impeccably barbered, manicured, and clothed, working out of a suite of offices with Queen Anne furnishings and Chippendale desks. But when Jack Petitcon spoke with the colorful aphorisms and profanities of his home, it was seen not as a manipulative affectation, but as The Real Jack.

He was universally described as a power broker in the Democratic Party. He had been its chief fund-raiser, chaired the rules and convention selection site committees, held a position of middling importance in a Democratic administration years ago. Every four years, the papers would carry breathless reports that he had rented a suite in the best hotel of the convention city, the better to help his fellow power brokers break the coming deadlocked convention. Otherwise insightful editors and producers would urge their reporters to line up exclusive "inside-the-room" features on Petitcon's wheeling and dealing.

The fact that there had not been a deadlocked convention for forty years, the fact that the delegates had all been committed to candidates in primaries and caucuses, these annoying facts were all swept aside in the collective amnesia that sweeps the political press in the grip of a colorful story. The hotel suites saw some splendid cocktail parties—all paid for by his firm—and as nominees came and went, Jack Petitcon prospered.

Now, on this Thursday after the election, Jack was accepting calls from the press and from fellow Democrats. Many sounded like condolence calls, mourning Jack's exclusion from the corridors of power. Jack muttered the appropriate words, marveling at the inability of these people to get it.

So Mack Foyle was a conservative Republican. So his administration would be staffed by lean and hungry young men and women determined to disassemble the massive federal bureaucracy brick by brick, to bring the wonders of free-market economics to the semi-socialized, encrusted sectors of American life such as health, agriculture, transportation, housing.

So what would happen when they tried to change the formula for Medicare and Medicaid reimbursements? The same thing that had happened when Reagan took the White House, and when the Republicans briefly took over both houses of the Congress. Endless hearings at the Department of Health and Human Services and in congressional committees. And who would the doctors and the hospitals need, to protect them from the ax now hovering over the neck of the goose that laid the golden checks? Why, a lawyer who knew the players; a lawyer like Jack Petitcon.

And what would happen when the farmers—not the Grant Wood

American Gothics with a peach pie cooling on the ledge and Lassie sewing the gingham dresses, but the agribusiness big boys with the grain silos and the freighters and the mechanized food factories—what would happen when they had to fight the proposed cuts in the subsidized food prices and water? Who would help them in the struggle to preserve their way of life? Yes.

And who would protect the truckers from paying the full cost of the wear and tear their rigs inflicted on the interstate highway system? Who would protect the owners of private planes from paying the real cost of tying up the runways of metropolitan airports so that the CEOs and CFOs could make it down to Boca Raton for one round of golf before darkness fell on a Friday evening? Who would shield the holders of broadcast licenses from paying the real market value of a TV license in a big city?

"Another four years in the desert," mourned the Ohio Democratic chairman, who dreamed of judgeships and postmasters and West Point commissions. Jack murmured words of sympathy, but he was seeing a different future: harvest time.

Soon, he knew, Marsh would be calling. Not because he wanted to—Marsh probably despised him, Jack realized—but because he would have to. Marsh would remember the lessons of other new administrations: You can follow any ideology you choose, but if you do not tip the cap and tug the forelock to the Washington that was and will be, you are doomed.

Jack Petitcon was a happy and contented man as he punched up the All News Network to find out what they'd be talking about at the two receptions and the dinner he had scheduled for that night. He saw crowds and horses, and men and women with cowboy hats, and banners and bunting everywhere.

I wonder what damn fool arranged this? he thought. *What a dumb way for a new President to start things off.*

Or finish them.

God it was so easy.

"This is a text . . . without a *con*-text . . . therefore . . . it is a *pre*-text. . . .

To suggest that we abstained . . . is a stain . . . upon our capacities . . . and our veracity."

Sure, he pushed it right to the edge sometimes. Maybe once in a while he half hoped that a questioner would slap his notebook shut, jump to his feet, and tell the Reverend W. Dixon Mason right to his face to cut the crap. But not this time. The young reporter's pen was flying across the four-by-eight-inch notebook, trying to keep up with the cadences, occasionally looking up to find himself confronted by the Stare, the Gaze, "the Laser Browns." That look had frozen schoolyard bullies, IRS auditors, gang leaders, corporate executives, and TV talk-show hosts across three decades. Aiming it at a twenty-nine-year-old reporter was like sending up a talented eleven-year-old Little League slugger to face Roger Clemens on a foggy night in Fenway.

Oh, yes, the reporter had done his homework. He had tracked down copies of the Election Day palm cards that had been distributed by the hundreds of thousands in North Philadelphia and South Central Los Angeles and Cleveland's Hough and Brooklyn's Bedford-Stuyvesant, listing all of the Democratic candidates for office, with the top slot blank, and emblazoned across the top of the palm card the slogan, "Say No! To Plantation Politics!" The reporter had learned that in city after city, the cards had been printed by companies that were principal suppliers to the Live the Dream Foundation, the organization founded and headed by W. Dixon Mason in the early 1970s.

And then there were the quotes gathered from sermons that had been preached in prominent black churches the Sunday before Election Day, preached in the Abyssinian Baptist Church up on 127th Street in Harlem, preached in the First AME Church at Normandie and Gower, sermons remarkably similar in theme, tone, even language.

"If Rosa Parks said that a segregated seat on a bus is no seat at all, then you can say that a choice between two bad men is no choice at all!" preachers had thundered. The reporter had uncovered a remarkable coincidence: all these churches had been funded in the recent past by Live the Dream.

It had the makings of an eyebrow-raising scandal: had W. Dixon Mason, the nation's most visible, most charismatic, most controversial black leader, the man who had proclaimed it as his life's work to "turn the voting booth into the sacred fount of freedom," helped elect a conservative Republican by discouraging his most loyal followers from going to the polls? Without question, turnout had been anemic in inner-city neighborhoods from one end of the country to the other. Post-election autopsies had already concluded that a more substantial black turnout could have moved Michigan and California from Foyle to Mueller; and with those states, the Democrats would have won the White House. Did Mason help engineer this result? And if he did, why?

Was it money? W. Dixon Mason lived comfortably, but by no means ostentatiously, and compared with the estates of the Sunday TV preachers, Mason's home, in a middle-class black neighborhood of Atlanta, was modest. He did travel first class, but he was tall, and suffered from chronic back pain. Only his clothes reflected a taste for the good life, his suits and shirts custom-tailored by a Boston craftsman persuaded into total secrecy. (At a charity roast some years back, Al DeRossa had turned to Mason from the podium and said, "Dix, you always were a man of the cloth—cashmere." Relations between Mason and DeRossa's network had never quite been the same.)

Normally, the eager young reporter would have not fretted a minute over the motives for what Mason seemed to have done. Normally, he would have dealt out his damning facts one after the other, like a poker player with a winning hand about to reel in the biggest pot of the night. Normally, he'd watch as his adversary squirmed under the relentless onslaught, confident of detecting the catch in the voice, the quickening of the eye blinks, the bead or two of Nixonian sweat.

But this was W. Dixon Mason. He was different.

He was one of the most physically imposing presences in public life. He was six feet, six inches tall; at age fifty-two, he still had the broad shoulders and slim hips of the All-American tight end he had been at the University of Illinois. His face was taut, chiseled, dominated by huge brown eyes. When he was sitting with a potential adversary, as he was today, with the earnest young reporter, he never sat behind a desk, but sat face-to-face, much closer than the normal space between two American men of heterosexual persuasion.

The more cynical inhabitants of the political world were firmly convinced that W. Dixon Mason knew exactly what he was doing with this technique. In a culture where the fear of big black men was primal, where it lurked as closely beneath the skin of the cultured white suburban liberal as beneath the skin of the Biloxi high-school-dropout truck driver, it was entirely predictable that Mason's technique would trigger an uncontrollable sense of apprehension. Mason, who had not raised his fists in anger since his high school days, would often joke to his intimates about his ability to induce his victims into putting on their "I Like Negroes" look, the countenance that seemed to say, "Why, yes, Mr. Mason, I do respect and admire you as an educated, cultured person of African-American descent, clearly well spoken and thoughtful, dedicated to the well-being and concerns of our disaffected minorities, and incidentally, would you please not hit me?"

Now W. Dixon Mason was putting the earnest young reporter through a Socratic dialogue that would have done the most sadistic Ivy League law professor proud.

About those palm cards:

Was there any evidence, any evidence at all, that the Live the Dream Foundation had solicited, or paid for, or distributed the palm cards? Was the reporter suggesting that black people were incapable of responding to political events on their own?

Not exactly, but . . .

Was it the reporter's implication that African-American clergy were incapable of drawing their own conclusions about the political interests of their parishioners, that they needed some kind of Big Brother to tell them what to say?

"Eighty-eight percent of the daily newspapers in this country endorsed the Republican ticket, and yet, if we were to suggest any kind of conspiracy or complicity, surely you would charge us with paranoia, and you would be right. Why, then, are we to accept paranoia when it is directed at our own people?"

No, but there's reliable evidence that . . .

"Reliability without credibility can be a liability without the ability to see the lie that lies within."

For just a moment there, just a split second, Mason thought he saw the reporter rise to the bait. Then the "I Like Negroes" look came back, and he knew he was home free.

By the time the reporter excused himself and left Mason's office, the story had disappeared. Perhaps it would wind up as a minor item in the magazine's "What We Hear" section, the leavings of rumor and gossip; but that would be all. No big story, no scandal.

So, how do you like your blue-eyed boy, Mr. Featherstone? Are you still proud of the way you stiffed me out of a prime-time speech at the convention? And what was that you told a reporter late at night after the convention was over?

"Mason wants a 727 as the price of endorsement—we're thinking about a Greyhound?"

Very funny, Mr. Featherstone. Why don't you have a good laugh over that little joke as you spend the next four years in a tiny office in some half-assed think tank, hoping each time the phone rings that it's Nightline *or* Crossfire?

"Electors! E-*lec*-tors!"

Mason spoke the word aloud, almost as a malediction. During one tense, brittle conversation, Featherstone had told Mason about all the Live the Dream allies, all the African-Americans, who had been chosen by the Mueller campaign as presidential electors, who would have the honor of casting the electoral votes for Mueller at their state capitals. Canny as Dixon Mason was, he could not decide whether the offer was another calculated insult or a mark of terminal stupidity. He also decided that it didn't matter. And he thought again of his favorite maxim: "Revenge is a dish best eaten cold."

FOUR

★ ★ ★

"It was that goddamn *e.*

"Bill Muller . . . people would have bought it, that sounds nice and clean. Bill Miller, now that was even better, even if it was also the name of Goldwater's running mate, but who the hell would have remembered that? Miller, Baker, Weaver, Smith, Cook, that's the ticket for the ticket next time, we'll find us two guys right out of a medieval guild. But 'Mueller,' see, the goddamn *e,* that was just enough to make it sound foreign, maybe like a Nazi spy from a World War Two movie, the kind of guy Conrad Veidt might have played, with a monocle screwed into his eye, a cigarette holder in his mouth, and a sneer in his voice: 'It iss known to uss zat you haf relatiffs on ze ozzer zide uff ze border.' It's that kind of country, Jack, and if you spent less time in Greenwich Village and Cambridge and North Beach, if you actually spent a night or two in the America where they don't really give a rat's ass about getting the *New York Times Book Review* four days early, maybe you'd know that in the real America they like Presidents with simple, clean, angular, Anglo goddamn American names; you know, Tru-man, Kenn-e-dy, John-son, Nixon, Ford, Car-ter, Rea-gan, Bush, Clin-ton . . . and Eisenhower, well, okay, I guess if you win goddamn World War Two it's okay to have a weird name, I mean, maybe Schwarzkopf fits, too, but I'm telling you, it was the goddamn *e* that did it. . . ."

"Okay, Joe, it'll make a great op-ed piece, but right now you're drunk and I'm tired, so I'm going home and let you think more great thoughts, okay? Take care, lover."

Pepper Days leaned across the desk, pecked Joe Featherstone on the cheek, slung on her oversized shoulder bag, and walked out of the office. Featherstone watched her walk away, noted for the record his approval of her form, considered for five seconds the possibility of a post-campaign fling, buried the idea in the toxic-waste section of his subconscious, and slumped back in his chair. He was thirty-five years old, twenty-five pounds heavier than he was a year earlier, estranged from his family and friends, more or less drunk (more), more or less broke (more), out of work, out of clean laundry, stranded in a city a thousand miles away from what once had passed for his home (a great song by the Heartbeats, remember, "You're a thousand miles away, but I still have your love to remember you by"), and immersed in the first phase of the death flush that imbues the men and women who run a losing campaign for President.

It wasn't as if he had strangled his grandmother. It wasn't as if he had lured an eight-year-old girl into the woods, or been caught wearing his sister's underwear, or pilfered the life savings of the widows and orphans of firemen. But the averted eyes, the silent telephone, the silence, the *silence* after all those months of relentless demands for his presence, his call, his attention, this was what they meant when they talked about a deafening silence. Wasn't there some old Fred Allen routine about a man who lived in a tenement right next to the Sixth Avenue El, and the day they tore it down he'd been sitting in his chair reading his paper, and at six-fifteen, when the express train didn't go by, he jumped out of his chair and screamed, "What was that?!?" *That's what this is like,* he thought, *I'm sitting here and the silence is bouncing off the walls, and I'm screaming, "What the hell was that?"*

Well, there was the press, of course, they were calling. Calling relentlessly, all wanting to know What Had Gone Wrong, What Would He Do Different. Well, that would be fun, wouldn't it? To grab one of those smart-ass, know-it-all bastards, throw him into a chair, and tell him, "What would I do different? I'll tell you what I'd do different. I'd find a candidate who had the political instincts of a clam, who knew better than to talk about the civil liberties of pornographers in the middle of a presidential debate. I'd find a candidate whose wife didn't think her master's degree in European literature made her a better speechwriter than the candidate's team, and who didn't rewrite his acceptance speech into a one-hour lecture that damn near emptied the hall.

"I'd find a Hispanic media consultant who actually knew how to speak Spanish, so that Mueller's slogan, 'A Man Who Loves His Country,' did not translate into 'A Man Who Is Horny for His Country,' giving us twenty-four hours of bad press, wiping Mueller's health-care program off the evening news. I'd find a time buyer in the Midwest who didn't spend all the TV money five days before the election, just about knocking us off the air in Michigan, Ohio, and Illinois the last week of the campaign. And did I mention the candidate's wife, who went to a county fair in the Central Valley of California and said—into a camera—that she didn't know why anyone needed to own a handgun, and she was sure her husband thought the same thing, and how that sent, oh, maybe seventy-five thousand gun owners out to the polls in California, waiting on line before the polls even opened. I'd like to have done something about that, like maybe putting the candidate's wife into a nice, long three months' sleep.

"And W. Dixon Mason, oh yes, I'd like to have done something about the Very Reverend W. Dixon Mason. Like what? Like maybe the tax-evasion charges that the U.S. attorney in Chicago had spent eighteen months preparing, until he was miraculously elevated to a judgeship. Or the extortion charges that a sacked BurgerTime executive had brought to the Atlanta FBI after Mason had ended a national boycott of BurgerTime with the promise of sixty franchises—financed with no-interest loans by the conglomerate that owned BurgerTime. Pretty remarkable thing, that canned exec suddenly finding himself running the sales and catering office of a five-star hotel in Anguilla, which just happened to be owned by a consortium including the minister of tourism of Anguilla, who had hired W. Dixon Mason's brother as a consultant three years ago."

And maybe none of this had anything to do with those sermons that had been preached in damn near every black church in America two days before the election. And maybe it had nothing to do with those leaflets that had popped up in Crenshaw in L.A. and the Hill in St. Louis and Hough and South Jamaica, and maybe that's why every time W. Dixon

Mason showed up all over the TV on Election Night with those sorghum-dipped words of sympathy and praise for Mueller he'd had to think very hard so that he did not put his fist through the Trinitron.

Featherstone wondered how that story would play in the hands of Al DeRossa, a network guy who actually understood politics without having to have a picture drawn with crayons. No, once the election was over, the TV guys cared about the inside baseball stuff about as much as they cared about the Federal Reserve Board. Maybe he'd give it to Klein, of *Newsweek,* or Kramer, of *Time,* let them put it into one of those minute-by-minute "how he won/how he lost" pieces. Yeah, that would be helpful. Mason would do one of his sorrowful let-us-heal-the-hurt speeches, Featherstone would be labeled a sour-grapes racist, and the guys who knew what Mason was like would just nod their heads and go on holding their noses while behaving like mistletoe was hanging from the back of his suit coat.

He leaned forward and stuck his arms into the mountain of paper that covered his desk, every scrap of it of incomparable importance three days ago, now all of it worthless—"Not worth the paper it's printed on," he said as he laughed mirthlessly. He picked up a paper, whose front-page analysis, the "dope" piece, explained portentously that Mueller's 233 electoral votes made him the narrowest loser since Richard Nixon in 1960.

Great. That's going to put me in the history books big time. I'm the genius who collected more of these useless votes than any campaign manager since 1960. The phones will really be ringing off the hooks with this baby.

And meanwhile, Marsh, that goddamn Marsh, would be putting the White House together, juggling the Cabinet, measuring the drapes on that corner office in the West Wing, breathing words of counsel into Foyle's ear—that's *President* Foyle to you. He could picture Marsh now, out there in some western town, waiting for his tiger to ride in some rodeo, watching the coins pour out of that slot machine all lined up with double bars, as the bells and whistles went off loud enough to wake the dead.

Well, there was his future to think about. He could write a book no one would read. He could get a fellowship for six months or a year. Maybe there'd be a job with a campaign for mayor or governor, with more bad food and bad air and bad sex or no sex. And there'd be seminars and panels for a few months. He could pick up a few bucks, keep his name around, be a C-SPAN regular. That's a good payoff for all the missed sleep and the marriage gone bad: heartthrob of the C-SPAN junkies and 233 electoral votes he couldn't swap for a thirty-two-cent stamp.

Of course, some stamps are worth a lot more than thirty-two cents.

Some stamps are worth a goddamn fortune.

FIVE

It was the greatest day of Old Doc Falter's life.

For half a century, Falter had tended to the horses of Cheyenne, Wyoming. From the day he had walked off the train after a five-day journey from Rochester, New York, armed only with a love for the West and a degree in veterinary medicine from Eastman College of Animal Science (sixty days' attendance and a fifty-dollar fee required), he had spent his life in the fields and barns of Laramie County. Once he had been called "Rusty," but his red hair had long ago turned to white, and his tanned skin had long ago taken on a shade of saddle leather, which was exactly why Old Doc Falter was standing by a golden palomino, syringe in hand, eagerly awaiting his date with history.

He had been plucked from his office, on the second floor above the Sears catalog showroom on Route 45, three miles outside Cheyenne, by Screech Katzman, a twenty-two-year-old advance man for the Foyle-Block campaign, acting on instructions that Marsh had detailed with compelling clarity.

"Let me spell this out for you," Marsh had told Screech three days before the election. "If we win this thing, and I can't figure out a convincing alibi, we are going to have to show up in Cheyenne, Wyoming, and our beloved leader is going to have to get on a horse in front of the entire world and ride down Main Street.

"This means we are going to have to find the nicest, gentlest horse in the state of Wyoming for Mr. Foyle to ride—a pastime in which Mr.

Foyle has never engaged. I mean, I do not think his beloved mother ever even put him on a pony for his birthday. So it is imperative that this horse be a very, very tranquil and relaxed horse. Because if he moves faster than five miles an hour, our beloved President-elect is not going to look at all confident and relaxed.

"So what we do need here, Screech? I will tell you. We need a veterinarian who knows every horse in the county; a vet whom we can trust to make sure this horse does not embarrass the new President by galloping down Main Street with Mr. Foyle hanging on his tail with his head banging along the street.

"And if it is possible—I myself am not very well acquainted with the physiology of horses—it would be very, very helpful if our friendly vet could somehow arrange for this horse not to take a giant dump in the middle of the Rodeo Days parade, as that will wind up on every piece of tape our friends in the media broadcast.

"Now I realize, Screech, that you would have preferred to spend Election Night in the bosom of our campaign family, sharing in the joys of victory. I realize that Cheyenne, Wyoming, is not your locale of choice. But look at it this way. You will be helping to plan the first trip of the President-elect—unless we can structure a plausible explanation for stiffing a couple of hundred kids in wheelchairs. So, happy trails to you, Screech."

Screech Katzman was not a man well acquainted with the ways of the West. What he did have was the telephone number of the Laramie County Republican chairman, who owned a 1,200-acre horse farm, and who met every workday at 7:00 A.M. at the L & A diner for breakfast and gossip with many of Cheyenne's worthiest citizens, among whom Old Doc Falter was one.

"He's your man," the chairman told Screech. "Stepped right out of *Gunsmoke*. Brought more horses into the world than anyone else around here."

(It did not seem right to bother the stressed-out advance man with the fact that the horses Old Doc Falter knew belonged mostly to the county chairman, who was not averse to the notion that the next President of the United States would be riding one of the chairman's steeds.)

From the time he left Foyle's campaign headquarters in Rosslyn, Virginia, just across the Potomac from Washington, it took Screech eleven hours and twenty-two minutes to reach Old Doc Falter's office in Cheyenne, Wyoming. It took Screech fifteen seconds to realize that Old Doc Falter was a gift from media handler heaven.

His office featured a rolltop desk, a hat rack, a battered but comfortable sofa, two wing-backed chairs, and framed photographs of Man o' War, Citation, Secretariat, and dozens of horses Old Doc Falter had cared for during his half century of labor in Wyoming. Other photos featured farmers and ranch hands, weather-beaten of face and lean of body. If any of the press wanted to interview Old Doc Falter they'd find themselves in a perfect setting.

Not as perfect, however, as Old Doc Falter himself. From his snow white hair to his twinkling brown eyes, to the wire-rimmed spectacles, to his brown cardigan sweater, complete with elbow patches, Old Doc Falter was the animal kingdom's version of Dr. Gillespie and Judge Hardy rolled into one, Gepetto with a western twang, a photo-op wet dream come to life. When Screech asked him whether he could find the right horse for Foyle to ride, Old Doc Falter put out a restraining hand and leapt to his feet.

"Say no more," he said. "This is your boy right here."

He pointed to a picture of a golden palomino framed in the place of honor over his desk: a picture that the Laramie County Republican chairman had personally delivered to Old Doc Falter twenty-four hours earlier.

"Foaled him myself eleven years ago; he's a gorgeous piece of horseflesh."

"Ummmm . . ." Screech paused, looking for the right way to frame his question. "Ummm, how . . . how *frisky* . . . ?"

"No worries on that score," Old Doc Falter said. "You know much about horses?"

"Ummm . . ."

"Well, eleven years old is pretty well up there. You're not likely to get a horse kicking up much of a ruckus at that age. Besides"—he grinned—"I can pretty much guarantee that Mr. Foyle will have a nice calm ride." He patted the battered black leather bag on the desk.

"Nembutal; I've got a bag full of preloaded syringes. Use it to sedate 'em if they're out of control. Only thing you need to worry about is whether the horse'll doze off halfway down Main Street."

Screech nodded.

"One more question. What's the horse's name?"

Old Doc Falter's grin would have lit up the night sky.

"Washington's Hope," he said.

"Yesssssss!"

Three days later, on a brilliant November day, Old Doc Falter stood in a specially constructed paddock just off Cheyenne's Main Street, patting the right flank of Washington's Hope, on the greatest day of his life. All along Main Street tens of thousands were lined up for the Rodeo Days parade, a substantial majority of them weighed down with portable tape decks and video cameras. Banners proclaiming "Welcome President Foyle" spanned the street; hawkers selling buttons, balloons, pennants, and stuffed dolls spilled out into side streets. At the head of the line of march, 216 children, in wheelchairs and on crutches, chattered excitedly. Four blocks away, in the designated demonstration venue, thirteen protesters waved signs reading "Foyle Exploits the Differently Abled," hoping to be interviewed by . . . anyone.

At the center of town, where Main Street and Western Avenue intersected, a set of bleachers enclosed by Plexiglas was rapidly filling up with the civic leaders of Laramie County, whose civic devotion had been calculated by the contributions they had made to Foyle's election campaign. Across Main Street, the giant parking lot of the Wal-Mart had been encircled by a chain-link fence whose entry was protected by four security guards, each of whom was between forty and seventy-five pounds overweight. This was the "media village," where the satellite trucks, portable editing facilities, and press filing center had been established. On the Wal-Mart roof, an elaborate if rickety wooden scaffolding held the pool TV camera positions and still photographers' perch. Screech and a three-person advance team had picked the site after scouring every conceivable rooftop along a mile-long strip of Main Street.

In the two days since Election Day, the press corps attached to Foyle had tripled; now, more than four hundred members of the press were following Foyle wherever he, his wife, his children, his pets, and his friends happened to be. The great majority of their efforts today would wind up as twenty seconds on the evening news, a single photo or a few paragraphs of text in a newspaper.

For Old Doc Falter, however, it was the greatest day of his life. In a few moments, the just-elected President of the United States would be escorted over to the paddock, where he would admire Washington's Hope and, before mounting the horse, would shake hands with the beloved veterinarian. As a news junkie, Old Doc Falter knew that TV news would cover—smother—every crumb of information about this appearance; maybe there'd even be a graphic thrown up on the screen when Foyle came over to the paddock, with Old Doc Falter's name, age, occupation, and picture filling the screen.

Old Doc Falter had spent hours preparing for his moment. He had washed and brushed his silver hair; he had sent his tweed jacket and cardigan sweater out for a rare cleaning and pressing; he had ironed his wide-wale corduroys; he had polished his dusty brown boots; he had dropped Visine into his eyes.

And he had carefully placed his wire-rimmed spectacles inside his breast pocket. Damned if he was going to look like some four-eyed geezer ready for the old folks' home, with the flashbulbs reflecting off his bifocals, making him look like Little Orphan Annie.

No doubt about it, Old Doc Falter looked a lot better without those spectacles. He just didn't see quite as well—not nearly.

So it was perfectly understandable that when he reached into his black leather bag for that preloaded syringe of Nembutal, he pulled out a preloaded syringe of adrenaline. Even when he had his specs on, the printing on the labels was so small that it was very difficult to read. Without his glasses, it was impossible for Old Doc Falter to tell them apart.

But Washington's Hope could tell the difference.

SIX

A stirring.

A first, faint hint, one neck craned, one head turning, searching for the source. Among the crowds behind the barricades, a sense that he is coming jumps almost telepathically from one spectator to another. Perhaps they glimpse the flickering in the eyes of the agents, the more urgent messages they whisper into their wrists; perhaps they sense the sudden urgency in the movements of the photographers penned into a strip of sidewalk.

Then all doubts vanish as the twenty-four-car motorcade cuts across West Sixteenth and the Ford Vanstar pulls up to the paddock ("No limo," Marsh had snapped the night before to the Laramie County Republican chairman. "I don't care how much the Caddy dealer greased you, if there's a limo, I swear to you on my mother's grave this whole deal is off; Foyle is not going to show up looking like a goddamn CEO"). MacArthur Foyle steps out, pivots slowly, raises his head up and holds out his left arm, waves his hand slightly to the crowd, and smiles broadly at an unseen presence up and to the right—a presence who would have had to be suspended some forty feet above the roof of the Wal-Mart, but an imaginary presence whose focus gives Foyle's bearing a distinctly more presidential mien.

There was now a Zone surrounding Foyle, radiating three or four feet out from him. It had started to form at about 2:00 P.M. on the afternoon of Election Day, when the network exit polls showed him the likely winner. It had intensified an hour after midnight, when California had moved—narrowly but clearly—into his column, giving him the presidency. Now, even the photographers, men and women who would trample a small child beneath them in pursuit of a better camera angle, men and women who had pressed in on him from Iowa to New Hampshire to California, held back when approaching the Zone. A year ago, he had been the Senator to his staff; then the Candidate; then the Nominee. Now he was something his advisers, even his friends, had difficulty speaking:

"Foyle, the Sena—the Pr-Pr-Pr—"

Now the man who was fast becoming the center of the known universe was covering his mouth with his right hand even as he continued to wave at the crowd with his left, and murmured a few words to Screech Katzman, who was standing beside him at the entrance to the paddock.

"Want to know how I feel?"

"Yes, sir," Screech replied.

"I feel like a fool—no, let me be more precise about this. I feel like an asshole."

"Yes, sir," said Screech.

"I look like an asshole, don't I?"

"No, sir, you look fine," Screech replied.

"No, I do not. I look like an asshole and in a few minutes I am going to look like an asshole in front of the whole world, because my staff, which is being canonized by every moron with a pencil and a notebook, could not manage to get me out of this nightmare."

He gestured to himself.

"Do you like this outfit? Do you think this is me?"

The outfitting of Mack Foyle for the Cheyenne Rodeo Days parade had consumed three staff meetings totaling six hours and forty minutes, involving fourteen people (not counting the conference calls with three Hollywood producers, the campaign wardrobe engineer, and Gordon Prickert, top salesman at Cheyenne Outfitters). After the transcontinental screaming match, four pieces of broken crockery, and a barely averted fistfight, the consensus outfit for Mack Foyle included a pair of Wrangler Cowboy Cut Jeans, a Roper Brand 100 percent cotton canvasback shirt featuring a bright Indian pattern of red and gold, a pair of Tony Lama boots, and a gray Resistol felt hat.

("What about chaps?" Alan Veigle had asked the clerk from Cheyenne Outfitters.

"That depends," the clerk said. "Do you want to look good in a parade, or are you looking to get picked up in a rough trade bar?")

Three young campaign aides had repeatedly washed, dried, and pounded the clothes, in an attempt to render them well worn. The Tony Lama boots had been dragged back and forth along a gravel path, the hat had been left in the sun all day. But as Alan Veigle sat in that crowded motel room in Cheyenne and watched the effect on his TV screen, the story came to him of a poor Jewish boy grown wealthy, who proudly displays to his mother his brand-new boat, blazer, white ducks, and cap.

"So what do you think, Ma?"

"I'll tell you," she says. "By you, you're a captain. By me, you're a captain. But, Benny, by a captain, you're no captain."

Al DeRossa barely looked up from his workstation two thousand miles away to consider the spectacle. Years of toil in the media vineyards had left him increasingly indifferent to the pictures on his television screen. When you have watched a dozen suits spend the better part of a morning screaming at each other through walkie-talkies and cellular phones, the better to frame a hand-painted sign over a candidate's left shoulder, when you have been handed a printed page detailing the time and place of spontaneous demonstrations, you tend to regard what you are seeing as a form of Virtual Reality. It may look like something real is happening, it may sound like it, but long ago DeRossa had concluded that if the operatives could somehow plant pictures directly into the minds of the voters, nothing at all would actually take place during a campaign. And maybe nothing did.

DeRossa's indifference, however, was by no means shared by his colleagues. They were watching the pictures from Cheyenne with the anticipation of a seventh-grade class eyeing the entrance of a substitute teacher.

Fresh meat! Fresh meat! Fresh meat!

A newly elected President in a cowboy suit! Riding a horse! Within minutes, the first acidic quip would be circling the room, phoned to a friend in a competing newsroom across town, faxed to a colleague a continent away. The hands of the political cartoonists were beginning to itch at the prospects: *We could have Foyle riding backward; maybe stepping in horse droppings if we could do it tastefully.* Comedians, who formed one of the most occupationally significant audience for all-news radio and public-affairs TV programs, were falling to their knees in prayerful thanks for the possibilities of a man born to wear a necktie about to mount a horse. Columnists were sniffing the distinct possibility of a new metaphor coming into view.

("President-elect Foyle found himself asking the new Congress to bury him not on a lone prairie last week. . . .")

Owners of dude ranches watched with their heart rates moving into the danger zone. A new President who rode a horse; maybe that would inspire a new clientele to leave their Ferragamos and Armanis behind; maybe emulation would set the credit card machines zipping back and forth across the green and gold plastic rectangles. Sure, it was only one appearance, but one never could tell.

As for MacArthur Foyle, anger at his staff was no longer his dominant sentiment. He had become a schoolboy again, alone in his room on a Sunday night, as the last light of day left the sky, and the inevitability of a Monday-morning French test roiled his bowels. He recalled long-ago prayers for a nuclear holocaust to break out, fleeting thoughts of phoning in a bomb threat to police headquarters that would force the closing of the school. Now he would mount the horse, knowing with absolute certainty that any slip, a hesitation, a grimace, would wipe out all that had gone before: the handshakes and hugs with the kids in the Wheelchair Rodeo procession, the grateful, teary thanks from the parents and teachers, all of the goodwill and emotion that he would earn from fulfilling a campaign pledge in his very first days as the incoming President.

Foyle stood for a long moment as the pool photographers snapped their last photos before he would climb aboard Washington's Hope. The TV camera moved in for a lingering close-up, capturing a near-solemn expression on Foyle's face. Perhaps, the correspondent mused aloud to his audience, perhaps the President-to-be was pondering the task ahead of him, or reliving the moving moments with his young wheelchair-bound charges he would soon lead in procession.

Actually, Mack Foyle was remembering a story that had been told to him long ago, a story about an Indian brave and an Indian maiden, members of warring tribes on the opposite sides of a lake, who fell in love with each other one day while out in their canoes.

They knew their love could never be because of the hostility of the tribes; and so, in despair, and to teach their elders the folly of their ways, the brave and the maiden paddled out to the middle of the lake, jumped in the water, embraced for the first and last time, and drowned.

And so moved were their elders by this act of sacrifice, that they named the lake after the two lost children: Lake Stupid.

That's me, Foyle realized. *I'm about to go out into the middle of Lake Stupid.*

"Mr. President! Mr. President!"

The chairman of the Laramie County Republican Party was being escorted over to Foyle, with a kindly, slightly befuddled Old Doc Falter in tow.

"Can't tell you how much this means to us, Mr. President . . . ," the chairman said; then, dropping his voice, he added, ". . . and don't worry yourself about this horse. Old Doc Falter made sure you're gonna have a smooth ride."

"Appreciate it, appreciate it," Foyle said absently.

"Dunno," Old Doc Falter muttered, glancing over at Washington's Hope. "He's acting a little frisky for all that Nembutal I pumped into him."

"It's nothing, nothing at all," said the Laramie County chairman, whose brain had been playing with the potential sales price of Washington's Hope all morning ("Yes, that's right, this is the horse President Foyle rode").

"It's the crowds and the music, is all. But, Mr. President," he said, turning Old Doc Falter with his left arm so that the three men were facing the pool camera head-on, "Mr. President, you may not be of the West, but you won the hearts of the West on Tuesday, and we are deeply grateful that you chose to return to Cheyenne and fulfill your promise to these great kids!"

As the chairman's words flowed through the wireless microphone clipped to his shirt and out over the crowd, cheers began up and down the line of march.

"And as you ride in this historic parade, on this magnificent horse, we know history will look back on this day as the beginning of a great adventure to restore our nation's greatness. And to commemorate this great day, we are proud to present you with this historic set of silver spurs, to help you spur the American people on to a brighter tomorrow."

The chairman produced a fine-grained wooden box, and, reaching in, he drew the pair of spurs—and the suspicious glances of half a dozen Secret Service men and women. The only thing suspect about the spurs was their historic nature; they had in fact been purchased by the chairman the previous day from Corral West. What would be historic, the chairman believed, was the price they would fetch after he retrieved them from Foyle at the conclusion of the parade. He bent in front of Foyle and fastened the spurs around his boots; then, with a sweeping gesture, invited the newly elected President to mount Washington's Hope.

With a barely convincing smile and a last wave to the crowd gathered across from the paddock, Mack Foyle swung himself onto the horse. Among his immediate entourage there was a sudden intake of breath. But they needn't have worried; the hour of practice earlier that day had paid off. Foyle mounted without a glitch, landing straight up, even waving his hat in the air with near enthusiasm.

And back in the motel room, Marsh, Alan Veigle, and the other members of the inner circle exchanged high fives and whoops of celebration. It was going to be okay, it was going to be all right.

And it would have been, it would all have been just fine, if it wasn't for the damned press pool.

SEVEN

Atop a flatbed truck waiting along Seventeenth Street, they waited, forty-eight of them, Hasselblads and Nikons, Sonys and Norelcos, Minolta Maxxums and JVCs, shoulders weighed down with battery packs, film canisters, light meters, frizzies, video packs.

Their presence was the consequence of a frank and open exchange of views between Alan Veigle and three representatives from Foyle's press corps—a frank and open exchange that had included many inventive variations on Anglo-Saxon nouns and verbs. The press secretary, acting under strict instructions from Marsh, had imposed a tight pool: one video camera, one still camera, all material pooled.

Outrageous, replied the photographers. What about the people's right to know? they yelled. Is this what Mack Foyle meant when he pledged to end the isolation of the White House? they charged.

"Someday," Marsh had said, "someday—just for my own amusement, mind you—someday I am going to find out *who the hell buys all these pictures those assholes keep taking!* How many goddamn newspapers and magazines are there in the world, anyway? You would think the simple laws of supply and demand would not permit *six hundred thousand* photographers to make a living selling the same goddamn picture of Mack Foyle picking his teeth! You know what? I just figured out what's causing the hole in the goddamn *ozone layer!* It's all those *chemicals* used to develop all those goddamn *pictures* nobody can possibly need!"

It was, by common consent, one of Marsh's better tantrums—a 6.8 on the Marsh Scale, campaign aides agreed—but in the end he gave in. There would be a loose pool of photographers covering Foyle's first post-election appearance; which is why there were forty-eight cameras waiting for Foyle atop a flatbed truck as he approached Seventeenth Street.

The most intriguing picture, of course, was the one almost nobody ever saw: the wide shot. It would not have shown Foyle at all. Instead, it would have captured Secret Service agents walking warily in front, alongside, and behind something, single-mindedly scanning the crowd for potential trouble, barely glancing down to spot a late deposit from the gallant steeds that had preceded the President-elect. It would have included the flatbed truck with the forty-eight photographers, each zooming in for the same tight shot of the President-elect on horseback. But only the crowds actually attending the parade could see the intrusive presence of the press. The view from the TV screen and the news pages was of the newly chosen leader of the land cantering confidently into the future. By now, MacArthur Foyle, like so many others of his vocation, had long since grown inured to the omnipresence of the cameras. Like a seventeenth-century king in the court of France, where courtiers attended the sovereign at his most intimate moments, Foyle had been offered the Faustian bargain—fame and power in exchange for the loss of privacy and a draft choice to be named later—and signed eagerly on the dotted line.

Washington's Hope, however, hadn't a clue about the deal.

He had spent his life under a big sky, well fed, comfortably stabled, groomed, and cleaned on a regular basis, the equine equivalent of a human with a trust fund, or a tenured faculty position at a well-endowed university. He had occasionally been pressed into service during a child's birthday party, or when a visitor from the East wanted a gentle ride. But he had never ridden in a parade, never heard the cheers of thousands assembled, and never, ever, confronted the phalanx of lights that suddenly shined into his face.

Washington's Hope was already feeling a strange sense of excitement, anticipation, anxiety. The adrenaline now pumping through his cardiovascular system was sending his heart rate up into the red zone. The Secret Service agents in cowboy gear who were holding his bridle had already had to yank down hard to keep the horse in line. Now, when the wall of light from the flatbed truck hit him squarely in the face as they turned, Washington's Hope reared up suddenly.

It was nothing an experienced horseman couldn't handle. But Foyle was nothing like an experienced horseman. And when Washington's Hope reared up, Foyle did what came naturally. He tightened his grip on the reins, while his legs squeezed inward along the horse's flanks.

And the historic silver spurs dug deep into the side of the horse.

The combination of sudden, sharp pain and the powerful stimulant now coursing through his body threw Washington's Hope into a frenzy. He bolted from the grip of the Secret Service man, reared up violently, wheeled around, and took off like a shot, back through the line of march, barely avoiding half a dozen of the wheelchair-bound youngsters in his path.

For an instant, there was no reaction. The reporters and photographers, many of whom had covered the political beat all their lives, and therefore had rarely witnessed a genuinely spontaneous event, assumed that this was a part of the program. Foyle, they assumed, must have practiced this maneuver, the better to win the cheers of the crowd.

Then they heard Foyle yelling.

He was not yelling "Yee haw!" or "Yippie-tie-yi-yay!"

He was yelling "Help! Help! Help, goddamn it, help!"

And suddenly lenses wheeled, and hands were banging frantically on the hood of the flatbed truck, as the press photographers screamed at the driver to "get moving, go! Go! Go! Follow that horse!" From their vantage point along the line of march, network correspondents were screaming into their cellular phones back to New York and Washington that "something's happened to Foyle!" It would take long, agonizing moments for the broadcast networks to interrupt their afternoon soaps and go live to Cheyenne, thereby incurring the wrath of 12,453 viewers who called the networks with their bitter complaints. ("Amber has just learned that the pool boy she's been sleeping with is her half brother, and you cut away?")

The All News Network had no such dilemma. All morning they had been running a split-screen shot of the Rodeo Days preparation in one box, and interviews in the other, principally with Dr. Sherman Gelt, ANN's resident expert on congressional relations, presidential debates, political advertising, international law, and polling. Dr. Gelt was just warming up to his discourse on the leading candidates for transportation secretary when Washington's Hope bolted, and the screen was suddenly filled with the image of MacArthur Foyle in full gallop.

To his credit, Foyle managed to stay aboard the horse for several seconds; indeed, for just one instant, when he held on to the reins with his left hand while waving his right high in the air in an effort to maintain his balance, he looked like a true son of the West. Had the moment ended right there, it would have made for a heroic snapshot in time.

Unfortunately for Foyle, the moment ended—and so did Foyle's ride. Urged on by the spurs that Foyle uncontrollably kept digging into his flanks, Washington's Hope wheeled again and bolted back toward the head of the march. The maneuver wrested Foyle's grip loose from the reins, and he went off into the air in a remarkably long parabolic arc—landing squarely on his left leg. The snap of the femur was clearly audible to the spectators near the point of landing.

Now, imagine for a moment that this is all that happens. A newly elected President is thrown from a horse, sails through the air, and breaks his leg. What comes next?

His brief flight is captured on tape, replayed again and again, becomes the front-page picture on every newspaper in America. Tabloid caption writers give thanks to whatever gods may be as they pen their brief commentaries: "What Man on Horseback?" or "Air Force Whoa!" Comedy shows dub rude sounds and comments on slow-motion replays of the accident. The footage becomes an inevitable part of every review of the week, every retrospective. Like Gerald Ford's stumbles down the steps of an airplane, like Jimmy Carter's collapse during a marathon run, like George Bush's hurl during a state dinner in Tokyo, Foyle's mishap turns into an instant international punch line.

All that would have happened—if that were all that had happened.

Here is what happened within the sixty seconds that followed Foyle's slamming down onto the pavement of Seventeenth Street.

• Nine Secret Service agents scattered along the line of march surrounded Foyle, guns drawn, alert to the possibility that someone in the crowd had fired a gun at Foyle or at the horse.

• One hundred thirteen spectators with videotape recorders pushed forward toward the ropes, heads filled with visions of large cash payments from grateful TV producers. "Is he bleeding?" one husband screamed at his camera-wielding spouse. "Get the blood, get the blood!"

• Four desk assistants, five secretaries, and nine news vice-presidents at four different networks lunged for telephones to locate their anchors, who were engaged in two power lunches, one racquetball game, and one act of conjugal relations not sanctioned by any major sectarian or secular authority.

• Thirty-seven correspondents and producers, on the scene in Cheyenne, scrambled to reach the feed point half a block away from the press bleachers, knowing that their networks would be switching live to the scene of the incident as soon as possible. One correspondent pulled a large can of hair spray out of his trench coat on the dead run, and was wrestled to the ground by a Secret Service agent, under the impression that it was some kind of dangerous chemical agent.

• The All News Network correspondent and the radio reporters were already on the air, jamming words into their microphones: "President-elect Foyle has been thrown from his horse! Foyle has been thrown from his horse! He landed on the ground! Secret Service agents are at his side! I repeat: President-elect Foyle has been thrown from his horse in Cheyenne, Wyoming, and is on the ground!" More than the words, which were repeated over and over again, the tone of just barely controlled hysteria instantly conveyed to every listener the sense that Something Big Was Up.

• The doctors, nurses, and technicians at the emergency rescue vehicle, alerted by the Secret Service that "Condor is down! Condor is down!" prepared to shock a stopped heart into beating, prepared for emergency surgery to remove a bullet, prepared for a tracheotomy to dislodge a food particle blocking Foyle's throat passage, flashed an alert to the Laramie County Memorial Hospital and Trauma Center that the next President of the United States would be on the way momentarily.

- Marsh leapt from his chair at the Golden Lasso Motor Court, stood transfixed in front of the television for several long seconds, and screamed at everyone in the room, "You are dead meat! Every one of you—dead meat!"
- And a tiny, undetectable microscopic globule of fat from the bone marrow of MacArthur Foyle's femur lodged tight into a capillary.

EIGHT

★ ★ ★

Imagine the stately home of a wealthy, well-mannered couple who have jetted off to the islands for a winter vacation, and given the help time off, leaving their estate in the care of their nineteen-year-old son. Imagine he invites a few friends over, who invite a few friends over, who invite a few friends over, who each have a few friends of their own. Now procure the key to the liquor cabinet, crank up the state-of-the-art sound system, and dispatch one of the partygoers to the nearest adult video store. Order in enough pizzas to feed the revelers—say, two dozen or so—and mix with an RV van full of potato chips, dips, pretzels, nuts, and beer. Now imagine this same stately home early on the morning after the party breaks up.

You haven't begun to imagine the scene outside the Laramie County Memorial Hospital and Trauma Center the morning after President-elect Foyle was brought in with a broken leg.

The parking lot was jammed with a dozen Satellite News Gathering trucks, each packed with half a million dollars' worth of digital editing and transmission gear, topped with an RCA Satcom II fourteen-inch-wide satellite dish that jutted up out of the sunroof, enabling the SNG truck to send and receive television signals from just about anywhere in the world. In normal times, they were leased and operated by local stations and regional news operations; now they had been subleased—"ransomed," in the words of one hysterical network cost-controller—by the major networks for coverage of President-elect Foyle's injury, and driven hundreds of miles to the site of the hospital.

On the grounds just in front of the hospital's imposing limestone entrance, a twelve-foot-wide patch had been given over to television. A series of elevated wooden stands marked the turf for each network. No one watching the reports would realize that Mark of NBC was barely eighteen inches away from Bill of ABC, who was close enough to Susan of CBS to be sued for harassment. Enough floodlights surrounded the area to suggest the imminent arrival of an alien spacecraft on the hospital lawn.

Here is where the famous faces would stand while taping their reports and chatting live with the anchors during the special reports that had shredded the networks' schedules all evening.

("What do you mean, 'preempt'?" one network entertainment chief had screamed at the news president. "It's November—it's Sweeps Month! I've got a four-part miniseries that starts tonight! Remember? The cheerleader who ran the S and M club in her church basement and then shot the gym teacher? Five point six million in production alone!")

Now, in the chill of a Cheyenne autumn dawn, the less famous faces, the second-string national correspondents who worked holidays, weekends, and the early mornings, whose salaries were often separated from the salaries of their prime-time counterparts by a decimal point, waited to feed the early-morning news shows. Their sour countenances, their slumped shoulders, were only partially attributable to the hour of the morning, to their lack of sleep, to their place in the broadcasting firmament. Mostly, it was the Desk.

All evening, all night long, they had been summoned by their beepers to conversations of teeth-grinding futility with the producers back home at the Desk: the men and women who never ventured any farther than the cafeteria and the rest rooms, but who lived under the assumption that once they had proposed a story, it was only a lack of initiative and gumption that prevented the reporter from getting it.

"We'd like you to effort a bedside interview with Foyle," they would suggest.

"See if you can get into the trauma room, and do a cinéma vérité thing with the folks who worked on Foyle—you know, like that *M*A*S*H** episode, the black-and-white one?"

"Can you get to the Secret Service guys who were on the parade route?

See if you can get to the driver who hit the kid in the wheelchair on the way to the hospital."

The reporters would explain that the Secret Service had cordoned off an entire wing of the hospital, that any attempt to bring a camera within two hundred yards of Foyle would end in violent death—"Does the term 'fusillade of bullets' ring a bell?" one of the reporters had snapped to his boss—that they were being spoon-fed medical bulletins every hour inside the hospital auditorium, and that was *it*—and from the Desk there would come a sigh of disappointment, and an alternative suggestion of equal plausibility.

"Well, what about the horse?"

In fact, Washington's Hope was history. A team of Secret Service agents had subdued the animal, dragged it down the street back to the temporary paddock, and dispatched it to horse heaven with three shots from a nine-millimeter Glock rapid-fire pistol. Unfortunately for the Secret Service, Mr. Lester Vinghis, a tourist from Oklahoma City, had lagged behind at the paddock after the crowd had streamed toward the parade route. He was taping the now-empty stall for want of anything better to do, when he found himself viewing an equine execution through his viewfinder. Lester Vinghis may have been a simple man—he had never heard of balsamic vinegar, hermeneutics, or grunge—but Lester Vinghis was no fool. Two and a half hours and $32,000 later, the tape was airing on a special edition of *Behind the Door,* America's favorite tabloid TV show—and 300 animal-rights activists were ringing Laramie County Memorial.

While the scene outside the hospital was approaching a decent working definition of chaos, the backstage disorder had hit full-tilt bedlam.

At least a hundred portable fax machines spewed out news copy, letters of agreement for emergency rentals of equipment, show lineups, hotel room reservations, and script rewrites. The remains of these communications littered the lawn and the parking lot. The Styrofoam coffee cups, the soda cans, the pizza cartons spilled over the rims of the trash cans placed around the hospital. The sanitary conditions inside and outside the three Porta-Johns would have staggered the imagination of Upton Sinclair.

The crowds that had moved en masse from the parade route to the hospital stayed on to watch . . . to watch . . . to watch. When they recognized a famous TV news star, they cheered, whistled, beckoned her over for autographs. When Foyle's campaign team arrived at the hospital, the news junkies pointed out Marsh and Veigle and "Screech."

Each time a portable light gun was aimed at the crowd, hands began to wave at the camera, smiles lit up the faces. The reporters, who were describing the crowds in near-funereal tones—"They came to stand vigil, to wait in silence, to pray for their new leader. . . ."—spat out muffled curses, finally prevailing with a simple warning: "Look—if you smile or cheer or laugh, we can't put you on TV. Okay?"

Most were there to gawk. A few were there to take their message to a waiting world.

"I know who tried to kill him! I know who tried to kill him!" a young man screamed over and over.

"I saw the whole thing!" a young woman yelled to the reporters, the camera crews, the hospital technicians, the paramedics taking a smoke break. "Put me on the TV! I saw the whole thing!"

But for all of the hysteria, all of the vast movement of people and equipment and money—millions of dollars in lost advertising revenue and overtime and emergency cash disbursements—the fact is that nothing of any real significance had happened. The President-elect had broken his leg. Now he was in traction on a third-floor suite of the hospital. The tape of the accident had been played so often that it had been committed to memory, frame by frame, by a working majority of the adult American population.

All of the resources of the great journalistic enterprises had been thrown into the service of a story that was smothered to death in its first minutes; and given modern communications technology, the coverage swiftly descended into absurdity.

Consider: Reporters are trained to cover an event, then distill it, then communicate its essence in a minute or two. But every briefing, by a doctor, a surgeon, or a member of Foyle's transition team, was being carried live.

Dr. Hawes, a noted orthopedic surgeon who had been flown in from Denver, described the President-elect's simple fracture of the femur, using a crude but effective drawing.

Then the reporters began to question Dr. Hawes. This is a procedure generally screened from the public eye for the reason best expressed by the old adage "If you love the law, and you love good sausage, don't ever watch either one being made." But now the journalistic community was in crisis mode. The All News Network had already been throwing its special graphic—"A Leader Injured"—on the screen every three and a half minutes, accompanied by the incessant musical signature of Hopi war drums. Great metropolitan newspapers had cleared whole pages for elaborate diagrams of the skeletal structure of the leg. And the reporters' never-ending search for the Truth was being beamed across America as it happened.

"Doctor, what can you tell us about the chances of this fracture reoccurring?"

"Doctor, when will we be able to see the actual X rays? Is there any reason for denying the public's right to see the X rays for themselves?"

"What assurance can you give us that the X rays have not been tampered with?"

"In the course of the treatment of the President-elect's leg, did you run across any evidence of any other health problem?"

"How would you assess the prospects for the President-elect to perform his duties without impairment?"

"How do you spell *femur?*"

As soon as the briefings ended, the reporters climbed on top of chairs, and began explaining to their viewers what they had just heard in exhaustive detail a moment earlier.

"Well, Ed, Dr. Hawes says it *is* a simple fracture, there *are* no complications, the President-elect *is* resting comfortably, he *is* in traction, he *has* been given a sedative."

The anchorman back in New York resisted the temptation to remind the reporter that the viewing public had heard precisely this information thirty seconds before. Instead, in the finest journalistic tradition, he tried to Advance the Story.

"Mark, what do Senator Foyle's advisers think this injury will do to the transition timetable?"

Mark resisted the temptation to remind the anchorman that he had been penned in with every other reporter and hadn't a clue.

"That's not entirely clear, Ed," the reporter offered.

In fact, the anchorman, whose name alone could gain him instant access to restaurant reservations, hot-ticket art exhibits, U.S. Open tickets, and corporate inner sanctums, had already spoken to Marsh, had already learned of the transition team's plans to move Foyle back to Washington within seventy-two hours. From a distance of 2,300 miles, the anchor had in fact been able to acquire infinitely more information than his network's reporter, who was 350 feet from the transition headquarters now established in the executive wing of the hospital.

"We understand that he'll be moved by the end of the week, Mark," the anchorman said in a tone of gentle reproach.

"We'll try to get confirmation from here, Ed," said the reporter, which could be loosely translated as *Why don't you go piss up a rope, you overpaid clotheshorse?*

By late night, it was clear that the story had run its course. MacArthur Foyle was sleeping, thanks to the day's exhausting events and the aid of a mild sedative. The transition team had worked hard on Dr. Hawes to have him minimize this point.

"See, Doctor," Alan Veigle explained, "once you talk 'sedative,' the next question is going to be 'temporary disability,' and then the next question is going to be 'Where's the Vice President–elect?' And then they're going to ask a lot of questions about the Twenty-fifth Amendment, and what kind of understanding does the President-elect have with Mr. Block, and by the way, is he on the way back from his well-deserved vacation, and so the more you can explain that this is simply a matter of a sleep aid, kind of like an aspirin, the better off all of us will feel after this genuinely unpleasant day, and the more grateful we will be, as well."

The television networks had already decided that one day of saturation coverage was enough. Apart from all the news specials, every other source of information and diversion had jumped into the act. *Hollywood Tonight* had the reaction from show business celebrities, who managed to offer get-well sentiments despite their loathing of MacArthur Foyle's conservative views. Only one celebrity, Scar, the lead guitarist of the hot group Plague, had broken with the pack, sneering into the camera, "Too bad it wasn't his pus-filled head."

All News Network's nightly half-hour *Slugfest* had featured a spirited debate about whether national leaders should risk their safety in pursuit of favorable publicity. *Carl's Place,* the syndicated prime-time call-in show, had devoted its entire hour to the story. Past footage of injured and hospitalized Presidents (Ike's heart attack, JFK on crutches from a back injury, LBJ's surgery scar, Reagan's recoveries from a bullet and from surgery) filled the screen.

So the story was done. Foyle's efficient transition team had manufactured feisty, gutsy, good-humored quotes attributable to the future President ("Did someone get the license plate on that horse?"), and excised his authentic sentiments ("When I figure out which one of you assholes got me into this, you'll be lucky to get a job inspecting whale blubber in Alaska"). It was time to move on.

Except that at 4:45 A.M., eighteen hours after that tiny globule of fat had entered MacArthur Foyle's bloodstream, a complex combination of chemical reactions to that intrusive episode triggered a sudden, undetected embolism in the left lung of the just-elected President—who gasped twice and died.

INTERLUDE: A RUMINATION ON CHANCE

★ ★ ★

It echoed through every living room, every den, every finished basement, every student lounge, every kitchen breakfast nook, everywhere a TV or radio could pick up the half-dissected pieties that the death of Mack Foyle demanded.

"A shocked nation" . . . "as a shocked nation" . . . "shock and grief shrouded" . . . "shock held a stunned nation" . . . "the shock was felt around the world" . . .

And in the millions of words that poured into America's living rooms in the first hours after the death of the newly chosen President, not one sentence was uttered that came close to the following sentiment:

"Why are we all so surprised? Don't any of us know the history of our own country?"

Indeed. If life turns on a dime, our political history turns on a plugged nickel. Epochal changes in our country have pivoted on the most whimsical events—a missed meeting, an ill-timed quip, a timely phone call. Sometimes these seemingly trivial events have meant the difference between life and death, tranquility and chaos.

Sometimes we do not even know what has shaped us. Were the votes that decided the 1960 election cast by the kind of voter who told a reporter that "there was something about Richard Nixon's eyes I just don't trust—especially the left one"? Does our political history owe more to the C-SPAN junkie who risks a good night's sleep to watch the Senate debate on the Supplemental Higher Education Act, or to the sort of voter who told a newspaper in 1964 that she would not vote for Barry Goldwater because he'd planned to sell her TV? When told that the Senator had been talking about privatizing the TVA (Tennessee Valley Authority), the voter replied, "I'm not taking any chances."

We cannot know why voters do what they do. What we do know is how few of them are required to change the story of a nation. Why did 5,563 people in Ohio and 7,242 people in Mississippi vote for Jimmy Carter instead of Gerald Ford in 1976? We do not know. But if that many voters in those two states had changed their minds by Election Day, then thirty-three electoral votes would have shifted, and Ford would have been elected President—even though Jimmy Carter would have received 1,682,740 more votes than the "winner."

Why did 55,458 voters in Ohio and Missouri choose Richard Nixon over Hubert Humphrey in 1968? Was it Mr. Nixon's ineffable charm? Did they conclude that anyone who, like Mr. Nixon, had so abandoned any pretense of inner peace and happiness deserved the job that had corroded his soul? We do not know. But had that fragment of the electorate—fewer than one-tenth of one percent of the 73,123,490 voters who shuffled to the polls that year, voted differently in 1968, Richard Nixon would have been deprived of thirty-eight electoral votes, which would have cost him his electoral majority. That would have left Alabama governor and third-party presidential candidate George Wallace with the balance of power, able to deal his votes to the high bidder, or plunge the election into the House of Representatives, gumming up the political machinery of the United States for months.

This history only begins to hint at the fragile foundations on which America has built its claim to political stability. Consider, for example, a few of those episodes where a trivial, utterly insignificant event has altered the course of history. It is as if a young lad, walking by a stream, skimmed a rock along the water—which hit a stone, which dislodged a submerged boulder, which altered the flow of the stream, which coursed into the river, which overflowed its bed and rushed into a whole new path.

- It is 1884. Republican James G. Blaine is headed for victory against New York governor Grover Cleveland, in large measure because the Tammany Democrats of New York, distrustful of Cleveland's reformist impulses, are sitting on their hands. Then, a few days before election, a passionate Blaine supporter addresses Mr. Blaine (in those days, followers often traveled to the candidate's home to pledge their fealty) and denounces the Democrats as the party of "rum, Romanism, and rebellion." It is unclear whether these remarks offended alcoholics and anarchists, but there is no doubt that New York's immigrant Catholics were incensed by the religious slur. They turned out despite Tammany's indifference, and Grover Cleveland won New York State by 1,047 votes. That gave him the state's thirty-six electoral votes, and those votes gave Cleveland, instead of Blaine, the White House.

- It is 1916. Republican Charles Evans Hughes, who has stepped down from the United States Supreme Court to challenge President Woodrow Wilson, is the heavy favorite to win the White House. Late in the campaign, Hughes finds himself caught in the middle of a ferocious internecine Republican feud in California, between the conservative faction, and the progressives, led by Senator Hiram Johnson. Hughes's plan was to walk a fine line by visiting both camps. But after making his peace with the conservatives, he went to visit Hiram Johnson—and could not find the senator's hotel room. The meeting never took place. Progressives, feeling slighted, sat on their hands on Election Day. The state of California went narrowly for Wilson, and that state's thirteen electoral votes kept Wilson in the White House.

(On Election Night, the story goes, a reporter called the Hughes home to get the candidate's reaction to his loss, and was told by a servant, "The President-elect has retired for the night." "Yeah?" the reporter replied. "Well, when he wakes up, tell him he ain't the President-elect anymore.")

- It is 1948. Republican candidate Thomas Dewey is so certain to be elected President that news magazines with pre-election deadlines prepare cover stories on the incoming Dewey administration—this, in spite of a stuffed-shirt pomposity that made him look, in Dorothy Parker's classic phrase, "like the little man on the wedding cake." Meanwhile, sure loser President Harry Truman crisscrosses the country, attacking the Republican Congress.

Late in the campaign, Dewey is whistle-stopping through the Midwest. At one stop, Dewey's speech from the back of the train is interrupted when the engineer, misinterpreting a signal, begins to pull the train out of the station. His dignity ruffled, Dewey snaps, "In Russia, they shoot idiots like that, but we'll let him off with a warning."

Among the several million Americans who worked on the railroads back then, or who were members of railroad families, the remark failed to elicit warm feelings. It sounded, in fact, rather like the lord of the manor rebuking the gardener for improperly pruning the azaleas. In key midwestern states like Illinois and Ohio, where the railroad was once a leading employer, Dewey's remark had roughly the same appeal as a compulsive overeater who rushes back from a hasty lunch at a Mexican restaurant, jams into a crowded elevator, and then proceeds to demonstrate the gastronomic consequences of ingesting the Acapulco Special in six and a half minutes. On Election Day, Illinois and Ohio swing to Truman by a combined total of some 30,000 votes. The combined electoral vote total of fifty-three keeps Truman in the White House. Had those two states gone to Dewey, the electoral college would have deadlocked—and the fate of the presidency would have rested in the hands of South Carolina governor J. Strom Thurmond, who had captured thirty-nine electoral votes as the candidate of the white-supremacist National States' Rights Party.

- It is 1960. Toward the end of a very close race between Richard Nixon and John Kennedy, word comes that Martin Luther King, Jr., is in a southern jail; his colleagues in the civil rights movement fear for his safety. Although King's father, a powerful community leader in Montgomery, Alabama, has endorsed Nixon (he fears a Catholic in the White House), Kennedy calls the jail to argue for King's release. When he is freed, King's father joyfully, if imprudently, declares, "I've got a suitcase full of votes, and I'm going to deliver them to this fine young man." Kennedy goes on to win the closest victory in modern history. It is hard to know whether last-minute black votes or very-last-minute creative arithmetic in the Chicago Board of Elections made more of a difference.

But surely, surely the fact that political fortunes rise and fall with such whimsicality cannot be compared to the first and last ride of MacArthur Foyle. Surely, the capricious casting of votes cannot be equated with the cruel fate that befell a man who gave his life for a photo opportunity, who ended his days on earth by taking a spill that led to a broken leg, that sent a fragment of fat on its deadly journey to a capillary that took from the nation the leader it had just chosen. Surely, the life and death of the most powerful people on Earth cannot be anchored in such flimsy harbors.

Oh yeah?

Well, let us journey back to Miami, Florida, in the winter of 1932. Look: there is the newly elected President, Franklin Delano Roosevelt, on vacation. There he is, riding in a motorcade with another prominent politician, Anton Cermak, the mayor of Chicago. A large crowd has turned out to cheer the incoming chief executive. The feeling, however, was not unanimous. In that crowd was one Giuseppe Zangara, who had come to Miami to kill Roosevelt.

Zangara was in the crowd at Miami's Bayfront Park, but could not reach the front of the crowd until after Roosevelt had finished speaking. By then, a crowd of dignitaries had gathered around him. So when Zangara climbed atop a wooden folding chair and opened fire, he hit five bystanders, and killed Mayor Cermak of Chicago. Had Zangara been at the front of the crowd, the presidency would have gone to the man the electors had chosen as the new Vice President: John Nance Garner, the Speaker of the House, a Texan of breathtaking reactionary bent, who would have guided this nation through the most troubled economic times in its history.

There would have been no New Deal, no fireside chats, no symbol of buoyant optimism in the Oval Office.

Now come back to 1960, when the newly elected President John Kennedy was putting his administration together out of his Georgetown home in Washington. Kennedy was, of course, being stalked by the full-court press, and by the swarm of lawyers, foundation executives, and third-level elected officials for whom a Washington appointment meant hope for a back door out of the lives in which they were imprisoned.

But there was someone else following the new prince's movements: a seventy-three-year-old former mental patient from Belmont, New Hampshire, named Richard P. Pavlick. He had concluded that Kennedy had bought the presidency through slick TV advertising and payoffs; he had also concluded that Kennedy had to die. Being an inventive gentleman, Pavlick stalked Kennedy while he vacationed at the family home in Palm Beach, Florida. Pavlick then bought several sticks of dynamite, and rigged it to his car. His plan was to follow Kennedy to church, ram his car into Kennedy's, and blow the newly elected President into the next world. On December 11, 1960, Pavlick drove up to JFK's home and parked across the street; the dynamite in his car was wired to a switch. But when he saw Kennedy emerge from his home with Jacqueline and Caroline in tow, Pavlick decided not to act.

"I decided to get him in church or somewhere else," he said. Nor did Pavlick act later, when he stood just a few rows behind Kennedy in church. Four days later, acting on a tip from a postal inspector back north, the Secret Service arrested Pavlick. But had Kennedy's wife and child had the sniffles that Sunday, or had Mr. Pavlick's sensibilities been less refined, Kennedy would have died before the votes of his electors had even been counted by the Congress.

And what then? If the votes of the dead Kennedy were discounted, Richard Nixon would then have had the most electoral votes cast for a living human being; would he then have been declared President-elect? Would the Congress have decided that not enough electoral votes had been cast to choose anyone, and thus thrown the election into the House of Representatives? Would they have counted Lyndon Johnson's vice-presidential votes, automatically elevating him to President-elect?

How can such close calls surprise any sentient citizen? If a shower passes through Dallas on November 22, 1963, the bubbletop stays on the roof of the presidential limousine, and John Kennedy travels from airport to trade mart without history pausing to blink. If Robert Kennedy decides to take the cheers of the crowd at the Ambassador Hotel on June 4, 1968, instead of choosing the relative peace and quiet of an exit through the kitchen, Sirhan Sirhan waits in vain.

If Squeaky Fromme and Sarah Jane Moore sign up with their local unit of the National Rifle Association and engage in some good clean family-fun pistol practice, before hitting the streets of California, then perhaps Gerald Ford's Vice President, Nelson Rockefeller, gets the lifelong dream that several tens of millions of dollars could not buy him. If

Ronald Reagan steps an inch to his left on March 31, 1981, or if Secret Service agents, unaware he has been shot, take him back to the White House instead of to a hospital which happens to have a trauma center, then Reagan bleeds to death and his presidency lasts eight weeks, not eight years.

The lesson is clear. Over the years, the American political system has resembled a scene from a classic Charlie Chaplin movie, where Chaplin roller-skates again and again to the edge of a fatal abyss, utterly unaware of his impending doom, righting himself at the last possible moment from what he fears would be an embarrassing pratfall, but what would in fact be a deadly plunge.

But this time, when President-elect Foyle mounted that horse in Cheyenne, Wyoming, there was no one to yell "Cut!"

NINE

★ ★ ★

This is what they lived for. This is why they did it.

This is why they spent their lives in rooms that never saw the light. This is why they worked amid the ambience of a landfill, breathing air redolent with the stink of printer's ink, tobacco, and a thousand half-eaten Chinese meals that sat glutinous in cardboard cartons that were never thrown away. This is why they tethered themselves to telephones and computer screens. This is why they labored for a free press and wore a prisoner's pallor.

This is why they could bolt from holiday hearth and home at a moment's notice, leaving their aged parents and stunned spouses staring mutely at the holiday turkey, hurling clothes into a bag, their faces flushed with a blend of guilt and lust. This is why they could leave a five-year old boy weeping over his birthday cake ("But you promised! You *promised!*"). This is why they could let the rush of true love, that blend of affection and desire, wither away into loveless nights and distant telephone calls heavy with recrimination, all of it ending not with a bang but a whimper.

What could possess anyone to lead such a life if not for a day like this? Look at Steve Baer, who had begun life at the Network fifteen years ago as a courier, weaving his way through the city traffic on a Harley, carrying tapes from the street to the newsroom. One day he had turned in his chopper for a job as desk assistant; after five years, he had begged, bluffed, earned his way into a producer's job. His reward for his talent, tenacity, and guts was a position on the late-night news program. For the Network, the show was a prestigious, award-winning money-making feather in the corporate cap. For Steve Baer, it was a life of 1:30 A.M. homecomings, a seven-year-old daughter, Hillary, who was in his life either as a blurred presence on weekday mornings, or as a stranger in a fluffy nightgown trying to drag him from his sleep on a Saturday morning. Steve Baer loved Hillary very much; it was simply in the nature of his work that he did not know the name of her teacher, her doctor, her stuffed dog, or the friends she played with.

One Saturday afternoon, Steve Baer had taken his wife and daughter to the National Zoo to fulfill a solemn parental pledge: a visit to the pandas that had been a highlight of the Parents' Day trip. Steve had missed that day, as he had missed every Parents' Day since Hillary had started school. (One airplane hijacking, two senatorial sex scandals, one anchorman's whim.)

As they made their way through the tropical birds, the monkeys, the penguins, and the reptiles, Steve's wife kept glancing over at him with the wariness of a bomb squad expert examining a ticking package. *For God's sakes, don't blow this one,* she silently begged him. *It's all right,* Steve smiled back. The beeper that seemed surgically attached to his belt was silent; the portable radios he was unconsciously monitoring as he walked through the zoo had none of the blare of Crisis, to which his senses were as attuned as those of a deer in the forest on the first day of hunting season.

"The pandas, Daddy, the pandas are over there!" Hillary shouted from atop his shoulders. Steve turned to follow the path, then spotted a pay phone. He crouched down and fished out a quarter.

"Honey, I'm just going to make sure nothing's happening, and then we'll go right to the pandas."

"No, Daddy, no! Don't call! Don't call!" Hillary began to pound on Steve's head in panic.

"It's all right, honey, I just have to check."

Hillary began to yank at Steve's hair, as passersby turned to gaze, shook their heads, and mumbled something about the epidemic of child abuse.

"Desk," came the voice through the phone.

"Baer here," Steve said, and the quick intake of air told him the temperature even before the words barked out at him.

"Jesus Christ, where the hell are you? We've been paging you for an hour!"

"My beeper—"

"Forget it, forget it. Beijing says your Anchor can have a no-limits interview with Li Peng Tuesday—*this* Tuesday. You've got a visa waiting at the consulate. Your flight leaves in three hours from Dulles. Move!"

And the line went dead.

"The pandas, Daddy. Let's go see the pandas!"

"Steve . . . ," his wife said.

And Steve Baer, his heart sinking and his knees buckling with the weight of his guilt and his daughter, began racing through the zoo, as Hillary wept and cried out, "Slow down, Daddy, slow down! This isn't *fun!*"

"See, honey, see, we're looking at *(huhn, huhn)* the pandas, and then Daddy has to run home and go all the way to *(huhn, huhn)* China, where the pandas live."

"Daddy, look at the straw! The pandas eat straw! I want you to look at the pandas eating the straw!"

"I am, honey, I *(huhn, huhn)* am."

Four minutes later, they were in the parking lot, Hillary hitting her fists on the back of the car. Fifteen minutes after that, they were home. Eight minutes after that, Steve was bolting from the house. Twenty-four hours after that, Steve was in Beijing, where he called home and learned that his wife had made appointments with a child psychologist and a matrimonial lawyer. Steve had spent those twenty-four hours without sleep, without rest, cutting a profile of Li Peng. When the executive producer returned from his lunch with the ambassador and his tennis game, he screened the profile, then screamed for five minutes at Steve for upcutting a sound bite. An hour after that, the Chinese authorities had canceled the interview.

Yet here he was now, support payments and unopened birthday presents forgotten, frantically searching the computer files, speeding tapes back and forth through the search mode on his VCR, stitching together the instant retrospective on the life and times of the late, lamented un-President Foyle, which would hit air the moment a break came in the flood of faces and voices that were filling the air. He would sleep for three hours in the next seventy-two; he would miss his weekend with Hillary; he had never been more fulfilled.

Or look at Diana Belzer. At twenty-seven, she was sleek, smart, funny, and had last had intimate contact with a person of the opposite sex four months earlier, when a well-dressed, personable-looking stranger had grabbed her left buttock in a crowded elevator at Macy's.

She had worked for the last two years as a researcher for the Network, spending her twelve- or fourteen-hour days verifying the death rate from famine in sub-Saharan Africa for the 1970s, or finding the percentage of women employed in policy-making jobs at the Department of Commerce during the tenure of Luther Hodges. It was also Diana's task to ensure the accuracy of the scripts the correspondents wrote; a task that often required her to assume the demeanor of the Angel of Death, as she reached a correspondent in the field three hours before air to inform her that the New Hampshire unemployment rate was eight, not seven percent, or to break the news to another that, no matter how terrific the sunrise looked over the lake during his stand-up, it was carbon *monoxide* that came from the exhaust of automobiles, not carbon minoxidil.

The job paid slightly less than what an entry-level secretary at a Wall Street law firm made; her closet-sized office was stacked with so many books, monographs, research folders, magazines, newspapers, and reference guides that she could barely make her way from the door to the chair; her earnest, carefully researched story proposals were met with a weak smile and palpable indifference by the senior producer; she had received three expressions of gratitude and twenty-six profane or obscene reprimands during her tenure.

And there she was, with her almanacs, and her *Congressional Quarterly* tomes, scattering files across the horseshoe rim of the newsroom, phone in each hand, verifying the rituals of presidential succession and state funerals, punching up medical databases to track down the nation's leading experts on embolism, in a state somewhere between bliss and hyperventilation.

And look at Dorian Wood, who forty years ago had rejected his family's 150-year-old commercial banking firm for a life in the press. He was a natural, so good that his colleagues from the working-class neighborhoods of Chicago and St. Louis and Milwaukee had forgiven him his breeding, his accent, his wardrobe, and his waistline. At twenty-eight, Wood had been managing editor of a prestigious Philadelphia newspaper; at thirty-two, he had been the wunderkind of *Time;* at thirty-seven, president of a major network news division. Then came a new corporate team at the top of the Company, and testy fights over budgets, and an extra gimlet at lunch, and wrangles with the Anchor, and the fight over the Watergate specials, and he was out, history, put a fork in him, he was done.

For three years, Dorian Wood suffered the mortifications unique to the Men Who Used to Be. There was the six months' Distinguished Visiting Professorship, the foundation-supported study on the "Moral Crisis in the Newsroom," the endowed lectures that were attended by C-SPAN cameras, and—invariably—small knots of lonely old women and lonely young men who came to fill their empty days in the empty halls. There were long walks through the city, and ever-so-casual bids for lunch dates that his colleagues promised to accept one day soon.

So when the job offer came from the Network, Dorian Wood did not care that it was a job without real power, or that he would spend his days dealing with the tasks no one else wanted, holding the hands of the lesser lights among correspondents and producers, who knew what such a meeting told them about their status ("A meeting with *Wood?* Oh, God, I'm finished"). Dorian Wood wanted the job so much his eyes welled up with tears of gratitude.

And here was Dorian Wood, roaming the newsroom in the Executive's Uniform of Crisis: the jeans, sweater, and sport coat that news executives always sported in moments like this one.

Look, the outfit said, *see how important it is that I am here. See how I bolted from the patio, from brunch, without a second thought, to be where my experience and my judgment are desperately needed.*

And it did not matter that Dorian Wood was snatching the phone from desk assistants, or ordering in sandwiches and sodas and coffee, or making sure that makeup and prompter people were properly staffed, all of which had been arranged hours earlier. If he had to, Dorian Wood would have been on his hands and knees, making sure the computers were plugged in, that the lights were on. Dorian Wood was *there;* he was marching in the parade, not watching it. He was *in the room.* And this is what they lived for.

It had begun with a phone call from Mark Khisoff, who had spotted Foyle's speechwriter on her way out of the hospital, and tried to strike up a conversation in the hope of gathering a nugget of news. The speechwriter, who shared with her political colleagues an innate ability to measure the importance of anyone she was talking to, quickly began the half-step shuffle that indicated an urgent desire to terminate the conversation.

Suddenly, one of her colleagues in the Foyle campaign raced over, grabbed her away by the arm, and hauled her off several steps, where he whispered something in her ear. The speechwriter had slumped to the ground, as if someone had hit her, hard, in the gut. An instant later, three Cheyenne Police Department patrol cars had pulled up to the entrance of the hospital, and seven grim-faced officers had piled out of the car, guns at the ready.

When Mark looked up to the third floor, where Mack Foyle was last reported "resting comfortably," he saw lights going on in every office, and urgent movement behind the curtains. Mark may not have been the most elegant stylist on the trail, or the most telegenic, but he knew enough to know that something was up. He ran over to the network trailer.

"Something's going on up there, I think something big," he said. He called New York to make the same report, and was greeted with a weary cynicism befitting a national desk that had not yet recovered from the hour of special reports on Foyle's injured leg, barely two days after the end of a presidential election.

"Look, guys, I'm not any happier about this than you are. All I'm asking you to do is stay hot; don't 'good-night' anybody, and be ready for an interrupt."

Mark walked back to the Network camera position on the lawn and explained to an extremely disagreeable camera crew that their long day and night were not yet over. At that moment, a motorcade pulled up to the entrance, and what appeared to be the entire senior staff of the Foyle campaign, who had left the hospital only four hours earlier, leapt out of the cars and raced back inside. Marsh, he noticed, was red faced, apparently in tears. That was enough for Khisoff, who grabbed a cell phone from the sound technician and began screaming to New York the moment the desk answered to *get him the hell on the air.*

(Later that day, the network's public relations staff would boast that they had been the first on the air with news of President-elect Foyle's mortal predicament, beating the competition by nearly fifty-five seconds. Khisoff's triumph led to profiles in *USA Today, Entertainment Tonight, Show Biz Today,* and *Newsweek,* which blasted him into a featured assignment on the evening newscasts for months after, culminating in a glamorous, danger-filled assignment to cover the drug wars in Colombia, where Mark was killed when a local *policía* mistook him for an American drug smuggler.)

There are not that many moments for the men and women of news when the air goes out of the room, when a sudden stillness is all there is. It does not happen at moments of great ceremony, for royal weddings, conventions, election nights, state funerals, and postgame Superbowl locker room calls from the President are scripted down to the last chuckle. Moments like this happen when a shock wave of the unexpected pounds the walls: when pictures of starving children in a land no one ever heard of suddenly fill the TV screens; when a spaceship on a routine launch suddenly disappears in fire and a plume of smoke; when the sounds of bombs falling signal the start of a war, live and in color.

And it happened when Mark Khisoff began his live interrupt with the simple words: "Something has happened to President-elect Foyle."

For the first twenty minutes, there was only rumor: Foyle had had a heart attack, they had found the AIDS virus in a blood test, he was hemorrhaging, it was cancer. By the time a haggard, unshaven Dr. Hawes walked unsteadily into the auditorium of the Laramie County Memorial Hospital for the formal announcement, you could hear the country quiet down.

"At about five A.M. this morning, Mountain Standard Time, President-elect MacArthur Foyle died of a . . ."

And as the news coursed its way across America, tens of millions of people, from the tiniest hamlet along Maine's seacoast to the always-crowded freeways of Los Angeles, from the mobbed streets of Manhattan to the farm on the lonely, windswept Dakota prairie, millions upon millions of Americans paused suddenly in their grief to share a common thought:

Oh, my God, Teddy Block is going to be the President.

Governor Theodore Pinckney Block had led a charmed life for every one of his forty-six and a half years. Then he was chosen as the Republican candidate for Vice President of the United States.

Part of it, of course, was money. From the time his great-great-grandfather on his mother's side had seized control of every iron foundry in Berkshire County, Connecticut, the Pinckneys had never had to worry where their next Tintoretto was coming from. And that was decades before Grandfather Block had turned his liquidity at the time of the Crash of '29 into a real estate empire.

But it wasn't only money. There were people with a lot more capital than Block who did not wear the trappings of privilege nearly as well. Their $1,800 Flusser suits creased and wrinkled by the time they had walked five blocks. Their $80 haircuts by Dominique were in disarray by the time they walked out the door. Their $4,000 tans from La Sammana faded into pasty white flesh within days.

Ted Block was different.

He was one of those people who had apparently been whisked off at birth to some top-secret medical facility in the mountains of Aspen, where hair follicles were treated with a process that kept their hair kempt in a hurricane. Their sweat glands were modified so that they could leave a squash court with barely a glow. Their bodies were coated with a chemical that kept their clothes creased and neat even if they had spent the night in a steambath.

Finally, some metaphysician placed around them an aura of animal magnetism and serenity. Such people did not stumble in doorways, spill coffee into their saucers, dribble canapes down the front of their suits, or pop a shirt stud in the middle of a black-tie dinner party. They were utterly free from any fear that they drove away women and attracted flies. Their bladders did not fill in the middle of a power breakfast, causing them to cross and recross their legs, or bolt from the room in mid-sentence.

Theodore Pinckney Block had been Born to Rule. And if he lacked a certain spark of genius or insight, if he was, indeed, a step or two slow out of the cognitive gate, then so what? He had but to turn elsewhere, to that legion of those who were Born to Serve, those who had been conceived under the watchful eye of a celestial committee who had looked down on the moment of creation and proclaimed:

"Another smart-ass Jew; another hungry Italian—a briefcase carrier, a memo writer. Stain him with eczema, frizz up his hair, billow his belly, and thicken his thighs. God, it's so hard to get good help."

Block had always worn the mantle of leadership comfortably. If he had been driven to achieve by the polite indifference of his civic-minded father, he had been drilled to courtesy and thoughtfulness by his mother. So frequently had she admonished young Theodore to "remember when it's someone else's turn" that his classmates at Mayflower Day School had nicknamed him "Your Turn." He was good enough at sports to win the respect of the boys, good looking and poised enough to win the hearts of the girls, cooperative enough to win the admiration of his elders.

Indeed, only once in his time at Mayflower Day did Ted Block find himself in a fistfight, and when he had driven his opponent to the ground with a sharp left jab to the nose, no one ever called him "Pinky" again. Only twice in the school years that followed—once at Lawrenceville, once at Princeton—did he find himself having to pay a scholarship student to take an examination for him.

His ascent up the greasy pole of politics was equally effortless; in fact, in the universe of Republican politics in Connecticut, the pole hardly had any grease at all; it was more like a thin, tasteful coating of aspic. His two years in the Peace Corps in Indonesia had given him a taste for international affairs (as well for for rare Balinese wood carvings) that attracted him to the Council on Foreign Relations, whose doors would have opened wide for him even without the council's appreciation of his charitable instincts.

His instinct for civic good works put him on the board of Connecticut's Conservancy Trust when he was in his mid-twenties, and ostensibly embarked on a career as a lawyer who specialized in trusts and estates. From that perch, he began a three-year-long tour of the state, speaking at high school assemblies, chambers of commerce, and anywhere else that would invite him. And everyone he met on those trips received a handwritten thank-you note, and permanent inclusion on the Block Christmas card list. That list had been begun by his feisty, witty, and very ambitious wife "Pebble," and kept up-to-date by an ever-increasing number of volunteers who were convinced that Teddy Block was the kind of young man who was going places, who was just the kind of fellow Connecticut needed.

His run for attorney general at age twenty eight seemed quixotic at first. But when nine members of the General Assembly were indicted for kickbacks and extortion by the U.S. attorney (a longtime colleague of Block's father) the incumbent state attorney general never had a chance. The clean-cut young man with the powerful slogan ("They've Had Their Turn; Now It's Your Turn") became a statewide catchphrase. His landslide victory earned Block his first picture in *Time* and *Newsweek* as one of the "25 Fresh Faces in Politics" feature. His capture of the governorship four years later would have been a near certainty even if a hopelessly divided Democratic Party hadn't produced a bitter primary and a third-party run by the loser.

By the end of three successful terms, Ted Block was forty-four and could have passed for thirty-five. Summer swims in the Long Island Sound and daily workouts on the tennis court kept his frame free of flab, and his face and brow were glowing testimony to good genes and his capacity to elude hard thinking. Block was one of those men whom acolytes describe as a "quick study"; this meant he was able to do as he was told. His speechwriters called him a "terrific editor," which meant that he reviewed speech drafts by drawing in big commas, periods, and capital letters. His operatives would sit in bars and lean across the table at an interviewer, confidentially revealing to them that Block was "really good in small groups."

In politics, this phrase is code. It carries the same meaning as when a schoolmate, trying to fix someone up, says: "She has a *wonderful* personality" or "He's really a lot of fun once you get to know him." In school, these compliments mean, "She has a face like a Nestlé's Crunch bar." When a political aide says, "He's really good in small groups," it means, *He is so completely incapable of understanding the power of words or ideas that I can barely restrain myself from leaning across his desk, grabbing his lapels, and screaming, "Wake up, schmuck!" into that lean, beautiful face of his.*

Such matters were of small consequence to Ted Block, who believed with quiet certainty that the presidency was his destiny. He had come from stock at least as venerable as the Roosevelts', far more upstanding than the Kennedys', far more affluent than the Bushes'. His brand of moderate-liberal Republicanism, so long out of fashion, was beginning to look appealing again, especially once the scorched-earth Republicans in Congress had lost their majority to the Democrats after only four years in power. Certainly his friends on the editorial boards of the great national newspapers treated him with near-deferential respect. (In fact, Block was one of the few people in public life who could, with a single phone call, arrange for a contrite *New York Times* editorial page apology for a reporter's acerbic observation the day before—an accomplishment usually available only to bankers with a net worth of more than one billion dollars, or corpulent, Teutonic ex–secretaries of state.)

So it seemed inevitable that Theodore Block would seek his party's nomination for the presidency. His Christmas card list now numbered well into the tens of thousands; his handwritten notes had by now reached at least that number of potential supporters, contributors, and convention delegates, and he had spent just about the whole year after his governorship ended touring the nation, speaking at any gathering of Republicans who would listen to him. He had gathered a staff of impressive fund-raisers, organizers, schedulers, media consultants, and political operatives who were attracted by his looks, his contacts, his ability to pay their five-figure monthly retainers.

The Great Mentioners among the political journalists tabbed him as an early front-runner. He charmed the crowds at the Iowa corn boils, the New Hampshire pancake breakfasts, the Illinois Lincoln Day dinner.

There was only one problem: Ted Block had nothing of interest to say to the voters—and the voters knew it. He talked about a "leadership commitment" to cut the deficit, and no one knew what he meant. He talked about a "restoration of civic stewardship" to end poverty, and no one knew what he meant. He talked about "the fixed star of flexibility" as the key to his political philosophy, and no one knew what he meant.

"Let me spell it out for you, Governor," his pollster told him the night before the Iowa caucuses. "It's like the story of the ad agency that had this dog-food account. So they got the best jingle writer, the best copywriters, the best marketing experts—and the dog food wasn't selling. So they had this big meeting, and everybody got to explain what was going wrong. Finally this messenger boy at the back of the room raises his hand.

" 'You know what's wrong?' he says. 'I'll tell you: *the dogs don't like it.*' "

The next day, Block finished fourth in the caucuses and made a graceful withdrawal speech.

So no one figured that Mack Foyle would ever pick him as a running mate. In fact, no one was quite sure what had happened in that Ambassador East Hotel suite in Chicago when Foyle gathered his advisers for a final decision. The sentiment seemed evenly divided between Helen Parkinson, the dynamic governor of Ohio, and Roger Bartlett, former secretary of state. When Alan Veigle told the group about Ms. Parkinson's youthful experiments with witchcraft back in law school, and Roger Bartlett's $3 million profit from a sweetheart investment deal, there was a long silence. Then Alan Veigle spoke up.

"I'm thinking a name you're not gonna like. I'm thinking Ted Block. Wait a minute, wait a minute," he protested as the groans began. "Let me put it on the table.

"He's young. He's cute. He's credentialed. He's too rich to steal. He's too dumb to lie. All those quiche-and-chablis assholes, the trust-fund boys who think Foyle scrapes his knuckles when he walks, they love him. *And he doesn't hurt us.* Give me a better name, and he's history."

There was another long silence. Then Mack Foyle spoke.

"Someday, when I'm done with the White House, I'm gonna campaign for a constitutional amendment that says you don't have to have a running mate. Well, what the hell. Once we win, put him in charge of the National Park concessions. Make the goddamn call."

The trouble began when Block showed up at the press conference the morning after Foyle's nomination to meet the press. There were 750 reporters in the Grand Exhibit Hall of McCormick Place, and this was the one piece of news to come out of the convention. For Block, who was indeed most comfortable in small, friendly groups, the combination of bright lights, body heat, and endless, endless questions produced an unaccustomed beading of sweat on his forehead and upper lip, and an outbreak of involuntary twitching in his eyelids.

It was this nervousness, no doubt, that led to Block's unfortunate comment when he was asked about his many differences with Foyle on matters of taxation, aid to the cities, abortion, and criminal law.

"Aren't you abandoning your principles for the sake of an office?"

"Of course not," Block said, eyelids blinking rapidly in the glare of the lights, looking to ease the tension with a quip. "I'm perfectly prepared to rise above principle."

No shark tasting blood in the water ever moved faster than the press corps sensing the debut of a new victim. That answer, that press conference, set the tone for the rest of the campaign. When Block told a crowd of Kansans how happy he was to be in Nebraska, it led the evening news. When Block bit into a taco and screamed in pain when the hot pepper hit his tongue, it was aired on every broadcast. When he forgot the lines to the national anthem at a baseball game, it was bad enough; but he topped himself when he spoke to a convention of backpackers, and nostalgically recalled "those splendid nights with my good friends, snuggled in a sleeping bag under the stars, feeling things I can still feel and taste."

What made it worse was the culture of the modern political world. The Foyle campaign operatives assigned to contain the damage had no loyalty to Block. By contrast, they traveled in the same social circles as the political press. The latest story of Block's misstep was negotiable currency in the world they lived in, and they didn't think twice about sharing a story with a columnist that, inevitably, found its way into print and onto the airwaves.

So Theodore Pinckney Block ended the campaign not just as Vice President–elect, but as the National Punch Line, the last refuge of desperate cartoonists and burned-out joke writers. He was destined to spend the next four years as the loyal lapdog of President Foyle, jetting from GOP fund-raiser to the funerals of second-rate world leaders. "Foyle's Assassination Insurance," one nasty editorial in the *Boston Globe* called him.

Unfortunately, Washington's Hope never read the editorial pages.

PART TWO

THE CENTER CANNOT HOLD . . .

ELEVEN

★ ★ ★

"Heckuva thing, Mr. Speaker, heckuva thing . . . uh-huh . . . absolutely . . . abso*lute*ly . . . soon as I . . . soon as I can . . . yes . . . yes . . . abso*lute*ly . . . well, I appreciate that. We're all praying right now, I'm sure. . . . 'Bye."

He passed the cellular phone to her.

"Topper thinks I should speak to a joint session the day after the funeral. Says we need to reassure the country, the world right away. Do an LBJ-after-Dallas thing. What do you think?"

What do I think? I think I'd like to be sleeping with a travel agent who books one-way flights to Australia, that's what I think.

"First things first, Gover—Mr. Pr—um, I think you'd better change right away. We need pictures of you on the plane ready for the press as soon as we can get them. Fax 'em to the nets so they're on the air before you land. And it doesn't look . . ." She gestured toward him with a wave of her hand. "You know."

Theodore Block, by virtue of the grace of God and a forgiving electorate the presumptive President-elect of the United States, was stretched out on a fully reclining leather airline seat, still wearing the Cacharel pullover and the knee-length Lacoste swim trunks he'd been wearing when a team of Secret Service agents had yanked him off the white sands of Gouverneur Beach on the island of St. Barthélemy's. A pair of Dior sunglasses rested on his head, and grains of sand were still sprinkled on top of his tanned toes. Little more than two hours before, he had been frolicking—Ted Block was one of the few men his age of whom it could be said he "frolicked"—in the warm surf of the French West Indies, happily indifferent to the political tempest he had created by choosing to vacation on a French possession, rather than an American resort.

("This is where my family's always gone," he said, and that had been that, the loud wails from the U.S. tourism industry dismissed as the wearisome griping of tradesmen.)

Little more than two hours ago, the most urgent concern of his exhausted staff had been the spate of jokes about the dress code at French beaches.

("So our new Vice President's going down to St. Bart's, where women bare their breasts on the beach," one late-night comic had said. "Makes for a good tabloid headline, doesn't it: 'Brainless Veep on Topless Beach.' ")

And little more than two hours earlier, Sharon Kramer, a thirty-nine-year-old strawberry blonde with eyes to melt the heart, legs to stir the loins, and a tongue to chill the blood, had been sitting on the veranda outside her bungalow oiling her legs and plucking dead skin off her arms while chatting with Alan Veigle and Marsh. The connection between Cheyenne, Wyoming, and St. Bart's was weak; the language was strong.

"Sharon," Marsh was saying softly, almost choking with the effort to remain calm, "what we have here is a newly elected President with a broken leg. What we also have here is a disaster in the making. I am less than thrilled to have the new commander in chief, the new leader of the world, looking about as presidential as Jerry Ford on a ski slope with his pole jammed up his rear end. What we need now is reassurance, Sharon. What we need now is good humor, the next President offering a worried nation a jaunty wave of his hand while three kids in wheelchairs and a decorated veteran are autographing his cast. If Block comes racing back, we aren't talking reassurance anymore, Sharon. We are talking goddamn crisis mode. This—is—not—what—we—want. *Is it?"*

"Of course that's not what you want," Sharon snapped. "What you really want is to dispatch a team of Navy SEALs to drown the poor sonofabitch."

"Since when have you become president of the Teddy Block Fan

Club?" Veigle had asked. "Jesus, my ear still hurts from all those phone calls about his latest balls-up."

"Well, I'll tell you something," Sharon had said. "When you guys told me I was going to be traveling with Block all fall, I knew damn well you were cutting me out of the loop. I knew damn well you were playing your 'whose-is-bigger' game. I've gotten that kind of crap from my first day producing local news right through every campaign I ever worked for. But I figure, okay, it isn't as if Block could do us any more harm than, oh, I don't know, lose us the election, maybe. So out I go. And then what happens?"

"Sharon, we—"

"Bag it. What happens is that every day I pick up a paper or turn on a TV or call up 'the hotline' and I see all these anonymous sources inside the campaign, trashing Block, pissing and moaning about what a moron he is, how maybe they'll ship him off to Guam to get out the absentee vote. Like it's hard to figure out who was talking. For God's sake, Veigle, what do you think I think when I see a Block speech compared to 'a treacherous trek across icy, barren terrain'? Who else in our campaign ever heard of Mencken, much less cribs from him—badly, I might add."

"Sharon, that's not—"

"I don't know, guys, I always thought during the campaign, you screw your enemies. I always thought we were supposed to wait for the transition to screw our friends. I thought maybe I'd get just a little bit of help."

"That's all water over—"

"So here we are, fellas. Here's Ted Block, who's a nice enough guy. In fact, some of his qualities are downright impressive. He's decent; he wants to be fair; and he's not in politics because he didn't get breast-fed enough. It's not his fault the brain fairy was giving out short rations when he was born. But I've got a flash for you: thanks to you geniuses, he's the next Vice President of the United States. And if the next President of the United States is lying in a hospital, maybe it's a good move to bring the next Vice President back; maybe it even makes it look like Foyle has a shred of confidence in him. Maybe—"

Sharon heard a scream, then a thud as the phone hit the floor, then more screaming. It sounded as if Marsh's hotel room had suddenly caught fire. Then she heard the utterly drained voice of Alan Veigle.

"He's dead," Alan said.

"My God, Alan, the poor dumb bastard hasn't even been sworn in yet, and you're already cutting him off at—"

"Not Block—Foyle. Foyle is dead. He died five minutes ago. In his sleep. We don't know why. But he died. You can bring Block back now, Sharon. He's going to be the President." Veigle started to laugh. "I must be in shock, right? I mean, that's why I'm laughing right now, isn't it? Teddy Block is going to be the next President."

By the time Veigle had hung up the phone, a Secret Service agent was pounding on her door, yelling that she had exactly *five* minutes, *five,* to throw everything in a suitcase before the motorcade left for the airport. Minutes later, lumbering out of her room laden with suitcase, travel bag, laptop computer, and briefcase, she saw the whole tableau of Official Panic spread out before her. Secret Service agents, some with guns drawn, were hollering at each other, at the bellhops, the petrified hotel staff, and into their wrists. That Mack Foyle had been felled by a horse and an embolism thousands of miles away was irrelevant; this was Mayday, Defcon One, the Balloon Was Up. Cars and jeeps were revved up, thrown into gear; staffers flung themselves into vehicles, and the convoy was off, snaking down the treacherous mountain roads of St. Bart's, careening down the canyon to Gouverneur Beach, pausing only to disgorge three blue-suited agents who raced into the water, all but pulled Block out of the surf, and dashed to the tiny island airport, where Block, four agents, and Sharon Kramer pushed themselves aboard the corporate jet thoughtfully provided for the post-election vacation by one of Block's old college friends who now ran several of the most highly leveraged companies in America. Seconds after the plane took flight, a dozen members of the traveling press arrived, some still tasting the flaky croissants of their expense-account breakfasts, cursing at the sky with threats of divine intervention and biting commentaries, as the biggest story of their lives disappeared into the fluffy white clouds.

Now Sharon Kramer was sitting in the paneled work area of Air Force Two, thoughtfully provided by the outgoing Vice President of the United States, whose sorrow at his failure to win the presidential nomination had long since faded in the prospective glow of forty-thousand-dollar speaking fees and offers from a dozen corporate boards. And now, as she fielded faxes and telephone calls from around the world, she found herself in the grip of a profound out-of-body experience. Even as she responded to the incessant chirping of the tiny cellular phones, speaking a few words into one and handing it to Block, snapping a curt rejection into another, turning to receive slips of paper from the communications staff, she was somehow looking at herself from a distance as she sat next to this lean, bronzed, empty shell of a man, and marveled at the conflicting emotions ebbing and flowing through her.

Shock, yes, of course, there was shock, yes, no doubt about it, Sharon Kramer was shocked. She had left Washington two days before with her battered political charge in tow, escorting him toward a future as bleak as any highly skilled political operation could design for a man soon to be that famed heartbeat away. Now she was sitting inside the center of the universe.

Fear; yes, because now the future was not going to be about chairing the President's Commission on Cable Television, or stepping in for the big guy at the annual convention of the National Association of Sink-Hole Drillers. Now it was going to be about choices about the Supreme Court, the tax code, our relations with the community of nations, and control over the nuclear arsenal, which could wipe life as we know it off the face of the earth, and all of this, all of it, was about to pass into the hands of a man most of the country would not trust to program a VCR. So chalk up fear if you're keeping score.

But what was this other emotion bubbling up to the surface? What are we sensing here? Could it be . . . yes, I believe it could be . . . are we talking here about . . . *exultation?*

Oh, yes, Sharon Kramer had spent too many years being brutally honest with her adversaries to be evasive with herself. She had called too many men on their hypocrisies, their horn-dog lust disguised as attentiveness, their condescension disguised as empathy, to be evasive with herself. She knew exactly where this rush of adrenaline had come from.

When victory had finally come on Tuesday night, Sharon had found herself in a funk of staggering proportions. She knew full well that, for all of the congratulations coming her way, she had been shipped off to political Siberia by Veigle and Marsh with a style that would have done credit to the wiliest of the Medici; she was to be doomed by her very success.

The care and feeding of Theodore Block would be one of the most delicate tasks of the Foyle administration. Memories of a sitting Vice President with a tainted reputation still roiled the bowels of those who had served in the administrations of Richard Nixon and George Bush, who shivered each time they recalled answering a telephone call with a strangled: "Agnew did *what?*" "Quayle said *what?*" And who better to be given that task than the operative who had so brilliantly contained the Problem throughout the campaign, who had kept the Problem confined to the level of a Liability, rather than a Disaster? Who better than the strategist who had fed Block enough self-deprecating one-liners to survive the morning talk shows and the radio call-ins? Of course the job would be hers: Sharon Kramer, chief of staff to the Vice President.

MacArthur Foyle would raise no objections, of course. The close bond they had forged in the primaries was, she knew, long since forgotten, swept aside in the wind tunnel of a general election campaign. The one time their paths had crossed, at a victory rally in Los Angeles one week before Election Day, Foyle had greeted her warmly and said, "We miss you, Sharon." It was little more than a rhetorical tic, a way of saying "thanks" that offered no reason for any hope that she would be beckoned back inside. (Besides, Mrs. Foyle had seen Mr. Foyle glance once too often at Sharon Kramer's legs, heard one snicker too many about "in-depth briefings." There had been nothing close to a sexual liaison between Foyle and Sharon. Sometimes, she thought, the smutty little jokes that accompanied any woman with real political power had become a national ritual, like the President thowing out the first ball of the season. But the distance imposed by Sharon Kramer's new role as Ted Block's top aide had its uses in easing the mind of the First Lady–to-be.)

So, for the next four years, she would be entrusted with the task of getting Vice President Block off the political respirator, slowly trying to adjust the perception of him as a public figure unsuited for high public office. No doubt this was a critically important task, but it was a job that would take her out of the loop, out of the West Wing, off the Air Force One manifest, out of the Inner Room.

And now it was all different. Sharon mourned the death of a man she had liked and respected, but she mourned him in the manner of a television newscast, which honors a just-departed soul with a slow fade to black and five seconds of silence, followed immediately by a commercial for hemorrhoidal relief. Now there was one person who had stuck with Block loyally, who had coached him, comforted him, protected him from the avalanche of scorn and contempt that had fallen upon this man whose most severe tribulation until this campaign had been the weakness of his backhand. Of course he would turn to old friends, school-days companions, comrades from his days as governor, aides from his abortive presidential bid. But there was only one from MacArthur Foyle's inner circle who had come to his side and who had stayed there.

No, Sharon Kramer would not throw Marsh and Alan Veigle and the others to the wolves; they were smart and tough and knew their way around the town and would be needed. But now, in the political theater that was about to begin, she would have more than a backstage pass; she would be helping to draw up the guest list. And so she watched herself juggling the phones and the faxes, and murmuring into Ted Block's ear, and she could feel the rosy flush in her cheeks. She felt a short, sharp pang of guilt—and then jumped back inside herself for the ride of her life.

TWELVE

★ ★ ★

"And now, the casket is being borne by a military honor guard up the Capitol steps, and what a tragic irony it is. Little more than two months from now, MacArthur Foyle was to have made this journey in triumph, as the forty-fourth President of the United States. Now, in a tragic irony, he—oh, for Christ's sake, will you get that goddamn cross talk out of my ear?"

The Distinguished Commentator yanked his earpiece out and hurled it to the floor, twenty-five feet below the makeshift platform that had been erected inside the Rotunda to provide the networks with a privileged perch. Below him, where a nest of cables and wires lay hidden from the crowds and cameras by a huge black cloth, the technicians jumped out of the way of the rapidly descending piece of plastic specially molded to fit in the ear of the Distinguished Commentator.

"What's the over-under on this one?" the assistant audio manager asked.

"I think it's six," the electrician answered. "You've got the long shift, the late hours, the blowup when he finds out he can't get sushi delivered during a state funeral . . . I'd say we're looking at half a dozen pieces of flying plastic before we're done."

Back in the network's Washington headquarters, in a control room packed with producers, engineers, assistants, and executives, Al DeRossa leaned forward and tapped the special-events producer on the shoulder.

"Why don't you tell our golden voice that tragedy and irony are two very different concepts."

"Because," Ken Crenshaw answered, "I don't want our Distinguished

Commentator to take a header off the platform in the middle of the run-through. I think it might mar the solemnity of the occasion."

DeRossa shrugged, rubbed his eyes, and turned back to the computer. He closed his eyes for a moment, leaned back, and pulled himself awake just before he slipped under. He had been awake for forty-three of the last forty-eight hours, and he had no idea how he'd remained conscious, much less alert. He remembered a famous piece of sports film, a black-and-white classic from the early fifties, that captured a marathon runner, on the brink of exhaustion, who had entered the stadium far in the lead, and had dragged himself across the finish line to the cheers of 100,000 fans—the wrong finish line, as it turned out. That was exactly what DeRossa and his colleagues, and the whole political world, felt like. Mack Foyle's death had violently disrupted the fundamental natural order of the campaign universe.

It started with The Summer Before, with long conversations with the potential candidates and their handlers, and you went to conferences in executive retreats and academic seminar rooms, talking about how the campaign would be covered differently this time, with depth, context, substance, perspective.

There were the early trips into Iowa and New Hampshire, and self-conscious jokes about how ridiculously early this all was. There were chats with the concerned citizens of Dubuque, Waterloo, Concord, Keene, who seemed every four years to try harder and harder to sound like the down-home, commonsense folks whose faces were most likely to pop up on the TV screen.

Then came the fever of the first straw polls, the first public opinion polls, and—finally!—the first actual event, the Iowa caucuses, with the streets of Des Moines crowded with enough satellite and microwave TV trucks to sterilize the whole town, with local news anchors trucked in by the dozen, with the first chance to get your mouth around some actual goddamn *votes,* for God's sake, real, measurable *data.*

Then came the morning after, the charter flights out of Iowa, which, like Brigadoon, would now go to sleep for another four years. Jacques, the maître d' at the Hawkeye Hotel, the man who for three weeks had been the most powerful restaurateur in America, returned to greeting hardware distributors and hog callers for another 205 weeks.

Then came New Hampshire, followed immediately by the ritual disemboweling of the failed candidates along the way, as they turned in their swords and shuffled off the stage with as much grace as they could manage, rewarded with praise by the same press corps that had banished them to the sidelines at the first stumble. Then the rush of primaries, one, two, three a week, with the solemn promises of The Summer Before swept away in a forced march across thousands of miles that yielded splendid views of airport tarmacs and the backs of a hundred bus drivers' heads.

Then the conventions, those splendid anachronisms that had become a blend of college reunion and camp meeting, the only places in the United States where Al DeRossa was a star, sought after by the comely young women of the European press, stopped a dozen times a night on the convention floor by C-SPAN addicts who thrust their Polaroids at fellow delegates and begged for a photo. Then the great treks across the country, and the debates, and Election Night.

And then you could rest. That was the way things worked. He was supposed to be on a beach, on a boat, in a bed alone, in a bed with a special friend, in a bed with a friendly stranger. He was supposed to be stretched out by an ocean, a lake, a pool, sweat dripping off his nose, devouring a book and a half a day and a bottle of wine a night.

Instead, DeRossa was scrunched up against a folding table jammed into a corner of the overcrowded, overheated control room, headphones on his ears and a microphone at his lips, surrounded by photocopies of *American Heritage* articles on the funerals of Harrison, Lincoln, Garfield, McKinley, Harding, FDR, and JFK, ready to feed instant wisdom into the ears of the anchors. At the same time, he and four desk assistants were speed-dialing across the country to anyone with any remotely plausible connection to Republican politics, trying to get a grip on what was to come.

When would the Republican National Committee meet to declare a vacancy? When Block ascended to the presidency, who would be his choice for Vice President? What kind of presidency would he design? He had thrown off his liberal leanings without a backward glance when he was asked to join Foyle's ticket, but the True Believers on the Republican Right had never warmed to him. One look at that profile, that posture, that forehead, that wardrobe, and dark visions danced in their heads, the same visions that had haunted the sleep of the followers of Robert Taft, Barry Goldwater, Ronald Reagan. They looked at Block and they saw the railroad magnate who had gouged their great-grandfathers, the banker who had taken the farms from their grandfathers, the effete lawyer-diplomat who had dispatched their fathers to wars they were not allowed to win. They saw thin wrists, crooked pinkies, pursed lips, pale skin, white wine, and they did not trust him. No matter how many country singers he embraced, no matter how many race-car drivers he shared a beer with, no matter how many moon pies and R.C.'s he consumed, he was not one of them.

But Block did have one saving grace in the eyes of the True Believers: the press despised him, and they despised the press. The battering he had received at the hands of the media made him something of a martyr; especially the moment that had come to be known as the Boy Scout Massacre.

Just after the convention, Block had been sent to Colorado to visit a Boy Scout encampment in Estes National Park. He had been sitting around a campfire on a bluff, surrounded by hundreds of eager young boys in their Scout uniforms, cooking hot dogs over the fire, when suddenly, sweeping up from below, a regiment of the national press began rushing up the hill, armed with cameras, lights, boom mikes, and tape recorders, shouting questions at the candidate. That night's newscasts captured the faces of the Scouts, at first frozen in fear, then flushed with anger, as Block sat calmly by the campfire, smiling and courteous, fielding the hostile inquiries.

"Had bad a liability are you?"

"Would you consider leaving the ticket if you thought it might cost Foyle the election?"

"What do you say to those who call you an embarrassment to the party?"

"When will you release your school transcripts?"

Finally, one of the Scouts jumped to his feet and yelled at the mob of journalists, with tears glistening.

"Why don't you guys back off? Why don't you let us have a little fun?"

It was Block's best day of the campaign. And it was a Sharon Kramer classic. She had never admitted to DeRossa that she had planned that ambush, knowing what the press pack in heat would look like on the evening news. But later that night, when DeRossa had confronted her over a late-night beer in the lounge of the Broadmoor Hotel, there was a glint in her eye that suggested barely concealed pride in what she had done. DeRossa understood it, even admired it. Unlike many of his colleagues, who found it shocking that guile was a major ingredient in political campaigns, DeRossa saw it as part of the game. Lying, no; slander, no, absolutely out of bounds. But shrewd tactical manipulation? You bet. And Sharon Kramer was one of the best. From her first leap from news director of a Chicago TV station to a campaign aide for a Senate candidate in Illinois, she had proved that, even to the Neanderthal operative who could not see past the packaging.

Not that DeRossa was indifferent to Sharon Kramer's appeal. In fact, a distinct hint of mutual lust had buzzed between them from the beginning. It had come to nothing, except for one night in New Hampshire a few campaigns ago, and that had been nothing more than a leisurely dinner, a second bottle of wine, and an hour of lubricious groping on a hotel bed, a tangle of arms and legs, a series of buttons and zippers undone, and the rush of blood to the appropriate parts of the bodies. When Sharon had suddenly jumped to her feet, pulled up her pants, and bolted from the room with a mumbled, "Not a good idea, kiddo," he had felt a sharp sense of frustration and a dull sense of relief.

Neither of them had been embarrassed by the encounter. Instead, the feel of her bottom in his hands, the press of his groin against hers, had knocked down whatever formalities had once existed. And so they had become casually intense friends, going months without seeing or speaking to each other, then exchanging the most intimate of revelations over a dinner table or telephone line without a trace of self-consciousness. Kramer knew that DeRossa's marriage was breaking up before he did, that the architect he'd professed undying love for was a doomed obsession. DeRossa knew when Sharon's candidates had behaved with particular stupidity or cupidity, when her latest White Knight on the Right had revealed himself as just another pretty face with a hunger for office. They carried each other's secrets faithfully, and when DeRossa had last spoken to her—a hasty Election Night call to tell her she had won, an explosion of anger at the future awaiting her in the service of the Vice President—they had promised each other a long, wet lunch. They would talk, they would sit in comfortable silence, they would embrace each other when they parted with warmth and heat, and with the knowledge that in another life, it might have worked for them.

There wasn't going to be any lunch now, though. As soon as a decent interval had passed after MacArthur Foyle was buried, the Republican National Committee would convene in special session to declare a vacancy, and Ted Block would be elevated to the presidency, awaiting only the formality of the electoral college vote in early December. Sharon Kramer would be in the White House, first mate to a captain who would rely on her to set the course, take the wheel, raise the sail, and point out the ocean to him. Had there ever been a woman in the White House (not counting spouses) who had ever held a fraction of the power Sharon Kramer would wield? . . .

"Al, could you help us out here?"

"What do you need, Ken?" DeRossa asked, in the vain hope that Ken Crenshaw would one day learn to modulate his voice. Not for nothing was he known as "Mr. Tylenol."

"When we come to a break in the memorial service, you know, sometime when it wouldn't look like we were pissing on the Trinity by talking politics, we may want you on camera or on a voice-over for a what-next—when they pick Block for President, who the Vice President might be, that sort of thing."

Which is when Al DeRossa reminded himself for the fourth or fifth time in the last two lunatic days, that he'd better find all this out—because as of now, he hadn't a clue.

THIRTEEN

★ ★ ★

All across this huge land, an invisible Army of the Over-Informed keep ceaseless watch on the press. They are everywhere. They are young men finding sanctuary in their parents' finished basements; they are old women attended by no other living thing save a house cat with scabrous breath and a regiment of cockroaches; they are assistant professors of history whose lungs have already been poisoned with the dust of a thousand monographs and ten thousand pieces of chalk. And they all have one thing in common: They know more about less than anyone else in the world. And they spend a significant portion of their waking lives waiting for the press to make a mistake.

Some among them knew the box office receipts of every movie commercially released in the United States since *Birth of a Nation.* And they knew that whenever a story appeared about all-time box-office-champion movies, those stories were fatally flawed; the writers never bothered to adjust for inflation, thus criminally underestimating the receipts for older blockbusters such as *Gone With the Wind.*

Or they could tell you how many of Babe Ruth's home runs in 1927 reached the stands not on the fly, but on one bounce, and were counted as homers under the rules of the day, thus undermining the argument that Roger Maris's sixty-one home runs during the 162-game season of 1961 was a less impressive feat than Ruth's sixty back in the 154-game season of 1927.

And what they could tell you, they did—instantly, eagerly, gleefully.

In 1992, DeRossa had called Ross Perot's withdrawal from the presidential race "the greatest missed opportunity since Napoleon failed to reach Moscow." Fifteen minutes after the broadcast, six faxes were on his desk informing him that in fact, Napoleon *had* taken territory within the city limits of Moscow, and had held it for several days.

DeRossa had felt the force of their numbers, and their zeal, from his first days in journalism. They wrote to tell him that his count of the presidents was wrong, since Grover Cleveland, who had won, lost, then won again, was counted twice in the official ledgers. They called to complain that the account of presidential popular votes was wrong, since he had failed to report the votes cast for the Socialist Workers' Party, the Socialist Labor Party, the Peace and Freedom Party, the Populist Party, the American Independent Party. They flooded his desk with telegrams when he referred to Vietnam as "the only war America ever lost," since the United States had never formally surrendered to North Vietnam. They demanded that he apologize to the memory of Harry Truman for saying that Truman had been defeated by Senator Estes Kefauver in the 1952 New Hampshire primary, since Truman had never formally entered the race. One year, DeRossa casually referred to the "first presidential broadcast debates in 1960." He was chastised by a media studies teacher for overlooking the 1948 radio debate in the Oregon Republican primary between Harold Stassen and Thomas Dewey. A few months later, he had carefully amended his reference to "the first *televised* presidential debates," only to be reprimanded by a mass communications graduate student, who reminded him of the 1960 West Virginia primary debate between John Kennedy and Hubert Humphrey.

For the Army of the Over-Informed, Election Night was Mardi Gras, Thanksgiving, and the Final Four rolled into one. Sometimes, as he prepared for another long night of numbers crunching, DeRossa would pause to picture the troops settling in for the night, bowls of potato chips and six-packs of Coke by their sides, armed with a remote control in one hand and a cordless phone in the other, flipping from network to network, waiting for the mistake that would trigger the closest sensation many of them would ever have to lust. So it was inevitable that when California had finally tipped into the Republican column, and the

Anchor had called Foyle "our new President-elect," the phone lines at the network's Election Night command post exploded.

"Yes," DeRossa's assistant had murmured a dozen times or more into the phones. "Yes, we know, he's not the President-elect until the electoral college meets, yes, we'll correct it at the earliest opportunity, yes, thank you for letting us know, thank you."

In the first hours after Foyle's death, the Army had been temporarily supplanted by the Conspiratorialists, who were now demanding that someone tell the real story of Mack Foyle's murder.

The radio call-ins were flooded with stories that a hospital security camera had actually captured the assassination on tape, that an orderly had been killed trying to phone in the real story to a popular radio talk show, that the autopsy records had been doctored, that the remnants of the Republican Party's eastern globalist/Wall Street/Council on Foreign Relations clique had shorted the stock market the day before—*before*—Foyle had climbed aboard that horse.

With all that raw red meat to feast on, there'd been no time to taste the sprouts-and-tofu dishes being served up by the Army of the Over-Informed. But during a rare moment of quiet, Al DeRossa had picked up one of the more reasonable-looking pieces of mail (no angry red crayon scribblings on the envelope), paged through it, and felt the first faint stirring of curiosity. By the time he finished sifting through the materials his own staff had gathered, his head was throbbing.

"Ah, gimme a break," DeRossa muttered as he pushed aside the half-inch-thick stack of papers and walked into the third-floor conference room for a working lunch. The run-through was over (with a very happy electrician pocketing $100 when the Distinguished Commentator hurled his telex out of his ear for the sixth time), the memorial ceremony was a day away, and DeRossa was supposed to brief the heavies—the Anchor, the reporters, the executives—on what to expect.

The third-floor conference room was packed with more than thirty people jammed around a large table, wolfing down dried-out deli sandwiches and warm sodas.

"DeRo," Ken Crenshaw bellowed. "Why don't you brief us on the ticktock?"

Why don't you try speaking English?

"Okay. The drill is supposed to go something like this. Tomorrow, they fly Foyle home right after the service. There's a burial at sunset. Next day, the National Committee meets at noon. Moment of silence for Foyle, blah blah blah. Then there's a formal vote on a vacancy, they pick Block to fill it—"

"And may God have mercy on us all," a correspondent muttered.

"Which is exactly, I mean *exactly,* what we do not need and *will not tolerate."*

Heads wheeled; eyes widened. Paul Howard, a network vice president for standards and practices, had rarely been seen in a news division meeting, and then only when someone had blundered badly, when an overly zealous producer had paid a group of protesters to hurl a rock at a cop. Now he was on his feet, face reddened.

"I am speaking at the express request of the chairman and CEO of this organization. So listen to me. Very carefully. The whole country is in a state of shock. If the market had been open these last two days, it's a safe bet that hundreds of billions of dollars in equity would have been wiped out—which would have left millions of people in this country, and most of you in this room, who hold our stock, significantly poorer. Not to mention the fact that we're about to get a President a lot of Americans wouldn't trust with the microwave. Above all"—he pulled out a piece of paper "... above all, and these are the chairman's words, we must do everything we can to convey a sense of stability in these uncertain days. No one is to do or say anything—*anything*—that would undermine this critical work. We must be the voice of reason and reassurance here."

Howard paused, folded the piece of paper back in his pocket, then looked around the room.

"Let me add a footnote of my own. I don't care what you think of Theodore Block. I don't care what you say, what you run, once he's sworn in. But the country's had about all the shock it can stand for a while. Don't add to it." He sat down to thick silence.

"Well," DeRossa said, "not meaning to do that, I have to tell you that we *do* have a small problem trying to reassure the country."

"What would that problem be, Al?" Crenshaw asked, in a disquietingly quiet tone of voice.

DeRossa took a deep breath.

"Okay. There's no mystery about what everyone *thinks* is going to happen. We've all looked at the rules of the Republican Party. And right there, Rule Twenty-seven, it says that 'the Republican National Committee is hereby authorized and empowered'—I love that, don't you, 'authorized *and* empowered'—okay, let's see, 'to fill any and all vacancies which may occur by reason of death, declination, or otherwise,' blah blah blah. The Democrats have the same rule; that's how they put Sarge Shriver on the ticket in '72, when McGovern kicked off Tom Eagleton. But the problem is, there *is* no vacancy."

"What do you *mean,* 'no vacancy,' " the Distinguished Commentator interjected. "In case you haven't noticed, Mack Foyle is lying in a box in the Capitol Rotunda, for God's sake."

"Yes," DeRossa said, "but that doesn't mean there's a vacancy. When the Democrats threw Eagleton over the side, there were three months to go until the voting. But *we* voted on Tuesday. It's *done.* It's over. We've voted for the five hundred thirty-eight electors who vote for the President."

"For God's sake, Al," the Distinguished Commentator said, "you're not seriously suggesting that this . . . *technicality* has anything to do with who's going to be President, are you?"

"I don't *think* so," DeRossa said. "I assume the Republicans will pick Block, put in some safely respectable senator or governor for number two, and everything will go along smoothly. I'm only saying that on Tuesday, we did what the Constitution said we were supposed to do; we've picked the people who will pick the next President."

"And they'll pick whoever the RNC tells them to pick."

"I guess," DeRossa said. "Look, I'm not trying to make life difficult for us. . . ." He paused. "It's just that—you all know how unhappy Foyle's people were when he picked Block in the first place. I mean, Senator Borax, who was Foyle's biggest supporter, wouldn't even go to the convention to listen to the acceptance speeches; he went off and played tennis. Well, those electors are Foyle's people. Are we really absolutely sure they're going to vote for someone as President that Foyle had to jam down their throats?"

Crenshaw rapped his fist on the table.

"Fair point. Look, this is probably a bucket of eyewash, but let's be safe; I want us to start checking in with those electors as soon as we can." He turned to the row of overworked, overqualified, underpaid desk assistants and researchers jammed against the back wall. "Get your lists out and start hitting the phones."

They looked, one to another, then to DeRossa, who smiled weakly.

"You know," he said, "I can go back and tell you about every delegate and alternate the parties sent to their conventions; where they're from, what they do for a living, how old they are. I can break down the voters into any subset you want, and I can tell you what they feel—working women with small children, Gulf War veterans with college degrees. I can go into our computers and tell you district by district, hell, precinct by precinct, how the vote went.

"But right now there are five hundred thirty-eight Americans with the legal power to pick the next President. And I can't tell you one damn thing about who the hell they are."

FOURTEEN

★ ★ ★

On what once had been the showroom floor of Swindell Oldsmobile, at the intersection of Route 40 and Vandenberg Avenue in Grand Rapids, Michigan, more than three hundred men, women, and children jammed into every square foot of space between the card tables, the chairs, the computer stands, and temporary office partitions, politely edging each other aside for a better look at the five large television sets positioned around the room. Many pinned Foyle for President buttons to their jackets, their dresses, and the straw campaign hats they had worn in celebration at the Election Night victory party. Now the buttons were bordered in black, and the faces that had been ruddy with drink and victory were stained by tears, strained by grief. A few in the crowd reached for the sandwiches and drank the coffee; they tasted like ashes.

In a small office in the rear of the building sat the brown-haired, brown-eyed forty-one-year-old woman who had rented the showroom, filled it with office furniture and supplies and telephones, organized the volunteers for three seven-day-a-week months, supervised the Election Day telephone bank, set out the Election Night refreshments—and then personally organized today's memorial vigil. Her name was Dorothy Ledger, and she was one of those people who made the country run.

She had spent the first seven years of her life as the only child of a high school shop teacher and a local librarian in a small town on Michigan's Upper Peninsula. Then, when she was seven, her father had left home for good, drawn by the show-business glamour of the movie-house ticket seller. Her mother then retreated to a universe bounded by the library and her bedroom, where she passed her evenings in a fog of television and Valium. Before she was ten, Dorothy had learned how to make a bed, vacuum a rug, make out a shopping list, roast a chicken, iron a dress. She had also begun to volunteer for all kinds of tasks at school and church: serving punch at the socials, selling raffle tickets, painting sets for class plays. All these tasks did not make her popular among the sought-after girls; they did not get her invited to the important birthday parties and sleep-overs. But they did get her out of the house. They did put her in places where it was likely that, sooner or later, the sound of laughter was likely to be heard.

Dorothy's tenacity, and the enthusiastic recommendations of her teachers, won her a full scholarship to Aquinas College in Grand Rapids, where she majored in business, with a heavy emphasis on accounting and bookkeeping—a suitable course for a woman whose social life gave strong indications that she would always be responsible for supporting herself. Two days after graduation, she walked into the First Colonial Bank and Trust, a one-story brick-and-colonial structure on the edge of a shopping mall, and began work as a management trainee. Nineteen years later, "Dot," as she had been called from the beginning, had become office manager. From her desk just outside the glassed-in executive wing, she ran the bank for a succession of increasingly younger bank officers, who shuffled in and out of the offices inside the glassed-in walls on their way up the First Colonial ladder.

Dot was treasured by these men. Every birthday, there were a dozen yellow roses on her desk; every Christmas, there was a piece of costume jewelry and a thirty-five-dollar gift basket of fruit and cheese. They treasured her with that special affection reserved for a highly competent worker whose gender and background posed no conceivable threat to their future.

"Our 'Old Reliable,' " the latest branch vice president had called her. That's what they called her at Kent County Republican Party headquarters, too, where Dot was officially the secretary-treasurer, and unofficially the heart and soul of the organization. No one made more telephone calls, gathered more petition signatures, baked more cakes for the fund-raising picnics, drove more people to the polls through snowstorms than Dorothy Ledger. The walls in her impeccably neat one-bedroom apartment were covered with signed glossies of Gerald Ford (Grand Rapids's only President), photos of Dorothy at long-forgotten Republican functions, parties at the Gerald Ford Museum, and other artifacts of a life of civic service. Aside from the customers of the First Colonial Bank and Trust, and the loyalists of the Kent County Republican Party, no one had ever heard of Dorothy Ledger. Yet she was one of those lonely heroines without which the Republic itself would cease to function.

Imagine our giant empires of commerce without the Tigress at the Gates, guarding the lair of the Great Man, booking his first-class seat on the aisle, bailing his son out of jail.

Imagine the halls of government without Dorothy's sisters in arms, defending the lonely island of order against the raging, chaotic sea of telephones, paper, and the cry of the supplicants for a moment of the Great Man's time.

Imagine the travel agency, the pediatric ward, the Department of Comparative Literature, the Committees to Save the Earth, the Associations to Despoil the Earth, without the kinetic energy of the women who make it all work. It is, literally, unimaginable. Remove the Great Man from his chair of rich Corinthian leather and the enterprise would roar down the tracks without a tremor; remove Dot Ledger, or her sisters, from their modest desks outside the inner rooms, and there would soon be nothing left but a twisted, steaming mass of wreckage.

In their less generous moments, the men Dorothy and her sisters worked for would mock them as lonely spinsters, making of their work the lovers, husbands, and children they never had. Dot, in fact, had been married for nineteen months to a driving instructor, a union that had uncoupled so dispassionately that they might have shared a table at a coffee shop rather than a life. Nor was she homely, or a recluse. Rather, Dot had been imbued from childhood with the notion that there was work that had to be done, and no one else but herself would do it. Everything about her, from her practical wardrobe to her sensible haircut, proclaimed Work, Not Play. If she resented the men who moved in and out of the glassed-in executive wing, if she grieved for the occasional man who shared her bed and did not call, she did not show it.

In fact, the man who now held her hand and cradled her shoulder had never seen Dot Ledger as broken as she was now. Charles Berlin, chairman of the Kent County Republican Party, had arrived at the Foyle-Block campaign office for the memorial service and found Dot weeping over a giant bowl of potato salad. He quickly escorted her into his office, pulled a monogrammed handkerchief out of his midnight blue suit jacket, and began gently patting her back.

"I know it's a terrible thing, Dot, but we have to be strong," Charles Berlin said. He was comfortable speaking such Rotary Club homilies, in large measure because he had been an officer in the Grand Rapids Rotary for the last thirteen years.

"It's just not fair," Dot said, breathing hard to hold back her tears.

"No, it's not," Charles said. "I know it's going to make that trip to Lansing very difficult now."

"What trip?"

"It's no wonder you forgot, with the shock of it all," Charles said. "You have to go down to Lansing to vote."

"Vote? For what? Oh," she said slowly, "oh God, that's right. Oh, God, no."

Last September, at the Republican State Convention, Charles Berlin had wandered over to her in a hotel hospitality suite packed with politically concerned citizens searching for free beer and cheese balls. He'd waved a sheet of yellow foolscap at her, and yelled so he could be heard over the clamor.

"We're two women short! I need you on the slate!"

"What slate?"

"The electors! If Foyle wins, you go to Lansing, and you vote in the electoral college! You'll be in the history books! Okay?"

"Yeah, I guess so," she'd said, and turned back to her conversation.

The next day, Charles Berlin had called her at the bank to laugh with her over the "nip and tuck" battle to select the electors.

"It was incredible," Charles said. "Just before the convention adjourned, your beloved county chairman and ten other worthies put twenty-one names in nomination for the twenty-one slots. It sort of moved things along that ninety percent of the delegates had already left. We found out that two of the folks we picked had died since the list had been drawn up."

"I'm deeply honored, Charles, and I hope to be worthy of your trust." They'd laughed, and Charles had briefly explained to her what she'd have to do if the Republicans carried Michigan. In the tension of a close election, Dorothy had not given her role a minute's thought. Now she turned away from the television pictures of the grim-faced dignitaries arriving at the Capitol for the memorial service.

"Charles, please; I don't still have to do that, do I? I thought they'd call it off, just have . . . I don't know, the Congress or a judge or somebody swear in Block as President, like with Ford after Nixon left. You're talking about a . . . formality, right?"

Charles nodded.

"Sure. But you have to do it, or we don't have a President next January twentieth."

Dorothy shook her head.

"So I do . . . what? I go up to Lansing and vote for a dead man for President?"

"No, no. In fact, in a couple of days, I'll be going to Washington for the National Committee meeting. We'll declare a vacancy, nominate Ted Block for President, pick somebody to take his place as V.P., and that's who you'll vote for."

Dorothy let out a deep sigh.

"What a mark to leave behind: 'I helped make Ted Block President.' "

Charles chuckled reassuringly.

"Let's be fair, Dot, the guy was under incredible pressure all during the campaign."

"Oh, right. I guess when he gets to the White House, and the pressure's off, he'll be fine."

"Hey, now, stop talking like a Democrat," Charles said in a wounded tone. "It was just the whole"—he waved his hands—"the whole media thing. Every time he opened his mouth, those bastards made him sound like some kind of idiot."

"Yes, right," Dorothy said, shaking her head. "But you know, Charles, I have this terrible feeling that maybe he keeps looking like an idiot because, once you get past the media distortions, he *is* an idiot."

Charles smiled weakly.

"Do me a favor, Dot. Keep those sentiments to yourself. We've been through the worst shock since Dallas, and the last thing in the world we need is for anyone—especially our people—to feel worse than they do now. Come on, let's go out with the others and watch the service. It'll do us all good."

Sure it would.

FIFTEEN

★ ★ ★

"Not sure, not sure about this," Ted Block said, and the little men with jackhammers went to work again inside Sharon Kramer's skull.

All during the campaign, Block had only to utter those words, and the little gang of cranial workers set to work breaking all productivity records. Block was never petulant, never whined, never exhibited any outward signs of temper or distemper. As he sat now in the back of the Lincoln customized stretch limo, one pin-striped leg crossed over the other, stroking his black silk tie and staring out the bulletproof windows, he displayed all the coiled tension of a boarding school house master arranging the sherry glasses. But whenever Ted Block uttered that phrase—"Not sure, not sure"—everyone around him heard the cry of "Mayday! Mayday!" on a storm-tossed ship of state. It meant that Block did not want to do what his staff thought he should do. It meant that he had experienced a primal sense of propriety, perhaps learned at his mother's knee, perhaps encoded into his DNA, that was telling him no.

Throughout his political career, Ted Block had been able to reduce every assistant, every special counsel, every high-priced political consultant to terminal helplessness by uttering that phrase. It meant that, no matter how powerful the reason might be behind a proposed course of action, Block was prepared to resist it—not by saying no, but by asking, again and again, "Why? Why should I do this?"

Much to the surprise of his subordinates, Block's obstinance proved politically valuable. Since he was possessed of a limited appetite for agonizing his way through complex questions, Block often resembled the living embodiment of Newton's Second Law of Motion; once having rested on a course of action, he remained at rest. Thus, he was rarely accused of inconsistency. As an exhausted Alan Veigle once put it, "Of course he doesn't change his position; don't you think finding *one* is enough of a challenge for him?"

Which meant that, unlike most public officials, Ted Block knew where he stood. He was rarely troubled by agonizing second thoughts, so he bore the weight of public office and political campaigning with rare good grace. The explosions of anger, the descent into depression, the torments of decision making were all but unknown to Block.

Throughout the campaign, Sharon had dealt with this side of his character with a mix of frustration and perverse admiration. As a child of her relentlessly self-conscious age, given to agonizing reappraisals of everything from her choice of career to her choice of lovers (the latter sometimes occurring within nine seconds of her partner's climax), she found it refreshing to be in the presence of someone for whom the unexamined life was damn well worth living. Moreover, it was a challenge for Sharon to maneuver Block into doing what had to be done.

Once, at a Teutonic Festival in Milwaukee, she found Block politely but firmly resisting his advance man's increasingly agitated advice to be photographed eating a bratwurst.

"Not a good idea . . . bad message for the kids, don't you think? Grease, fat . . . bad message."

After all the normal appeals to tradition and political necessity had failed, Sharon Kramer had taken Block aside.

"Sir," she said, "I understand you had a mother who was pretty firm about good manners."

A smile of recollection had broken through.

"Yes, indeed," he said.

"Well, so did I, sir. And I can tell you, if I'd been invited as a guest in someone's home, and I'd refused to eat what I was offered, I wouldn't have been able to sit down for a week."

Block stood for a moment, then nodded and went off to down half a dozen bratwursts. And the fact that Sharon Kramer's mother had never once raised a hand to her? Well, politics is war, and in war, truth is the first casualty.

Today, however, was not some political ritual. In a few minutes, the car would arrive at the East Front of the Capitol, where the memorial service for MacArthur Foyle would be held. A line of mourners estimated at 400,000 was lined up to pay tribute, to express their own sense of shock and sorrow, to be a part of history, to have a set of slides for their neighbors back home. More to the point, a few hundred million Americans, not to mention the leaders, parliamentarians, and currency speculators of dozens of other nations, were waiting for some sign of reassurance from this decidedly unreassuring figure. Today, Block would appear, for the first time, in the role of President-to-be. What he said and how he said it would either reassure, or unsettle, a nation, and an international community, with a bad case of nerves.

And now Theodore Block was, in his own way, digging in his heels. For Sharon Kramer, that was very bad news.

"Not sure about this, not sure," Block mused. "After all . . . Mack's day. All that attention . . . unseemly, maybe. Why say anything?"

He paused to examine the idea, as if it were a jacket he might buy.

Well, why not? Sharon thought as she turned to his perfectly sculpted face. *Why not this one last slight hitch as we prepare to mourn and then soldier on?*

A few hours earlier, she'd returned DeRossa's phone calls, and vented her outrage.

"Al, you can't believe this place."

"I can imagine—"

"I don't think so, Al, I really don't. You would think even in this town that the egos must conceivably be checked at the door, just for a day or two. You might think people would let up just for a little while so that we might give the man we just elected President a decent burial. And you know what, Al? If you thought that, you'd be a complete simpleton. Here: you know that New York billionaire real-estate schmuck wants to come to the funeral with his bimbo? And you know what he wants? He wants to sit on the right side of the Rotunda because he photographs better from that side."

"You're—"

"Kidding? I wish I was. Then I got the Reverend W. Dixon Mason's message, which strongly suggests that *he* be invited to give a eulogy so that the funeral will be . . . how did he put it . . . 'a celebration of inclusion.' Oh, and if I could arrange it so that he spoke just *after* the President and before Block, that would be 'a sign of sensitivity.' Then the Mueller campaign wants twenty-five seats at the service. That's so we can all 'come together in common grief.' I don't know what the hell that's about. Maybe Mueller wants another twenty-four hours in the spotlight before we forget about him. I've got three—make that five—TV magazine shows who want to make sure this doesn't turn into a 'media circus.' And I swear to you, Al, every goddamn one of them suggests that if we just let Diane or Connie or Tanya or Muffie follow Mrs. Foyle around for, oh, the day of the ceremony—you know, at the house, in the limo—that way there'd be 'taste' and 'restraint.' I hung up on them before they could explain how dignified it would be if they could get a peek inside the coffin."

"I guess this isn't the right time to ask you about what happens—"

"No, it isn't, Al. I'm sorry, but you know what happens when we elect a President and he ups and dies on us."

"No, I don't. That's what—"

"Well, don't worry, DeRo, neither does anyone else."

There was, however, one thing Sharon knew. This was Theodore Block's chance to wipe out the first four months of public ridicule totally and forever. The same media organs that had painted Block as a stumblebum had already begun supplying a heavy dose of reassurance into their round-the-clock coverage. The ghost of Harry Truman was repeatedly summoned to prove that a public figure scorned as a bumbler and a fool ("To err is Truman") could rise to greatness. The mantle of Ronald Reagan was draped around Block's shoulders. Reagan had been ridiculed as an actor, a simpleminded robot who could not recognize his own Cabinet, yet who had presided over the endgame of the Cold War. Legions of onetime Block aides spoke of his "solidity," his "graciousness," his "quiet presence." True, these were encomiums that might have summed up the most admirable qualities of a fine maître d', but they were the nearest ports available in a storm of doubt.

Similarly, Block's every word, every gesture, were now being seen through a rose-colored glass, gently. When his plane had touched down at Andrews Air Force Base, Sharon had urged him to give voice to the national sense of shock and loss, to ask for the nation's prayers. So he had stepped to the bank of microphones and said, "I share your sense of shock and loss. I ask for the nation's prayers."

"A simple, eloquent statement of the nation's sense of shock and loss," the Anchor intoned.

That evening, the world got a look at America's presumptive new leader through a ground-floor window at Blair House, the official White House guest quarters, as he huddled with advisers and worked the phones.

"A candid glimpse of the next President at work," the Distinguished Commentator had said. Sharon Kramer had silently offered a prayer of thanks to the advance man who had positioned the two dozen photographers across Pennsylvania Avenue for that candid glimpse.

Now the world wanted more. For Sharon, the memorial service was the perfect place to provide it. For one thing, people loved funerals. Look at what Pericles pulled off when they were burying the heroes of the Peloponnesian Wars. Look at Marc Antony when Julius Caesar got the ultimate veto from the Roman senate. Look at Ronald Reagan after the *Challenger* exploded. Make them cry over an open grave, and you are a leader. Besides, what was the competition here? The outgoing President had been rendered all but invisible by age, infirmity, and lame-duckery. The congressional leaders had long forgotten how to speak English. It was not beyond the realm of possibility that the Speaker of the House would conclude his tribute by saying, "Let us pray for the soul of MacArthur Foyle. Hearing no objection . . ."

In such a setting, a short, simple eulogy by the next President would be a slam dunk. Two of Foyle's best speechwriters had crafted just such a eulogy, inspired by their genuine feelings for Foyle and their genuine hopes for future White House employment. From its poignant opening line ("There is a fifty-first star in our hearts today") to its inspiring, simple close ("Mack Foyle cannot make this journey; so we will take him with us as we go"), the speech was crafted to bring its speaker and the audience to tears. Sharon could already hear the TV pool director barking out the orders that would enhance the words with appropriately moving images.

"Cut to Joseph! He's losing it! C'mon, dammit, cut to Cannon! He's got his head in his hands! Shit, pan up to the Speaker, the Speaker! I want the tear trickling down his fucking face! Let's go, he's at the *'e pluribus unum'* bit, I need a *schvartzer,* I need a *schvartzer!"*

And Ted Block still did not want to do it.

They had arrived at the Capitol now, the east front draped in black and purple bunting. Despite the huge crowds, shivering in the chill of a gray November day, the silence was so prevalent that the shutters of the clicking cameras sounded like a mob of enraged crickets. Sharon thrust the speech at Block, and once again he demurred.

"Not the right moment," he said, "doesn't feel right, shouldn't stand in the other guy's spotlight. Not the right thing to do."

Sharon had thirty seconds or less. *All right, fourth and twenty-nine, clock running down, throw the Hail Mary.*

"You know, this isn't about you at all. It's about what you owe to Mack."

"Don't follow . . ."

"What is his legacy, Governor? It's *you.* He chose you as the leader of this country if anything should happen to him. You need to prove to America—to the world—that this man chose well, that his legacy was a good one, a wise one. He can't defend that legacy now, Governor, but you can." She handed him the speech again. "You must. It's your duty."

Slowly at first, then more rapidly, Theodore Block began to nod. Sharon began to nod along with him encouragingly. For a moment, the two of them looked as if they were watching a yo-yo demonstration. Then Block gave one final nod.

"Yeah, okay, right, for Mack. Okay, yes, yes."

One more second and he would have turned into Molly Bloom. Here, take the speech and go be a hero.

As the driver opened the limo door, as half a dozen Secret Service agents began talking into their wrists, President-to-be Theodore Block extended his long, lean legs and swung gracefully out of the limo.

And then, in a moment Sharon Kramer would remember for the rest of her days, Block turned back to the open door, leaned down and spoke to her words she had never heard him speak before, words that chilled her marrow, froze her blood so that, like the victim of an impending disaster, she could see the horror of what was about to come even as she was powerless to prevent it. For the rest of her life, not a moment would go by that she did not hear those words of Ted Block as he turned to ascend the steps of the Capitol to honor his fallen leader.

"You know, Sharon, I was thinking . . ."

SIXTEEN

★ ★ ★

Deep in the heart of every public figure lies the impulse to prove that he is not the sum of his handlers. The more their words, gestures, wardrobe, travel schedules, offhand remarks, and moral values have become products of professional operatives, the more anxious they are to demonstrate that they are, in fact, self-directed human beings. At times, the lengths they go to create this appearance are astounding. In 1933, President-elect Franklin D. Roosevelt copied the typewritten draft of his inaugural address in longhand, the better to prove that he had, in fact, written it himself. The only thing he had to fear was an overly inquisitive historian.

But not until former governor Theodore Block decided to speak a few words of his own did the impulse of a political figure to be his own man set off the most serious constitutional crisis in the history of the Republic.

No one should have been more immune to the virus of self-expression than Block. He had been born and raised to believe that a staff of loyal subalterns was the natural order of things. From childhood, the day had begun with clothes laid out, with breakfast on the table. Beds were stripped, laundry was done, cars were gassed, vacation cabins were stocked as a matter of course. One of the few abstract concepts Block had grasped instantly was Adam Smith's Theory of the Invisible Hand, since these hands had attended him since birth. And yet, as he sat in the Capitol Rotunda at Mack Foyle's memorial service, he returned again and again to the thought that had troubled him during the short ride to the service. Sharon was right; this was his chance to prove that Destiny had not played a cruel joke on the United States. And how would he do this? With a tribute crafted by other hands? Not a chance; the way things worked these days, the speechwriters would be on national television explaining why they had chosen the words they had. Everyone would know that Ted Block had no more uttered his own thoughts than a trained seal had composed the tune he was playing on the air horns. He found himself thinking of the phrase his mother used when she discovered that the pachysandra had begun to grow over the cobblestone walkway, or when her brother had deflowered and impregnated the downstairs maid during his semiannual visit, or when black marchers had been hosed in the streets of Birmingham, Alabama. "This is unacceptable." And then he remembered the many witty toasts he had offered during holiday dinners, and bachelor parties, the many tributes he had spoken at funerals and memorial services for school chums and political colleagues. And so he resumed thinking. . . .

"Whatever we can do, Ted . . . Mr. Presi . . . whatever we can do . . . you have our prayers. . . ."

The Speaker, the majority leader of the Senate, and the minority leaders greeted Block at the ceremonial Capitol entrance muttering the platitudes that were safe enough to be overheard by a surreptitious pool microphone, or a particularly eagle-eyed lip-reader. Together they began the slow, stately walk through Statuary Hall, where the revered congressional leaders of the past flanked their path, until they came to the Rotunda, where the outgoing President of the United States sat, virtually immobilized by his afflictions. The President had been brought to the Capitol's underground entrance and escorted to a side entrance to the Rotunda, beyond the reach of the pool cameras; in this time of national grief and shock, it was universally understood that the sight of the current chief executive painfully trying to walk the short distance to the Rotunda would not be an image in conformance with the meaning of today's event.

In the center of the Rotunda, resting on the same catafalque that had borne the bodies of Abraham Lincoln and John Kennedy, lay the flag-draped casket of MacArthur Foyle. Ringing the Rotunda, behind a simple red velvet rope, sat the dignitaries whose political power, social power, financial connections, or special link to Foyle entitled them to this ringside seat. Even in their grief, Marsh, Alan Veigle, and other key aides to Foyle had stage-managed the funeral as if it were a State of the Union speech, where a select handful of Ordinary Americans sat in the gallery proximate enough to the First Lady to remain in constant TV range.

Here was the widow of the Brooklyn firefighter who had died saving two babies in a tenement fire in the heart of the Bedford-Stuyvesant ghetto. There were the three children from the suburbs whose parents had been killed in the cross fire of a gunfight in the middle of a Chicago street while leaving the circus. Here were the Navy SEALs who had stopped terrorists from kidnapping an American cultural attaché on the streets of Rome. Each had played a key role in the Foyle campaign commercials; they were here now because the political instincts of MacArthur Foyle's team had survived the death of the candidate himself, much as the body of a chicken is said to race around the barnyard even after its head has been severed.

As the magisterial ceremony progressed, Theodore Block continued to muse. He barely remembered to mumble along with the hymns of the Marine Band, he scarcely heard the words intoned by the dignitaries. And by the time the Speaker of the House called his name, Block knew what he was going to do.

He strode the few steps to the simple podium with the few pages of text in his hands, the words printed out in oversized type, the edges of the pages raised so he would not fumble when he turned them. And then, with a small, reassuring smile, the future President of the United States began to speak to the world.

"I have asked others to write the words I would say here," he began. "They are good words. Fine words. But on this day, you have the right to hear *my* words. And so, I will put these words aside, and speak to you—from my heart." And he turned and handed the prepared text to a startled Marine guard.

In the temporary holding room under the bowels of the Capitol, Sharon Kramer froze in her chair, and uttered an involuntary gasp.

And Ted Block continued.

"Times like this—bad time; tough, tough time—you go back to basic things. You go back to the words that got you through the bad times. I go back to the Bible."

Sharon Kramer began to exhale again.

"I go back to Ecclesiastes: 'To every thing, there is a season . . . time to be born . . . time to die.' We may not understand . . . may not 'get it,' as the kids say. But if you believe in the Lord God Almighty, then this was Mack Foyle's time to die."

Not even the lightning reaction of the pool director could wipe from eighty million television screens the sight of the Senate majority leader's jaw dropping open.

"Do we know why the Lord chose that horse, at that moment, to throw Senator Foyle, our newly chosen President, to the ground? Don't know . . . can't say. When I was a boy, I spent one whole summer training for a show . . . meant the world to me. The night before, tripped on a rake left out by the pool. Never got that chance to ride. Thought the world was going to end. Didn't, of course. Never got a chance to get that medal. But I never let that setback get me down. And we're not going to let this setback get us down, or stay us from moving forward to . . . to our journey."

"In the words of the late, great Daffy Duck," Crenshaw mumbled to Al DeRossa, " 'Shoot him now, shoot him now.' "

As he paused at the lectern, Theodore Block could sense that things were not going the way he had hoped. His leap into spontaneity had apparently stunned his audience, but from the expressions on their faces, Block could tell that he had not made himself as clear as he would have liked. So he regrouped.

"This loss will weigh heavy on our hearts. But remember, my friends, this is America. We lost Lincoln and we fought on. We lost Roosevelt and we fought on. We lost Jack Kennedy and we fought on. And if we could survive *those* horrible losses, we can certainly survive this one.

"And so," Block said, "we pledge ourselves to carry on the work that MacArthur Foyle set out for us; we pledge ourselves to make real the dream he dreamed for a better America."

Wrap it up, you're almost there, Sharon Kramer urged him silently. *Wrap it up. Just stop. Maybe it will be okay.*

"And to the man who should be standing here—well, not here, because if he were here, we wouldn't have to be here—to Mack Foyle we say"—and here Block struggled for the alliteration that he knew was the hallmark of every fine speech—"we say, go to God, good friend, Godspeed, good-bye . . . and good luck." And Ted Block sat down.

"Good *luck*?" Marsh screamed. "Did he say good fucking *luck*?"

"Oh, yes," Alan Veigle said, nodding very slowly. "Oh, yes, indeed. That's what he said. Which is exactly what we are all going to need."

SEVENTEEN

★ ★ ★

It is an article of faith among millions that the first instinct of the contemporary American political press is to eviscerate the leaders chosen by the American people. This is not true. The lust for blood is the second instinct of the contemporary American political press. The first instinct of the contemporary American political press is its preternatural fear of whatever lies beyond the security perimeter of conventional wisdom.

In part, this is a question of fairness. When you are about to comment on a make-or-break political event with 30 million people listening, it is only reasonable to ask yourself how confident you are of your instant first impression. In part, it is a question of prudence. If you are standing on a convention floor surrounded by howling partisans in the grips of near-religious ecstasy, it may be the better part of valor not to refer to the just-concluded speech as "designer bilge."

And it is also a matter of timidity. For all of their self-assured, Olympian style, political journalists are often plagued by self-doubt. This is why, after a campaign debate, the phrase most likely to be heard is "Well, there were no knockdowns for either side," unless one of the participants foamed at the mouth and began to sprout fangs.

Imagine, then, how the chill hand of caution clutched at the heart of the reporters covering MacArthur Foyle's memorial service as Ted Block finished his eulogy and returned to his seat, as the Marine Band struck up "The Doxology." They sensed that what had happened was more or less what would have happened if Winston Churchill had taken to the radio in the fall of 1940, as the German bombs were raining down on London, and declared, "Quick! Everybody learn to like sauerkraut!" But was that what the nation wanted to hear, was that what it needed to hear, at this moment? Was anyone about to stand up and hurl a whipped-cream pie in the face of a weeping Statue of Liberty?

"Ted Block told us he would speak from the heart, and no one can deny that is exactly what he did," the Anchor said over the Marine Band.

"A remarkably personal tone, a remarkably . . . human speech," said the Distinguished Commentator.

"If you had the opportunity to cover Governor Block, as I have, over the last few months," said the Second-String Correspondent, whose banishment to the vice-presidential campaign had suddenly turned into the career opportunity of a lifetime, "you know that you often have to look beneath the words to find the real sense of what he means. Superficially, those words may have sounded . . . inappropriate. But when you come to better understand Block"—an open bid here for the job of White House correspondent—"you know him to be a man of deep personal faith, whose confidence in God's will is truly rock solid. And what you can hear in that last 'good luck' is a kind of prayer for the soul of Mack Foyle."

Such sentiments were heard by an estimated 175 million Americans who were watching the memorial service, the largest television event ever for a single event. They were translated into dozens of languages and heard by a billion and a half people who were watching around the world, transfixed by signals beamed to 117 countries from two dozen geosynchronous satellites that girdled the globe 22,000 miles high. And of all these witnesses, all the kings and queens, popes and priests, sheikhs and warlords, moguls and magnates, history will record that the single most important of these was sitting on a folding chair in a vacant Oldsmobile showroom on Twenty-eighth Street in Grand Rapids, Michigan, clad in a silk-polyester dress purchased for $39.95 at the Wardrobe Outlet, clutching a tearstained handkerchief, staring at a TV screen.

When Block had gotten up to speak, Dot had felt a twinge of sympathy for him, a decent enough man without any evident evil or malice, about to be placed in a job he was so clearly unsuited for . . .

. . . and then the duck had come down and hit her on the head.

From childhood, Dot Ledger had lived her emotional life between the forty-yard lines. She'd played the hand she was dealt even if she suspected that the dealer was silently chuckling as he pulled another joker from his gartered sleeve. The men had come and taken the corner office at the First Colonial Bank that was rightly hers; the men had run for the legislature and the Congress as she labored in the cramped, grimy offices of the Kent County Republican Party and spent her weekends stuffing flyers in mailboxes; the men had taken her dreams of marriage and family and crumpled them like a paper napkin, and the next morning there was work to be done. She had lived her life checking her resentments at the door.

But now Fate had aimed its kick in the pants at the national posterior. Now it was the whole country that lay prostrate in the dust. This was not another private sorrow. Now Dot Ledger was being asked to ratify another raw deal—only this time the joker was going to wind up in the White House.

"Charles," she said, "suppose I don't want to vote for Block for President? Suppose I think it would be the wrong thing to do?"

"Don't even think about it, Dot," Charles said offhandedly. "Not even as a joke; don't even think about it."

But that was exactly what Dot Ledger was doing. She'd begun to think about it. . . .

EIGHTEEN

★ ★ ★

A major airport on a stormy evening. A jumbo jet has called in a "Mayday!" message: the landing gear has locked. The three hundred petrified passengers are braced, their heads between their legs, hands locked behind their necks. On the ground, emergency crews respond to the urgent alarm. Their trucks line the runway, spreading foam to contain the likely fire. Medical crews are at the ready; emergency surgical teams race to unload the plasma, the oxygen, the mobile heart and lung machines that will save lives in the midst of the impending disaster. This is what it was like in the first minutes and hours after Ted Block had paid his unique tribute to the fallen President never-to-be.

Even as the casket was being borne from the catafalque, even as it was being walked out of the Rotunda, down the Capitol steps, and onto the waiting horse-drawn caisson, the minority leader of the House was beckoning Sharon Kramer to him with a flick of his prominent eyebrows. At forty-seven, Connor Doyle was a cartoonist's dream, with a haircut shaped by a Kennedy acolyte on acid, a leonine head atop a tall, lean body, and a mirthless smile that often emerged at particularly inauspicious moments, as when he was denouncing "the liberal, permissive mentality that had set thugs and hoodlums loose to wreak havoc"—smile!—"on innocent citizens." His energy and single-mindedness had propelled him into the Republican leadership in his second House term. When the party lost its House majority, and the outgoing Republican Speaker traded in his office for a nationally syndicated satellite talk show, Connor Doyle was the all-but-unanimous choice to become Republican leader.

Sharon Kramer had never seen Doyle as the kind of man she could have a real conversation with, but she was impressed by Doyle's preternatural political instinct for the right gesture at any moment—even this one. As she came to his side, he spoke to her with the barest movement of his lips. As far as the probing cameras were concerned, he might well have been offering up a bemused observation about the awful mysteries of life.

"Get in the car with me—we'll talk on the way to Arlington."

"Mr. Leader, the governor wants me—"

"He'll be fine. There's no possible place for him to open his mouth between here and the cemetery. We *have* to talk." Connor turned to Sharon and put a fatherly hand on her shoulder. He seemed to be offering a kindly act of consolation as he casually turned her out of camera view.

"I begged him. I *pleaded* with him not to put him on the ticket. You know what he said to me? He said: 'Sometimes you can just look a man in the eye and know he has what it takes. That's what I see in Ted Block.' So because Mack Foyle thought he was some kind of psychic optometrist, we've got . . ." Connor shook his head—a gesture that would later be described by *USA Today* as "a silent, eloquent testimonial to the vagaries of chance"—as he climbed into the car, gesturing Sharon in with him.

"He had a fine speech," Sharon said. "A terrific speech."

Connor Doyle reached over to the armrest and pressed a button. A thick glass partition rose to block off the driver's seat from the rear. He pressed another button and a metal shield followed. The driver, who had been ferrying celebrities around the capital for nineteen years, simply assumed that a pre-interment act of fellatio was occurring a few feet behind him, and returned to his recurring fantasy of finding thirty thousand dollars in small bills in the wallet of a deceased passenger.

"That's great how good his speech was," Connor snapped. "Maybe he can stand up at the grave site and apologize for trying to think of something to say on his own. Maybe then we can all go back to the Capitol and run the memorial service over again so he can give the speech somebody else wrote for him." Doyle gazed out the window at the crowds lining the route to Arlington: youths in Scout uniforms, old men in either World War II khakis or Vietnam-era camouflage shirts saluting the cortege; families clustered together, holding up handmade signs reading

Goodbye, We'll Miss You. One couple, a white-haired man wearing a tweed jacket and bow tie, the woman in a flowered shift and cardigan sweater, stood, coatless and shivering, bearing an inscription from a gate at Princeton University, built to honor a son of wealth who had died in World War I: "His sun is set 'ere it was noon."

"I was in junior high when they shot JFK," Doyle said. "I remember two things. One, I had a French test scheduled for Monday that I knew I was going to flunk. When they told us what had happened over the P.A. system I almost cheered, I was so relieved. But I also remember thinking that Lyndon Johnson was going to make everything all right. He was old and ugly, and his face sagged like a basset hound's, but that was okay, he was . . . a grown-up. He would hold it together."

He pointed to the crowds and the signs.

"You have to make that happen for them," Doyle said to Sharon. "You have to help them think Block is going to be able to make it all right."

"I can't make him something he isn't," Sharon said.

Connor Doyle smiled, and the temperature inside the limo dropped twenty degrees.

"No? I thought that's what they paid you to do. Forget it. Here's what I'm thinking about. I'm thinking of asking the Speaker to address the National Committee just before we vote to make Block the President. What do you think?"

In spite of herself, Sharon smiled.

"Sure, why not ask the highest-ranking Democrat in the United States to endorse the selection of a Republican President at a partisan Republican gathering? You really think he'd do it?"

Doyle nodded.

"Yeah, I do. Know why? Because I thought what would I do if I were the Speaker and it was me someone was asking." He began to count on his fingers as if he were recalling a list of picnic items.

"One: I'm owed big—and I mean *big*—for the next four years by the President. In fact, maybe I'm owed bigger than anyone else in the whole country. Because right now Ted Block is bleeding from a hundred cuts, and I'm the guy who can bandage him up.

"Two: It makes my job in Congress a whole lot easier, because at the other end of Pennsylvania Avenue is a President who can deliver me maybe two dozen Republicans whenever the clowns in my own party start making life tough for me.

"Three: In one day I go from being a politician to a statesman. Suddenly I'm Arthur Vandenberg—"

"Who?"

"What did they teach you in history, Sharon? All the words to the *Monkees' Greatest Hits*? Vandenberg—the Republican senator who walked away from isolationism and backed Truman on the Marshall Plan and Point Four and globalism. Bingo! All at once he became the hero of the editorial boards and the Council on Foreign Policy and the Trust Funders for Peace and *Time* magazine. So if I'm the Speaker, maybe I'm tired of all those cartoons that make my nose look like a Christmas light. Maybe I'd like to become the tough-nosed pol who stood tall in a moment of great national crisis. Maybe I'd like to be 'Person of the Week.' Maybe I'd like to be the good guy on *MacNeil-Lehrer*. Maybe I'd like half a dozen honorary degrees from universities that most days wouldn't let me into their football stadium. So that's how I'm thinking if I'm the Speaker. I assume he'd be thinking the same way."

Sharon stopped nodding.

"Okay—I get it. That's why he'd do it. Now tell me why *we'd* do it. Why would we want to make a hero out of the Speaker when we're going to be throwing stones at him in six months?"

The funeral cortege was moving across Memorial Bridge. Ahead of him, just beyond the Circle, was the rise of Arlington National Cemetery. Connor glanced up at the metal shield, then leaned forward and spoke in a tone so low that Sharon could barely hear him.

"Because if you don't," Connor said, flashing that smile again, "you may not ever get that chance to throw stones at the Speaker or anybody else—at least, not from the White House."

"Oh, please, Mr. Leader, let's get a taxi back to Planet Earth, okay? We won, remember? We won the election. We get the White House, we get the airplanes, we get the helicopters—"

Connor grabbed Sharon's forearm, hard.

"Listen—just *listen*. You—we—haven't won anything—yet. What we've won is three hundred five electors, just about thirty-five more than we need. What do you know about them?"

"Not a thing," Sharon said. "But who cares? You're talking about some technicality."

"That's right," Connor said. "I'm talking about a technicality—a stupid formality. But without it, Ted Block doesn't get to be President. And if there's a hint—the least hint—that some of those electors get it into their heads that they don't want Block to be President . . ."

"What? *What?* What are they going to do?"

"That's my point, Sharon. We don't really know what they can and can't do. Maybe they can do *anything they want to do.* Maybe some of them will vote for Foyle. I know he'll be six feet under in a few minutes, but they can. Or maybe some of them will find somebody else to vote for. One thing I'm sure of: a whole lot of these electors are true believers, which means they think Block is some kind of international socialist. Or maybe—maybe—there are thirty-five and a half of them who are liberal Republicans—I think that's how many are left in the country—and maybe they started out liking Block, but now they think he's a moron, and maybe a Democrat like Mueller would be safer in the White House."

"Come on, Connor"—Sharon was exercised enough to drop the courtesy title—"a Republican elector *can't* vote for a Democrat."

Connor Doyle shrugged.

"Maybe—maybe not. Maybe they vote for their brother-in-law, or their dentist, or Madonna, and then the courts or the Congress or somebody can sort it all out. But the only way to make sure it doesn't happen is to make a vote for Theodore Block an act of patriotic duty. We have to make that National Committee meeting a cross between the Constitutional Convention, the Superbowl, and a National Prayer Breakfast—I wonder if Mother Teresa would fly in?"

The limo pulled past the gate and swung into the VIP parking area. Two Secret Service agents moved to the doors and pulled them open. One muttered into his wrist, "We have Chestnut confirmed on the ground with an unaccompanied female." Connor and Sharon sat for a moment in silence. Then she shook her head.

"You're serious, aren't you? You're not kidding."

"Would I kid about something like this?" Connor Doyle said—and his smile frosted the window.

NINETEEN

★ ★ ★

It might all have been different if Jack Petitcon had been out of the office when the Speaker called. If he had gone down to Boca Raton, to the sumptuous home he discreetly shared with the Senate minority leader, a justice of the Supreme Court, and the owner of a major cable conglomerate, if he had been out on the eighty-five-foot cruiser they jointly owned (technically owned by a Costa Rican charitable foundation and chartered out of Ecuador), perhaps the Speaker would have listened to Connor Doyle's appeal to patriotism, to the need for national unity. A sentimental man, known to cry at every wedding, funeral, confirmation, and circumcision he attended back home—and he attended hundreds, thousands of them—he might well have been moved to tears, and then to act.

But of course, that is exactly why Jack Petitcon had slipped away from the memorial service and returned to his office to watch the funeral of MacArthur Foyle on television, instead of following the procession out to Arlington. It wasn't that Jack knew that the Speaker would be calling; it wasn't that he knew exactly who would be calling him, or why. But as he leaned back in the LeCorbusier chair, his five-hundred-dollar hand-tooled brogans resting on the desk that FDR had used at his Warm Springs, Georgia, retreat, Jack Petitcon knew that someone was likely to be looking for him, someone might be calling for somber words of counsel that he would offer up out of friendship and patriotism—for future consideration.

So when the television cameras caught the Speaker of the House in whispered conversation with Connor Doyle, and followed him as he beckoned an aide for a cellular phone and urgently punched out a number, Jack Petitcon was hardly surprised when the private line in his office rang. Gratified, of course, but not surprised.

"How dew, Mistah Speakuh, how dew?"

There was a short silence. On the TV screen, the Speaker could be seen looking up sharply, then shaking his head.

"What are you doing, Jack, tapping the cell phones now?"

"Bettah than that, Mistah Speakuh, I got me a friend at Comsat who owed me big time? So he got me mah own personal transponder with a cellular intercept? Jus' watch out you don't call one of those 'nine-seven-six' numbers on the taxpayers' dime."

Jack chuckled, then abruptly changed tone. As his voice dropped several registers, so did the intensity of his Bayou accent.

"Goddamn terrible day, Mr. Speaker, a goddamn terrible day. Remember what they said in Ireland when Jack Kennedy died? 'They cried the rain down that night.' I think that's what we'll be doin' tonight . . . cryin' the rain down."

"What a wonderful way to put it," Topper Huggins said. "Maybe I can use it in one of my eulogies. Thanks, Jack."

And Jack Petitcon recorded another entry in his "accounts receivable."

"Tell you why I'm calling now, Jack."

"Mr. Speaker, you might want to take a few steps to your right, behind those Secret Service men. It might be a good idea not to let the camera see you on the phone right now."

"What? Oh, damn, damn, damn! Vultures, they're all a bunch of good-for-nothing vultures!" The Speaker moved, and in a few seconds he had disappeared out of camera range.

"You still there, Jack?" The Speaker came from an era when people yelled during long-distance telephone calls, on the theory that the farther away the call was coming from, the louder one had to speak.

"Right here, Mr. Speaker."

"Anyway, I just had a . . . remarkable conversation with Connor."

"Was he smiling?"

"Lots."

"Hmnnnn. Sounds bad. What'd he want?"

"I'm not sure you'll believe this, Jack, but he wants me to speak at their National Committee meeting when they nominate Block to the presidency."

Jack Petitcon said nothing.

"He said it would be . . . I'm trying to remember his exact words, Jack, he said it would be 'an act of national healing.' Said it 'would put this wounded country back on its feet.' I told him I'd think about it. He said he'd be grateful if I could give him an answer before the burial's over. Said he'd like to leak it to the *Times* and the *Post* so it could hit the front pages tomorrow."

The Speaker paused.

Jack Petitcon said nothing.

"Can you imagine that, Jack? Going to the other guy's hall to nominate their guy for President? Boy, that'd be one for the history books, wouldn't it?"

The Speaker paused.

Jack Petitcon said nothing.

"You have any ideas on this, Jack?"

Now.

"I'm jes' pickin' mahself off the flo', Mistah Speakuh," Jack said with a slight chuckle. "That's 'bout the weirdest idea ah evah *hurd.* Do me a favuh an' run it by me one mo' tahm. Jes' how is this sposeda happun now?"

The Speaker began to explain: as the House minority leader, Connor Doyle would convene the Republican National Committee into session, to act as a committee on vacancies. He and other top Republican officials would offer a resolution inviting the Speaker of the House, as the ranking national Democrat, to address the committee. The Speaker would explain that, at this time of national shock and grief, at this time of national and international crisis, nothing was more vital to America than a clear demonstration of national unity. Therefore . . .

Jack Petitcon wasn't listening to a word.

He was a man who had come to his wealth and power by understanding, as well as anyone who had ever come to Washington, the presence of weakness. No, not understanding; it was more like the innate ability of a predator to detect the faintest sense of blood in the water. Jack could hear it in the slightest quaver of a voice in a hearty greeting. He could see it in the few rapid blinks of an eye. Others had this gift, of course, but Jack Petitcon had something else, something very rare. He could sense this weakness secondhand. It wasn't the Speaker's uncertainty that fascinated Jack—it was Connor Doyle's. There was something about Block's ascension that wasn't going the way it should. He'd made a fool of himself, of course, but by that calculus the House and Senate chambers would be three-fourths empty on a permanent basis.

Jack waited until the Speaker had finished explaining Connor Doyle's proposal.

". . . so then Block accepts the nomination and he promises a 'government of national healing.' That means a couple of Democrats in the Cabinet, with a promise that I'll be actively consulted—I don't pick 'em but I can veto 'em. And that's it."

The Speaker paused.

Jack Petitcon said nothing.

"You got any ideas on this, Jack?"

"Tell you what, Mr. Speaker, lemme get back to you on this. No—I don't think it'd look all that good for you to get a phone call while they're putting Mack Foyle in the ground. Give me . . . give me a half hour or so on this, and call me back when you get someplace private."

Jack hung up—and turned his private line off.

In the last decade, Jack Petitcon had turned off his private line exactly twice. The first was when an urgent call from the White House informed him—forty-eight hours before it had become public, and twenty-four hours before the President had been told—that the United States had been secretly selling arms to an officially designated terrorist nation. The second time was when a call from a pay phone in Des Moines informed him that the leading candidate for President was about to be accused of rampant infidelity by a high school cheerleader who had taped their encounters. The result of the first call was a special tax ruling for a European-based holding company that saved it $4.7 billion over nine years.

The second call had resulted in a winning bid for a mobile phone franchise in the eighth-biggest market in North America.

In both cases, Jack had cut off the phones, lowered the electronically controlled blinds, turned off the lights, and sat in darkness until the outlines of The Problem—it was always A Problem, never A Disaster, never A Scandal—sharpened into a clear picture.

The outline here was obvious enough. There was no way a party that had just retained control of the White House was going to make a hero and a partner out of the de facto leader of the opposition. No matter how big a shock the country had sustained, no matter that a just-elected President had dropped dead, the Republican offer was inexplicable . . . unless they were worried about their hold on the White House. Was it Block's performance during the campaign, his unchallenged position as the nation's kick-me boy? That was a problem, no doubt about it. But in a country where incumbent Presidents have gone on morning radio talk shows to joke about their insatiable appetite for fast food and fast women, would that be enough for a party to offer a couple of Cabinet seats to the man their ads had called "a living symbol of isolated, insulated arrogance"?

No, something else was on the mind of Connor Doyle and Company. There was something out there, a potential threat big enough to tempt them into the political equivalent of a preemptive nuclear strike. The Republicans wanted a gesture big enough to suck all the air out of the room, to make Block's selection a question almost of national security. It was the kind of "Hail Mary" play that a trailing candidate might try in the closing days of an election. But the election was over. It wasn't as if there was any real suspense about the electoral vote . . .

. . . And it was as if Jack Petitcon had been flying a helicopter in a dense fog, headed toward treacherous mountain terrain, when a sudden updraft pulled him a thousand feet straight up, clear of the clouds, and suddenly a huge valley opened before him, as far as the eye could see. It was a rich, fertile valley, green with the promise of a harvest of confusion and chaos. It made all the vineyards in which he had toiled—the halls of the Congress, damp with the fear of loss of office; the marbled corridors of the moneyed classes, slick with the fear of higher tax rates;

the teak and paneled homes of the lawyers and lobbyists, who wore all manner of uniforms when they appeared in public, but who all carried the same king's shilling in their pockets—it made all that he had seen pale before this valley of opportunity.

He paused for a moment, like a chess master seeing an unguarded path to the king. Then he gave a quick nod of approval to himself and flicked his finger at the speed-dial console next to his phone. He chuckled as the digital tones gave off their high-speed chirps.

"Wonder how my picture's gonna look on a five-dollar bill," he mused aloud, and reached for the speakerphone button.

TWENTY

★ ★ ★

"Jack, I wish I could say it's a pleasure, but under the circumstances, that doesn't sound quite right."

"Hoo, boy, you got that right. This town was broken up plenty when Frank Roosevelt died, and it was catatonic when Jack Kennedy got killed, but this . . ."

I love it, Al DeRossa thought. *I love how he calls Roosevelt "Frank"—especially since Jack Petitcon was about fourteen years old when FDR died, and was fetching coffee for his father's clients in Baton Rouge when Kennedy was murdered.* DeRossa was exhausted from the coverage of Mack Foyle's funeral, punchy from the lack of sleep, desperate for a hot meal, a hot shower, and a warm bed, but there was something about Jack Petitcon that was almost irresistible—emphasis on the "almost." There was hardly a story, a recollection, an offhand remark from the man that was not shaped and polished like a fine piece of sculpture to reflect the greater glory of Jack Petitcon. He could begin a conversation by talking about an Italian restaurant he'd dined at, and within a minute or two, he'd been comparing the risotto there to the dish he'd been served at a private dinner with the Pope. DeRossa knew one other thing about a chat with Jack Petitcon: anyone who tried to grasp its import simply by listening to the words being spoken was likely to wind up with egg on his face, and with a treasured part of his anatomy in Jack Petitcon's pocket.

"Al, I ever tell you the story Larry O'Brien told me about when he and Jack Kennedy were down in Palm Beach right after 1960?"

"Not that I recall, Jack." *Maybe this is about how he'd passed Marilyn Monroe over to JFK.*

"You got to picture this, Al. There's Jack and the family, and Larry, down in Florida, right after the election. They're lyin' in the sun, and catchin' their breath, and tryin' to put together a gummint. Suddenly they get a call from one of their guys in Louisiana. You remember what happened in Louisiana that year?"

"Not offhand, Jack."

"Shoot, and they pay you all that money to be their political director? Okay—well, in Louisiana the Democratic Party was all split to hell and gone over civil rights. It wound up that half the electors were pledged to Kennedy, and the other half said they'd vote for whatever redneck they could find who'd swear that segregation was the holy writ of God Almighty himself. I'm not proud of that time, Al, not at all."

"It's okay, Jack. Go on." *Where the hell is this going?*

"Okay—so this guy in Louisiana tells O'Brien that the Kennedy electors are gettin' all these calls, tellin' 'em not to cast their ballots for Kennedy at the electoral college. And he says the same calls are bein' made to the Kennedy electors in Georgia, and Alabama, and South Carolina, and Arkansas . . . So Larry starts thinkin': 'Jesus Christ, we only got three hunnert and three electoral votes anyway. If these guys put their heads together, maybe they could get thirty-five, forty guys to vote for somebody else!' You see what got 'im so panicked, don't you, Al? There goes JFK's majority, and there goes the election: right into the House of Representatives, with all those southern Democrats to tell Kennedy: 'Lay off the civil rights stuff or you don't get to be President.' Or maybe the electors take a walk over to Nixon and say, 'How'd yew like to be President?' Hell, the popular vote was just about a tie, he could've figured out a way to make it look good. Or maybe the electors cut a deal with Jack: 'If you want these votes, we get to pick the federal judges down here.' Larry said it was pretty tense down there before they managed to put the fire out."

"Would've been a hell of a show."

"Well, that's just fine and dandy for you TV people, I guess. Nothing like a force-five natural disaster to get the blood going, right, Al?"

DeRossa smiled for the first time in days; there were few experiences more delicious than Jack Petitcon in the midst of a patriotic outburst.

"I guess you would've had a real blast in '68 if George Wallace had pulled it off, right? 'Member his idea? Win a bunch of southern states—he did that—deadlock the electoral college, and the deal: no more Voting Rights Act, no more federal troops in the South, the whole damn civil rights revolution stopped dead in its tracks. Remember how close he came? Dick only won by half a million votes over poor Hubert. One or two states the other way and Mr. George Corley Wallace would have had his fist wrapped tight as a tick around Uncle Sam's family jewels. That make a good show for you?"

DeRossa hit the "mute" button on the phone and let out a whispered "Jee-sus." Petitcon's act was beginning to wear just a bit. DeRossa had spent the day in a makeshift studio that was nothing more than an oversized closet packed with electrical gear and three stupefyingly bored stagehands, staring at a monitor while tethered to a microphone and a plastic earpiece. Ken Crenshaw, the special events producer, had told him to be ready with any political news he might have about the impending presidency of Theodore Block: when the Republican National Committee would meet, who the vice president would be, who might wind up in the Cabinet or on the White House staff. When DeRossa asked Crenshaw how he was supposed to gather such information while sitting in front of a television set, Crenshaw had patted his shoulder and said encouragingly, "Make it happen, Al, make it happen."

DeRossa had been cued exactly twice in the eleven hours of continuous coverage to be ready to go on the air. Once, he'd been preempted by an Air Force "missing man formation" flyby; the other time, the network had cut away to the grieving Foyle family approaching the casket for a final farewell. The only saving grace was that DeRossa had been spared the temptation to come off as an insensitive lout, so consumed by political calculations that he might as well have been jumping up and down on MacArthur Foyle's casket to get a better look at the spectators.

And now, with a throbbing headache, a sore backside, an empty stomach, and a mildly wounded ego, DeRossa was being subjected to a meandering lesson in political history by a Washington player whose personality could single-handedly supply the petroleum needs of New England. Why? At which point Al DeRossa sat up straighter and pressed the phone closer to his ear. *Pay attention—he is trying to tell you something.*

"Believe me, Jack, we've had all the great television we can stand for a while. I bet right now there are three producers back in an edit room, putting together the retrospective we'll run in three or four days. You know: 'Do you remember where you were when you heard the news?' Of course, if they can't remember, they've probably come down with Alzheimer's."

"Lissen, you dumb sumbitch, there's a few of us in this town who think the country's been through just about enough. What we're tryin' to do is to make sure nothin's comin' down that's gonna throw us into holy confusion about who happens to be the next President of the United States."

Petitcon's voice lowered to a conspiratorial level.

"Have you done your homework, Al? Are you sure those Republicans have got their ducks lined up behind Ted Block?"

"I can't imagine the National Committee—"

"Not the *committee,* dammit, the e-*lec*-tors. What the hell you think we've been talkin' about? The e-*lec*-tors. Foyle and Block only won three hunnert and five, just about what Kennedy got back in '60. They've only got thirty-five to spare. And Jack Kennedy won fair and square, if you don't count Chicago. But these guys never thought they'd be voting for Block for *President.* They thought the same thing we all did, that Foyle would take his Vice President and make him so damn invisible he'd be on milk cartons by the next election. And you know somethin', Al? As far as I can tell, they don't have to vote for Block for *President* at all, unless they feel like it. And jes' between us, I hear from some of my Republican friends that they're soilin' their shorts over this."

"I can't see it, Jack. The electors are good Republicans, they're not going to—"

"Really? You got any idea who they are, Al? Or are you like ever'-body else in this town? You got any head count about how any of 'em are so conservative they want to wipe out public schools? Or how many of 'em think Ted Block is a paid agent of the international banking conspiracy? Or how many just plain do not want to see a walking whoopee cushion with his finger on the button?"

While Jack Petitcon was talking, DeRossa was frantically waving his hand in the direction of Kathy Conicki, who was staggering out the door in search of the nearest horizontal surface. He flagged her, motioned her over to his cubicle, and scribbled a note: GET ME SHARON KRAMER, GET ME CONNOR DOYLE, WHERE ARE THOSE ELECTORS' LISTS? Conicki gave DeRossa her patented "What the hell now?" look and hurried off.

"Jack," DeRossa said with studied indifference, "I think maybe you've been hitting the Glenlivet a little too hard. It's a nice fantasy for somebody's column, but if you think the Republicans are going to throw away the White House—"

"Tell you what. Don't give it another thought. Don't bother yourself to make a phone call to find out whether they've asked the Speaker to show up at the Republican National Committee. Don't track down Marsh and Veigle to see whether they're gettin' flooded with calls from true-blue Foyle folks tellin' 'em to keep the Blockhead out of the White House. And don't even bother tryin' to see how many electors are already checkin' in with their state party to see whether they have to vote for Block if the committee says they should." *Hell,* Jack thought to himself. *Maybe they* are *being flooded with calls.*

"Pardon my indelicacy, Jack," DeRossa said, "but just what's in it for you?"

There was a pause.

"I'll tell you, Al, if you were one of those baby-boomer pundits who thinks he should be whispering advice into the President's ear, maybe I'd give you the cynical spin 'cause that's all those guys can deal with: you know, tell you that it's bad for business, or I'm lookin' to make friends with the Republicans. But this is you an' me, Al, and I'm just telling you straight as I can that you guys have just got to not let this get out of hand. If that's not good enough for you, well, you can go take a flying leap. I gotta go."

Of course he doesn't believe me, Jack thought as he hung up. *But it doesn't matter. He's got to follow it up. It's too good a story.*

Damn right that's not good enough for me, Al thought as he hung up. *But it doesn't matter. It's too good a story.*

So Jack Petitcon began calling DeRossa's counterpoints at a dozen different news outlets, urging them to keep the lid on a story of monumental political significance for which he was the principal source. And those counterparts began doing precisely what Al DeRossa was doing, precisely what Jack Petitcon knew they would do.

They went ballistic.

TWENTY-ONE

★ ★ ★

What Jack Petitcon had done is best explained by an old story. Some years back, a transcontinental railroad train was speeding across the Great Plains when the engine suddenly gave out.

"We're in luck," the conductor told the engineer. "The man who designed this engine just happens to be a passenger on the train."

Summoned to the locomotive, the inventor probed for a few minutes, then asked for a hammer. He struck the engine a single, sharp blow—and the train started up again.

A week later, the president of the railroad company was shocked to receive a bill from the inventor for five thousand dollars. He demanded a more precise accounting. A few days later, this itemized statement crossed his desk.

> Hitting engine with hammer—$1.00
> Knowing where to hit engine with hammer—$4,999.00

Jack Petitcon had simply known where to apply the hammer to the engine that drives modern politics.

Oh, yes, perhaps in an earlier time, when political discourse was controlled by relatively few gatekeepers, Jack Petitcon's hammer might have struck nothing but his thumb. Back then, when wise and prudent men of the same stock, from the same schools and universities, from the same law firms and clubs and summer retreats firmly held the reins of power, it might have been possible to keep the national conversation muted, to sweep to the side unseemly speculation about what was going to happen now that Mack Foyle was in his grave.

But this is our time, and there are no gatekeepers anymore. This is our time, when millions of us no longer believe what the press tells us, when tens of millions more no longer care. This is our time, when mendicants by the hundreds sell their wares on the radio and cable-TV street corners, and when there is no cop on the beat to shoo them away. It is easy to say our Founding Fathers would have been appalled by this, but they must have known it would happen, one way or another. After all, they wrote the Bill of Rights when there was no such thing as an "objective" political press, when the papers were owned lock, stock, and barrel by the political parties that paid the bills, when accusations of treason, popery, bribery, and murder were routinely aimed at political foes.

So they would hardly have been shocked at the stream of misinformation and invective pouring out of the radio and the TV, speeding its way back and forth through the telephone lines that linked millions of computers in a worldwide web with no center, no headquarters. In the midst of the chaos that blossomed around the sudden death of the just-elected President, it was hardly surprising that there would be tales of millions in gold paid to traitorous medical technicians by a band of New York bankers in league with the Block family. The ties between Block, a Bolivian drug-smuggling cartel, and a top executive of the International Monetary Fund were direct descendants of the early nineteenth-century newspaper allegations that charged Thomas Jefferson with lusting to bring the anti-Christian terror of the French Revolution to American shores, that reviled Andrew Jackson as a murderous bigamist, that scorned John Quincy Adams as the man who, during his tenure as American envoy to Russia, procured women for the czar's pleasure.

So, would our revered Founders have blanched at the calumny that passed for political discourse in the last days of the twentieth century? Not a chance. In fact, they had cobbled together the complex mechanics of the American government precisely because they understood the need to insulate it from the wilder winds of public debate.

"If we're going to let everyone say pretty much what they want," they had decided, "we'd better make sure that however decisions are made, they're made inside a structure that provides shelter from the storm outside."

And here was where these revered Founders slipped up. It just never occurred to them that, two centuries or so after they had done their work, the power of public conversation would be strong enough to breach the wall of separation they had built between the passions of the public and the pulleys of power. But now the whole force of that public conversation was being aimed at just such a wall: the power of presidential electors to choose the President.

In the eyes of the traditional press, the electoral college had always been one of those Quaint Perennials, a story that emerged every four years, only to sink promptly into the mist, something like a constitutional Brigadoon. Sometime after the November elections, a handful of local TV stations and newspapers would run a story that began: "You may have thought you voted for Ronald Reagan last Tuesday, but actually, you elected Alie Straithorn, a sixty-three-year-old Chevrolet dealer from Canton, who . . ." And on the first Monday in December, there'd be feature stories following these obscure men and women as they posed self-consciously on the steps of the state capitol, had a nice lunch, posed with the lieutenant governor or the secretary of state, and joked about voting for their brother-in-law. Like Groundhog Day, like the swallows coming back to Capistrano, like opening day of the baseball season, the story of the electoral college was covered—when it was covered at all—with a faintly amused nod to ritual and tradition.

But now, across the radio dial, and out there on the higher, more obscure end of the cable television universe, and out there in cyberspace, where the computer communities gathered electronically, a radically different conversation had been going on for the last thirty-six hours. While the traditional organs of mass communications had been frozen in place by the sheer magnitude of the story, while they had been pressured by their own sense of propriety and restraint to paint the succession of Theodore Block in as reassuring a light as possible, the more freewheeling voices out there had been restrained by no such concerns.

"My friends," bellowed Avi DuPoir, the most-listened-to radio host in the land, "I don't know what to think about some of these wild rumors flying all over the country about what really might have happened to President Foyle . . . maybe it's all hot air, maybe it's smoke from a real forest fire. I do know that if there *had* been *any*thing suspicious about this tragedy, our liberal friends in the media would have done anything and everything in their power to minimize it, trivialize it, 'put it in context,' do everything but take a hard look at whether someone—or some*ones*—wanted to keep a tough, committed conservative out of the White House. But I'll tell you *this:* put aside the so-called conspiracy talk for a minute, and ask yourself: What's going to happen when the people of this country start to understand that there is a chance—even a theo*ret*ical, *tech*nical chance—that the five hundred thirty-eight people none of us ever *heard* of actually have the legal, the constitutional power to elect the President?

"Well, I'll tell you what I think: I think once the American people realize that this power is actually being held—right now—by these strangers, I think you have the real possibility of a national uprising: a de*mand* that these electors follow the will of the American people as manifested on Election Day. And what was that will? It was to *put* a real con*ser*vative into the Oval Office. And the question we have to ask ourselves is simple: Is Theodore Pinckney Block that kind of conservative? Never mind the talk about his IQ, you'll always get that from the liberal media about any Republican. I'm talking about his 'CQ'—his 'conservative quotient.' Let's talk about that, after this from Rainbow Precious Metals, the investment of choice for today's daring financial planners."

"Let's talk about what's right here," murmured Jade Mandelbaum, the famed feminist–criminal-defense attorney–centerfold model who had traded in her shingle for a network cable chat show.

"What happens in a horse race when the first horse across the finish line is disqualified? The runner-up is declared the winner. What happens if the woman elected Miss America is unable to fulfill her duties? The first runner-up succeeds her. What happens if the low bidder on a government contract can't do the job? The second low-bidder steps in.

"So isn't it obvious," Ms. Mandelbaum continued, with the same earnestness that had once deadlocked a jury deciding the fate of a brother and sister who had plotted for seven months to poison their parents in order to collect on an $8 million insurance policy, "doesn't it stand to reason that, since Mr. Foyle will . . . ah . . . be unable to fulfill his duties as President, the job must go to the man who finished second, Bill Mueller? I mean, let us be honest about this: does anyone seriously contest the fact that if the American people had been asked to choose between Mueller and Teddy Blockhead, there would be any doubt about the outcome? We're going to talk all afternoon about this, folks, because it is about the very future of our form of government. First, though, this from Snugs, if the spirit is willing, but your kidneys are weak."

"Lissen, lemme tell you exactly what's going on here," rasped Mort Fillmore, the longtime conservative polemicist who first gained fame by labeling the House Democratic Caucus as "the Kremlin's Auxiliary Sewing Circle."

"This is the same game that worked at Watergate. It's the same game they tried during Iran-contra, until Ollie North ate their lunch; it's the same game they tried with that 'October Surprise' fairy tale—and I *do* mean fairy tale—about how Ronald Reagan and George Bush flew over to Paris in a jet plane and told the Iranians to keep our hostages locked up. Look, the Republicans won the election, and some crackpots out there are trying to use this tragedy to reverse the results of that election. Mack Foyle was going to be President. He picked Theodore Block as the man to succeed him if anything should happen to him. *And the American people ratified that choice.* In the face of the most vicious attack on the character and decency of any candidate for high public office in my lifetime, the American people said, 'Okay, Mack, that's the man you picked, that's good enough for us.' If that horse had bucked thirty days from now, after the electoral votes had been counted, we wouldn't be hearing a word about all this nonsense. So let's not get ourselves hysterical about a two-hundred-year-old formality. The Republican National Committee will name Governor Block to fill the vacancy; they'll choose a good, rock-solid conservative as Vice President; and that will be that. Now this from Pep-Up: if your doctor won't prescribe the lift you need to get through the day, don't give up—Pep-Up."

"I'm gonna give it to you straight," barked Slim Chance, the cowboy-philosopher whose *Straight Shootin'* talk show was quickly becoming the hottest new contender on the circuit, and who had become even more famous as a guest dispenser of cracker-barrel wisdom on the prestigious Sunday interview shows.

"It's like what happens in a ballgame, when it's a close game, and there's two out and three men on, and then the skies just open up, and down comes a gully-washer. Sure, the umpires might try to keep the game going until it's official, but suppose it's the seventh game of the World Series? There's only one thing to do: call the game and play it tomorrow. We need for our congressmen to get off their big fat recesses, and get back to Washington, and call this game off and run it again."

Not that long ago, this part of the national conversation did not exist. Even just a few years ago, it might as well not have existed as far as those on the upper reaches of Washington's greasy poles were concerned. And even now, most of the more important members of the House, the Senate, the executive branch, most of the men and women who were perched on the tonier printed pages and airwaves, knew of this conversation inferentially, as when a sudden explosion of popular anger flooded the mail rooms, and phone lines, and fax lines of the Establishment, protesting the latest outrage that their tribunes had unearthed.

By the time of Foyle's election, though, these voices had grown insistent enough so that attention had begun to be paid on a regular basis inside the halls of power. The younger congressional aides and agency paper shufflers, the young network desk assistants, and newspaper gofers had grown up listening to these voices, and their bosses wanted to know when to expect the next avalanche of calls and letters. Some of the younger, and young-no-longer media types, the ones who self-consciously inserted old rock lyrics into their commentaries to prove their hipness, listened every now and then to reassure themselves that they could still find the cutting edge of popular culture.

And so when Al DeRossa finished his conversation with Jack Petitcon, and summoned his exhausted staff with a request—all right, a demand—to sniff out any signs of defection among the Republican electors, he found fertile soil for the seed Jack Petitcon had planted.

Oh sure, Al, it's all over the radio, I heard it on my way over here at five-thirty in the morning.

Yeah, they were talking about it late last night, sounds like there might be some trouble even when the National Committee meets tomorrow.

DeRossa looked around the room.

"Great—so can I assume you're all tracking down these electors to find out how serious this all is?"

The silence was not merely pregnant; it was the Dionne quintuplets of silence.

"Al," Kathy Conicki said quietly, "we can't find out who they are."

"What do you mean?"

Conicki shrugged helplessly.

"I called the National Committee; you can imagine what kind of chaos it is over there. When I finally got one of the researchers, she told me she had never seen a list of electors, not this year, not ever. She thought the state parties might have them. Most of them were closed for Foyle's funeral; I got through to Missouri, Florida, and California; they had no idea, and one of them thought I was trying to get my kid into electrical college. I tried the state capitols, mostly the governors' offices, or the office of secretary of state; you know, the folks who issue commemorative driver's licenses. They were all closed for the funeral, too."

"I don't suppose our computers . . ." Conicki shook her head.

Al nodded.

"Of course not," he said. "When has it ever mattered? Well," he added, "I guess the good news is, if we don't know who they are, nobody else does, either . . . although, come to think of it, maybe that's the *bad* news."

TWENTY-TWO

★ ★ ★

They had tried; Lord knows, they had tried.

All along the sidewalks on the Connecticut Avenue approach to the Shoreham American Hotel, bands of Young Republicans were holding up signs reading, Welcome, Delegates! The lobby of the hotel was festooned with red, white, and blue bunting. Around the wrought-iron railing of the balcony that bordered the lobby, blown-up photographs of past Republican Presidents beamed down at the National Committeemen, the Committeewomen, the alternates, the press, and the 2,250 befuddled members of the American Gastro-Intestinal Association, whose annual meeting had been thrown into chaos by the hastily convened emergency session of the Republican National Committee. (A dozen or so specialists had almost instigated an ugly incident by prying open a meeting room door where the Christian Coalition was gathering, and inquiring, "Is this the flatulence group?") Powerful lights beamed down upon the makeshift wooden platforms from which the broadcast press fed live coverage of the comings and goings.

Inside the Grand Ballroom, a miniature convention floor had been constructed, with a podium, three hundred folding chairs with state standards and floor microphones. On the second level of the ballroom, small-scale skyboxes had been erected for the two networks that had been willing to fork over the $25,000 to the foreman of the hotel construction crew.

("Extortion!" the NBC executive had screamed. "This is a time for sacrifice," the foreman had replied calmly.)

The Republicans were trying their hardest to convey a sense of soldiering on, a great party, indeed a Grand Old Party, tending to the nation's business while brushing away a last tear for MacArthur Foyle. Unfortunately, the combination of the circumstances that had made the gathering necessary, combined with the unsettled state of party affairs, lent an air of forced enthusiasm to the session even before it began—a condition symbolized by the Missing Photo.

Three huge black-and-white photos were supposed to dominate the makeshift podium. On the left, a somber, heroic portrait of Foyle, bordered in black. In the middle, a somber, heroic portrait of Theodore Block. On the right . . . on the right there was an empty frame. It was supposed to be filled by a somber, heroic portrait of the candidate who would be offered by the Republican Party for the vice presidency. Half a dozen bored workmen stood, sat, slouched, and smoked around the ladder, ready to mount the photo in place as soon as it was delivered to them. Thirty-five floors upstairs, in an anteroom outside the presidential suite, a cluster of young suits waited with satchels full of photographs, of every conceivable candidate for the vice presidency, including the former governor of a large industrial state now residing in a federal halfway house. One of the suits had a cell phone grasped in hand, programmed to ring a dedicated line in Murray Roman's House of Photos, where Mr. Roman himself, on retainer at eighty dollars an hour, was waiting to blow the appropriate photo up to somber, heroic size.

The workmen, the suits, and Mr. Roman had been waiting for more than eight hours for the group inside the presidential suite to provide the name to go with the photograph. It was not going well.

All told, there were a dozen people inside the presidential suite. Four of them were crowded into one bedroom, attempting to compose the speech that Block would deliver to the National Committee once his selection had become official. Each of the speechwriters had come armed with a draft, and each was fighting for every word, every metaphor, with the intensity of a parent trying to get his son into a Little League starting lineup. They had spent forty-five minutes arguing about whether Block should declare this a moment of national grief or a moment of national redemption.

("Redemption?" the Pragmatist had screamed at the Lyricist. "What the hell is redemption? That's what my mother used to do with Green Stamps!"

"You have the soul of a Department of Motor Vehicles clerk!" snapped the Lyricist.)

The eight others, who regarded speechwriting as the playpen of modern politics, were grouped in the living room area of the suite, doing the grown-up work: running down the list of possible Vice Presidents. Sharon Kramer, Connor Doyle, the Senate minority leader, Marsh, Alan Veigle, the campaign pollster, and the party chair all looked as if they had been trapped in a smoky subway tunnel on a hot August afternoon. Their hair was plastered to their scalps; their shirts were soaked through with sweat.

Across the spacious living room Theodore Block sat, leafing through a book of *Treasured American Homes.* Not a hair was out of place, not a drop of sweat glistened on his brow. He had been utterly untouched by the storm that had broken over every member of the group hours before. A storm? No; more like a force-five hurricane. Last evening, all of the networks had reported "unconfirmed signs of discontent" within the Republican Party over the elevation of Governor Block. Each had reported that "informed sources" were hinting at "reported hints of concern" among some Republican electors. The resulting flood of telephone calls to anyone remotely connected with the Republican Party, the Foyle campaign, Ted Block, or any first-term Republican congressman with a listed home telephone number had almost paralyzed the District of Columbia phone grid. The chaos had also made it impossible for Marsh, Veigle, Doyle, Kramer, and company to call each other for the purpose of finding out what the *hell* was going on, and had anyone on God's green earth actually managed to *speak* to a single elector anyway?

By the time the group convened for a dinner of leathery steak sandwiches and pale green salads, nerve endings were throbbing like the speakers on a jukebox.

"Has everyone out there gone completely out of their minds?" Alan Veigle asked. "Do you know how many calls I got in the first fifteen minutes—the first fifteen *minutes*—after the evening news? I stopped counting at fifty; that's when I took the phone off the hook. I remember because it was forty-five minutes after that that I had to sneak out of the basement to duck the three news crews that were parked outside my house, blocking my driveway. Jesus, what kind of lunatics are these people?"

"It was almost as bad as what happened to the Vice President's staff after that Unfortunate Incident with the Flight Attendant," Marsh said. "If I recall right, the chief of staff was trapped inside his condo for eighteen hours; he had to call the cops to get him out."

"What I cannot fathom," Veigle went on, "is that I don't think any of those putzes even talked to an elector. If we don't know who they are, how do they know who they are? Wait, wait, I take it back. There's a guy out in Utah, a retired state senator who sent Foyle his first campaign contribution. I think he asked us to see if we could get him picked, and we did. He's, I don't know, eighty-eight, maybe eighty-nine, with a very bad case of cataracts. Hey, maybe he doesn't know what happened to Foyle. You could call him, I guess, but he might drop dead when you tell him the news."

That was the tone that pretty much carried through the night and into the dawn. Under the best of circumstances, when you know you've won a presidential nomination and the convention is still weeks away, picking a running mate is a nettlesome piece of business, an exercise comparable to moving a case of nitroglycerin. Turn away for a brief moment, and you wound up with a running mate who forgot to mention that, every few years or so, he checked himself into a big house on the hill with soft, rubber walls, where he got himself wired up to a generator to clear out the cobwebs in his head. Oh, and didn't the distinguished nominee ever bother to correct that pesky financial disclosure form? Darn, how had she forgotten to mention that her husband had a long and happy business association with a few gentlemen who stored and shipped a few hundred million dollars a year in sophisticated adult video entertainment?

And those were the sorts of things that happened under normal circumstances. Now, with the country still trying to deal with what had happened to their new President, and with Ted Block's unfortunate missteps in presenting himself to the country as the leader for this troubled time, the job of finding the right Vice President was infinitely harder:

whoever they picked would have to be prestigious enough to win the applause of the elites, conservative enough to satisfy Foyle's supporters, diffident enough to be willing to play second fiddle to an out-of-tune President, and safe enough to withstand the intrusive inquiries of the press—and all that was before Jack Petitcon's labors had borne such ripe fruit on last night's evening newscasts.

Some possibilities were dismissed within seconds. The President? There was something daring about the gesture, but the same two-term limit that barred him from seeking another term made him ineligible for the vice presidency; and the fact that he was a near invalid, while posing no substantive threat to his ability to carry on the duties of Vice President, was not what the nation needed right at this time. The sitting Vice President? No, that Unfortunate Incident with the Flight Attendant was enough to put that idea to rest.

"Should we be thinking about a Democrat?" Sharon Kramer asked. "Symbol of national unity at this time of crisis?"

"It's a seventy-thirty," the pollster said. "We asked last October; seventy percent said it was time for a bipartisan government."

"In a pig's eye," said the national chairman. "You wanna go make the *New York Times* happy, go adopt a baby seal. What about you, Connor? You're on TV every week, you're a national leader—"

"No way," said Connor. "I've spent eight years throwing everything I could find at our friends on the other side of the aisle. I've called 'em tinhorn dictators, bullies, fat and corrupt. They love it at the fund-raisers, and they love it on the Hill, but there's not one damn thing that's presidential about me—yet."

"Same here," said the Senate minority leader. "Only you can forget about 'yet.' "

So they slogged on.

- The governor of Ohio was great; son of a plumber, a Democrat turned Republican (just like Reagan!) who had won reelection by a landslide. But he was pro-choice, and he'd been through a not-very-pleasant divorce.
- The secretary of the interior was a veteran of Congress with a great personality, the best sense of humor in Washington, and a public life free

of scandal. But everyone in Washington knew about her "roommate," a college chum she had lived with on and off for more than thirty years . . . named Margaret.

- The senator from California was a rare breed: a working politician who not only read books, but wrote them. He was the most informed, articulate member of Congress—as long as you spoke to him before he returned from drinking his lunch.
- The former Vice President was quite likely the most distinguished-looking man in the United States, with a face off a Roman coin, silver hair, piercing blue eyes, and a deep, soothing voice that could deliver a stump speech, a sermon, or a quarterly report with equal power. At seventy-one, he was in fine health, and his reputation was still good enough to win him a seat at the table of a dozen boards of directors. And that was the problem; since leaving office eight years earlier, the former Vice President had traded in a life of government salaries for the best life money could buy: he spoke for forty thousand dollars a pop, he fronted for everything from a gold bullion trading company to a "Madison Collectibles Museum." He would have charged for his autograph if his wife hadn't threatened to leave him.

"No way he takes the job unless we jack up the pay to three and a half million a year," Alan Veigle said.

By six o'clock in the morning, after only eight or nine shouting matches and three near fistfights, the group had narrowed the choice to two: Mark Hennigan, the three-term senior senator from Florida, and Peter Wilkes, the Senate whip from Missouri. All through the night, squads of fog-brained lawyers had been working their way through tax returns, financial statements, TRW credit ratings, newspaper clippings, and completely groundless rumors about the two men.

"Let me make it easy on everybody," Sharon said. "We have to make the decision within an hour."

"What decision?" Ted Block had been sleeping for the last six hours; he emerged from the second bedroom in the presidential suite in an impeccably fresh sweat suit.

"Your Vice President," Sharon said.

"I know, I know, only kidding here, people." He poured himself a glass of orange juice from the side bar. "God, I hate pulp. I don't know why these companies advertise 'Pulp in! Pulp in!' Our cook used to spend God knows how long every morning trying to strain the darn stuff out." He took a long, deep gulp.

"I hope you're not forgetting Sherwood," he said, and walked back into the bedroom.

There was a long moment of silence.

"Sherwood?" Connor Doyle asked.

"Sherwood Phelps," Alan Veigle answered in a monotone. "The congressman. Upstate New York; Princeton; Oxford; family had a place up in Maine; I think that's where they met; very big on national parks; very big on intercity rail subsidies; very big on international family planning."

"Could we have him call Block and tell him he won't take the job?" Marsh asked. "Could we set fire to his hair?"

"Probably," Sharon said. "It's just going to delay us an hour, that's all. It's just going to give us one more reason to look like a bunch of amateurs."

Sharon looked around the room.

"Anyone else got an idea to keep us locked in here until the inaugural address? No? Good. Let's see if we can get through the next hour without an airplane crashing into the hotel."

As it turned out, Sharon Kramer's imagination was both too vivid and too pinched. It wasn't that an airplane was about to crash into the Shoreham American; it was that, thirty-five floors below this enclave, Dorothy Ledger of Grand Rapids, Michigan, was checking in.

TWENTY-THREE

★ ★ ★

By the time she reached the registration desk, Dorothy Ledger had become convinced that this was all some terrible practical joke, a twisted, psychotic version of *Candid Camera* or *People Are Funny.* Any minute she expected Art Linkletter or Alan Funt to pop up from behind the desk with a frozen smile and gift certificate for a year's supply of soda. *I must have been crazy to let Charles drag me into this,* she thought. Charles Berlin was just as edgy, but for very different reasons.

He'd thought of this trip as a masterstroke. Troubled by her doubts about Theodore Block taking over the most powerful office on earth, he'd used every ounce of juice he had to get Dorothy designated as the temporary National Committeewoman from Michigan. He'd assumed, logically enough, that immersing her in the solemn majesty of the moment would settle whatever qualms she had about Block's ascension. But as an old political maxim has it, assumption is the mother of fuck-ups.

First, the connecting flight out of Grand Rapids had been three and a half hours late, grounded by a "surprise" snowstorm.

("Imagine that," Dot had snapped to Charles Berlin. "Snow in the Midwest in November. Who could have imagined such a thing?")

So they'd missed the flight from Detroit to Washington, and had to spend three and a half hours in Metro Airport, with Dorothy repeatedly threatening to bolt to the Budget Rent-a-Car counter and drive straight back to Grand Rapids. The next flight to Washington was delayed another ninety minutes by what the pilot called "a mechanical event," and arrived not at National Airport, but at Dulles International, a convenient thirty-five-dollar cab ride to downtown. All that was the warm-up; the main event began the moment Charles and Dot stepped out of their cab at the entrance to the Shoreham American.

On both sides of the entrance, crowds of protesters, supporters, witnesses, and onlookers pressed behind police barricades, hurling prayers, obscenities, and leaflets at Charles, Dorothy, and anyone else entering the hotel. The Capitol police, their anxiety honed to a fine edge by the tumult of the last few days, were in no mood to make fine distinctions. They were seizing anyone trying to enter the hotel, and demanding they produce some sort of credential. By the time Charles Berlin found the right set of papers identifying himself and Dorothy as National Committee members from Michigan, the cab had driven off—with Dorothy's garment bag in the trunk.

If the street outside the hotel was chaos, the lobby was bedlam. Camera crews took up every square foot of space, stacking tape decks and gear on the lavishly upholstered chairs and polished-oak coffee table, snaking wires across carpets, around pillars, up to the mezzanine, where compact editing and transmission equipment was piled high. The behavior of the camera crews had long ago been raised to the level of a primal instinct: as soon as the revolving doors began to move, the crews swarmed toward the entrance, forming a narrow, barely passable corridor. As Dorothy discovered, it did not matter that the victim was completely unrecognizable; print reporters and producers tried to dig out this information, by yelling, "Who are you?" at the hapless guests. Dorothy would have found all this unsettling even if she hadn't been blinded by the lights of the cameras, and even if a boom mike hadn't hit her a solid smack on her forehead.

Charles knew he had a problem on his hands; despite her low-key surface demeanor, a dyspeptic Dorothy Ledger was not to be trifled with. He'd once seen her drive a state senator, a former All–Big Ten tight end, out of a meeting in tears when the senator had scheduled a fund-raiser on the same date as the county Republicans' picnic. As he waited at the registration desk—there seemed to be "a computer situation" with their reservations—he maneuvered to get Dorothy out of the line of fire.

"I don't know about you, but I'm starved," Charles said. "That airplane snack was awful. Why don't you get us a table at the coffee shop, and I'll join you as soon as we get our room keys. And don't wait for me; just go ahead and get yourself something to eat."

Chalk up another slam dunk for Fate.

Dorothy managed to fight her way through the mob in the lobby—and found a line of at least thirty people waiting for a table in the Roman Hruska Room. With a rumbling stomach and a grinding headache propelling her to action, she strode past the line, until she spotted a booth where a lone diner was working on a sandwich and a cup of coffee. She never broke stride.

"I beg your pardon," Dorothy said, "but would you mind if I shared this booth? I've been on airplanes and cabs and—"

"Don't say another word," the stranger replied, with a welcoming gesture. "You look normal enough, and right now that would be a blessing." He put out his hand.

"I'm Walter Ames, Jr., from Lodi, New Jersey."

"Dorothy Ledger, Grand Rapids, Michigan."

After she'd flagged down a harried waitress and ordered a cheeseburger and strawberry milk shake, they began exchanging the compulsory pleasantries. Walter Ames, Jr., was a well-preserved man of sixty-nine, owner-manager of the wholesale plumbing supply business his father had started in 1925. "I suppose it seems foolish for a man my age to be 'Junior,' " he said, brushing back his silver hair, "but my dad lived to be ninety-three, and by that time, that's how everyone knew me."

Dorothy decided she liked Walter Ames, Jr. His face was open, agreeable. His eyes did not wander over her shoulder, looking for a more useful person to talk with. His clothes were simple: a tweed jacket, a flannel shirt. She guessed he'd be wearing chinos or corduroy pants. He wore no jewelry, smelled of no cologne. His only outward mark of distinction was the beribboned badge pinned to the lapel of his jacket.

"Are you the committeeman from New Jersey?"

Walter laughed.

"Ma'am, you couldn't get me to take a job like that with a stick. No, I'm the guy they come to when they want somebody to raise a little money. I've got a lot of friends who do pretty much what I do, small businessmen, you know, and it's not that hard to scare up some campaign money; nothing big, you know, but between the breakfasts and the galas and whatnot, I guess I raised pretty close to a million dollars for the ticket."

Dorothy whistled softly.

"I guess you're pretty good at it."

"Well," Walter said, "think for a minute. Would you want to get on the wrong side of the guy who installs your plumbing?" He held up a hand. "Just kidding."

"So this was your reward? A trip to Washington? Oh, thank you, thank you," she said to the waitress as her food came. She took a huge bite out of the cheeseburger, washing it down with a gulp of the strawberry milk shake. "I know it's bad for me," she said apologetically, "but where I'm from, this is comfort food."

"Don't apologize," he said. "I don't care what they say, a healthy appetite never killed anybody. Anyway, I guess I'm here on political business. See, the party wanted to do something for me, so they made me an elector. You know, one of those—"

"Really? Me, too."

"You don't say. Six months ago, I never heard of it. Now I am one and I met one." Walter shook his head. "I'll be honest with you, though, Dorothy—may I call you Dorothy?—okay, then, I was a big fan of Foyle's, *big* fan. I'd met him a few times at fund-raisers, when he'd come in and help us draw a crowd. I liked what he said about—you know, too much government, too little citizenship? I don't mind telling you, when he was killed, I cried for the first time since I lost my wife, and that was 1981. But this Block fellow . . ." He shook his head. "But I guess we just have to hope for the best. Anyway, I think the boys down in Trenton got a bit nervous, wanted to make sure I was feeling all right about this, so they invited me down here. I'm going to be at the reception for Block after the vote. You going to that? Dorothy? You okay?"

She looked at Walter Ames, Jr., and it briefly struck him that the last time he'd seen a glint in the eye like that was at Pork Chop Hill, when a second lieutenant told his platoon to fan out.

"Do we, Walter?"

"Do we what?"

"Do we have to just 'hope for the best'?"

"I don't follow you."

Dorothy took a deep breath, then leaned forward again and began speaking in a voice so low Walter could barely hear her.

"What did they tell you about what you were supposed to do when you got to cast your vote?"

Walter thought a minute.

"Uhmmm, well, I'm supposed to go to Trenton—if I drive, they'll reimburse me thirty-five cents a mile, plus tolls—I go to the state capitol, the governor gives a speech, we have a lunch, then they give us ballots, and we put them in this box, they count them, give us back the ballots as souvenirs, and we go home. Then they mail us a certificate, and I guess if we go the inauguration, we get to sit in a special section."

Dorothy put her hand on his.

"Walter, that was when you were going to vote for Foyle for President. But he's *dead.* What did they tell you about now?"

"I . . . uh, I don't think they said *anything.* But I don't get your point. I'm a Republican. I'm a good Republican. If that's who I have to vote for . . ."

"Ah, but that's my point, Walter."

She suddenly jumped up from the booth and grasped his wrist, pulling the taller and heavier Walter Ames, Jr., with her.

"C'mon," she said, "we've got work to do."

"Where are we going?" Walter said, as he threw a bill down on the table.

"I'm not exactly sure," Dorothy said. "But the first thing we're going to do is to find out how many others of us are here." She led Walter out of the still-packed coffee shop, past a startled Charles Berlin, who had just entered the room.

"Dorothy! I finally got our keys!"

"Later, Charles," Dorothy yelled over her shoulder. She turned back to Walter Ames, Jr., and laughed for the first time in days.

"What's so funny?"

"That's our county chairman. When he made me an elector, he told me I'd have a little piece of history. I think it's starting to look a little bigger!"

TWENTY-FOUR

★ ★ ★

It is impossible to be counted as a sophisticated observer of American culture unless you enthusiastically embrace the idea that our mass media define reality. As Bishop Berkeley might ask today: If a tree falls in the forest and it did not make the six o'clock news, did it make a sound? Did it, in fact, fall at all?

So it may come as a surprise to realize that many of the shaping moments of American political history, even many that took place during the Era of Mass Media, began in obscurity, unattended by camera, microphone, or pen. Why? Because in the arena of politics, the mass media are best understood as a giant radar system, capable of tracking any object in its path, but blind to those small, critical events that take shape beneath its radar screen.

The first stirrings of the civil rights movement, the first cluster of voting rights workers huddled in church basements, the knot of suburban housewives and political science professors agonizing over the war in Vietnam, the small-town churchgoers furious at the assault on their culture, the women who first wondered why they could not fight fires or fly fighters, the longtime Democrats turning pale with rage and fear as they read their property-tax bills all took up their battles at first without benefit of press coverage. They fought their fights for many reasons: because they were angry, because they burned with a sense of justice, because they were bored, because they wanted to be part of something bigger than their own lives, because they found warmth and friendship in a cause, because they wanted to get laid.

But they did not do what they did because they wanted to be on television.

Now, as hundreds of press people jammed into the corridors of the Shoreham American, Dorothy Ledger was sitting in her hotel room, perched uncomfortably on her bed, working the phones, looking for the most elusive citizens in the land: the presidential electors. Unlike the employees of the multibillion-dollar media conglomerates who had been trying to track the same information, Dorothy had no WATS lines, no fax-modems, no high-speed data banks, no phalanx of workers scattered across the continent. What she had was her imitation-leather phone book, her purse stuffed with phone numbers scrawled on the backs of business cards, scribbled on cocktail napkins and credit card receipts, envelopes and laundry tickets. And in a nearby room, Walter Ames, Jr., was calling his children, his secretary, his friends back home, asking them to rummage through his den, his office, to root around in dusty drawers and shelves, looking for the numbers of friends, acquaintances, and passing strangers gathered over a lifetime.

"John, if you look up on the second or third shelf, I think, you'll see an appointment book . . . black, maybe brown . . . okay, tan, yeah. Now, see if there's a number for a Kellner or Kellman. . . . No? Damn, I could swear it was—wait, how about a Hellman, Martin Hellman? . . . Great, that's it. Okay, wait a minute . . . Yeah, I've got it. Now, what about Stewart . . . Last name . . . E-W, I think, but I'm not sure. . . . Nothing, huh? John, do you see a card file anywhere there? . . ."

After an hour and a half of this, Dorothy Ledger's wrist hurt, her back was aching from sitting unsupported on the side of the bed (where did hotel architects think people were supposed to sit when making their calls?), and she had run into half a dozen brick walls. But she'd also managed to make contact with four people who actually knew people who'd been chosen as Republican electors. Three of them had hung up on her as soon as she began to ask them about their intentions.

("Of *course* I'm going to vote for Block," one of them had snapped at her. "Do you think I want to go to jail?")

Another had asked her whether she was working for a TV network, and volunteered to continue the conversation as soon as she was wired five hundred dollars.

But the fifth person she called, a retired state assemblyman from Indiana named Andrew Hays, listened attentively.

"I'm not making you any promises, understand," Hays said. "But when Foyle chose that moron, I swallowed hard, told myself I was a good, loyal Republican, and figured, 'Okay, they'll send Block off to count the trees in the Sequoia National Forest.' But Teddy Block with his finger on the button? Hell, I wouldn't trust him with sharp scissors. I can't wait to see who he picks to run with. Look, I don't know what I'm going to do, or even if I have the right to do anything, but keep me posted."

Better than nothing, Dorothy figured as she gathered her things and headed down to the bar. Across the lobby, in the Grand Ballroom, the members of the National Committee were gathering to formally nominate Theodore Block as their presidential candidate, and to enthusiastically embrace whomever they were told to embrace as Block's Vice President. And a nervous Charles Berlin had already knocked on Dorothy's door, reminding her not to be late for the nominating session.

"I'll be there, Charles, I promise. I just have to take a care of a few phone calls . . . you know, the bank."

"Okay, okay. I'm slipping your credential under the door. Just make sure you're there when they call the roll."

An old gospel song, isn't it? "When the Roll Is Called Up Yonder, I'll Be There." Don't you worry, Charles. I'll be there.

"All right," she said ten minutes later, as she hurriedly sat down next to Walter Ames, Jr., at a table in a dark corner of the hotel bar. The room was rapidly emptying as the National Committee members, alternates, political operatives, and members of the press streamed toward the Grand Ballroom. "I've got one who says he's willing—Walter, who's this?"

She pointed to a short, blond thirty-something woman with bright brown eyes.

"This is Faith McCoy," Walter said. "Ran into her in the lobby about a half hour ago. To tell you the truth," he said with a blush, "I thought she might be a . . . professional woman."

"I am, I am," Faith laughed. "Assistant professor of history at Rice University."

"I apologize," Walter said gallantly.

"Don't bother, Walter," Faith said. "Compared to the way they treat a conservative Republican on your average university campus, it'd be a lot better for me if I were dispensing head instead of stuffing them."

"Did you . . . um . . ." Dorothy stopped.

"It's okay, Dorothy. The only reason Walter let me in on your cabal is that I started running off at the mouth about how Teddy Block stood for everything I despised about the Republican Party. I'll take an honest left-wing Democrat any day over those blue-blood bastards like Block."

"Are you an elector?" Dorothy said.

"No," Faith said, "I'm here with three graduate students doing a content analysis of the rhetoric at the committee meeting. Complete bullshit, but it's what they want on the tenure-track publications. However," she added, pulling a yellow legal pad out of her purse, "I remembered this guy in Odessa—Texas, not Russia. Oliver Giddens. Shows up at every state convention I've ever been to, usually demanding the repeal of the Fourteenth Amendment. I know, I know, you don't have to roll your eyes. The truth is, they put him on the slate of electors to shut him up, so the convention could adjourn—turns out Giddens is one of those *Robert's Rules of Order* freaks. In fact, one of the chairmen went ballistic when she saw Giddens's name; figured he might wind up voting for Cardinal Richelieu, or maybe himself. But that's the point: he can't be bought, he can't be threatened, and he's damn well not going to vote for Block to be loyal to the party. I suggest you take your allies where you find them—like any good revolutionary."

"Anything else?" Dorothy asked.

"Yeah," Faith said, motioning to a gawky young man seated on a barstool to join them at their table. "I want you to meet Ben Weinstock. He's a dropout from CalTech, who handles a laptop like Heifetz with a fiddle. Met him at a conference two years ago, and we've kept in touch ever since. Pull up a chair, Ben, and tell us what you've got."

Weinstock settled uneasily into his seat. He had the volcanic face of a sixteen-year-old, and a death pallor proving that he had not set foot out of doors in the California sunshine for months.

"Hi, Faith, hi . . . uh . . . hi. Okay, well, I chatted up this friend of mine who's a real politics freak. He's on-line with maybe a dozen boards a night . . . bulletin boards . . . you know, computer bulletin boards. . . .

Anyway . . ." Weinstock pulled out a sheet of paper and handed it to Dorothy.

"Turns out they've been chatting away on the boards about all this since about five minutes after Foyle kicked—after he died. There are . . . let me see . . . eleven names on this list who say they're electors, and who've been asking everyone on-line whether they have the legal right to vote for somebody besides Block."

There was a moment of absolute silence around the table.

"Good heavens," said Faith. "You see what you've got here, don't you, dear?" she said to Dorothy.

"I'm not sure," she said.

"Well," Faith reflected, "here you are, all by yourself, trying to stop what certainly looks like an oncoming locomotive. Now it turns out that, completely unknown to you, there's this . . . movement that's been trying to take shape out there in cyberspace. Out there is this . . . this movement brewing. All they're looking for is someone to show them what to do."

"I haven't the vaguest idea what to do," Dorothy said.

Walter Ames, Jr., nodded.

"I think we can solve that dilemma. Ben, you have a laptop with you?"

"Are you kidding?" Faith asked.

"Sure," Weinstock said.

"Fully loaded, modem and everything?" Ames asked.

Weinstock looked like Ames had asked him whether he'd remembered to bring along his liver.

"Fine. Fire it up. Call up your political friend on the double. Tell him to find every political freak he knows. We've got some research to do for Ms. Ledger here, and we've got"—he checked his watch—"about a half hour to do it."

Weinstock smiled.

"No problem," he said.

"May I ask what's going on here?" Dorothy said.

"Simple, Ms. Ledger," said Faith. "If Ted Block doesn't give us a damn good reason to stand with him, you're going to try to bring this locomotive to a stop. And you're going to need one hell of a monkey wrench."

TWENTY-FIVE

★ ★ ★

As soon as the live feed of Theodore Block's vice-presidential announcement popped up on a monitor in the network's Washington bureau, Al DeRossa knew that something had gone terribly wrong with the selection of a Vice President. Only the All News Network and C-SPAN were airing the feed in the minutes before the formal announcement, but the faces of the operatives spoke volumes. Marsh, Alan Veigle, Sharon Kramer had filed into the Wayne Hays Room of the Shoreham looking grim, angrily turning away all questioners.

Even more telling, there had been no official leaks, no conference calls to the networks and the bigfoot columnists and commentators, alerting them to the vice-presidential selection, and offering the reason why the selection was a thoughtful, sensible, politically astute pick. In the past, no vice-presidential choice had gone uncelebrated. DeRossa well remembered that in 1988, Bush campaign chief James Baker called the choice of Dan Quale "a bold leap across the generations." Only the next day, when the assault began, did Mr. Baker remember to inform the press that he had not even been in the room when the selection had been made. The silence now suggested that something very strange was about to occur.

From his perch on a metal box in the back of the Hays Room, the Distinguished Commentator was fuming.

"I cannot be*lieve* the complete and total in*com*petence of these idiots! I have to go on national television *live* and I haven't the foggiest *idea* of who they've picked. I may be about to make a *fool* of myself!"

"Talk about dog bites man," muttered a desk assistant.

"I wonder if he knows that about a hundred thousand folks who own satellite dishes can hear every word he's saying," replied a production assistant.

"Do you love the way his face turns purple?" said the desk assistant. "I thought that was only a figure of speech, but look, it's really turning purple."

"He goes on the air like that and half a million people are gonna be hitting the tint button on their remotes."

DeRossa leaned forward from his chair along the back wall of the control room and tapped the technical director on the shoulder.

"Gary, punch up Ed's IFB," he said. "I need to talk to him." The TD flicked a small switch on his console labeled "Anchor."

"It's DeRossa," Al said. "I think you might want to open with a hint that there's a surprise coming."

Ed Steele glanced up from his notes, staring blankly into the camera, listening to DeRossa through his molded earpiece.

"What do you know, Al?" said the anchor.

"That's just it, Ed. There are no calls, no tips, no 'guidance.' I've gotta believe we're getting a major-league curveball here."

"Well," the anchor said coolly, "I'm not entirely persuaded that your lack of information is an infallible political signal, but it's worth knowing. Thanks, I suppose." He lowered his eyes to his note cards.

"I dunno," said Ken Crenshaw. "Every time I turn around, some media consultant asshole with an Armani suit and a computer printout is talking about 'warmth,' all the focus groups say they want 'warmth,' you can't make it on camera without 'warmth'; the audience wants a daddy, an uncle, a big brother, a dutiful son, a peppy daughter . . . 'warmth, warmth, warmth.' So you tell me how we wind up with the coldest sonofabitch in the history of broadcasting and he's number one across the board?"

"Maybe we underestimate the audience," DeRossa replied. "Maybe they don't care if he won't help their grandma across the street if he knows what he's talking about."

"A comforting thought," Crenshaw said. "Hey—we got the hard 'two.' "

In front of the main pool camera, a disembodied hand was wagging a

V sign back and forth, the universal two-fingered symbol that the main event would begin in two minutes. The three broadcast networks were breaking into the midday programming, each signing on with a Voice of God announcer. ("*This*—is a *special* report—the vice-presidential *decision*. Here, reporting *live* from the Capitol . . .") The cameras played on the rear entrance to the hall, trying to give viewers a glimpse of the man Theodore Block had chosen.

"As soon as the door opens," the Distinguished Commentator was saying, "we'll know who Governor Block has chosen as the man to fill his shoes, as he takes on the awesome responsibility that has fallen on his shoul—wait, now the door is opening, and here comes Governor Block and—who the *hell* is that?"

Block strode onto the platform, tall, lean, elegant, followed by a middle-aged man at least a foot shorter, a man so smooth, so pink, so natty that he at first appeared to have been removed bodily from a window display at J. Press. Every strand of his yellow-blond hair was perfectly in place. Not a wrinkle furrowed his brow or chin. His tiny body was clothed in a blue, double-breasted blazer with a crest on the breast pocket and a paisley handkerchief jutting out, gray worsted flannel slacks, a red-and-blue rep tie, and tasseled loafers. His dimpled cheeks framed a set of incandescently white teeth. As he strode to the platform behind Block, one hand in his trouser pocket, he gave a jaunty wave with the other.

"This is not possible," DeRossa muttered. "Open me up to the team," he said, then leaned into the control room mike.

"It's Phelps—Sherwood Phelps."

"I don't have any notes on this guy," Ed Steele whisered back sibilantly. "Not a line."

"Fourth-term congressman from upstate New York," DeRossa hissed back, his *Almanac of American Politics* in his hand. As he began to speak, Steele was already on the air, spinning out perfectly modulated sentences as DeRossa poured more information into his ear.

"In what will surely be regarded as a surprise—even a shock—Governor Ted Block has chosen an obscure fourth-term member of the House from upstate New York, Sherwood Phelps, as his running mate. He is regarded as a moderate-to-liberal Republican, and chairs the . . . uh . . . Congressional Collectibles Caucus. Let's listen."

"My fellow Americans," Block began.

"In the days since the tragic death of President-elect Foyle . . ."

"Okay, okay, good start," Marsh whispered to Alan Veigle, "at least he didn't call it a 'fortuitous circumstance.' "

". . . I have had to face my first critical decision: the choice of a Vice President. But to make that choice, I first had to make a different choice: whether to listen to a dedicated, able, hardworking team of advisers, or to make this choice the way our greatest Presidents of the past have made their choices: by listening to my own head and heart."

"Ah, the sounds of silence," Crenshaw whispered to DeRossa.

"I have looked over the likeliest of possibilities; and I can tell the American people with pride that the Republican Party has a remarkable range of talent and wisdom to offer this country. I intend to rely greatly on their guidance in the coming days. But in the end, I made a determination to select someone who could fulfill a critical obligation of a Vice President: someone with whom I felt comfortable."

"Geez, why not pick a cocker spaniel while you're at it," said a videotape editor.

"The man I have selected is more than a distinguished member of the House of Representatives. While he may not be the most visible, or the loudest, he is one of the most thoughtful, reliable, loyal political leaders we have."

"Geez, he *did* pick a cocker spaniel," said the videotape editor.

"I'll bet Bush inducted Phelps into Skull and Bones," said the voice of National Public Radio.

"He has had experience in the business world . . ."

"Dad left him financial control of Niagara Glass," Marsh told Sharon Kramer.

". . . but he devoted most of his energies into the philanthropic works, for which he is perhaps best known."

Kathy Lester, the best researcher in the Washington bureau of the network, was kneeling at DeRossa's feet with a sheaf of paper that had spewed out of the Lexis/Nexis printer.

"Executive vice president of the Phelps Foundation," she summarized rapidly. "About one hundred fifty million in assets, big on civic improvements: fountains, gardens, that sort of thing."

"This guy's gonna be gangbusters in the Kmart parking lots," said DeRossa.

"Just as important to me," Block concluded, with a broad smile, "is that throughout his life, Sherwood Phelps has come to embody a quality we need a lot more of among our leaders—a sense of *excellence.* His family: excellent. His education: excellent. His record: excellent. Everything about him says to us that Sherwood Phelps is a man who was born to lead: and believe me, as one who's seen him handle an eighty-five-foot cabin cruiser in those choppy waters off Providence, I'm delighted to welcome the man I know as 'Skipper' as first mate on our ship of state. Welcome aboard, Skipper."

Sherwood Phelps bounded up to the podium, and greeted Block by playfully cuffing him on the shoulder.

"Permission to come aboard, Captain," Phelps quipped, with a voice that suggested he had secreted two good-sized plums in his cheeks.

Standing in back of the duo, grouped with the Republican congressional leadership, House minority leader Connor Doyle forced his smile in place.

I was in college when Richard Nixon won the "bubba" vote, he thought. *I was a state senator when Reagan took the blue-collar vote. I watched the sons and daughters of plumbers, cops, longshoremen, sales clerks move into the Republican Party. Can these two twits really undo it all in an hour?*

Dorothy Ledger was thinking very different thoughts as she sat in the Marion Barry Cocktail Lounge at the Shoreham American, next to Walter Ames, Jr., Faith McCoy, and Ben Weinstock.

"What do you think?" Walter asked her.

In the back of her mind she saw a regiment of smug, beefy men who had picked her brains, signed their names to her work, put their names on the embossed executive stationery at the First Colonial Bank and Trust of Grand Rapids, dined at the country club while she threw packaged dinners into the microwave and looked through *TV Guide* each week, marking the late movie listings.

She reached for the printouts piling up next to Weinstock's laptop.

"What the hell," she said.

TWENTY-SIX

★ ★ ★

Dorothy Ledger entered the Grand Ballroom at the worst possible moment: the moment of silence in memory of MacArthur Foyle. Throughout the hall, the only noises that could be heard were the shuffling of feet, the occasional muffled sob, and the sibilant hissings of the Distinguished Commentator:

("Almost *total* silence engulfs the room . . . there's not a sound to be heard . . . not even a whisper to mar this farewell to the fallen leader of the land. . . . You can actually sense the stillness. . . .")

She hadn't expected the ballroom to be so packed; with only 108 voting members of the committee, she assumed it would be a more or less intimate gathering. But in an effort to lend the event presidential weight, the committee had packed the floor with staff, interns, volunteers, and press. It took her fifteen minutes to navigate the short distance from the ballroom entrance to the Michigan standard on the floor.

"God, you had me scared," Charles Berlin whispered to her. "I thought you'd decided to go home."

"You may wish I had," Dorothy whispered back. Charles looked at her sharply.

"What are you—hold it, I want to hear Doyle."

The House minority leader was at the podium, invoking God's help and the will, strength, and purpose of the American people, to lead us out of this time of tears.

"Today," Doyle said, "there is no battle of party, no clash of ideology.

Today, we are one people. One band of mourners. In that spirit, I am pleased to welcome the Speaker of the House of Representatives to say a few words."

That was the deal Speaker Topper Huggins had struck with Doyle, with the advice and counsel of Jack Petitcon. No seconding speech for Block, no formal endorsement by the highest-ranking Democrat in the land of a new Republican administration—not the way Ted Block had performed so far. But a symbolic appearance? A few grace notes? Sure. And, thanks to a Yale graduate fellow spending a year in the Speaker's office—courtesy of his father, a major campaign contributor—the Speaker had even come armed with Whitman's famous elegy on the death of Abraham Lincoln, "When Lilacs Last in the Dooryard Bloomed." It would have been a moving reference, had not the Speaker chosen to quote Whitman's line about how "the great star early drooped in the western sky," which conjured up unfortunate images of Mack Foyle flying off the back of a horse.

Dorothy Ledger ignored the ritual mourning; she was shuffling through the papers Ben Weinstock had handed her minutes ago—printouts of scholarly writings and old newspaper articles downloaded by Weinstock onto his laptop and printed out in the hotel's business center. She also had a copy of the rules of the Republican National Committee. Now she was waiting for Connor Doyle to utter the magic words. Here they were:

"I will now entertain a motion to declare a vacancy on the Republican Party's ticket for President of the United States, and to direct the Republican electors to cast their presidential ballots for Theodore Pinckney Block, and their vice-presidential ballots for Sherwood Phillip Phelps," Doyle said.

As Senator Ellen Barrett of Kansas strode to the podium to make the formal motion, Dorothy jumped to her feet and grabbed the floor mike with her left hand.

"Point of order, Mr. Chairman!" she said.

There was no reaction at all, except for the turning of heads in her immediate area. The microphones, placed by each state standard to emulate the look of a real convention, had not been turned on—graphic testimony to the fact that no delegate to a national convention had made a motion from the floor since 1976. Dorothy found a small switch on the microphone's head and flicked it on.

"*Point of order,* Mr. Chairman!" she bellowed.

"*Dorothy!* What the *hell* are you doing," Charles yelled, trying to grab her and pull her to her seat, as his words rang out in the hall through the now-open mike. As a hundred cameras swept the hall, trying to find the speaker, as a thousand heads now snapped around, Charles quickly retreated to his seat.

Connor Doyle was no fool, and did not panic easily. He could, of course, have simply ordered all the floor mikes turned off, ordered the intruder escorted out of the hall, and gone on with the performance. But his political instincts told him that if there was an unexpected break in the script, he had no choice but to play along with the improvisation. The sight of armed guards hustling someone out of the Grand Ballroom was the last thing he, or Ted Block, or the Republican Party, or the country needed.

So he stood at the podium and looked out with an indulgent smile on his face.

"On a point of order, the chair recognizes the . . . the gentlewoman from . . . is it Michigan?"

"Yes, Mr. Chairman, my name is Dorothy Ledger."

"The gentlewoman from Michigan will state her point of order."

"Mr. Chairman, as temporary"—she shuffled her papers against the microphone, and a ripple of nervous laughter flew around the room.

At the Anchor desk, Ed Steele reached for a phone and punched the direct line to DeRossa.

"What *is* this?" he snapped.

"Haven't a clue," DeRossa said.

"As temporary national woman . . . I mean, as temporary National *Committee*woman, and as a Republican elector from Michigan, may I ask on what authority this committee instructs the electors to vote for Sherwood Phelps for Vice President?"

Connor Doyle blinked for a moment, then leaned forward at the podium with a reassuring palm held high.

"Ms. . . . Ledger? Yes. Ms. Ledger, there is obviously, tragically, a vacancy on the Republican ticket for the presidency. Under the National Committee's rules, we are authorized to fill that vacancy. Should Governor Block be selected to fill that vacancy, as I expect, that will create a vacancy for the office of Vice President. Is that clear?"

He turned to welcome Senator Barrett to the podium.

"Mr. Chairman! Point of order!"

Now a rumble began to build from the floor. A cry of "Throw her out!" was clearly heard in the hall. Dorothy flipped the pages of her notes.

"Mr. Chairman, with all due respect, you are missing the point. As an elector, I am pledged to vote for MacArthur Foyle for President, and Theodore Block for Vice President. I am simply asking how this National Committee can argue that it has the power to force me to cast a vote for Vice President for someone I never heard of in my life."

Dot's last words were almost drowned out by a din of boos and shouts.

Connor Doyle pounded the podium with his gavel.

"Fellow delegates, this has been a painful time for all of us. But let us remember why we are here; we are here to reaffirm our faith in the rule of law, in our great system of free government. Let us not permit the sorrow of this occasion to divert us from this path. The gentlewoman from Michigan will be heard."

And then I'll run that bitch out of here so fast it'll make her hair hurt.

"Thank you, Mr. Chairman." Dorothy took a breath, then resumed.

"In the first place, it is far from clear whether anyone has the power to bind presidential electors *at all*—even when they simply refused to vote for the candidate under whose name they ran. The Congress had a big fight about this in 1969, after a Nixon elector from North Carolina voted for George Wallace. They wound up counting that vote."

She stopped and looked up politely at Connor Doyle, who was urgently conferring with the House minority parliamentarian.

"Perhaps, Ms. Ledger, you are unaware that in that case, North Carolina had no statute binding their electors. Since that time, a majority of states require their electors to vote for the candidates they represent."

Gotcha! Dorothy exulted silently.

"Mr. Chairman, with all due respect, the overwhelming weight of scholarly opinion seems to be that statutes binding electors, or pledges that they may give, are unenforceable. I'll send these papers up to you now, if you'd like." The still photo of Dorothy clutching a sheaf of papers in her hand made the front page of seventy-five major daily newspapers the next day.

"And anyway, that says nothing about those electors in states that have no such laws on the books."

"Shut up and sit down!" a voice boomed from the balcony.

"Throw her out!" cried the National Committeeman from New Jersey.

"Let her speak! Let her speak!" thundered Walter Ames, Jr., as he wrenched the microphone away from the New Jersey National Committeeman.

"Let her speak!" yelled Faith McCoy from the rear of the hall.

"We will be in *order!"* Connor Doyle said, and slammed the gavel down again. He smiled in Dorothy's direction, causing several of the delegates near her to turn white.

"Ms. Ledger?" Connor said.

"Just one more point, Mr. Chairman," Dorothy said, squaring her shoulders.

"Putting aside whether we can be bound at all, I will simply point to the facts today: since the presidential candidate I pledged to vote for is *dead*—since in fact such a vote for a deceased person would likely be rejected by the Congress when it meets to count the votes in January, it seems to me perfectly clear that this National Committee cannot place the electors under *any* obligation *at all,* except, perhaps, to vote for Governor Block for *Vice* President, since that's what we promised to do.

"If this . . . horrible tragedy had happened a month ago, *before* the election, yes, fine, the National Committee would have declared a vacancy, it could have put Governor Block at the top of the ticket, if that had been its decision," she added pointedly, "and we electors would have had the choice of committing ourselves to the ticket, or resigning. *But that is not what happened here.* As far as we're concerned, *there is no vacancy.* The election is over. *We've been elected.* And I suggest to you that the death of MacArthur Foyle has put us in the position that the Constitution originally conceived: to exercise our judgment about how to carry out the people's will. Maybe a vote for Governor Block is the right thing to do. I suspect most of the electors will likely make that choice. All I am asking is this: On what constitutional or legal authority does the National Committee deny me the right to exercise my authority under Articles Two and Amendment Twelve of the United States Constitution?"

And Dorothy Ledger sat down.

Within a few seconds, the scene inside the Grand Ballroom of the Shoreham American Hotel took on the exact look of a courtroom drama just after the mystery witness fingers the real killer as he testifies on the stand. Delegates and alternates sprang to their feet, yelling imprecations at Dorothy Ledger. In the press section, reporters, acting on decades of instinct, picked up their phones to yell the news to their editors, who had been watching the TV coverage, but who urgently questioned their men and women on the scene, as though they could possibly have learned anything useful in the four seconds since Dorothy Ledger had stopped speaking.

In the network's Washington control room, Ken Crenshaw leapt out of his chair.

"Get me every constitutional lawyer in your Rolodex!" he screamed at the bookers. "Call Carey Limousine! Have every car they've got booked on emergency standby! If anyone with a history or law degree answers the phone, get 'em the hell over here! And who the hell is that Ledger woman! Call the Detroit affiliate!"

The TV networks cut live to their reporters inside the ballroom, who reported that "pandemonium has broken out here," "a bombshell has just exploded inside the Republican National Committee," "this incredible, unbelievable post-election season just got a lot more incredible." Up on the stage, Connor Doyle was pounding his gavel for order, while conferring with party officials.

And in his office, Jack Petitcon and the reverend watched, and nodded, and smiled.

And in another office, three and a half miles southeast of Jack Petitcon, so did the Reverend W. Dixon Mason.

TWENTY-SEVEN

★ ★ ★

In the fifty-one minutes after Connor Doyle returned to the podium, the following events occurred in rapid succession:

- A pack of reporters tried to rush down the aisle toward the Michigan standard where Dorothy Ledger was seated; they were repulsed by a phalanx of private security guards wielding billy clubs, one of whom exclaimed that he hadn't had this much fun since '68, when he'd "slammed Dan Rather one good lick upside the head."
- Charles Berlin told Dorothy Ledger she had ruined her career, ruined his life, and inflicted the most grievous injury to the Republican Party since Watergate. He then marched out of the ballroom, out of the hotel, and into the Golden Shamrock Saloon, where he ingested five scotch and sodas and fell asleep on a barstool.
- Connor Doyle announced that, after conferring with the party parliamentarian, he had determined that in fact a vacancy existed on the Republican ticket, and immediately asked for a voice vote on his ruling. A chorus of ayes filled the hall. A few scattered voices shouted "No!" Dorothy Ledger among them.
- Doyle then asked for nominations to fill the vacant presidential slot. Mrs. Ted Gunderson of California nominated Theodore Block. The nomination was seconded, and nominations were then closed. Mr. James Jackson Johnson of Missouri moved that Theodore Block be nominated by acclamation; a motion he had been strongly urged to make by a top

aide to Connor Doyle, thus precluding a roll-call vote. Block's nomination as the Republican nominee for President of the United States was thus approved.

• Connor Doyle then announced that, with the elevation of Block, a vacancy existed on the ticket for the nomination of Vice President. Mr. Anthony Lamotta of New Jersey nominated Sherwood Phelps. The nomination was seconded by a relatively thin chorus of voices, and it did not escape the attention of the press that when the chorus died down, a voice from the rear of the hall could be heard distinctly, shouting, "Who the hell is Sherwood Phelps?"—a phrase that, within twelve hours, was seen on lapel buttons all across the country. Phelps, too, was nominated by acclamation.

• Sherwood Phelps gave an acceptance speech that lasted one minute and eighteen seconds. In it, he declared that this was a time not for celebration, but for remembrance and reflection. He asked his fellow Republicans, and the nation, to say a prayer for MacArthur Foyle. The speech had been given to him three minutes before his appearance on the stage by Sharon Kramer, who told Phelps in a single sentence composed of simple one- and two-syllable words that he was to give the speech *exactly* as written if he wanted to have any semblance of staff waiting for him when he got off the stage.

• Theodore Block gave an acceptance speech that lasted two minutes and five seconds. In it, he spoke of a wounded nation, spoke of the strength and resiliency of a nation that, even in this dark moment, retained its tradition of debate and devotion to the rule of law, and pledged that he would answer the doubts of some Americans by working to be the President of all Americans. The speech had been given to him five minutes before his appearance by Sharon Kramer, who said to him that the future of the two-hundred-year-old American political experiment depended upon his delivering these words, in this order, without so much as an extemporaneous clearing of the throat.

• The committee meeting ended with the singing of "God Bless America" as the hall darkened and red, white, and blue lights swept the ballroom's ceiling. Dorothy Ledger slipped out of the hall and jumped into a taxicab. Six minutes later, she hurried through the lobby of the

Monroe Arms Hotel, took an elevator to the fifth floor, and joined Walter Ames, Jr., and Company.

• Block, Phelps, Doyle, Marsh, Alan Veigle, and Sharon Kramer, surrounded by Secret Service and hotel security, exited the Grand Ballroom and took a service elevator to the fifty-third floor, where they retreated to the living room of the presidential suite and, joined by a cluster of campaign operatives, grouped themselves in couches and chairs around a huge glass coffee table.

"I thought that went rather well," said Sherwood Phelps.

"I respectfully disagree, Mr. Vice President," said Connor Doyle. "In fact, I think we have a problem."

"No," Alan Veigle said, shaking his head. "Custer had a problem. The *Titanic* had a problem. We have something else. Call it, oh, I don't know . . . a disaster, maybe?"

A thin young man cleared his throat.

"According to a flash poll we just completed, sixty-four percent expressed 'serious reservations' about Theodore Block's qualifications to be President."

"How many people could you call in an hour?" Sharon Kramer asked.

"Twenty-two," the pollster said. "But it was a very tight screen."

Marsh picked up the remote-control clicker and began surfing the channels, stopping for a few seconds at each one to listen to scraps of conversation.

". . . normally unthinkable, but not impossible, Roger, when you consider that legally . . ."

". . . hard to believe, Bob, but we're in mostly uncharted legal waters, so . . ."

". . . voted for somebody they weren't supposed to, Sally, but it's never *mattered* before . . ."

". . . think about all the gaffes, the stumbles, the perceptions, well, Mai Lee, you begin to wonder . . ."

Marsh hit the mute button, and gestured dramatically toward the television set.

"*That's* what we're fighting. Every hour that goes by that we don't squash this talk like a bug is one more hour when some genius from Armpit, Oklahoma, decides that he's really James Madison in a hundred-thirty-five-dollar suit. Can you imagine where that might lead?"

"We don't have to imagine," said Connor Doyle. He looked around the room impatiently.

"Where's Oates? *Oates!*"

From the far corner of the living room, a slight man with wispy hair and a prominent mustache waved uncertainly. Harold Oates, at fifty-nine, had been the Republican parliamentarian for twenty-nine years. He had stood by Republican congressional leaders, guiding them through the thicket of the House rules, devising strategies to tie the Democrats in knots with non-debatable motions to adjourn, privileged resolutions, and rules that could open and close at the whim of a floor leader. During those increasingly rare moments at nominating conventions where a platform or a rules fight erupted, Harold Oates could be seen in the rear of the rostrum, back to the camera, counseling the usually befuddled man with the gavel.

"Harold, let's get clear on where we are. What do we need to nail down the presidency?"

"You need a majority of electors, Mr. Leader," Harold said.

"Is that an absolute majority?" Doyle asked.

"Absolutely—sorry, this is no time for humor. Yes, Mr. Leader. You need two hundred seventy votes for Block to make him the President-elect."

"So, let's say a bunch of our electors decide to vote for Foyle, as a gesture of affection, as a fitting tribute to the fallen leader. What happens?"

Harold smiled and nodded enthusiastically.

"A fascinating point, Mr. Leader. They had a *big* fight about this in 1872, when Horace Greeley—he was the Democratic candidate for President—died. You see, whether a dead man is a 'person' under the Constitution"—he felt Doyle's gaze—"perhaps I'll move on. Whether the Congress counts those votes or not doesn't really matter, because you *still* need those two hundred seventy votes for a majority. Same thing if they vote for you or me or anybody else. Without two hundred seventy votes, no electoral majority."

"And then?"

Harold chuckled.

"Then the House of Representatives gets to pick the President, and the Senate picks the Vice President."

"Christ!" Alan Veigle said. "The Democrats control the House! *They* get the White House after all this?"

"No, no, no, no," said Harold Oates. "It doesn't work that way. Each *state* gets one vote. A majority of states is what you need to win once it goes into the House."

"Each *state?*" said Alan Veigle. "You mean, Alaska has one vote and California has one vote? A state with fourteen hundred Eskimos and a million seals has the same vote as thirty-four million Californians? That's nuts."

"No," said Harold. "That was the deal—that was how the big states got the small states to sign the Constitution; like the Senate."

"So who comes out ahead if we count that way?" asked Connor Doyle.

"Let me think about this for a second," said Harold. He stared up at the ceiling, eyes open.

"What's he doing?" Marsh whispered to Sharon Kramer.

"I think he's counting the Congress in his head, one by one, and then figuring out how the state delegations add up. Hey," she added, "it's a living."

"As far as I can tell," Harold said, "we've got fifteen states, the Democrats have nineteen, and the rest split evenly."

"So they win!" Alan Veigle said. "What a crock!"

"No, no, no, no, no, no," Harold said. "It takes an absolute majority—just like with the electors. If a state's vote is tied, it doesn't count—but somebody still needs twenty-six votes to win."

"And if nobody wins?"

"Well, they just stay in session, and they keep voting until somebody gets a majority. Jefferson and Aaron Burr in 1800, it took eleven weeks. Took almost that long with Quincy Adams and Jackson in 1824." Harold Oates's eyes all but danced with delight.

"Meanwhile," he went on, "with the Vice President, it's one senator, one vote. So with our majority there, we could elect Phelps with one ballot. Of course," he said with a frown, "if the House deadlocks, that could mean we have a Vice President come Inauguration Day, but no President, in which case I suppose Sherwood Phelps would become acting . . ." His voice trailed off, as every head in the room turned toward the dapper man with the double-breasted blazer, curled up in a large armchair, fast asleep.

Connor Doyle got to his feet.

"Look, people. Let's get a grip on ourselves. We're not going to take this ride to hell, because we're not going to let this happen. Not any of it."

"First thing," said Marsh, "first thing, we need to call every state party official we can find. In fact," he added, snapping his fingers at a twenty-something interfraternity president poster boy, "get back down to the hall and round up every state chairman and chairwoman you can find. Put 'em in the holding pen next door; tell'em the ticket wants to thank 'em for their support. And while they're waiting, tell 'em to get on the phone back home, round up their electors, and have 'em show up for press conferences tomorrow—tonight, if they can do it—backing this ticket. We need to kill this with a stick. By this time tomorrow," Marsh said grimly, "this whole thing will seem like a bad dream."

Then he glanced toward the master bedroom, where Theodore Block, Republican nominee for President of the United States, was happily working a double-crostic puzzle.

"Well, most of it anyway."

TWENTY-EIGHT

★ ★ ★

Nine and a half minutes after Dorothy Ledger finished making her point of order, Al DeRossa was in Studio A of the network's Washington bureau, sitting in a narrow semicircle that included Professor Richard Muttle of Georgetown University Law School, and Professor Leonard Griese of American University's Department of Political Science. Both men had been all but dragged from their offices by teams of young men and women dispatched by Ken Crenshaw, hurled into waiting cars with such speed and force that it might have qualified as a criminal abduction, sped through the streets of Washington to the network's studios, then propelled into their chairs as sound technicians and makeup artists worked to make them audible and photogenic.

That last presented two different challenges. Muttle was a tall, tanned, immaculately coiffed man in his mid-thirties, who looked more like a headwaiter at a trendy Malibu restaurant than an academic. Griese was a walking cliché: a sixty-something, doughy man with dusty gray hair in disarray, a tie ending two inches above an entirely too substantial belly, horn-rimmed glasses perched unevenly on a bulbous nose. Muttle sat with his right foot balanced on his left thigh, helping the sound man thread the microphone through his tie loop. Griese had twice yanked the mike off his frayed jacket as he reached for his notes, his pencil, and a glass of water.

From the control room, Ken Crenshaw was fast approaching full orbital stage, breathing so hard and sweating so profusely that one of his secretaries had slammed a blood-pressure cuff onto his right arm, and was monitoring his condition with increasing anxiety.

"DeRossa!" Crenshaw bellowed into the IFB. "You guys are on in one minute! One minute! I want them to explain *exactly* what's going on! I want it clear! I want it *right*—and I want it short!"

DeRossa nodded, then turned to the task of setting his guests at ease.

"Here's what we'll be doing," he said. "The convention—"

"Actually, it's not a convention; it's a National Committee meeting," Muttle interjected helpfully.

"Right. Thanks." *Oh, brother.* "The—committee will be in recess for about ten minutes while they try to sort out this point of order. Right now, our floor reporters have been interviewing the delegates, the office-holders, whoever we can find. We've just gone to commercial—"

"Very nice, very nice," mumbled Professor Griese. "The fabric of the Constitution is shredding by the hour, and you're selling flatulence cures."

"Trust me, Professor, I'd rather be selling de Tocqueville on CD-ROM. Anyway, they'll come to us, and I'll ask you some questions about what the law says these electors can and can't do."

"Laws," Griese corrected. "Laws. There is no 'law.' That's the point."

"You understand," DeRossa said quickly, "that we don't have a lot of time to get into the complexities of the electoral college."

"No problem," said Muttle. "I do *Wake-Up Call* on Channel Eight once a week; I'm on retainer to Fox for celebrity bust commentary; I take time cues."

"Yes, but you see," Griese said, "it doesn't work—"

"Coming to us in ten," yelled the floor manager.

"Just relax, forget the lights and the cameras, it's just a conversation," DeRossa said. *And if you screw up, you'll make a fool of yourself in front of ten million people—no big deal.*

"As you can see," Ed Steele was telling his audience, "what was to have been the formal conclusion to these days of national trauma with the designation of Governor Theodore Block as the all-but-official President-elect has instead become a scene of unprecedented confusion, as an elector from Michigan, Dorothy Ledger, has challenged the party's power over the presidential electors. Political director Al DeRossa is in our Washington studios to try to sort this out. Al, I think most Americans think the electoral college is one of those schools they see in a bowl game on New Year's Day."

"Yes, Ed." (God help you if you ever said "No, Ed," or "You're wrong, Ed" or "What a lame joke, Ed.") "Once upon a time these electors were among the most prominent men in their states, chosen because of their stature or reputation. Now, they're more often picked because of the envelopes they've licked, or the money they've raised, or the years they've spent in the state legislature or the Congress. As long as you're a citizen, and as long as you don't hold federal office, you can be an elector.

"But what's really at issue here, gentlemen, is whether Dorothy Ledger is right—can she ignore the Republican National Committee and vote for whomever she wants to?"

Muttle had begun to speak the instant DeRossa finished his question; there wasn't a chance he wouldn't be first to answer.

"Well, Al," he began smoothly, "we've had a number of cases in our history where electors did not vote for the candidate they said they would—the so-called faithless electors. Most states have laws on the books to punish them, but if an elector decides to vote for somebody else, there's no way to stop them, unless Congress decides not to count that vote when it meets in January—and they've never done that."

"You're wrong," Professor Griese said.

Oh, boy, DeRossa thought. *Here we go. Food fight.*

"I beg your pardon," Professor Muttle said sharply. "I happen to have a doctorate in law with a specialty in constitutional legal history. I've published—"

"Sorry, Professor," Griese said, and DeRossa thought he detected a sparkle in the older man's rheumy eyes. "You're forgetting what happened in 1873, when Horace Greeley, the Democratic candidate who lost to Grant, died before the electors could meet. The Georgia electors cast their votes for him, but the Congress was split on whether a dead man was 'a person' within the meaning of the Constitution, so they never did count those votes. It's clear that the Congress is the sole judge of the electoral vote count, and—"

"That's hardly on point here," Muttle snapped. "The question here is whether the victorious party has the power to declare a vacancy. The rules of the Republican Party are clear; there clearly is a vacancy; the rest is just academic pixie dust."

"Gentlemen," DeRossa began, "I wonder if we could get—"

"I don't know what they're teaching these days, *Professor,"* Griese said, "but in my day, we learned that the people don't vote for President; as Mr. DeRossa said, they vote for *electors.* If a journalist can understand that, I don't know why an alleged scholar can't. And we've voted for them. The election is *over.* The American people voted for electors who were pledged to vote for MacArthur Foyle, and that's what they got. Period. If he'd died before November fourth, yes, absolutely, there's a vacancy, and there'd have been time to replace any of the electors who didn't like the new candidate—although you can't begin to imagine the legal nightmare *that* would be. But now? I mean, the committee can vote on who they would *like* the electors to vote for, but compelling them? No way. And even with the states that think they're forcing the electors to vote in accordance with their party, it's a complete mare's nest no matter where you look."

DeRossa was beginning to like this Professor Griese, especially when he looked over at Muttle and saw a few beads of sweat popping out on his forehead.

"Professor Muttle, is that the situation?"

Muttle shrugged.

"These technicalities are made for small minds," he said. "The fact is, these are loyal Republicans, who are going to—"

"You are talking about a potential constitutional crisis, Professor," Griese said, and he seemed to grow taller as he spoke. "Let me give you a few examples."

"Don't let him start talking about all the goddamn laws!" Crenshaw bellowed. *"I'm starting to lose consciousness!"*

"Here's just a taste." Griese began reading from a stained, crumpled piece of yellow legal paper. "Okay, Connecticut: they say an elector has to 'cast his ballot for the candidate under whose name he ran on the official ballot.' Sounds like, if you're an elector in Connecticut, you have to vote for a dead man."

"Oh, for—"

"Hold, it, Muttle. Now, Nevada: they say the electors have to vote for 'the nominees'—get that, the *'nominees'* for President and Vice President of the party that prevailed in his state. . . . Okay, so in Nevada, it looks like the Republicans can nominate a replacement, and the electors are bound."

"Professor, we're running out of time—"

"Wait, wait 'til you hear California! This is a real gem! California says the electors have to vote for the candidates of the party they represent *'if both candidates are alive'!* But guess what? It doesn't say *what* they can or can't do if they're not both alive. And if one of them is alive, does that mean they're allowed not to vote for that guy? If the party puts in somebody else after the general election, is that new guy 'a candidate'? We don't have a clue!"

"Enough!" Crenshaw screamed.

"Okay, thank you, Professor Muttle, Professor Griese, I think we've gotten a sense of just how confusing this is. Ed?"

"We're clear," said the floor manager.

"I'm not," DeRossa said. He turned to Professor Griese, who was trying to remove his microphone; a thick strand of fiber dangled from his jacket.

"Bottom line, what's the odds on electors bolting because they don't like Ted Block?"

"It's a ridiculous question," Muttle said angrily. "This is academic masturbation. It's faculty lounge stuff. It's for losers who call into C-SPAN on New Year's Eve. The Republican National Committee has nominated Block and Phelps. And that's who the electors will vote for. Okay, maybe a half dozen will try to get their names into the history books as a footnote and vote for Senator Morris, or Connor Doyle, or Clint Eastwood, or Elvis. But it isn't going to *matter!"*

Muttle threw down his earpiece and stalked off the set.

"All this bullshit, and not even a consultant's fee," he said.

DeRossa motioned Professor Griese to follow him back to the cubicle he'd commandeered for his temporary office, gestured to one chair, shut the door, and perched on the edge of the desk.

"You really think this could happen, Leonard?" DeRossa asked quietly. "Understand, after what we've been through the last week, the last thing I want to see us do is start scaring the hell out of the country with some banana republic fantasy."

Griese sat quietly for a moment; through the glass walls, DeRossa could see and hear the frantic movement in the offices and corridors: *book the guests, book the satellite, order up the microwave relays, order in the pizzas and sodas.* All the signs of Crisis.

Griese looked up at DeRossa and smiled sadly.

"Would you think it a completely predictable sign of academic dementia if I told you I've been afraid of something like this happening since I was in high school?"

DeRossa shook his head.

"No, I remember a lot of talk about this back in '68, when George Wallace ran third party. But other than that, I never gave it a minute's thought."

"That was the real reason Wallace ran that year," Griese said. "Deadlock the electoral college, deal with Nixon or Humphrey: 'My electors in return for an end to the civil rights push.' And he almost pulled it off. James Michener—you know, the writer?—he was a Pennsylvania elector that year. He spent a lot of time trying to cut a deal with some Nixon electors that they'd cast their votes for whoever won the popular vote, so Wallace couldn't be kingmaker. It didn't get to that, of course. But there was a lot of talk in Congress that it was time to abolish the electoral college, pick the President by popular vote, that sort of thing. And then it all went away, like it always does."

He shrugged.

"There are . . . oh, I don't know, a few hundred of us who actually *worry* about this sort of thing. We actually know why they call it an 'electoral college.' "

"You know, I never thought about it."

"Why should you?" Griese said. "One of the Constitutional Convention delegates—Charles Correll—he'd studied in Europe, and picked the idea up from the way the Holy Roman Empire, in Germany, picked electors from its regions to choose the emperor back in the fourteenth century. Pretty exciting stuff, huh?"

"Maybe if they were having sex with each other, we could get it on a prime-time magazine show."

"I know, it's the kind of hopelessly boring stuff you can't even think about without getting a coughing fit from all the chalk dust. Who cares why the Founding Fathers came up with this scheme? Who cares about the big states and the little states, and the fear of a king, and the fear of the mob? Who cares that they thought the electors would almost *never* choose a President; that they'd winnow it down to three, and the Congress would figure it out?"

Griese paused to listen as Ken Crenshaw accosted two production assistants in the corridor, and explained to them his strong distaste for roast beef sandwiches without Russian dressing. When he was done, the two strapping young men bolted to the men's room to deposit their lunches.

"But you know, some of them knew they'd left a time bomb ticking. Jefferson said the whole electoral college system was 'the most dangerous blot on our Constitution, and one which some unlucky chance will one day hit.' "

"And if it has . . . ," DeRossa began.

"Well, as another American President once said, 'You ain't seen nothin' yet.' "

TWENTY-NINE

★ ★ ★

Connor Doyle's wish for a speedy end to the chaos might have come true were it not for the overweening ambition and determination of Rick Russell, a communications major at George Washington University working his way through school as a room-service waiter at the Monroe Arms Hotel.

It was a good job: indoor work, good tips, and an occasional, if fleeting, encounter with famous and semifamous people. More than once, he had wheeled up a lunch or breakfast order for two, to find a very familiar figure signing the check, while a quickly closing bedroom door revealed a glimpse of flesh.

Rick Russell's fantasies, however, were fueled by different yearnings. Whenever he read a journalist's account of "How I Made It in the News Business"—a story all of them seemed breathlessly eager to relate to a waiting world—he was struck by how often luck played a starring role in the drama. *I happened to be there when the fire broke out, the river flooded over, the governor was shot, the hostage was freed.* Mind you, these big-time journalists also managed to make it clear that when luck kicked in, they were ready with their incredible talent, drive, wit, brains, energy, courage, and wisdom. And Rick took this to heart. He would be ready, he told himself, when opportunity knocked.

It was, in fact, not opportunity that came knocking, but Rick Russell himself, standing at the door to room 541 of the Monroe Arms Hotel, with a tray of club sandwiches, hamburgers, sodas, coffee for five, and half a dozen beers. The door was opened by a pleasant-faced senior citizen who seemed to be in a state of considerable anxiety. Three or four other people were crowded into the single room, a crowd that would have aroused his suspicion under most circumstances. But would anyone really put together an orgy that linked two older gentlemen, a nerdy kid who looked to be barely college age, a thirty-something woman, and—

And the woman he'd seen just a few hours ago on the TV screen in the employees' lounge, going toe-to-toe with the entire establishment of the Republican Party.

If you worked in a Washington hotel, one of the first things you learned to do was to wear a poker face no matter what you confronted on the other side of the door. A famous movie star in tears, a United States congresswoman in leather, nothing was supposed to shake that impassive demeanor that silently communicated the message: *I am not seeing this, your secret is safe with me, now turn your relief and gratitude into a huge tip.* So Rick never so much as acknowledged the woman's presence—was it Dorothy, yes, Dorothy something—but instead set about finding someplace in the crowded room to put all the food and drink.

"Excuse me, thank you, sir, I'll just get your lunch all set up—"

"That's really fine, waiter," said one of the older gentlemen. "But could you just make sure you leave a church key for the beer?" He smiled, slipped Rick a ten-dollar bill, and looked lovingly over at the beaded bottles lying in the Styrofoam ice bucket.

"And I'll take the check," said the apparent host of the luncheon, one "W. Ames," if Rick could trust the imprint on the bill. A few seconds later, Rick was outside the room with an exorbitant tip scribbled on the bottom of the check, and an urgent conviction that he'd better get to a telephone, fast. But what for? In the old black-and-white newspaper movies he'd grown to love, the hero-reporter always called the city desk and yelled "Rewrite!" Rick hadn't a clue what "rewrite!" meant; more important, he didn't know anyone at a city desk. What he did remember was that he'd recently met an intern who worked at a major television network, a Smith College senior named Ann . . . He reached for his wallet, pulled out a crumpled piece of paper, and . . . oh, God, a water stain blurred out most of the last name. He thought he could make out a

"Mc . . ." something or other. Well, isn't this how all those million-dollar-a-year guys got started?

Rick took the service elevator down to the kitchen, dropped off the room-service check, and ducked out of the kitchen before he could be given another run upstairs. Just outside the employees' men's room was a pay phone, where room-service waiter Andrew Hamilton, better known to talk-radio listeners as "Andy from Anacostia," was haranguing a local radio call-in show—a hobby that took up the greater part of his waking life.

"See, this whole thing is ridiculous," Andy from Anacostia was saying. "You know, I mean, we voted for the Republicans, now this lady is saying, well, she don't wanna vote for the Republicans, well, she should, like, be quiet, you know, or they should fire her, and then get somebody who will vote like the way we the people told her she should vote, right? Because we the people wanted a Republican, and like, from my particular point of view, if the guy we voted for picked this guy to be the President if anything happened to him, and now something happened to him, and he can't be President, so like, they should have the guy that this guy wanted us to have, okay?"

It was hopeless. Rick raced up the stairs to the hotel lobby and ducked into the gift shop. Alice Meehan, a grandmother in her late fifties, had a mild crush on Rick, who traded her smiles and kind words for an occasional magazine or candy bar.

"I've *got* to use a phone," he said.

"You sick? Girl trouble?" Alice asked. "Never mind. Just make it quick. You know how they feel about the help."

"Right," Rick said. Directory assistance gave him the number of the network, but then what? Ann McWhatshername worked . . . where? . . . *Yes,* the political unit. But what the hell was her name?

"Political unit." The voice on the other end of the line was harried. Rick could hear loud voices in the background, along with an unsettling crash.

"Ann Mcblmphng, please."

"Speaking," she said.

Remember this for the memoirs, Rick thought.

"Ann, it's Rick, Rick Russell. We met at Walter's party?"

He thought he detected a small, exasperated grunt.

"Rick, I can't talk now. It's insane over here, so—"

"Wait! Wait! This isn't a social call!" Alice was looking at him curiously, motioning her head toward the lobby, where the concierge was peering in suspiciously. "Ann," Rick said, "I know you don't know me very well—"

"I don't know you at all. Now, please—"

"*Listen* to me. You have to trust me on this—aren't you guys looking for that woman who caused all the fuss this morning at the National Committee meeting?"

"Dorothy *Ledger?* Are you kidding? They've got us calling every airline, every hotel, they've sent everybody they can spare out to cruise the downtown streets. The Shoreham won't even put calls through to her—"

Rick dropped his voice to a whisper.

"I know where she is."

"What?"

"And what are you doing here?" The concierge was tapping Rick on the shoulder.

"It's an emergency," Rick begged. "Give me two minutes."

"We have plenty of facilities for you people," the concierge said. "Two minutes," he said, with a wag of his fingers.

"Are you still there?" Ann said. "Where is she?"

"Ann, put one of your bosses on the phone—the bigger the better." There was a long moment of silence, during which Rick could see the concierge at his desk, holding up one finger.

"Yes," said a voice on the phone. "This is Al DeRossa. Who's this?"

"My name is Rick Russell. I work at—I work at a hotel here in Washington. I know where Dorothy Ledger is."

"Where?"

"Mr. DeRossa, you need to know two things: First, I want to work in news; I'm desperate to work in news. Second, if I stay on this phone another thirty seconds, I'm probably going to get fired."

"Congratulations," DeRossa said. "You've done great on your job interview. Now, where is she?"

"You're not jerking me around here, are you?" Rick looked up again and saw the concierge draw a finger slowly across his throat.

"Look, Rick, it'll be a while before we can get you on the air, but a job? Yes, I think it's safe to say that getting us to Dorothy Ledger is an impressive beginning to your career. Now, where is she?"

It all began for me on a fateful November day, Rick thought as he looked up at the concierge and held up a finger of his own.

THIRTY

★ ★ ★

At twenty-four minutes after six in the evening, one of Connor Doyle's bright young aides turned on the four television sets that had been hooked up in the living room of the Shoreham America's presidential suite. The day had been a jumble of special reports, news updates, and live interviews, alternating between reassuring messages of loyalty and support for Theodore Block from Republican officials across the country to bet hedging from a wide variety of talking heads. Every time a state party chair or well-known Republican governor or senator dismissed Dorothy Ledger as a "disgruntled dissident," Dr. Sherman Gelt would note that if only twelve percent of Republican electors—thirty-six, to be exact—decided not to vote for Block and Phelps, there would be no electoral college majority.

Dr. Gelt, the resident political analyst for the All News Network, had spent the whole afternoon and early evening guiding his audience through the swamp of the potential constitutional crisis. After a quarter century of obscurity teaching political science at Van deVanter College in Tennessee, after three years as a distinctly B-list scholar at Washington's Fleigle Institute, Dr. Gelt had become a media celebrity through his daily appearances on ANN's *Washington Today* talk show. He analyzed polls, provided historical analogies, and spun off catchy phrases heavily laced with pop culture references. "A slam dunk!" he'd call a clever political ploy. "It's 'Forrest Gump Meets Jurassic Park!' " he'd call an upcoming debate. During major political stories, Dr. Gelt seemed to be on the air constantly; according to one popular Washington rumor, he was fitted out with a "motorman's friend" tube device, to provide for his personal relief while ensuring his constant presence on the set.

"It's ridiculous!" Alan Veigle complained. "That windbag is on in every newsroom in the city—make that the country. We got five thousand reporters covering politics, so figure maybe twenty of them have had an original thought in the last five years. So they listen to this schmuck, and they think some whack-job lady from Michigan'll turn the presidency into *Wheel of Fortune.* Meanwhile, we got every state chair standing behind Block and Phelps, saying it's the greatest ticket since Tippecanoe and Tyler, too."

"Not quite everyone," said Sharon Kramer. 'Not Wyoming, not Minnesota. Not California—as Dr. Gelt and his colleagues reminded us several times an hour."

"A mix-up," said Alan Veigle, dismissively. "In all that confusion, I'm amazed we only missed three. Anyway, those anchor pops Connor is doing should put the cap on it. Has he got a hard count from two hundred seventy electors yet?"

"No," Marsh said. "But it's close enough for government work. We've got at least two forty we can cite by name and hometown right now. The rest is just a matter of logistics."

"I hope that's not what Connor's going to say on TV in a minute," said Sharon Kramer. Hours of work on the telephone, cooped up in a crowded hotel suite, had left her neck sore, her eyes itchy, her legs cramped, and her disposition as sour as her stomach. Moreover, she regarded the presence of Marsh and Alan Veigle with a deep sense of ambivalence. During the fall campaign, they had banished her to the care and feeding of Ted Block; they had consigned her to a job with the Vice President–elect, a position as desirable as the FBI office in Butte, Montana. Now, with their champion dead and buried, they had found a way back in: as damage-control experts. All she could do now, she realized, was to keep a sharp eye out for more political minefields, and to keep her back to the wall.

"What's wrong with a little upbeat news, for a change?" Marsh asked.

"There are two possibilities," Sharon replied. "If Connor claims we have the electors locked up, and doesn't produce two hundred seventy names, the headline is, 'He's Bluffing.' If he's honest, and gives the real hard count, the headline is 'Block Lacks Votes to Win.' "

She paused to let the next sentence sink in.

"That's why I told him that the best he can do is to say there's been an 'outpouring of support,' that nobody's had time to actually add up all the votes, but there's no possibility—*no* possibility, *none,* not one chance in hell—that there's any doubt about who the next President is."

"That's what *you* told him to say?" Marsh asked.

"Yes," Sharon said pleasantly. "On the elevator on the way down. With Block and Phelps over at Blair House—we put out the word that they're working on the Cabinet and the White House staff—Connor Doyle is our public point man. Let him tell the story straight, with no room for nit-picking by the press, and no room for any other outcome to this story line. As long as there's no competing story, we'll be okay."

"Speaking of which," Alan Veigle interrupted. "Has there been a Dorothy sighting? Or did she click her heels three times and go back to Kansas?"

"I know what they're saying on the talk shows," the head of the Young Republicans piped up. He'd been serving as a bartender, coat holder, telephone operator, and gofer, and regarded his presence in the room as not only the most important moment of his life, but as the *only* important moment of his life.

"What are they saying?" Sharon asked.

"They're saying she has a history of mental disorder; that she's been hospitalized for shock treatment."

"Is that really what they're saying?"

"Well," the young man said, "that's what I told my people to call in and say. Let her deny it."

"Settle down," Alan Veigle said. "Let's see the nets."

At precisely six-thirty, the four network news broadcasts began with a dazzling array of computer-generated special effects and portentous music, all bearing a vague resemblance to the sound tracks of *Star Wars, Rocky,* and *Superman.* The graphics dissolved into head-on shots of four attractive middle-aged white men, one attractive middle-aged Caucasian woman, and one woman of (very little) color. All began with headlines that promised an in-depth examination of the day's "startling," "shocking," or "bombshell" events; all promoted "exclusive" interviews with House Minority Leader Connor Doyle.

"Good, good," Marsh muttered at the TV screens, then sat bolt upright.

"Punch up Steele! Punch up Steele!"

". . . with the mystery woman who's at the center of what just may be the most serious constitutional crisis in a century—Dorothy Ledger of Michigan."

The camera cut to a huge monitor behind Steele. In the frame a nervous but composed woman wearing a white blouse, gray skirt, and black cotton jacket was blinking into the camera with a small smile on her face.

"Oh, Jesus, we're gonna be sandbagged!" Alan Veigle yelled. "It's Rather and Bush all over again!"

While the other networks were playing their taped interviews with Doyle, Steele was executing a half-turn away from the camera, toward the monitor.

"Dorothy Ledger is a lifelong Republican, longtime executive with the Kent County Republican Party. She's also a presidential elector, pledged to vote for the Foyle-Block ticket. She was handpicked as Michigan's temporary Republican National Committeewoman for the express purpose of coming to Washington for this meeting—where she made her lonely stand.

"Ms. Ledger, what happened? What made you stand up to your own party this way?"

"Gee, Ed, why don't you just throw her a bag of marshmallows while you're at it?"

Dorothy Ledger took a breath. She remembered the conversation she'd had with Al DeRossa, after the newsman had tracked her down at the Monroe Arms Hotel. He did not patronize her, did not try to win her confidence with endearing stories, did not conceal his personal and professional interest in her appearance on his network.

His point was simple: either you get your story out your way, explain your point of view so that no one can misunderstand it or distort it, or you're going to be painted as a cross between a lunatic and a traitor by sundown. Come on our newscast, and you'll get a fair shake, time to make your point, and a chance to be heard the way you want to be heard.

She'd looked around the room, and found Walter Ames, Jr., Ben Weinstock, and Faith McCoy all nodding in agreement.

"You've got nothing to lose, Dorothy," Faith McCoy said, grinning at her. "They're going to be tearing you a new—they're going to be ripping you to shreds no matter what you do. You've already jumped off the high board; might as well hit the water your way."

Now, staring into the camera, Dorothy started to talk. *Keep eye contact, relax your body, try to smile, be concise, be clear, don't get angry, don't get defensive, and—oh, right—be yourself.*

"Mr. Steele," she began, "I've been a Republican all my life. I worked very hard to get MacArthur Foyle elected President. I would have been proud to have cast my vote for him. When he was killed, I was . . . devastated,"

"Aw, Christ, that bitch is going to cry," Alan Veigle barked at the screen. "I'm gonna be sick."

"I was prepared—I *am* prepared—to fulfill my obligation to my party. But I'm asking whether the Republican Party has fulfilled its obligation to me, and to the millions of people who voted for Senator Foyle. Does Governor Block stand for the conservative principles Mack Foyle stood for? Does he have the qualities we need in a President? Suppose I think the answers to these questions are no. What am I supposed to do?"

"You're supposed to shut up and vote," Alan Veigle growled.

"Well," Ed Steele said, "it's a fact, isn't it, that your candidate, Senator Foyle, *chose* Governor Block to be his successor in case anything happened to him. Don't you show disloyalty to the memory of the late President-elect by rejecting his own candidate?"

"Unbelievable!" Marsh shouted. "A fair question!"

"I haven't decided to do anything—yet," Dorothy answered. "The whole reason I raised my points of order was to find out what legal rights I and the other electors have. One thing we've already discovered is that the law here is one big mess.

"But one thing I think we already know," she went on, "is that the original Founding Fathers wanted us to be free agents. A lot of us have seen in the recent conduct of Governor Block some very disturbing qualities. In fact, I wonder whether if MacArthur Foyle had been able to see this side of Governor Block, he ever would have picked him as his running mate."

"But, Ms. Ledger," Ed Steele asked, "it's been understood for years, for decades, that you folks aren't *really* free agents. Ninety-nine out of a hundred Americans didn't even know there *were* electors until a couple of days ago. Do you really think you have the right to deprive your party of the White House?"

Dorothy smiled.

"Mr. Steele, wasn't it John Kennedy who said, 'Sometimes party loyalty asks too much'? All I want to do is to ask some very hard questions about what we should be doing." Now she looked right into the camera. "And if there are any other electors listening to me, that's what I want them to do as well. I want them to stop—and think—and ask themselves whether we really want to be personally, morally responsible for making Mr. Block President. If they answer that question yes, well, okay. But all I can say is that, in my own life, I've seen firsthand what can happen when unqualified men are given power and responsibility they aren't equipped to handle. I can't imagine ever wanting to have anything to do with putting someone like that in the White House."

"Dorothy Ledger, thank you very much. I have a feeling we'll be hearing a lot more from you."

"I can't believe it," Marsh said. "It's the 'Checkers' speech. It's Reagan at D-Day. It's 'I Have a Dream.' Who gave her that crap?"

"I think that's the problem," Sharon Kramer said. "She did it all by herself. And I've got a hunch that's exactly what they're going to think out there in Regular Guy Land." She looked around the room, her eyes fixed on Marsh.

"Do me a favor, okay? Next time you elect a President of the United States, have him ride a bike."

THIRTY-ONE

★ ★ ★

'Preciate your comin' by, Joe," Jack Petitcon said warmly, as he beckoned Featherstone into his office. "Get you a drink? Single-malt scotch, maybe some bourbon?"

"Just some Evian if you have it," Featherstone said.

"You young sumbitches really plan on livin' forever, don't you?" Petitcon said with a chuckle. "I remember once Phil Harris—you don't know who he was, do you, 'course not, no way you would. Well, he was a character on the old Jack Benny radio show—you've heard of Jack Benny, haven't you, Joe? Thank God. I'd be checkin' into the home if you hadn't. Well, Phil Harris was the bandleader, a real carouser, you know? They were always jokin' about how much Phil liked to drink. Guess you'd get thrown off the air for that today. Well, one show, he's askin' a guest, 'Do you want a cigarette?' 'No,' says the guest, 'I don't smoke.' 'Well, then,' Phil says, 'how about a martini?' 'No,' the guest goes, 'I don't drink.' 'Do you mean,' Phil says, 'you're one of those jokers who's gonna die of *nothin'*?' "

Petitcon chuckled, handed Featherstone a glass—cut crystal—then settled into a richly upholstered red leather chair facing Featherstone's, a chair whose seat was built up five inches higher than his guest's. Featherstone sipped at his water, wondering the same thing he'd been wondering for the last three hours: *What is this all about?* He'd been sitting amid the ruins of Mueller's campaign office, surrounded by cartons of résumés, speech drafts, Federal Election Commission forms to be filled out, and a rapidly rising pile of bills, glancing occasionally at the television to watch the tragedy-cum-farce the Republican Party was performing, letting his voice mail accumulate the messages. When his private phone rang, he was surprised to hear Jack Petitcon's voice; more surprised when Petitcon invited him over for a drink, today, actually, if he could fit it into his schedule; then baffled when Jack's voice dropped almost to a whisper as he suggested that it would probably be a very good idea if Joe didn't mention this particular visit to anyone.

"So, Joe, you believe this circus they're puttin' on? If it weren't so damn serious, it'd be like what happened in '56 with Joe Smith. You weren't even born then, were you? Well, I'm talkin' 'bout the Republican Convention, when they were renominatin' Eisenhower and Dick Nixon. This one delegate from Nebraska, Terry somebody, got a little ticked off at all the stage managin'. So he got up and said he wanted to nominate 'Joe Smith' for Vice President as a symbol of an open convention." Petitcon took a healthy swallow of his drink.

"Carpenter," he said. "Terry Carpenter, the name was. Well, the chairman didn't appreciate the ad libbing, and TV was too new for him to remember that the cameras were on. So he bellows, 'You take your Joe Smith and get out of here!' Well, you'd have thought the Democrats had gotten hold of a smokin' gun. They had all these buttons printed up, you know, 'I'm for Adlai, Estes, and Joe Smith.' And what happened? A big fat landslide for Eisenhower and Nixon." Petitcon nodded emphatically, took another swallow, and sat back with a sigh of satisfaction.

"I see," said Featherstone, who didn't at all. "So Dorothy Ledger is our Terry Carpenter?"

Petitcon shook his head and offered an indulgent chuckle.

"Oh, Lord, Joe, you're too smart to b'lieve that. You damn near won yourself a President. You know better'n I what's going on here, right?" He paused for an instant, set his glass down on the brass-and-glass coffee table, and leaned forward intently. On the wall behind him, Featherstone glimpsed a picture of Lyndon Johnson in the Oval Office, talking with a much younger Jack Petitcon, his body in the precise posture Jack was now assuming.

"Joe, when I was a boy, my daddy'd take us Sunday driving out to

Lake Charles. We'd catch catfish all day, fry 'em up over a fire at night. I can still taste 'em—wish I could, but the doctor'd kill me. Anyway, ever' once in a while, a storm would start to build over there, on the western edge of the lake, an' head right toward us. We'd be standin' under a bright sky, but over there you could see it movin' right toward us—a sheet of rain, the water churnin', the sky all gray an' angry.

"Buddy, when Miz Ledger stood up there in that hotel ballroom, that storm began to build. And you know what kind of storm it is?

"It's a *shitstorm,* Joe. The biggest, nastiest *shitstorm* we have ever seen. An' everyone in this town has two choices: you can set out ahead of it, or get ready to be hit right in the face by it. Hell, I bet you've got all this figgid out by now, but les' just spell it out."

He stuck out a huge hand, palm up, fingers splayed out an inch or two from Featherstone's face, and ticked off his points one by one.

"One: if we reran the election tomorrow, Mueller versus Block head-to-head, for President, how do you figgah it'd go? Sixty-forty? Maybe two to one? That's a dead cinch, right?

"Two: nobody has to guess, 'cause I guar-ahn-tee they'll be puttin' those numbers out on every network tonight.

"Three: that dog-and-pony show the Republicans put on has about as much chance of stickin' as a snowflake on the bosom of the Potomac."

"Ev Dirksen, right?" said Featherstone.

"Hey, you are one smart S.O.B. Can't diddle you for a minute, right? So while all the chairmen are lined up smilin' and shakin' hands here in Washington, just what do you suppose those electors are doin' back home? Tell you what I figure, you set me straight where I screw it up. Count up how many of the Bible-thumpin', snake-handling', no-secular-humanist-public-school folks got to be electors 'cause they spent twenty hours a day, seven days a week, workin' for Mack Foyle. You think maybe a few of them have a few problems linin' up behind a guy whose ancestors crewed on the *Mayflower?*

"Now, how 'bout the folks that had their diapers pinned with Goldwater buttons, who spent their lawn-mowin' and baby-sittin' money on Reagan bumper stickers, with *National Review* centerfolds on their walls? You think they want Nelson Rockefeller's love child in the White

House? You think they're happy about a President who sang a song about clean water with a bunch of Communist folksingers on public television? An' I'm not makin' this up, Joe. The guy's a liberal Republican. You believe that? In this day an' age? It's like bein' the head of the Flat Earth Club after Columbus came home.

"Now finally," Petitcon said, and Featherstone leaned so forward to hear him he almost slid off the chair. "Think about somethin' you're not supposed to talk about in this town. Think about how many of those electors just think it would be *wrong* to make Teddy Block the President of the United States. I know, I know, it's all supposed to be about climbin' the greasy pole, and winnin' and losin', but you know that's not always how it happens. You know when Harry Truman got the Marshall Plan through the Congress? When the *Republicans* were in control, and a sorrier bunch of know-nothin' metal-heads you never saw. But enough of 'em understood that you had to put Europe back on its feet to vote with Truman.

"You know who got the Civil Rights Bill through the Congress? Mr. Everett McKinley Dirksen, a small-town Taft Republican who never met a retainer or campaign contribution he didn't like, and who prob'bly never knew a colored man who wasn't pouring him a drink or helpin' him into his coat. But he knew it was the right thing to do. He got up on the floor of the U.S. Senate, an' said it was 'an idea whose time has come,' an' that was the end of that tune.

"You know who got Richard Nixon out of the White House? No, not those reporters, an' not the judge, an' not that woman on the House Committee with a voice like she was about to break into 'Lay Down My Sword and Shield.' It was all those *Republicans,* Joe, the *Republicans.* I'm talkin' before the tapes came out, and ever'body realized he'd done it. If those Republicans hadn't had enough brass in their pants to say, 'He did it,' this town'd have torn itself in two."

Petitcon jumped to his feet and strode to the window.

Oh, no, Featherstone thought. *Don't do the Jimmy Stewart bit. For God's sake, don't do the Jimmy Stewart bit.*

"That's what saves us ever' time, Joe," Petitcon said. "We're not just in it for the money and the glory, Joe, and God knows I've had more'n my share of both. But when it matters—when it really, really matters—it's the stand-up folks that hold it all together." He stopped, and looked for a long moment at Featherstone.

"You wonder what Walter York must be thinkin' right now, right, Joe?"

In fact, Walter York had not made the slightest entrance onto the disordered slum of a stage set that was now Joe Featherstone's mind. And why would he? The retired four-term Republican senator from Vermont, silver of mane, firm of jaw, whose tongue was as sharp as his eye, was the semi-official national symbol of rectitude. He divided his time between teaching at Middlebury College back home and running a tiny office in Washington. There he spent several hours a day turning down offers to chair bipartisan, nonpartisan, and antipartisan commissions on government spending, campaign finance reform, immigration policy, monetary redesign, and a dozen other vexing policy issues that would determine the very course of our national future, and that no one in any position of real power wanted to think about for more than two and a half consecutive minutes.

"Bet I know where that mind of yours is homin' in," Petitcon continued. Featherstone wished he could take that bet, but since much of his mind today had been homing in on Pepper Days's delectable backside, he chose to nod sagely and to listen.

"Bet you're wonderin' what would happen if Walter York and a bunch of other Republicans got up in front of the cameras and said that, come Election Day—or Elector Day, or whatever the hell they'll call it—they'd vote for Bill Mueller for President."

Featherstone slammed his glass down so hard it cracked the coffee table.

"Goddamnit, Jack, I knew I'd be swimming in a cesspool once we lost, but I didn't expect this of you. I'm a punch line for every backstabbing snake in town, my wife kicked me out of the house weeks ago, I'm owed seventy-five thousand in salary and expenses from the campaign that I'll never see again—and now this? What, are you videotaping this for the next Alfalfa Club smoker? Is this going to make a dandy anecdote for your next off-the-record lunch with a bureau chief?" He started to get up when Petitcon pushed him back with a short, sharp jab of his forefinger.

"Glad to know what you think of me, Joe, it always helps clear the air," Petitcon said, indignant that Featherstone would confuse his normal practice of taping every office conversation with some sort of malicious practical joke.

"But you listen to me, you third-rate excuse for a campaign manager. Maybe you're too blind to see it, but *Billy Mueller can still be the President.* He ran, what, two percent behind in the popular vote? Thirty-seven in the electoral count? And the guy that won is dead. So logically, who *should* be President? The guy that almost got elected in the first place? Or some bozo that most of the country wouldn't trust on a White House tour?"

"But the rules—"

"There *are* no rules, Joe. Don't you get it? It's never happened before. We're all makin' ever'thing up as we go along. I'm telling' you: watch the news tonight an' check out those polls. If you can find a few statesmen like Walter York who'll get up and praise Miz Dorothy Ledger as a gutsy, courageous heroine—you know, Dolley Madison, Barbara Frietchie, standin' up for what's right—if you can find enough Republicans to talk just a handful of those electors into choosin' country over party—well, Joe, you know I don't bet long shots. But I'd put some serious milk money down that you could pull this off."

By now, Petiticon had his hand on Joe Featherstone's left shoulder. He was breathing hard from his words, and his face was slightly pink. His eyes were boring in on Joe, who was very glad he was not some government regulator standing between Petitcon's clients and a mineral-rights permit on federal land. But in another, darker corner of Featherstone's mind, a string of buried fantasies were reanimating: a West Wing office, where Others answered his phone, sorted his mail, booked him tables, concerts, playoff games at the merest flick of an eyebrow; small conferences in the Oval Office, with cameras outside probing for the smallest glimpse of his face; Sunday mornings in Washington television studios, with a cluster of microphones waiting for him outside; the sidelong, frank appraisals of sleek women, maneuvering around the waiter for a personal chat with so powerful a man. . . .

These daydreams had been buried on Election Night; and now Jack Petitcon was peering into the ruins with a flashlight and a ladder.

"Even if this was at all possible," Featherstone said, "what makes you think someone like Walter York would even dream of doing such a thing?"

Jack Petitcon thought back on the conversation he had had an hour ago with Walter York; his old friend, his co-chair on the National Commission on Presidential Debates, his occasional golf partner, and his slightly more frequent partner on nineteen initial public offerings over the last six years.

"Call it a hunch," Jack said.

THIRTY-TWO

★ ★ ★

"It's *Godzilla,* Alan Veigle said to no one in particular.

"You want to be a little *more* cryptic, Alan?" Sharon Kramer said. "You know, just in case someone might conceivably know what the hell you're talking about?"

"You know—all those movies, *Godzilla, Mothra, Megalon, Godzilla Meets Mothra,* all of the 'Monster Eats Tokyo' movies," Alan Veigle said professorially. "Or did you spend all your Saturdays in the library?"

"Could we all just keep our tempers in check, please," Marsh said, pulling the telephone away from his ear and covering it with his hand. "Let's just remember that we're all a little frayed around the edges right now."

The atmosphere was in fact downright dank. The air inside the presidential suite of the Shoreham American had the faint reek of trapped air, discarded food, the stray cigarette butt, and too many bodies occupying too little space for too many hours. Outside, rumor had it, the sun had shone on a crisp fall day that had now become a bracing autumn evening. For all that some of the best minds of the Republican Party had seen of it, they might as well have been a claque of vampires hiding from the light. They had spent the day surfing through the television channels, watching the story of Dorothy Ledger's challenge being transformed into an instant legend. By midafternoon, the All News Network had designed an arresting graphic, featuring a heroic sketch of her face, that popped up behind the anchors each time a new nugget of information was found: her high school yearbook photo, pictures of her at a dozen different Republican Party lunches and dinners, enabling the news heads to ask "why this devoted Republican Party loyalist stood up to her own party and said 'No!' " They had watched as a Detroit-based correspondent, dispatched to Grand Rapids, interviewed her colleagues and co-workers:

"Kind of quiet, but a real can-do person . . . don't know how the bank would ever run without her . . . never thought of Dorothy as a trouble-maker . . . if I was in a fight, I'd sure want her on my side . . . I always said Dorothy never got a husband, 'cause she already had two lovers: the bank, and the Republican Party. . . ."

Inevitably, the coverage was glazed with a bias deeply embedded into American pop culture: the underdog is always right. For the press to take the side of the Republican establishment against Dorothy Ledger would be like a newspaper running a story about an ailing widow about to be evicted from her family home by a hotel and gambling casino, and concluding that it was high time the old bag got out.

Not that this spin was the only problem. Now armed with a list of presidential electors disgorged from the sleepy state capital bureaucracies, the vast armies of the mass media were beginning to fan out in search of potential allies who might rally to plucky Dorothy's side.

And, to the growing dismay of the occupants of the presidential suite of the Shoreham American, they were beginning to find them:

- Hugh D. Luce, a retired United States congressman from Wyoming, who had been given an elector's slot to help dissuade him from endorsing the Income Tax Abolition Party, announced that he intended to cast his vote for the late Senator Foyle, because "Mack Foyle six feet under would be a better President than Ted Block six feet over." In any event, Luce went on, he would have no part of putting another Trilateral Commission poster boy into the Oval Office.
- Etta Bunyon, longtime postmaster of Withering Springs, Mississippi, said she thought the Republican National Committee owed Dorothy Ledger an apology, and intended to see that she got one.

"If they don't say yes," Ms. Bunyon said, smiling sweetly, "I guess I'll just vote no."

- From the village of Seals Point, Alaska, in the farthest reaches of the Aleutian Islands, came a fax, zapped to all likely news organizations from one Theodore Roosevelt Treebark, who declared his intention to cast his electoral vote for his cousin, Cecil. Most of the news organizations held up on this development, having been unable to obtain any confirmation of Mr. Treebark's status as a presidential elector, or indeed, the existence of either Theodore Roosevelt Treebark or the village of Seals Point.

It was all more than enough to feed the story of a budding electors' revolt into the next news cycle, and to strain further the nerves of some of the shrewdest Republican strategists money could buy.

"See, here's what happens," Alan Veigle was explaining to an increasingly impatient Sharon Kramer. "Godzilla's always tucked away somewhere, nice and safe: they're buried under the sea, or they're frozen in a glacier, or they're trapped inside a volcano. Then something happens. Maybe it's an A-bomb test, maybe it's some arrogant scientist trying to drill to the center of the earth, maybe it's a meteorite, or a comet. It really doesn't matter. So anyway, the bomb goes off, the drill cuts through the white-hot rock in the earth's core, the meteor slams into the volcano, and *bam!*—out comes the monster, and we get forty-five minutes of complete and total destruction before the scientist with the horn-rimmed glasses and his beautiful daughter figure out that Godzilla's allergic to rayon or something, and they drive him back into the ocean until the next sequel."

The room was utterly silent.

"Don't you get it?" said Alan Veigle. "That's what happened here. We've had this monster buried for more than two hundred years now. Every now and then somebody says, 'Hey! I think I felt the ground tremble a little bit. Maybe we should check it out.' And then the ground stops trembling, and we forget about it. This time, Godzilla woke up—and he's coming right for us."

Sharon nodded.

"Great rant, Alan, genuinely great rant. If the boys on *Crossfire* could hear you now, they'd be green with envy. The fact that it's a great steaming pile of nonsense notwithstanding. Marsh, what are the state chairs telling us? Have they got it under control?"

Marsh spoke a few words into the phone, hung up the receiver, then shook his head and rubbed his hand across the stubble of beard that made him look even more like a mob hitman than usual.

"They think they're okay, but the truth is . . . the truth is, who knows? Most of our electors have called in, they're all saying this is nuts, they're one hundred percent with Block and Phelps, but the best I can figure . . ." He paused to look at a page of indecipherable handwriting. "What we know is we absolutely have somewhere between two thirty-five and two fifty votes—fifty or sixty less than we won on Election Day and around twenty to thirty-five short of a majority. Maybe that doesn't mean anything; they're out fishing, or they don't have an answering machine. And maybe it means some of them may be thinking about going AWOL. In which case . . ." Marsh sighed, and his face sagged a bit further.

"Which reminds me—permit me to share a delightful conversation I just concluded with elector R. Charles Cashin, recorder of deeds in Key Banyan, Florida. Mr. Cashin wants very, very much to stand foursquare with the Republican Party, to which he has devoted countless hours of unremunerative labor since the days of Dwight D. Eisenhower."

"Uh-oh," said Sharon.

"Yes, indeed," Marsh said grimly, with a single, sharp nod of his head. "Mr. Cashin has long had a dream . . ."

"A small business, perhaps?" said Alan Veigle.

"A shopping mall on a bird sanctuary, perhaps," Sharon chimed in.

"A golf course on an ancestral burial ground, financed with a Small Business Administration loan?" Alan trumped.

"More or less," said Marsh. "I asked him if he realized he was probably committing a federal crime. Know what he said? Said as far as he could tell, he was free to vote any way he wanted, for whatever reason. Said it was no different than somebody else voting for a senator who promised to keep a shipyard open. It was just that Mr. Cashin's desires are more . . . *concrete,* more . . . *targeted.*"

Marsh looked around the room.

"Anybody want to bet on whether that's the only call like that we get? Jesus, I wonder what the going rate is for an electoral vote?"

"Actually," one of the Young Blue Suits piped up, "if you figure that we spent about one hundred ten million dollars in the primary and the general to win three hundred five electoral votes, it works out to about a third of a million each. But if the universe is, say, the thirty or so we'd need to get to a majority, then the market price would be about three to four million apiece."

The Young Blue Suit stopped, looked around, then turned beet red.

"Sorry," he mumbled, "I thought you . . . um . . . really might want to know . . ."

Marsh suddenly jerked forward, and snapped his fingers at the muted TV set.

"Hey, hey, what the hell is *that?"*

Behind the All News Network anchor desk, a "NewsFlash!" graphic appeared—the signal that a breaking story was in the works. Next to the graphic was a black-and-white photo of a distinguished, almost noble face: the face of Walter York.

Marsh flicked the mute button on the remote, and the anchor's voice swelled, filled with that edge of urgency and hesitation that signaled: Hey—Something Big Is Going On.

". . . can remember a press conference so hastily called, on barely fifteen minutes' notice, at the York Institute here in Washington. We don't know what Senator York plans to say, only that one aide who refused to be identified says it concerns, quote, 'the current situation,' and that it concerns, and again we quote, 'a major announcement of potentially historic consequence.' Of course, ANN will be there, live, and we'll be back after this short break."

As the picture flipped from a graphic demonstration of hemorrhoid relief (a forest fire cooled by a soothing blast of water) to a feminine hygiene demonstration (a sponge miraculously absorbing a viscous fluid) to an intestinal distress remedy demonstration (a balloon pumped full of air until it noisily exploded), half a dozen hands groped inside their pockets for the cellular phones that began to chirp all at once, like a field full of maddened crickets.

"No . . ." "How the hell do I know? . . ." "Not a clue . . ." "You tell me!"

"It's trouble," Sharon Kramer said quietly to Marsh. "York is the favorite Republican of everybody who hates Republicans; they put him on PBS for 'balance,' he's always in those *New York Times* roundups. I'd love to know the last Republican he actually voted for. Flip to C-SPAN, Marsh, at least we can check out the room."

C-SPAN, the television of choice for the terminally civic minded, had built a fanatically loyal following with its gavel-to-gavel coverage of the Congress, and of every speech and panel on public policy held anywhere in the country. For the truly obsessed, C-SPAN offered a special treat. It often began a moment or two before the start of the speech on interstate fishing disputes, or the panel on White House staff management reforms. The result was that viewers often learned that blue tickets for the Sunday buffet would be available at the registration desk *only* until 4:00 P.M., or that the hospitality suite would be strictly nonsmoking. And after a banquet speech, the C-SPAN cameras would pan the emptying hall for long moments, so that viewers sometimes got a glimpse of a United States senator as he bade good night to his table companion, allowing his hand to linger just a moment too long on the back of the comely wife of the undersecretary of state.

Now, Sharon Kramer was desperately trying to discover who was attending Walter York's press conference. She found what she was looking for—or rather, what she was desperately *not* looking for—almost immediately.

"Oh God, take a look: it's Charles Barrow."

Four years ago, Barrow, a Republican congressman from rural Virginia, took to the pulpit of the Silver Falls Baptist Church to denounce the shocked congregation for its "racist way of life." The next day, he resigned his seat to devote himself to the passage of a Federal Housing Rights Act, barring discrimination on the basis of race in all public and private housing. He had also spent the last four years attacking the leaders of the Republican Party as "night riders of repression." This was not a happy portent.

"And isn't that . . . Jesus, it's Mary Margaret Schuyler," Marsh said. "Remember? They booted her off the National Committee eight years ago after the platform fight on abortion—you know: 'Every woman's right is every woman's fight.' "

"Couldn't this be good?" asked a Young Blue Suit. "I mean, if they're liberals, and Block is sort of liberal . . ."

"Don't kid yourself," said Sharon Kramer. "Forget the voting records, forget the issue. These people believed they ruled by Divine Right; they've never gotten over losing their party to the sons and daughters of plumbers and cops and furniture salesmen. I don't know what's up, but it's—okay, here's York."

The former senator strode to the podium, and with a nod of his patrician head, began to speak.

"This is a painful and wrenching time for our country. We have lost the man we had just chosen to lead us—and now the choice to succeed MacArthur Foyle has been plunged into controversy. It is a time when the normal rules of political behavior will no longer serve.

"I have spent my life in the Republican Party . . ."

"No!" Marsh screamed. "Jesus God, no!"

"Oh, yes!" It was Connor Doyle, who had just rushed into the presidential suite. "He called me three minutes ago in the car—wanted to give me a 'heads-up.' I told him it sounded a lot more like 'up yours.' Know what he told me? 'We don't need language like that at a time like this.' 'Okay,' I said, 'How about "go fuck yourself"?' But he's really gonna do it."

"By his conduct during the campaign, by his inappropriate and often disturbing behavior since the tragic death of President-elect Foyle, Mr. Block has demonstrated his unfitness for the office of President. Nor is there any doubt that, were an election held today, Mr. Block would lose overwhelmingly to the Democratic nominee, William Mueller.

"Therefore, I am urging my fellow Republicans who have been chosen as electors to use the power given to them by the Founding Fathers; to exercise their best, independent judgment, and to cast their electoral votes for Bill Mueller. It would be my hope that, in recognition of these extraordinary circumstances, Mr. Mueller would agree to replace his vice-presidential candidate with one chosen from the ranks of the Republican Party, and would agree to form an administration that was truly bipartisan and nonpartisan.

"I know some will say this act would be an attempt to reverse the results of the election. But that has already happened; the President America picked was taken from us by a tragic act of fate. The question now is whether we are willing to take extraordinary measures in defense of our system and our future. Thank you."

Then came the questions, shouted out with all the clarity and decorum of a trading pit at the Chicago Commodities Market. No, he had not talked to Mueller; yes, he had talked with a few Republican electors, but he had no idea of what they might do; no, he'd given no thought to which Republican Mueller should pick; no, he doubted that he, Walter York, was the one. . . .

"That's enough," Connor Doyle said. "Oates! Where the hell are you?"

"Right here," the House Republican parliamentarian said brightly. "My, this *is* a day for the history books, isn't it?"

"I'll tell you what day it is, Harold. It's a day to get on the goddamn phone, get every nerd at the Congressional Research Service you know into the law libraries, and start finding out what the law says about what can and can't be done about any of this. Can we do anything about an elector who won't vote for the party's nominees? If we can't, can anybody else? What about the governors? What about the Congress?"

"If I remember right," said Alan Veigle, "this is the part in the Godzilla movies where they figure out that they can't kill the monster with nuclear weapons."

"And then . . . ?" asked a Young Blue Suit.

Alan Veigle smiled.

"Then he eats Yokohama for lunch."

THIRTY-THREE

★ ★ ★

By the time Walter York had stepped down from the raised platform in the auditorium of the York Institute, the following acts had been taken by the men and women gathered in the network's command post on the seventh floor of the Washington bureau:

- The news division president had called the network president and asked for clearance for an indefinite time to cover the story. Informed by the network president of the cost in lost dollars, the news division president suggested to the network president that he convert that sum into nickels and quarters and store them in a highly unusual place. The time was cleared.
- Ken Crenshaw, the producer of special events, told the director of the Bureau of Technical Operations that he did not care how much time the other networks and news organizations had already booked, he didn't care what the Comsat and the K-Band people were saying about no transponder space available, he wanted microwave and satellite linkups with affiliates in all fifty state capitals within fifteen minutes, or he would personally see to it that every last employee of the BTO, union or otherwise, would never be employed by the network at any level higher than a weekend security guard.
- The head of news research sent every available body to the law libraries of George Washington University armed with cellular phones and laptop computers equipped with internal fax-modems, to start gath-

ering every scrap of information about the way states regulated their electoral machinery, a field of law that had been so monumentally inconsequential for so long even the public relations officers of the universities, normally given to near-orgasmic pleasure at the mere possibility of placing one of their faculty on a television talk show, had to mumble apologetically when asked for names.

• Anchor Ed Steele, whose wardrobe had been flown to Washington by chartered Lear Jet, and which now occupied the entire office of the assistant travel manager, was seated in a high-backed conference chair, legs stretched out before him, feet propped up on the conference table, twirling a $7,500 solid gold fountain pen in his fingers, while his executive assistant and a nervous young man from the network's legal affairs division quietly, urgently briefed him on the nuances of constitutional law. He appeared vaguely distracted, at times indifferent; but during the next five hours of continuous news coverage, the Anchor flawlessly touched on almost every point the two covered.

("What is it, a trick?" the lawyer later asked the executive assistant. "Is it like a photographic memory for words, or like those idiot savants who can't tie their shoes but can multiply hundreds of numbers in their heads?"

"Much simpler than that," said the executive assistant. "When they absolutely *have* to be better than anybody else, they are; it's how they get there, it's how they stay there.")

• The Distinguished Commentator suggested, in the *strongest possible* terms, that he be moved on set next to the Anchor, the better to provide instant context, perspective, analysis. This was the biggest political story of the *century,* maybe *ever.* It was a time for a cool voice of reason, from someone who knew the town inside and out.

"Here's the problem," said Rich Chapman, executive vice president for news, a man who did not work on the premise that a soft answer turneth away wrath. "Right now, we have no idea what the story is, or where it will break wide open next. We don't know whether fifty electors will follow Walter York, or three. We don't know whether there's a cabal brewing in Colorado, or Pennsylvania, or Kansas, or everywhere, or nowhere. And we don't know how to find out, or who to talk to, or whether Dorothy Ledger is having a nervous breakdown, or what Bill Mueller thinks about becoming President despite inconveniently losing the election. And we do not know what anybody might try to do to stop these electors from bolting the Republican ticket, or if they do, whether it'll hold up in court—provided the courts have anything to say about it.

"Now, under these circumstances, just how do you propose to provide context, perspective, and *goddamn fucking analysis?"*

• And Al DeRossa was starting to get scared, big time.

He had never been in combat, never been shot at, except for the time, very early in his newspaper days in Chicago, when a drunken off-duty cop accidentally shot his service revolver off in a bar and missed DeRossa's ear by five inches. And unlike his colleagues in dozens of other countries, neither the stories he used to write nor the comments he sometimes offered over the airwaves exposed him to any risk greater than a letter smeared with excrement, a threatening message on his voice mail, or temporary banishment from insider briefings. Working in politics, he'd realized a long time ago, was like being a sportswriter, only better: not only was it a game played within clear limits, but the game actually mattered. Along the way, DeRossa had developed a strong sense of respect for the men who'd gathered in Philadelphia two hundred–some years ago to hammer out the rules of the game. It had bent and buckled plenty of times when the winds of hysteria had kicked up . . . but it had not broken. It had produced plenty of Joe McCarthys, but never a Joseph Stalin. The only men on horseback that showed up when a new President took office were the ones riding in the inaugural parade.

But this one scared him—in good measure, thanks to Professor Leonard Griese. Before Griese could leave the network news bureau after his verbal coldcocking of Professor Muttle, DeRossa had signed him up as a paid consultant for the duration of the crisis.

("Two thousand dollars a day?" Griese had exclaimed. "I feel like a vulture, cashing in on all of this chaos."

"The chaos began before anybody ever heard of you," DeRossa had replied. "Just cash the checks and show up—and make sure your clothes are cleaned and pressed. You don't need to reinforce the stereotype.")

Even before Walter York's bombshell, Griese was painting a near-apocalyptic picture of what was coming.

"Let's just take one small example," he told DeRossa. "The Constitution is very clear about who has the power to decide how electors are chosen: it's the state legislatures. Nobody else. Not the Congress; not the governors; and not the *people.*"

"What do you mean, 'not the people'?" DeRossa said.

"Just what I said," Griese answered. "Legally, the legislatures could choose the electors all by themselves; or they could give the power to the governors; to the Alcohol Beverage Control Commission; or anyone else—anyone. It would be impossible politically, of course; the people would never stand for it—at least, not usually. But suppose something weird happens."

"Like if the guy who wins dies," DeRossa said dryly.

"Well, yes. Suppose Indiana or New Mexico decides that Foyle's death wipes out the electors' commissions. Suppose they appoint a whole new slate. Nobody quite knows what the Congress would have to say about that sort of thing."

"The *Congress?*" DeRossa said. "Didn't you just say it's completely up to the state legislatures how these people are picked?"

"Yes, I did," said Griese. "But the Congress has total power over how the votes are *counted.* When they meet that first week in January. You know about 1876, right? The 'Stolen Election'?"

"Yeah," DeRossa said, uncertainly. "Tilden-Hayes, right?"

"Yup. Three states send in disputed vote counts. If Tilden gets one—*one*—of those votes he wins. But the Congress forms a special commission, Hayes promises to end Reconstruction, all the southerners vote with him, he gets all the disputed votes, and he's President."

"Couldn't Tilden have gone to the Supreme Court?"

Griese shrugged.

"Back then, no way. Today, I'm sure it would have happened. In fact, with TV, I don't think the Congress could ever get away with anything like that. But that leads you right into another swamp. If the Constitution says the state legislatures have all the power, can they meet to disqualify an elector? Maybe yes, maybe no. What about *after* the people have voted, and an elector says he won't vote for the candidate he's pledged to? Can he be replaced? North Carolina says sure, the minute an elector casts a 'faithless' vote, the other electors can declare the vote null and void and replace him. Is that constitutional? Who knows?

"There's a New York State court decision—about fifty years old or so—that says the winning party could go to court and get a writ to *force* an elector to vote the way he promised. But most of us academics think that no matter what anybody says, the Constitution says they're free agents. And by the way—what about when an elector keeps his mouth shut, *then* goes to the state capitol and votes for somebody else? Can the state legislature void the vote? Can Congress refuse to count that kind of vote?"

Griese rubbed his hands together. DeRossa wondered whether it was out of anxiety or intellectual stimulation.

"And none of this, mind you, touches on the situation we've got right now, where none of these electors promised to vote for Block for President. Suppose they vote for Foyle—or somebody else—for President, and then vote for Block for Vice President. Couldn't they argue that's just what they promised to do?"

DeRossa suddenly remembered Freud's classic "examination dream," in which a student finds himself in a classroom, looking at a test in a subject he has never studied, in a language he doesn't understand.

"You must feel like Cassandra right now," DeRossa said.

"More like Jor-el," Griese said. "Don't look so surprised. I cut my teeth on *Superman* comics just the way everybody else did. I even saw the original movie. There's Jor-el, standing in front of Krypton's Council of Elders, telling them they'd better hurry up and build spaceships before the planet blows up, and do they listen? Of course not. So he was right. Big deal. He got blown up, too."

"You really think it could come to that?" DeRossa asked.

Before Griese could answer, the news president held up his hand.

"Quiet! It's Farrell up in New York—says it's an emergency. Put him on the box."

An assistant pressed a button on a sleek octagonal box on the center of the table, and Farrell's voice filled the room.

"You guys hear me?" he said.

"Yeah," Crenshaw answered, "but what the hell is the foreign editor doing in the middle of this story? We don't need what the man in Piccadilly thinks about—"

"Oh, right," said Farrell. "I'm sorry to bother you with this bit of trivia, but the Nikkei index has fallen twenty-seven hundred points in the first two hours of trading—that's about eleven percent of book value, and no sign of stopping. Tokyo says the government may order the Nikkei shut down—which would probably mean a wave of panic selling of every Japanese stock around the world. And I guess nobody cares that every central bank in Europe is waiting for the biggest run on the dollar since '71—probably worse."

"Because of the Block situation?" the news president asked.

"Better believe it," Farrell said.

"Why?" Crenshaw said.

"Nothing mysterious," said Farrell. "All those European zillionaires, all those South American plutocrats, all those Arab sheikhs and African despots and ex-Communist commissars, they've always kept their money right here in the good old U.S. of A., no matter what they said in public. Why? Because *we were the grown-ups.* Maybe they didn't like our music, or our culture, or our fast food, but they sure liked the way we paid our debts."

"Okay, Farrell, thanks." The news president cut the connection. "Anybody want the good news?" he said.

"Please," said DeRossa.

"I think we're gonna get a whole lot of airtime this week."

THIRTY-FOUR

★ ★ ★

"Well," Faith McCoy said to Dorothy Ledger. "Do you want the good news or the bad news?"

"Give me the bad news first," Dorothy said. "I was the kind of kid who always ate all my vegetables before dessert."

"Right," said Faith. "Scoot over to the other bed and let me stretch out a bit. Hunching over that damn phone threw my back out."

On the other side of the hotel room, Walter Ames, Jr., watched with intense curiosity as Ben Weinstock tapped on his laptop computer, which was plugged into a cellular phone no bigger than a small flashlight. Even as the foursome was sneaking out of their Washington hotel in search of a locale where the relentless media would be less likely to find them, Weinstock had been busying himself in the backseat of their taxicab, posting a new e-mail address for his allies out in cyberspace. By the time they had checked into two rooms at the Silver Spring Inn ("HBO, Pool, Free Local Calls"), Weinstock had made contact with two dozen invisible colleagues from one end of the country to the other. In the meantime, Faith McCoy had taken on the more mundane task of checking Dorothy Ledger's answering machine back home.

"Okay, first, the bad news. The bank has put you on unpaid leave; they say they're issuing a statement about your 'disturbing and unprofessional behavior.' Your friend Charles Berlin has gotten the State Republican Executive Committee to demand your resignation on grounds of disloyalty. They may have voted on this already. Also, your aunt called—she says she's going into the hospital for tests."

"She's probably asking her doctor to X-ray her nerves," Dorothy said. "Oh, Lord, I hope she's not really ill."

"She said two men from *Behind the Shades* tried to sneak into your house disguised as meter readers. She figured something was up when they opened their mouths—never heard an Australian accent in Grand Rapids, she said."

"I guess she must be okay," Dorothy said with a chuckle.

"Maybe not after you hear the next news," Faith warned. "There are at least two dozen calls from the media just in the last—when did you clear your last batch?"

"About an hour ago."

"Okay, then, just in the last hour. They want to know: (a) whether you were a patient at a drug-and-alcohol rehab center two years ago, (b) whether you had an intimate relationship with Charles Berlin, (c) whether you are hiding out now with your 'special woman friend'—hey, I guess that's me," Faith said.

Dorothy buried her head in her hands.

"For heaven's sakes, I'm a *Lutheran*—Missouri-Wisconsin synod to boot. This is *crazy.*"

"It'll pass. Now," Faith said, "here's the good news—sort of. Somebody named Lionel Schubert called. Says he wants to talk to you about a book."

"I know that name," Walter Ames, Jr., said. "He did all those jailhouse books—*The Butcher of San Jose, Hollywood Massacre,* you know."

"That's the guy," Faith said. "He says he can get you at least half a million, not counting the money from the nine-hundred number you could set up to tell your side of the story."

"That's the *good* news?" said Dorothy.

"Oh, it's only the beginning, sweetheart—you don't mind if I call you sweetheart after all we've been through, do you? Yes, indeed, tomorrow, if you so choose, you are cordially invited to appear on *Today, Good Morning, America, CBS Morning News, Good Day, New York, Good Day, Chicago, Good Day, Los Angeles*—maybe I should just skip the local morning shows, okay—so let's see, *Talkback Live, Inside Politics, Feedback, SpeakOut, Macneil-Lehrer,* all the evening news shows, *Equal Time, Hard Copy, Inside Edition, Current Affair, Beyond the Pale, Nightline, Late Night, Late Show, Wired,* . . . shall I go on?"

"This is still the good news, right?" said Dorothy.

"I haven't even gotten to the more . . . intimate offers," Faith said with a wicked smile. "Honestly, Dorothy, you folks back in Grand Rapids have been holding out on the rest of us. Two men called to tell you they've been *very* naughty boys. Two other men—and a woman, I think—called to say *you've* been a *very* naughty girl. Maybe you can guess what they had in mind. Then there are a few marriage proposals, invitations for weekends in Vegas and Disney World . . . you did say Missouri-Wisconsin synod, didn't you?"

Then Faith saw the look on Dorothy Ledger's face.

"I'm sorry, Dorothy. It must feel like a crazed mob chasing you down the streets with clubs and torches. At least they don't know where you are—yet. Maybe there's a way to see the humor in all this."

"Right," Dorothy said. "Let's see . . . the man I worked my heart out for gets elected President and he's dead four days later. The guy who's next in line turns out to be everything I despise in politicians, and men. I try to find out if there's anything I can legally do about my opinion, and I wind up hiding out in a hotel room. I can barely stop from laughing my head off."

Walter Ames, Jr., walked over and handed Dorothy a Coke.

"No Diet? No caffeine-free?" she asked.

"Come on, Dorothy, you're going to need all the cheap energy you can find," said Walter Ames, Jr. "If Ben's e-mail is any indication, there are lots of folks out there who are waiting to hear from you."

Weinstock walked over and turned the screen of his laptop to face Dorothy.

"Let me tell you what I've been doing," he said eagerly.

"No cyberspeak," Faith McCoy said. "Nobody here but us liberal-arts types."

"Business administration," said Dorothy.

"It's a joke, honey, chill just a bit."

"She's right," said Walter Ames, Jr. "I can do my inventory and my accounts and that's about it."

"Okay. First, I set up a triple-blind mail drop—sorry, sorry. Let me think about this in plain English. Okay; it's like if someone would mail you a letter at an address, and then the letter was sent to a second address, then another one, in a way that no one could possibly follow the letter. Well, it's the same thing, only with a computer. All of this e-mail gets kicked to San Diego, then Macao—"

"Macao? Near *China?"* Ames said.

"Sure," said Weinstock. "It doesn't matter. Once you're on the web, it doesn't cost any more to zap the stuff down the street or around the world. Then from Macao, it comes right back here," he said, patting his laptop with obvious affection. "But if anybody should happen to start looking for communications to you, it would take them quite awhile to link you up with Benwa.@web.zapata." He grinned shyly. "My e-mail address. If you know what benwa balls are, you'll know why any snoop would think this was a weird sex forum."

"Forget it," Faith said to Dorothy. "Missouri-Wisconsin synod, remember?"

"Okay," Ben went on. "I also asked some of my more politically minded friends to try to surf the web for presidential electors. You'd be amazed, Dorothy," he said. "There are half a dozen Dorothy Ledger news groups, bulletin boards—lots of argument about you, Dorothy. But the big news is, my buddies have managed to make contact with twenty or so real, live Republican electors, and about the same number of Democrats, if that means anything to you."

"I don't know what anything means anymore," said Dorothy. "What do they want?"

"Why, they want to hear what you want them to do," Ben Weinstock said.

"Right on!" Faith McCoy said, jumping to her feet and dancing around the cramped hotel room.

"Oh, this is wonderful! This is absolutely spectacular! Don't you get it, Dorothy? You're the fantasy of all my academic revolutionary friends turned inside out! The delicious *irony* of it all! Inside their bleeding hearts they've nurtured their revolutionary wet dreams all these years . . . the sixties would *live* again! They would all be young again—trashing the administration building, seizing the dean's office, balling the night away in the library stacks with Janis screaming her sweet heart out on the P.A. system.

"And who shows up to turn the system on its ear? Who rises from the heartland to speak truth to power? Our 'Pasionaria' of the Infobahn! Our taxpaying, casserole-cooking, law-abiding Republican with a picture of Ronald Reagan close to her heart! God, I'd love to be back on campus, listening to those tenured Maoists gnash their teeth."

Dorothy looked at Faith with her mouth agape.

"Does it bother you," she finally said, "that I don't have a clue what you're saying?"

"Not a bit," Faith said. "That's what makes this country great—tens of millions of people who haven't any idea what their fellow citizens are talking about, and don't really care. Any other culture, they'd be at each other's throats.

"Forget it," Faith said, moving to Dorothy and clasping her left hand with both of hers. "The point is, you touched something out there. You had a nice, scripted part you were supposed to play, and instead you stood up and said no! You weren't nasty, you didn't say 'fuck you!', you didn't set fire to anything or shoot anybody—you just said no. So now they want to hear what you have to say next."

"That sounds right to me," said Walter Ames, Jr. "They think you speak for them. They want to know whether you're going to follow Walter York and vote for Bill Mueller, or whether you're going to try to deadlock the electoral college and let the Congress pick the President, or whether you've got another candidate in mind."

"This is *nuts!*" Dorothy yelped. "I don't want to tell *anybody* what to do. I want somebody to tell *me* what to do!"

"Okay," Faith McCoy said. "So we have to think." She reached into her bag, pushed several pounds of contents one way and then the other, shut the bag with a brief oath, and looked up beseechingly.

"Anybody got a cigarette? Oh, c'mon, we're *Republicans,* it's allowed."

"Sorry," said Walter Ames, Jr. "Even Republicans have lungs."

"Smoke makes my eyes gag," said Ben Weinstock. "Besides," he said, gesturing to the computer, "it can really screw up the drives."

"Okay, forget it," she said, reaching for a bag of corn chips. "This much we do know. If you don't want Ted Block to be President, you have to deny him a majority in the electoral college. That means you *can't* vote for Foyle—even as a tribute or whatever—because the Congress could decide not to count those votes, and require that Block only get a majority of *valid* electoral votes. They might do that, they might not, but you don't want to take the chance."

"Okay," Dorothy said, "that's clear."

"And you have to make it clear to them that they can't vote for Mueller. We have no idea whether anybody's going to follow Walter York, but we have to assume he'll persuade some of the Republicans to jump the fence. Do you want that to happen? Do you want Mueller to be President?"

"Me, help the Democrats take the White House?" said Dorothy. "God would strike me dead."

"Okay—so no votes for Mueller. We have to get that word out."

"But that's not enough," Ben Weinstock said. "Not according to what my buddies have said. If you tie up the electoral college, it goes to the Congress, all right—but they only get to choose among the top three finishers. That means it's critical to figure out who you *do* want, so that he, she, whatever, can be in the running when the House meets."

Dorothy Ledger began to chuckle.

"Oh, yes, this is where I always thought I'd be someday: overthrowing the government with a telephone, a laptop computer, and three lunatics—I mean, four."

"That's my girl," said Faith McCoy. She took another handful of chips, then slapped her left flank sharply.

"I don't know if the country's going to survive all this," she said, "but this butt of mine's a goner."

PART THREE

MERE ANARCHY IS LOOSED . . .

THIRTY-FIVE

★ ★ ★

The signs were everywhere: the American body politic, once the Charles Atlas on the world's beach, was now starting to display the unmistakable signs of a breakdown.

- In Fargo, North Dakota, longtime Republican Party official and presidential elector Elmer Sidell was having a cup of coffee at the Cafe de Bistro with his old friend and fellow Elk, Parker Lundine. Mr. Sidell expressed to Mr. Lundine his uncertain opinion of Theodore Block's presidential qualities. Counterman Wellesley Mundt, whose hostility to Mr. Sidell wound back through the years to a brief high school brawl, called his state senator to warn him that Mr. Sidell was "talking betrayal." Armed with a hastily acquired understanding of the law, the state senator telephoned Sheriff Edgar Winokur, demanding that the sheriff serve Mr. Sidell with a writ of mandamus, commanding him to cast his electoral vote for the candidates of the Republican Party.

Mr. Sidell, who had every intention of doing just that, inquired of Sheriff Winokur whether he was under the impression that he was an official of the former Soviet Union. Mr. Winokur, in turn, demanded to know whether Mr. Sidell was calling him a Communist. Upon being informed that if the shoe fit, he should wear it, Sheriff Winokur engaged in a lengthy series of blows with Mr. Sidell, resulting in two bloody noses, a broken wrist, several injured ribs, a charge (dismissed by the Justice of the Peace and fishing buddy of Mr. Sidell's), and a lawsuit that dragged on for four and a half years.

• Among the most prestigious newspapers and news magazines, a feverish competition broke out to see which of these mighty organs of communication could offer the most comprehensive possible account of the current crisis.

The *New York Times* provided readers with a twenty-four-page insert, entitled "American Dilemma," featuring short essays by seventy-five prominent writers, intellectuals, politicians, and performance artists, from every conceivable angle ("Founding Fathers' Flaws—A Latino Perspective"). The *Washington Post* provided a breakdown of the potential votes of every member of the House and Senate should the contests for President and Vice President be thrown into the Congress ("Outcome Uncertain, Experts Agree"). The *Wall Street Journal* published the longest editorial in its history, asserting that the crisis was rooted in the moral sewer of the 1960s, and the tyrannously high marginal income-tax rates. And the *Los Angeles Times* on Sunday published a 125,000-word account of the crisis—a story that began on page 1, then jumped to pages 12, 13, 16, 22, 24, 26, 37, 39, 44, 45, 51, and 55–59. One irate reader responded by calling the paper's "Readerline" and reciting the entire article into the paper's voice-mail system, disabling it for six hours.

• The speaker of the California State Assembly called the body into special session, in order to pass the Emergency Voting Rights Protection Act, requiring all electors to sign a loyalty oath or forfeit their offices immediately. Berkeley assemblyman Kwami X (original name Richard Fleischer, who had taken his new name as an act of solidarity with all oppressed people) and three fellow progressives launched a three-day filibuster, arguing that the post-election oath amounted to an ex post facto law, as well as a blatant attack on the First, Ninth, Thirteenth, Fourteenth, Nineteenth, Twenty-fifth, Twenty-sixth, and Twenty-seventh amendments. The filibuster ended when Kwami X and his colleagues were forcibly removed from the chamber in Sacramento, as five thousand protesters were swept from the steps of the capitol with fire hoses. The assembly and the state senate then passed the bill, which was immediately vetoed by the governor. The assembly speaker then asserted that, under Article II of the U.S. Constitution, only the legislatures had power to choose the electors, and therefore the governor's veto was void. When the American Civil Liberties Union filed suit in federal court, both the governor *and* the speaker argued that the federal courts had no jurisdiction over the matter at all.

- The Alabama State Legislature passed similar legislation with far less dispute, a result foreordained when Governor Earl Blessingame ordered the National Guard to ring the capitol as a symbol of his determination to act forcefully if anyone attempted to thwart the will of the people and install a left-wing proto-socialist Democratic presidential wannabe who had been rejected by the voters. The gesture had a tragic outcome; seeing the live television coverage, Aryan survivalist Bo Pepperdane instantly concluded that the long-prophesied Illuminati Conspiracy to seize the United States had come to pass. He drove to the capitol with his fourteen-year-old twins, three AK-47s, and fifteen hundred rounds of ammunition. Pepperdane and his sons shot and wounded three Guardsmen before being cut down in a hail of bullets.
- The New York Stock Exchange shut down for forty-eight hours following the collapse of the Nikkei index and the run on the dollar. When it reopened, it lost 150 points in the first twenty-five minutes before trading was suspended again. On the unregulated world markets, the price of gold jumped $150 an ounce in a day; at the request of the White House, Wilbur Mullett, the folksy, homespun investor genius, gave a rare press conference from the front porch of his family home in Muncie, Indiana. When asked to offer the ritual vote of confidence in the market, Mullett laughed, shook his head, and said, "I'm damn sure glad I'm liquid." The market remained closed. In working-class neighborhoods of Buffalo, Pittsburgh, and Cleveland, there were brief runs on local branches of large banks. After those runs, and with no public announcement whatsoever, four small government jets were kept on standby alert at Andrews Air Force Base, each loaded with $37 million in currency.

• The President addressed the nation, appealing for calm, and assuring his fellow citizens that the country's political institutions were rock solid, and that whatever temporary upheaval there might be, the Constitution was more than adequate to carry out the task. The President's remarks were somewhat undercut when the public learned that the chief executive's health was so poor that the remarks had to be taped and heavily edited, and that the President had been flown to the estate of a close friend in Coral Gables, Florida.

• Al DeRossa was asked to moderate a conversation among half a dozen members of the House of Representatives, in an attempt to explain to viewers what might happen should the election be thrown into the House.

Representative Alice Carruthers of New York said she planned to vote the way the voters of her congressional district did, since that was who she represented.

Representative Mike McPhee of Missouri believed he was morally obligated to follow the will of the voters of the State of Missouri.

Representatives "Ace" Stoker of Louisiana and Martha Lewis of Vermont believed they should cast their vote in accord with the *national* popular vote.

Representative Lou Abbott of Ohio agreed, but said that, since Governor Block had not been on the national ballot for President, he would cast his vote based on an average of the national public opinion polls taken closest to the vote in the House.

To that, twenty-three-term representative Carroll Garden suggested that Representative Abbott be named House chaplain, since he was acting with all the moral courage of the Vicar of Bray. No harsh words followed, since the twenty-nine-year-old Abbott, a product of the nation's contemporary public education system, believed that Representative Garden was paying him a compliment.

And through all of this confusion, Sharon Kramer and Joe Featherstone sat in their campaign offices, and spent twenty-hour days trying to figure out what in heaven's name they were supposed to do next.

For Featherstone, the task was to keep the possibility of a Mueller presidency alive without permitting the slightest inference that Mueller or the Democrats were trying to pull off an American version of a coup. In the wake of Walter York's bombshell announcement, Mueller had refused even to appear before the television cameras, instead issuing a brief written statement, fully translatable only by reading between the lines.

"The American people gave Senator Foyle their votes," the statement said. [*I know how to lose gracefully.*] "I respect and honor those results [*ditto*] and I mourn the tragic events that thwarted the will of the people. [*In your wildest dreams, you never even imagined that stumblebum Block would be President, did you, folks?*] It is now critically important that the constitutional process go forward [*Let's permit those fine electors to vote for the very best man they can find*], so that whatever the result, we remain the strongest, most stable, free, and independent nation on earth." [*Just like those electors were meant to be free and independent, right?*]

What gave Featherstone heart was that the utter unfamiliarity of the terrain made any argument at least worth hearing. Even the regular Sunday talking heads, who skipped from currency reform to Southeast Asian politics, to African crop-rotation strategy, to abortion, based on a thirty-minute Nexis search, were slogging through completely unfamiliar terrain. The arguments had not been diced, sliced, extruded, and re-formed into conveniently sized aphorisms and insights; this time, people really had to *think* about what they thought, a process that proved quite daunting among many of Washington's best-known faces and voices.

Was it really unthinkable that we might have a President who lost the popular vote?

"Not at all," said Walter York, who was rapidly becoming a fixture on television talk shows. "In fact, many of our leaders were actually minority Presidents, in the sense that more people voted for other candidates: Woodrow Wilson, Harry Truman, Richard Nixon, Bill Clinton. . . ."

"It's absolutely true that Bill Mueller was not the choice of the American people," said Senator Adrian O'Donnell. "But was Ted Block the choice of the American people?"

It was enough to draw dozens of Mueller campaign workers back to the cavernous campaign headquarters, now littered with cardboard cartons and the wretched refuse of a thousand pizza deliveries. Oddly, a surprisingly large number of anonymous cash contributions had appeared at Mueller's campaign offices, a sum big enough to turn on the lights and the telephones.

("Shouldn't we report this?" asked the campaign's chief accountant."

"Report what? To whom?" Mueller had replied. "The campaign's over. There's no transition. The hell with it.")

Instead, the staff spent most of its time phoning in to talk shows around the nation, faxing letters to newspapers around the country, and swapping rumors.

In a formal sense, they had nothing to do, nowhere to go. But if the political version of a nuclear bomb went off, they wanted to be right there at ground zero.

And a few miles away, at Foyle-Block headquarters, Sharon Kramer went about the business of preservation in something of a daze. In the large first-floor bullpen, a huge banner reading "We Did It!" still hung limply from one pillar. Four huge cardboard boxes labeled Résumés sat atop a large folding table. More than five thousand had arrived *after* Foyle's fall from grace, mailed before he had stepped out onto that Cheyenne street in search of the perfect post-election photo op. Overhanging the room was a huge black-and-white portrait of Foyle, draped in black, with another oversized photo of Theodore Block now peering down on the room.

Along with Marsh and Alan Veigle, Sharon had listened as Connor Doyle explained their task.

"For the next two weeks," he said, "you must reduce the political vocabulary of the United States to these words and phrases: 'the people's will'; 'fair play'; 'betraying their trust'; 'political treason.' This has got to be communication through the gut. 'America chose Foyle; Foyle chose Block.' If there's any money we can scrape up, I want an ad campaign running within thirty-six hours; I want to see those Americans raising the flag at Iwo Jima, and dead soldiers on the beach, with something like, 'They Died for Your Right to Vote; Don't Let Them Take It Away.' We have to make the very thought of any other outcome absolutely un-

American. Oh, and one other thing—no more 'Ted' or 'Teddy.' From now on, it's *'Governor* Block.' We have to remind people that not so long ago, he was a reasonably respected politician. Right now, half the voters think the first thing Block said to Foyle was, 'You want fries with that?' "

They had gotten those ads out, all right, and the Republican partisans were rolling out their rhetorical clubs and rocks as well.

"This is the end of the twentieth century, not the eighteenth," argued ex-governor W. B. Spackle of Texas, who had chaired Democrats for Foyle during the campaign. "We can't possibly be serious about letting a handful of nonentities erase fifty-three million votes!"

"Are we serious," said Connor Doyle, "about overturning an election in which one hundred ten million Americans voted because of a tragic accident that happened to fall at the wrong time in the electoral cycle?"

At times, Sharon found herself utterly unable to believe this was happening. How was she, or anyone else, supposed to run an "election" when the only people who could vote were a few hundred people nobody had ever heard of? Wasn't anyone thinking about the minor problem of forming a new government? Not that many days ago, she had been flying back from the Caribbean with the President-to-be by her side; visions of Cabinets and White House staffs had danced in her head. Now even to think of the normal business of a transition might seem like an act of arrogance to a nation that wasn't all that sure that Governor Block was even going to *be* the President.

Of course, the more the tumult and the shouting went on, the greater the chance of renewed panic and financial bloodletting.

In which case, she thought as she reached to answer the phone for the hundredth time in the last hour and a half, *the White House wouldn't be worth that famous warm pitcher of . . .*

"Connor Doyle on line two."

"Yes, Connor, it's Sharon."

"Can you be here in fifteen minutes? I think we may have figured out how to cap this thing."

"Really?" Sharon said. "Does it involve the use of a nuclear warhead?"

She was surprised at how hard he laughed.

"Actually, Oates has been calling it 'The Fifty Megaton Option.' "

"That dangerous?" Sharon said.

"I hope that powerful," said Connor. "I'm not the melodramatic type, but I don't think we're talking about winning the White House anymore. Now I think we're talking about saving the country. You understand what I'm saying? *Saving the country."*

As she rushed out of the room for the Capitol, Sharon realized that she had just heard a powerful American politician speaking an entire sentence of absolute, unadorned, complete emotional authenticity.

It was the most terrifying thing she had ever heard.

THIRTY-SIX

★ ★ ★

It was the first Friday in December, five days before the members of the electoral college were due to appear in their state capitols to choose the next President of the United States, and three days before the post-election session of the United States Congress was due to convene. Connor Doyle and the Senate majority leader were holding an emergency meeting with the Speaker of the House, the Senate minority leader, the secretary of the treasury, and the chairman of the Federal Reserve Board. They gathered in the ornate offices of the Speaker at six o'clock in the morning, along with Sharon Kramer, Alan Veigle, Marsh, and Harold Oates, all of them sworn to total and absolute secrecy.

By 6:20 A.M., thirty-seven reporters and fourteen camera crews were surrounding the Speaker's office.

Whatever was said inside the meeting, it was enough to fuse the congressional leaders into a united front. At 10:30 A.M., the four top House and Senate leaders invited the press into the Speaker's lobby, where for only the second time in history, live television coverage was permitted, as a grave Speaker Topper Huggins, flanked by the entire congressional leadership from both parties, announced that "the first act of business in the new Congress will be the consideration of the Emergency Presidential Election Voting Rights Protection Act."

Under the law, the Speaker explained, electors would be forbidden to cast a vote for candidates other than the nominees of the political party under whose banner they ran.

"In other words," the Speaker ad-libbed, "this law would regard a 'faithless' electoral vote as the same kind of act as blocking the entrance to the registrar's office, or trying to physically harm a voter on the way to the polls."

Further, the Speaker explained, the law would authorize electors in every state, by majority vote, to nullify any "unlawful" vote, and to appoint immediately a replacement elector. Congress, the Speaker concluded, would regard all "faithless" votes as not "regularly given."

"That means they will not be counted," Topper explained.

Having been presented with a carefully crafted, dramatic, constitutionally challenging proposal to resolve the most serious domestic crisis since the Civil War, the assembled Washington press corps homed in directly on the profound questions of constitutional powers and governance.

"Mr. Speaker, does this mean that you believe Governor Block would not now receive an electoral majority?"

"What promises have been made to you by Governor Block or the Republican congressional leadership in exchange for your support?"

"What do you say, Mr. Speaker, to those who will regard today's statement as a betrayal of Bill Mueller—your party's designated nominee for President?"

"Could you tell us how you arrived at this decision? Who was in the room? Who chaired the meeting? Were food and drinks served?"

"Don't you regard this as an ex post facto law?"

Indignant heads whirled around to stare down the last questioner: Casey Davis, a twenty-seven-year-old reporter for a congressional news wire who had attended law school for a year.

"Let me take that question," said Connor Doyle, "since it seems to be the only one of substance on the table right now. Obviously, we're not talking about punishing past behavior. What we're talking about now is regulating the conduct of electors who *haven't done anything yet.* They've simply been chosen to vote. Now, this law will tell them the rules under which they will vote. Okay?"

A chorus of other questions followed:

"What commitments has Governor Block made to you, Mr. Majority Leader, for including Democrats in his Cabinet?"

"Can we expect that as President, Governor Block would support your efforts for legalized gambling in National Parks?"

The press conference ended, and the networks began their briefings with their respective talking heads, with ANN's Dr. Sherman Gelt declaring that the leaders had "thrown a Hail Mary pass that looks a lot like Joe Montana hitting Jerry Rice in the end zone—it may well bring the curtain down on this Superbowl of political melodrama."

"What do you think?" Al DeRossa asked Professor Leonard Griese as they sat over coffee in the cafeteria. Griese, DeRossa noted, had shed his dusty tweed sports jacket and chinos for a muted blue Bucatina jacket, a wide-striped tab-collared dress shirt, and a Natalie Michael hand-painted floral tie. "Nice threads, by the way."

"Oh, thanks," Griese responded, with a distinct blush. "One of my . . . colleagues . . . graduate student, actually . . . suggested, um . . ."

"Hey, whatever; I just hope you don't wind up being chased across campus by a camera crew if you get sued for harassment."

Griese's blush deepened.

"Well, no . . . it's . . . to get back to your question—I don't know if it's constitutional, I don't know if you could make an argument that the electors were chosen under at least a technical understanding that they could cast a free vote for President, but I think the bill could work; right now, I can't imagine what could stop it."

But nobody had to imagine United States Senator Billy Doggs of Tennessee. He was on Interstate 95, somewhere between Jackson, North Carolina, and Richmond, Virginia, at the wheel of a 1983 Chevrolet Nova when he heard the press conference; and he damn near swerved right into the path of a speeding Crunchin' Chips semi, he was so angry at what he heard. And when Senator Billy Doggs got angry, which usually happened between five and twelve times a week, the earth trembled.

Billy Doggs was a child of the Tennessee hill country, the eighth son of a railroad track–repair foreman who had left home at fifteen and spent his youth traveling with a succession of vacuum-cleaner salesmen, circuit-riding evangelists, and repo men, who reclaimed furniture and household appliances bought on time. His gift for gab had caught the ear of the owner of a string of small-town radio stations, who'd signed up the twenty-year-old as an announcer, disk jockey, and daytime personality. Boggs had been a hit from the start, offering recipes for rhubarb pie, homegrown remedies for colds, fevers, and the monthly miseries, even singing a lick or two from songs he'd learned as a child. Within a year, Doggs had become known as "the Arthur Godfrey of the Volunteer State," and moved over to the still-new medium of TV as well.

It soon became clear that underneath the affable exterior of Billy Doggs beat the heart of a true son of the Confederacy. When the civil rights movement began to pick up steam, Doggs began to salt his record introductions and weather reports with caustic comments about the Supreme Court, guilelessly ignorant coloreds in the service of New York agitators with unpronounceable names, and the network news programs. The station owner soon moved Billy Doggs to a regular spot on the local radio and TV newscasts, which provided a perfect springboard into the United States Senate.

Once in the Senate, Billy Doggs became one of the most polarizing figures on the national scene. Beneath the surface—his face was gray, his hair combed straight back in a pompadour held in place by Wildroot Hair Tonic, the bags under his rheumy brown eyes were big enough to carry a week's worth of groceries, his teeth were permanently stained from forty-eight years' worth of chain-smoking unfiltered Chesterfields—beat the heart of an authentic zealot. Doggs thought nothing of holding his fellow senators hostage for hours-long diatribes against all of the forces of collectivism, moral relativism, federal arrogance, cultural barbarism, and globalism that were threatening the good people of Tennessee and the rest of America. He pulled no punches. When denouncing the culture of permissiveness, Doggs declared on the Senate floor, "God's handwriting is on the wall, and it's spelling out A-I-D-S."

Senator Billy Doggs was, in fact, a classic leader of the Resentment Party, which had proclaimed from the very birth of the United States that the nation was under siege from enemies of infinite cunning, evil, and power. And it did not matter whether the agents of intrigue and deception called themselves liberal Democrats or conservative Republicans. Billy Doggs was absolutely incorruptible in his vigilance. He would make no deals with the devil no matter what cloak the devil wore.

And now Senator Billy Doggs heard a new threat, from a new quarter.

From the center of federal power came a proposal for a law to take one of the Constitution's fundamental commitments to state autonomy—the power to supervise the choice of presidential electors—and wrest it from the states, placing total authority in the hands of federal officials, federal judges, federal agents. And for what? For the rise to power of a wellborn blue-blooded son of the American aristocracy!

By noon, Senator Doggs had parked his car in the capacious lot of the Rebel Yell Home Cookery off Interstate 95, just south of Cumberland, Virginia, polished off the $4.95 blue-plate special (pork chops, mashed potatoes and gravy, wax beans, brown Betty), lit up a Chesterfield, pulled a chair over to the pay phone, and dialed up Paul Shwinn, the talk-show host whose nationally syndicated midday program was heard on 650 stations coast to coast, and where Billy Doggs always had an open microphone waiting for him.

"It's crystal clear to me that the leaders in Congress mean well," Doggs began, "but you know what road is paved with good intentions. The sad fact is, liberty is always the first casualty when a crisis leads to a hasty decision. In this case, we're talking about the most outrageous act of federal usurpation since the Supreme Court took God out of the public schools—the idea that we need to rip apart the whole delicate balance of the United States Constitution to prevent the process from going forward would be funny if it weren't so sad—and so frightening."

Senator Doggs might as well have shot off a starter's pistol, as far as the members of the Resentment Party were concerned. By sundown, the Capitol switchboards and fax lines were hopelessly jammed; Mailgrams by the tens of thousands were flooding the post offices of Washington. Cable call-in shows were receiving so many communications that the long-line divisions of four major long-distance companies announced they were suspending all traffic until midnight. And the ANN's Dr. Sherman Gelt was now shaking his head and commenting that "what had seemed at first to some so-called experts as a brilliant stroke to cauterize the political wound of uncertainty now looks like a clumsy stumble by a band of political quacks that accidentally poured salt into that now–rapidly abscessing wound."

"All right, it's a bad hit, I grant you," Connor Doyle was saying to the half dozen people grouped around him in the presidential suite of the Shoreham American. "Maybe it's God's punishment for letting that primate lead the charge for us so many times. I mean, we liked him when Doggs was talking about how the Democrats could use a good shot of testosterone, didn't we?"

"So what do you figure?" Marsh asked. He looked white enough to be admitted to the cardiac care unit of any major hospital.

"Well," Connor Doyle said with a sigh, "there'll be blood all over the floor, but I think we can do it. We can wire the House with a closed rule—Speaker says it's okay as long as we Republicans are out front on it—and that'll be that. A lot of screaming, a lot of scars, but it's doable.

"The Senate? If they try to invoke cloture, shut off any filibuster, after two hours or so, I think it'll come down to two or three votes. But with the right deals, I think we can squeak by. I wouldn't necessarily want to try to get tough on 'needless pork' in the next federal budget"—Connor shrugged, with a nod to the tall, lean man sitting to his right—"but I think we can make it happen."

"Don't do it," said Theodore Block.

He was smiling, but shaking his head slowly, firmly.

"I beg your pardon, Governor?" said Connor Doyle.

"Don't do it. I'm no fan of Senator Doggs, but he's right about one thing: you don't go fidoodling around with the Constitution just because it makes life difficult. My dad was very big about that: 'Maybe you bend with the wind, but you don't break in the wind.' "

"Speaking of breaking wind . . . ," whispered Alan Veigle.

"The best ideas aren't always all that popular," Block went on. "It doesn't mean they're bad. I don't know about you, but I think the folks who wrote the Constitution did a pretty impressive job. . . ."

"Of course he thinks that," Alan Veigle said. "He's related to half of them."

"So I suggest, Connor, that you and the other boys in Congress just pack it in—say you know you can't get the legislation that would just add to the ill feeling already out there, that there's too much suspicion and bad vibes out there already. And then you'll just withdraw the bill, and we'll all pick ourselves up, dust ourselves off, and get back to fighting with the rules of the game we were given. Besides," he added, "I'd hate to think of becoming President owing half the gold in Fort Knox to a bunch of hustlers."

"You understand what you're saying, Governor," Sharon Kramer said. "It means we have to fight on fifty, maybe a hundred fronts, against enemies we can't see. And it could wind up costing you the presidency."

"But I'll sleep at night," Block said, with an indulgent smile.

That's good, Sharon thought. *Because for the next five days, none of us will.*

THIRTY-SEVEN

★ ★ ★

Once the chance for a decisive end to the crisis had passed, the opening bell rang for what historians would come to call the "Great Turkish Bazaar." It was precisely what the Constitution had been crafted to minimize, not just in the selection of the President, but in the operation of the national government. "Factions," James Madison had called them in the most famous of all the Federalist Papers, those groups "who are united and actuated by some common impulse of passion or of interest, adverse to the rights of other citizens, or to the permanent and aggregate interests of the community."

Madison and his colleagues thought they'd designed a government to keep those factions—"special interests," as they are called these days—in check. But after decades of a political process driven more and more by organized money and power, it had become the norm for voters to think of themselves as an interest group; indeed, the most deserving of all interest groups. So it was inevitable that the spirit of faction began to infect a substantial number of presidential electors. They had been around long enough to understand that, in a political sense, they were the owners of a tiny plot of useless land that just happened to be smack in the middle of the 100,000 acres that Gargantua Enterprises was hoping to turn into the world's third-largest indoor mall.

And, as Professor Griese said to Al DeRossa, "Why would it occur to them to not use that power?"

"Maybe they'd think about what's been happening to the country,"

DeRossa offered. "And what will happen if we don't find some way out of this."

"I see," said Professor Griese. "You want them to restrain themselves, to put aside this unbelievable clout on behalf of some abstraction called 'the common good.' Is that it?"

"Okay, something like that," DeRossa said. Griese laughed out loud.

"Let's get real here, Al. We've been pandered to, coddled, frightened, soothed, and bribed on the basis of how we pray, our tax brackets, where our grandparents came from, what we do for a living, you name it. So why shouldn't a bunch of people who suddenly find themselves with all this power think any other way?"

And so they did:

- Four Republican electors from Wyoming and Idaho appeared at a press conference called by the Federalist Land-Use Association. They declared their "present intention" to vote for Governor Block—but pointedly asked for a "commitment written in stone" to abolish all federal restrictions on logging and grazing on publicly owned western lands.
- Seven Republican electors from California and Florida were flown to Washington by the American Life Support Coalition, to express their "confidence" that Block and Phelps would stand by the right-to-life platform of the Republican Party and the campaign pledges of the late MacArthur Foyle, and to express their support for the ticket "on the basis of that understanding." Three hours later, four Republican electors from New England announced their "deep concern at the prospect of the next President turning back the clock on a woman's right to choose. We will," they concluded, "be no part of any such effort." They refused to expand on this last comment.
- From Washington State, two Democratic electors flew to Los Angeles, to stand with three hundred of the movie industry's most famous stars at a luncheon of the Hollywood Human Rights Caucus. There, after an uplifting speech by the writer-director of the highly popular *Spatterguts* series, the two participated in a "Ceremony of Perpetual Commitment," exchanged rings, and demanded that Bill Mueller "earn the courageous support tendered to him by Walter York and publicly

declare that he would sign the Federal Human Rights Act, extending full civil rights protection to all people, regardless of sexual orientation or preference."

• At a "Satellite Town Meeting," organized and funded by the National Firearms Organization, nine Republican electors from the Great Plains and the Northwest unveiled a "Pledge of Allegiance to the Second Amendment," calling for a complete, total, and irreversible end to all federal restrictions on the right to keep and bear arms. Pointedly noting the "checkered record" of Block and Phelps on this "life-and-death" issue, they demanded that the Republican nominees earn their electoral votes by signing the pledge, in front of the press, and in the presence of a notary public.

The sheer press of events was beginning to take its toll on the most hardened veterans of news coverage. At the network's control room in Washington one day, Ken Crenshaw was trying to coordinate the coverage of three electoral press conferences, while fending off the sharp buzzing of the red phone directly over his head. The phone was linked to the offices of the network president, who was undoubtedly demanding that the news division let the goddamn soap operas on the air once, just *once,* without cutting into the critical first five minutes of plot development. The satellite link to Phoenix was down, the computer graphics were coughing up slides from the last Olympics—and then news vice president Dorian Wood walked into the control room, an enthusiastic smile on his face.

"God, this is *wonderful*!" Wood said, beaming, to no one in particular, as he bounded up and down on the balls of his feet. "I haven't seen anything like this since October of '64. You will remember, I take it, that we had a presidential election, a coup in the Soviet Union, a Chinese nuclear bomb, a World Series . . . I mean, those bells were going off, *auuughh*!"

Dorian Wood found himself pinned against the glass wall of the control room by Ken Crenshaw. On the other side of the glass, a public relations functionary, taking a television critic on a tour of the bureau for an in-depth piece on news crisis management for *Video Week,* barely managed to avoid disaster by hurriedly whisking the critic down the hall for a look at the network's three-dimensional model of the United States that they would soon deploy to cover the electoral count.

"Listen to me, you desiccated turd," Ken Crenshaw hissed at Wood, his face barely two inches from Wood's. "Nobody *gives* a shit—do you hear me, nobody *gives* a shit about the time you gave Edward Murrow a light, or what Eisenhower said to you, or your goddamn stories about the time you got pissed on by a police dog when you covered Martin Luther King in Birmingham. Okay?"

Crenshaw began to pound Dorian Wood into the wall to punctuate his points.

"There are giant cracks opening up on the Earth's surface right now, okay? A spaceship bearing life on other fucking planets is landing on the White House lawn, okay? You get it, *asshole?* It's the biggest story in the history of the world, it's bigger than anything I've ever done in my life, and *I don't know what to point the cameras at!* I don't know how to take a picture of five hundred people I never heard of, who may or may not be plotting to pick a President! I don't know how to do it, so please, Dorian, go give a lecture at the Columbia School of Journalism or something, but go away or I will hurt you very, very badly!"

Dorian Wood pulled himself free of Crenshaw's grasp, straightened his sport jacket, murmured "Good luck," and left the control room. Neither of them ever mentioned the incident again. And Crenshaw returned to his command chair in the center of the second row, just behind the two dozen technicians at the master control board.

"More power!" he yelled at his team, as he had a hundred times before.

"We canno' gi'e ye inny more power, Cep-tahn!" they chanted in unison. "The ship is gonna blowwww!"

And the tension in the room dissolved for at least forty-five seconds—which was a lot better than they were doing in the election headquarters/presidential-transition/inaugural-planning/crisis-management offices of the Foyle-Block campaign committee.

The entire wall opposite Marsh's desk was covered by a gigantic map of the United States. Within the borders of each state—or on the outer edges of the map, in the case of states like Rhode Island, Delaware, Connecticut, and West Virginia—sheets of paper listed every elector, and their current voting intentions. The map had been up for only little more than a day, but the sheets of paper already were filled with so many penciled-in alterations that they looked like baseball scorecards after a game had entered the fourteenth inning. Every time a new report was phoned in to Marsh, he barked out instructions to the four Young Blue Suits who were working the map, cell phones cradled to one ear, a fistful of multicolored pens and pencils in each hand.

"Jesus, God, Almighty," Alan Veigle said to Sharon Kramer when they came into the room. "It's a cross between the Shanghai Commodities Exchange and a Jerry Lewis telethon."

"How's the candidate?" Marsh said to Sharon, who shook her head.

"He flew home," she said. "His family has some traditional gathering between Thanksgiving and Christmas—says there's no way in the world he'd miss it."

"What about the calls to California?" Marsh demanded. "What about the video?"

Sharon shrugged.

"Said he'd try to call from Woodlot—that's the name of his mother's estate. As for the video, he didn't think much of the idea."

"*There's* a fucking surprise," said Alan Veigle. "Like he thinks much about anything."

"No, he doesn't," Sharon said. "And it's not as if I enjoyed pulling his foot out of his mouth all fall. But I'll tell you something about him: in some weird way, he knows who he is. When he gets a fix on something he believes, you can't move him with a stick of dynamite."

"How reassuring," said Alan Veigle. "How genuinely *reassuring* to see how you can find admirable attributes in the man who is your meal ticket to a corner office in the West Wing."

"It wasn't *my* idea to spend three months holding Ted Block's hand," Sharon snapped. "And it wasn't *my* idea to put Foyle on a drugged-up horse and send him through the streets of Cheyenne. And I'm not saying this guy is Forrest Gump with a Windbreaker and a trust fund, much less Harry Truman. I'm only telling you what you saw with the Election Protection Act. Is he a little dull, a little tone deaf on the politics? Of course he is. But there's something else going on—"

"*Speaking* of which," Marsh interjected, "it might be a dandy idea right about now to figure that out—what's going on, I mean." He gestured to one of the Young Blue Suits, who held a shiny palm-sized rectangle in his hand. "Barrett," he said, "what do you know?"

"Is that your first name or last?" Alan Veigle asked, a little too politely.

"Forget it," Marsh said. "C'mon. Where are we?"

Barrett pushed his thumb down two or three times, squinted at the screen, then held the device up to his ear.

"It's the latest PDA—you know, 'personal digital assistant,' " Marsh explained. "Voice, data, images, video, all sent, retrieved, stored—all wireless, too."

"If they were voting today," Barrett began, "we're sure, absolutely sure, of two hundred fifty-five votes."

"Fifteen short," Sharon said.

"If you count the votes we won on Election Day, it's more like forty-eight short—which is good news, in a funny way. If we can get a third of the holdouts to stay with us, we're over the top. And we think most—*most* of the public negotiations aren't going anywhere. They were more about fifteen minutes of fame, that sort of thing."

"What about the *thirteen—thirteen*—calls I've gotten asking about specific government contracts and appointments in the last seventy-two hours?" Marsh asked. "How do you count them if I tell them to go take a flying . . ."

"I've checked the names, sir," said Barrett, "and my best estimate now is that the . . . uh . . . counter-pressure will work."

"What's that?" said Sharon.

"Employers, mortgage holders, that sort of thing," Marsh replied. "And don't even *begin* to give me any grief about playing hardball here—unless you're prepared to make up the, I don't know, half a trillion in equity loss the Fed anticipates if this thing drags on for another month or so, and we wind up picking the President in the House. I've talked to every state chair we have—except for that rat bastard in Delaware," he added grimly, referring to the state party official who had fallen off the face of the earth, leaving only an answering machine message that he was "on vacation, out of the country."

"What I've told them," Marsh said, "is that anything goes here—*any-*

thing. If one of our reluctant electors is playing 'hide the salami' with his secretary, use it. If there's a gay son, a crazy aunt in the attic, an IRS investigation, use it. To be honest with you, I don't think Barrett's numbers would be that high without the rough stuff. What else?" Marsh asked. "What about defections to Mueller?"

"Just the one in Maine that we know about." Barrett said. "And the Executive Committee is meeting tonight to replace her. I doubt there'll be any other defectors."

"Any we'll *know* about," Alan Veigle said. "If there are any others out there, they'll shut up until they actually vote—not to mention what that Ledger woman is up to. To think nobody's been able to find out where she is . . ."

Which was when another Young Blue Suit pushed open the door to Block's office with a look on his face that hinted at a personal communication with God.

"On the phone," the Young Blue Suit said, "Jack *Petitcon. Himself."*

THIRTY-EIGHT

★ ★ ★

There was a time not so long ago when a major event had the power to pull us together, to share history side by side. Our grandparents flocked to the telegraph office and listen to the telegrapher shout out the latest news clattering in, one letter at a time. They stood, shivering outside the newspaper office, watching the numbers chalked up on a blackboard, to learn who had won the presidency. They crowded together on a downtown street, craning their necks up at the skyscraper around which electronic bulletins flashed. Our parents surrounded parked cars, leaning in to catch every muffled, tinny word blaring from the car radio, or they huddled outside an appliance store to watch the flickering images of a baseball game.

We lack most of that communal sense of drama today; we sit at home, alone, to watch spaceships explode and wars begin and earthquakes shred a city. Gathered in our separate shelter, it is not always easy to connect with the common grief or joy or lust or fear.

But the chaos now enveloping the choosing of a President was different. You could walk through the parking lot of a suburban shopping mall at midmorning, wander through the aisles of Vons, into the Sears, stop at the Baskin-Robbins counter, and plug into the common conversation. You could walk down the Santa Monica Pier, through Bloomington, Minnesota's cavernous Mall of America, down the mile of State Street that links the University of Wisconsin to the state capitol, and you would not miss a moment of what had become the National Topic. It was the two-stroke watercooler chat at the office, the obscenity-laced lunchroom jabber off the factory floor, the commiserating head shake between $95-a-day Fifth Avenue doormen and $750-an-hour corporate attorneys; and more than a few highly compensated professional companions had exchanged a few words about the vagaries of constitutional policy with their clients before taking matters in hand.

It is true that, in normal times, Americans tend instinctively to tune out the political chatter. But now the natural rhythms of the post-campaign system were gone, wiped out by sudden death and by the disintegration of anything approaching an orderly succession. Now, somehow, a handful of nobodies were actually threatening to use the power they had been given only on the express understanding that they would never, ever use it. A hundred years ago, Kansas senator John J. Ingalls had said that presidential electors were like "the marionettes in a Punch and Judy show." Now, the marionettes had cut their strings, picked up the cudgels, and were racing through the audience, threatening to pummel the crowd to death. Like news of a massive comet heading straight for the Earth, the impending chaos of the electoral college vote for President was concentrating the national mind wonderfully.

Which made it all the more remarkable that one of the key players in this national melodrama had managed to remain beneath the radar screen of public attention. Dorothy Ledger remained the target of an increasingly frantic full-court press by the press; the five major networks had expended thousands of man-hours on the hunt; the syndicated tabloid shows had offered rewards of up to $200,000 for her whereabouts, and when that ploy failed, they had resorted to highly unsubtle innuendoes in an attempt to force her into a public denial. (One show had gotten hold of a home video of Dorothy performing in a Republican Party variety show, clad in a modest one-piece bathing suit, and featured the tape with the headline: "Dottie's Naughty Peep Show!" Another asked: "Is it Booze? Pills? Men? Tonight: The Dark Side of Dorothy Ledger.") But Dot and her tiny troupe had remained at the Silver Spring Inn, convening their group of electors twice a day—thanks to the magic keyboard of Ben Weinstock.

It was, in fact, Weinstock's wizardry that had kept the vultures at bay.

Through his worldwide hacker friends, Ben had left a bogus, tantalizingly easy-to-trace trail of Dorothy's purported travels. Recorded messages from Dorothy were zapped by Weinstock to his allies, then phoned into news organizations, which eagerly reported that Dorothy Ledger had been traced to Chicago, St. Louis, Seattle, Buffalo, Stockton, and Gstaad. Phony credit-card receipts, which miraculously appeared in newsroom faxes, located her at a Four Seasons Hotel in Beverly Hills, a sporting goods store in Cleveland, an airport gift shop in Philadelphia, and an erotic boutique in Thailand.

In his efforts to protect Dorothy, Weinstock had allies he did not even know about: a mob of parasites who were ready and willing to provide incendiary information about political controversy, celebrity perversity, or paranormal phenomena. For instance, Chaim Ben Schnoreman, a retired Israeli intelligence agent (he had been in charge of custodial services), had spent nine years and earned tens of thousands of dollars peddling the tale of a secret deal between high White House aides, Afghanistan drug smugglers, South African neo-Nazis, and renegade CIA agents involved with the Kennedy assassination—in fact, both Kennedy assassinations. Now, he claimed to have had a series of personal conversations with Dorothy Ledger, who was being held at a safe house on the Caribbean island of Anguilla. He would deliver her, he promised, for a fee of $25,000 plus expenses, including but not limited to a $2,200-a-day villa at Cap Juluca. And a highly rated daytime talk show featured a panel of psychics who each claimed to be able to divine Dorothy's hideout (the show turned into an ugly brawl between the astral projectionist who had spotted Dorothy in Detroit, and a channeler whose twenty-thousand-year-old Norse warrior claimed to have received oral sex from her at a basketball arena in Ottumwa, Iowa).

Eventually, Dorothy's support group shrank: Walter Ames, Jr., had to return to his job and his home in New Jersey, but promised to keep in daily computer touch, and to say absolutely nothing that would arouse the suspicions of the New Jersey State Republican Executive Committee. Faith McCoy said she had to return to her campus for at least a few days; there were papers to read, exams to prepare.

"I'll be back as soon as I can, Dot," Faith promised. "I may have to tell the school that I've got a drug problem; that way, I can tell 'em I'm going right into rehab, and they can't touch me. Drugs are an addiction, which is a disability, which is now a federal civil right; if they so much as make a move on me, I'll slap 'em with a discrimination suit so fast they'll never know what hit 'em. Meanwhile," she said, hugging Dorothy, "*you* have been one inspiring woman. In fact, I've made myself a resolution; if you had the courage to stand up to the entire political-financial-cultural establishment of the United States of America, I just may have the courage to actually flunk one of my illiterate, drunken, tail-chasing students this semester."

So for the last two days, a woman whose name was on the lips of every journalist, late-night comedian, and political junkie in the country; a woman who was being hunted by more than 2,400 reporters, researchers, book agents, and talent bookers; a woman as admired and reviled as any individual in the land had spent her every waking hour in a sixty-five-dollar-a-night hotel room less than seven miles from the Capitol on whose steps the next President would stand to take the oath of office—whoever that might be. Her only human companion was a socially inept, incomprehensibly brilliant Ben Weinstock and the twenty-six presidential electors, the latter twenty-six only available by way of messages on a computer screen. Every morning and every evening for an hour and a half, they greeted each other, counseled each other, argued with each other, encouraged each other to keep their own counsel and no one else's. They had come up with a name for themselves: the Committee of Cyberspace Correspondence, after the men who two and a quarter centuries ago had formed the loose confederation of colonials organized to protest the depredations of the British. They talked about the incredible pressures they were under to commit themselves to Block and Phelps, and wondered whether they could be prosecuted for perjury if they signed such an oath, and then withheld their votes. Could they ask for a secret ballot if their state's ritual had always been for ballots to be preprinted, then ceremoniously dropped into symbolic ballot boxes? What about calling for a caucus before the vote, so that they might have a chance to persuade their fellow electors to deprive Block of their votes, and push the choice into the House of Representatives? And when, when were they going to decide who their dissenting votes should be cast *for,* so that their choice would be one of the top three finishers; and thus eligible to be chosen as President by the House.

It was heady, even exhilarating stuff. And late one night, Dorothy Ledger woke up in a cold sweat, convinced she could not do this anymore without help. She rummaged through her purse, dug out a crumpled piece of paper, found the number she had jotted down so hastily that she misread it, and dialed a wrong number on her first try. Then, recognizing the sleepy voice at the other end of the line, she began at once to speak.

"Hi, I'm sorry to wake you, do you know who this is? It's me—I mean, it's Dorothy. No, yes, really. I'm fine, nothing's wrong—well, that's not true, what's wrong is that there are these people who think I'm leading some kind of moral crusade or some political . . . revolution or something, and the truth is, I don't know what I'm supposed to be doing here. I work in a *bank,* for God's sakes. In Grand *Rapids.* I live in a two-bedroom house with a guest room as big as a closet, and a quarter-acre patch of grass out in the back. I've got nineteen thousand dollars in the bank, and a pension that will be worth seven hundred seventy-five dollars a month when I'm fifty-five years old. I've been out of the country four times in my life, and that's counting Canada and Mexico. And you know what my political experience is? When the county Republican Party wants to hold a picnic, I organize phone banks to get people to turn out. I rent the tables and chairs, and I make sure the tablecloths are clean, and I yell at the barbecue guys when the hot dogs are cold or when the beer is warm or when the rolls are stale, and I make sure the band can play Glenn Miller and Benny Goodman and Elvis and the Beatles and the Carpenters. I make sure the mike doesn't go out when the congressman and the governor get up to speak. And then I make sure the checks clear, and the bills get paid, and the pamphlets get printed and go in the envelopes and the stamps get stuck on, and the envelopes wind up in the mailboxes, and then on Election Day I make sure the phones are answered and the courtesy vans are clean and gassed up and my people get to the polls, and we get to keep the courthouse and City Hall.

"That's what I know how to do—I do not know how to decide who gets to be the President of the United States, for heaven's sakes. And now I'm sitting here like a prisoner, I can't go outside, I'm afraid to go home to Grand Rapids, for all I know I'll be arrested for . . . I don't know, *treason* or something, I know it's unfair even to ask you to help, it's not like that's what you do, but there are bills piling up, my aspidistra's probably *dead* by now, oh God, I just don't know what I'm going to do next. . . ."

Dorothy Ledger dissolved in tears. And at the other end of the phone, Al DeRossa realized that he didn't know what the hell he was going to do next, either.

THIRTY-NINE

★ ★ ★

And he didn't. In fact, all that Dorothy Ledger's late-night call for help had done was to pile another slab of confusion on Al DeRossa's increasingly inadequate shoulders.

All day, he'd sat in the network's Washington command post, packed with the network's highest-priced talent: eleven executives, the Anchor, the Distinguished Commentator, nine correspondents, seven off-air reporters, three researchers, four graphic designers, three floor directors. All day, he'd tried with an increasing sense of desperation to offer some coherent guidance for the coverage of Electors Day, or whatever they were going to call it.

"I hate that name," the news president said. "It sounds like some festival at a New England prep school. Can't we come up with something better than that?"

Around the room, brows furrowed; lips pursed. When the news president so much as hinted at dissatisfaction, it was as if the finger of God had scrawled a warning on the wall: *"You have been weighed in the balance, and found wanting."* Network veterans often told the tale of a royal wedding, when the president had shown up in London six hours before the coverage was scheduled to start, and murmured something about how unbalanced the London skyline backdrop looked; within ninety minutes, three graphic artists had moved Big Ben the equivalent of three miles up the Thames. Now the alternatives began to fly.

" 'Election Day Two'?"

"What's that? A sequel to a horror flick?"

" 'The Choice'?"

"Nah—that's a nine-hundred-page novel they turn into a miniseries for the sweeps."

"Maybe, 'Day of Decision.' Nope, forget it. That's what they called those film strips we saw in fifth grade assembly about how Joey says no to the drug dealer."

"How about 'Kollege Kapers'?" asked Jerry Griffin, the sixty-four-year-old floor director known as "TNS" ("Takes No Shit"). "You know, like all those black-and-white college musicals of the thirties where Jack Oakie's the dumb football player who can't pass his exams, so Priscilla Lane is hired to tutor him, and Kay Kyser and his band is stuck in town, so they play at the prom . . . ah, screw it, it's a generational thing, you wouldn't understand."

"God, I love that thing ANN does, with that 'Countdown to Crisis' logo, and that . . . *thing* they play in and out of commercials with the drums. What is that, some Eskimo war dance? '*Boom*-buh-buh-buh-*boom*-buh-buh-*boom.*' Great stuff."

"I want something with a lot much punch than Electors Day," the news president said. "So—Al—where are we going to be tomorrow morning?"

Al drew a deep breath and smiled weakly.

"Okay. As far as we know, Mueller's electors are going to hold. Now that the two gentlemen of the gay persuasion out in Washington State have been coaxed back into the fold, the only Mueller holdout we know of is up in Maine."

"Miss Esperanto," the Anchor murmured.

"Exactly. Says she will not vote for Bill Mueller unless he agrees to order the publication of all official government documents in Esperanto, to encourage world peace. The state Democratic Committee says she's forfeited her place on the electoral slate, and they'll be replacing her. *She* says she'll be in Augusta to vote. I think we'll be okay with the live affiliate feed."

"Sacramento?"

"Absolutely. I mean, you run down the list of the Republican electors out there, it's like a time-travel machine. You've got a ninety-three-year-old retired state senator from Oakland, helped Bill Knowland with the China lobby fifty years ago."

" 'China lobby'?" a young researcher asked.

"Ancient history," said another one. DeRossa winced.

"Thanks for that, Juliette. I'll just get my warm milk and shawl and check out the Lawrence Welk reruns. Ah hell, you're right, it is ancient history. But so are some of those California Republicans. I mean, we're talking folks who go back to Nixon for senator, folks from the Goldwater campaign in '64. I can't believe we're not going to see one or two defections out there."

"Okay," Crenshaw said. "Augusta, Sacramento, Albany. What else do we know about?"

"Like Michigan," the news president said. "We still have nothing on Dorothy Ledger?" It was not hard to detect the heavy-handed hint of dissatisfaction.

Crenshaw smiled weakly.

"We've had Metro Airport staked out for the last seventy-two hours," he said. *Us and about twenty other outfits,* he thought to himself. "We've got her place in Grand Rapids staked out, too, just in case she doesn't come home through Detroit. And Lansing, obviously—if she tries to cast a vote tomorrow, she's got to be there in person. And the Republicans will be waiting to serve her with a 'show cause' order, demanding she show why she shouldn't be removed as an elector for 'implied breach of obligation.' "

"Can they do that?" one of the political correspondents asked.

"I'm glad you asked," said DeRossa. "Because now we begin to leave the Earth's gravitational field and start our journey to Planet Mongo," he said. "Let me introduce you to Steven Weiss," he said, gesturing to a lean, hawk-nosed man who sat to DeRossa's left. "Some of you may know him as the chief of the network's legal affairs division."

"Oh, *yes,*" snarled the Distinguished Commentator. "You're the one who said I couldn't do those informational videos for the Hydroponics Association. Cost me a hundred seventy-five thousand."

"Sorry, but a conflict of interest's a conflict of interest." Weiss was in his middle forties. He wore his charcoal gray Armani like a second skin.

"Right, like I spend my days covering the controversial world of underwater *plants,*" said the Distinguished Commentator.

"As it happens," DeRossa said, "Steve taught at Stanford Law before joining the company. He was considered one of the country's leading authorities on election law—he's the guy who helped John Anderson get on the ballot in all fifty states. Steve?"

Weiss shot his cuffs, and looked around the room.

"Let me put this in highly technical legal terms. What we have here is a grand clong."

"What the hell is a 'grand clong'?" the Distinguished Commentator asked.

"A 'clong,' " Weiss explained, "is best defined as a sudden rush of shit to the heart. Usually, they fall into the category of 'petty clongs.' That's when you wake up and realize that you haven't paid your property tax bill, and if you don't get to the county by six P.M., they could take your home. A 'grand clong,' on the other hand, is when you wake up and see them auctioning off the house, because you were supposed to pay the bill last month. When you folks start trying to figure out what's going to happen tomorrow, you will discover you are facing a grand clong of the first magnitude.

"You want to talk about Michigan? Fine, yes—Dorothy Ledger is supposed to be served with a 'show cause' order. The state committee got one from a superior court in Grand Rapids. But the Michigan Civil Liberties League went to *federal* court and got an injunction forbidding the state from issuing that order: they claimed it violated her First Amendment right of free speech, there's a Fourteenth Amendment due-process claim, a Ninth Amendment claim—don't ask—and the federal judge out there agreed."

"So," Crenshaw said, "the Republicans won't be serving Dorothy if she shows up, right? I mean, it's a federal court order."

Weiss shook his head.

"Not so fast—the leaders of the Michigan State legislature—they're both Republicans, in case you couldn't figure this out—went to the Michigan Supreme Court yesterday. They argued that since the Constitution very clearly gives the *state legislatures* the *sole* power to choose electors, and since Michigan law gives the power to the party committees, the federal courts have no jurisdiction at all. And they got an emergency order reaffirming the show-cause order."

"I'm totally confused," said the Anchor.

"Congratulations," Weiss said. "You understand the situation. But I have to tell you," he said, shaking his head, "it's going on all over the country. You want to hear about Tennessee?"

"Probably not," the news president said.

"You're right," Weiss said. "Okay: the state legislature passes an emergency loyalty oath: any elector who doesn't sign a promise to vote for the Republican nominees is yanked off the slate; anyone who signs and breaks his word is automatically in criminal contempt, and his vote is thrown out. The governor—who's a Democrat and an old golfing chum of Mueller's, by the way—the governor vetoes the bill—says it's unconstitutional, violates the spirit of the Founding Fathers, blah blah blah. He calls out the National Guard to protect the electors' rights. *Then* the speaker of the Tennessee house says, 'Wait a minute—the Constitution doesn't say jack shit about the governor. It's up to *us*—the state legislature and us alone.' *He* says the governor can't veto it—and he's called out the state capital police to enforce the new rules."

"Are you telling me," the news president said, "that we might have a . . . an armed confrontation at the state capitol the day after tomorrow?"

"I doubt it would come to that," Weiss said. "But you know, back in the forties there were three different governors of Georgia for a week or two—honestly. Armed guards blockading the governor's office, everybody ordering everybody else thrown in jail—of course, there was no national TV coverage."

"Lucky us," said Crenshaw. "So let me see if I got this right: we're going live to Albany; Sacramento; Augusta, Maine; Lansing, Michigan; and Nashville, Tennessee."

"Maybe," DeRossa said.

"Maybe," Crenshaw repeated, and he began to tap the conference table with his forefinger. Those who had worked with Ken Crenshaw over the years had seen this gesture only four times before; they eyed each other nervously, and one of them scurried out of the room.

"Why, 'maybe'?" Crenshaw asked, with excessive politeness.

"Because," Weiss answered, "we're only talking about states where we know, or strongly suspect, that there will be some kind of defection or confrontation. My own guess is that those electors most likely to defect are keeping their own counsel; it would be much harder to undo their acts *after* they've voted. To be safe, you'd need to pick up the actual vote in all fifty states."

Crenshaw's face was rapidly assuming the color of a sunburn victim.

"You're telling me I need the capability of *fifty simultaneous-remotes?"*

"Fifty-one, if you're counting the District of Columbia, but that should be a reliably Democratic vote. Still—"

Hours later, when Crenshaw had been restrained and sedated, when the meeting finally adjourned, Al DeRossa fell into his hotel-room bed, desperate for a few hours' sleep and a clear head—which was when he picked up the telephone to find a desperate Dorothy Ledger at the other end of the line.

As he listened to her disjointed monologue, DeRossa found his own emotional state careening almost out of control.

First came Daffy Duck mode, the response of DeRossa's cartoon hero when confronted by the prospect of sudden wealth: *Ohmigod, it's The Story, I've got it, it's fallen right into my lap, it's the biggest thing since Watergate, and it's mine, mine, mine.*

Then came the sudden, sober second thought: *It's a trap, it's a phony, it's the twelve-year-old junkie who never existed, it's the truck they rigged to make it blow up. If I touch this, I'm dead.*

But by the time Dorothy had finished her disjointed tale of woe, DeRossa's exultation and fear had been supplanted by a different emotion: complete and utter confusion. What was he supposed to do? Many of his colleagues, he knew, would have hustled Dorothy into an exclusive interview within minutes, exchanging a sympathetic ear and the promise of help for a thirty-minute slice of prime-time air. He could no more do that than he could stick a camera into the face of a mugging victim's mother and ask if she'd like to share her feelings with her fellow citizens. For now, he guessed, what she most wanted was the sound of a friendly voice—and a sentiment a little more reassuring than his initial comment to her that he hadn't a clue about what to do next.

"Are you okay, Dorothy? Are you safe? We've had you spotted everywhere from the top of the Washington Monument to a monastery in Sri Lanka."

"No, I'm fine, really," Dorothy said. "I'm actually—Mr. DeRossa, do you really think it's safe to talk?"

"I don't think you have to worry about phone taps on my line," DeRossa said. "And you've done pretty well eluding the media mob."

"I've had . . . help. But I need to talk to someone. By tomorrow we . . . I . . . a decision has to be made, and I know I'm not up to it. I know you're a reporter and all that, but you seem like someone I could trust. Also, I've been watching your coverage, and that professor you have?"

"Griese?"

"Yes—what a terrible name for someone like that. Anyway, he really sounds like he understands what a terrible mess this all is. If I could just sit down with you and him, I think I might be able to figure out what we—I—should do."

"Dorothy," Al asked. "What do you mean, 'we'? Is there some kind of organization you're part of?"

He was surprised at her laughter.

" 'Organization'? That's the *last* word I'd use to describe—Al, I really don't feel right talking about this over the phone. What I'm wondering is whether you think you and Professor Griese would sit down with me and help me figure this thing out."

Aha, DeRossa thought. *Bingo. The very thing I need. Right in the middle of the biggest political mess in American history, a nice fat personal dilemma that could cost me my job.*

"I know you're not supposed to get involved, Al, I really do. 'No cheering in the press box,' I heard a reporter say once. But there isn't anyone else, Al. God, that sounds dramatic, doesn't it? 'There isn't anyone else.' But it's true. The man I worked with for twelve years in Michigan is telling the press I've turned into some kind of pre-menopausal whack job; the people who say they're on my side, half of them are con artists out for a buck and the other half sound like they're from another planet. At least with you, you didn't pretend, you were absolutely straight with me, and God, I haven't had one straight conversation with anybody since I stood up in that hotel room and made that point of order."

She let out something between a sigh and a shudder. And for Al

DeRossa, that did it. More than a shower of tears or racking sobs, that sound of utter helplessness did it.

"Tell me where you are," he said. *This is crazy, this is crazy, don't do it, this is trouble, ah shut up.*

"Do you know Silver Spring?" she asked.

"Not that well," DeRossa said. "But I'll get a crew to drive me—I promise you, no videotaping, no interview. But the fact is, it's eleven P.M., and I'd feel a lot safer if we keep it in house. Give me forty-five minutes."

"Oh, God, thank you. Thank you. You can't imagine how much I appreciate this, Al."

Great. Maybe you can keep me company on the food-stamp line.

DeRossa ended the call, then dialed up the assignment desk.

"I need a crew and a truck—right now," he said.

"We don't have—"

"Sure you do. You've got three crews sitting on their butts in the lounge waiting for somebody to shoot the President or blow up the Capitol. Well, nobody's going to shoot the President, because he's a thousand miles away and five-eighths dead anyway. I'm telling you, I need this crew—now."

"Where are you going?"

Where am I going? I'll tell you where I'm going. I'm going to track down a story that'll blow the lid . . . oh, get a life, DeRossa.

"It's a clandestine interview with a source. That good enough, or do we have to call the suits in on this? Have the crew swing by the Jackson Arms in ten minutes. I'll be downstairs."

His last call was to a decidedly unsleepy, clearly out-of-breath Professor Griese. Judging by the mix of embarrassment and frustration in his voice when he'd picked up the phone after hearing the start of DeRossa's urgent message, Professor Griese had been interrupted in the middle of some strenuous exercise.

"I know, I know," DeRossa said. "You and your capable assistant were going over some last-minute footnotes—or headnotes—or something. I need you, Professor. No, right now. As in this minute. Get your pants on and meet me in front of the Jackson Arms as soon as you possibly can."

Fifteen minutes later, DeRossa and Griese were speeding up Massachusetts Avenue on their way to the Silver Spring Inn.

"She wants advice?" Griese said, rubbing a hand through his disordered hair. "I thought you folks weren't supposed—"

"That's what you're doing here," DeRossa explained. "I don't know what Ms. Ledger has been doing, but it's my very strong hunch that one way or another, a slice of these Republican electors are depending on her for guidance. From the way she sounded on the phone, it may be a case of the blind leading the blind."

Griese shook his head as the crew truck pulled into the parking lot of the Silver Spring Inn.

"Imagine," he said. "You suddenly find yourself with the power to affect the lives of millions and millions of people—and you look up and you're completely alone."

But when DeRossa and Griese knocked on her door, they found that a very frightened Dorothy Ledger was not completely alone; sitting on the bed were two men in dark suits, who looked up curiously. Dorothy looked at DeRossa, then at the two men, and shook her head.

"You know what I think we have here?" DeRossa said. "What we have here is the living embodiment of one of the Three Great Lies in the World: 'I'm from the government and I'm here to help.' Have I got that right, gentlemen?"

"Close enough," one of them said. The other one just nodded.

FORTY

★ ★ ★

"They knocked on my door five minutes ago," Dorothy said, gesturing with a blue-bound sheet of paper. "They gave me this."

"First things first," DeRossa said. "Do you gentlemen mind if I see some identification?"

"Are you her lawyer?" the taller, thinner one said.

"No, but we could have one here in about fifteen minutes," DeRossa said, wondering just who in hell he had in mind.

"It's okay," the shorter, stockier one said reassuringly. "Nothing to hide here, right?" He reached into his suit coat and opened a leather billfold. The taller, thinner man did the same.

"Federal marshals?" DeRossa said. "Is there some kind of crime you're accusing Ms. Ledger of?"

"No, no, no," the shorter, stockier one said. "No, we're simply serving Ms. Ledger with an injunction; it was obtained in federal district court in the Eastern District of Michigan this afternoon by the Republican State Committee, the Republican National Committee, and by a Mr. . . ." He pulled a paper out of his breast pocket and consulted it for a moment. "A Mr. Edward Mack, who avers under penalty of criminal law that he is a duly registered voter in Michigan who cast his vote last November for MacArthur Foyle and Theodore Block. He avers further that Ms. Ledger has been violating her obligations as a Republican elector by conspiring to communicate across state lines in such a way as to render his vote null and void. What we've served Ms. Ledger with is an injunction forbidding her from engaging in any such communication." He tucked the paper back in his breast pocket.

"Do you understand what kind of gibberish they're talking about?" DeRossa said to Griese.

"Actually, yes." He nodded. "This goes back to the theory that the electors are supposed to gather in their own states, and make their own judgments. The Founders were scared to death of some kind of cabal among electors; that's why they rejected the whole idea of gathering the electors together to pick a President. In fact, they assumed they would rarely ever *pick* one—just narrow the field, and let the Congress do the picking."

"But not letting an elector make telephone calls to other states?" DeRossa said. "That's crazy."

"Not just telephone calls," the shorter, stockier one said, looking at the paper again. "Also, 'any and all communication by mail, wire, telegraph, telephone, cellular or satellite communication, electronic device, computer"—he paused and looked at Dorothy for a beat—"or other device."

"My God, they know," Dorothy said.

"What do they know?" DeRossa asked.

Dorothy picked up the phone, and punched out three numbers.

"Ben, could you come over right away? . . . No, I mean *right* away. Now."

A moment later, Dorothy answered the knock on her hotel room door to find a half-asleep Ben Weinstock, wearing a rumpled Van Morrison T-shirt, pajama bottoms, and ratty athletic socks.

"Little late for a party, isn't it?"

"Ben, this is Al DeRossa—"

"The news guy, right? You interviewed Dorothy." He pointed to Griese. "And you're on the TV, too. But who are they?"

The taller, thinner one smiled slightly.

"I'll bet you're Ben Weinstock." He reached into his pocket and handed Ben another blue-bound sheet of paper. "This one's for you, my friend."

Ben read the paper, then looked up in a state of shock.

"This is impossible," he said. "There's no way you could have found me. It's *impossible.*" He looked around the room, trying to put back the broken pieces of his virtual universe.

"If you *knew* the protections we built into this . . . it would have to have been . . ." He looked up as it hit him.

"Jesus," Weinstock said. "It would have had to have been the National Security Agency at *least;* probably one of those black-bag agencies only the hackers believe exist."

Weinstock was caught between total outrage and total fascination.

"You understand what they must have done?" he asked no one in particular. "They must have run a total surveillance on every presidential elector: phone taps, mail intercepts, and cellular eavesdrops. Then they would have had to trace the communications back to us. But . . . to follow the pulses all over the world . . ." He shook his head.

The shorter, stockier agent stood up.

"Mr. Weinstock," he said with polite formality, "this injunction also asserts that you have aided and abetted a continuing illegal enterprise in violation of the statutes of the United States that constitutes a violation of the Racketeer-Influenced and Corrupt Organization Act. This injunction authorizes us to seize all assets and equipment used in pursuit of that illegal enterprise: to wit, one personal computer—"

"You can't do that, man," Weinstock said. "That's my *life* in there! You *can't.*"

"We are also authorized," the shorter, stockier one said, "to return Ms. Ledger to the Eastern District to respond to this injunction. Under the law, her continuing refusal to respond to subpoenas and other official communications constitutes obstruction of justice. We've booked you on a six A.M. passenger train leaving Union Station for Detroit, with connections in Chicago. We'll remain outside the hotel to ensure that you do not attempt to flee."

DeRossa walked over to the shorter, stockier one. The taller, thinner one stood up quickly and began to move toward DeRossa.

"Oh, get serious," DeRossa said. "Do you think I'm about to get physical here? No, no, I just want to let you folks know that you have just stepped into the biggest, steamiest pile of equine excrement that you have ever imagined."

He turned to Dorothy and Ben and gave them a wide smile intending to communicate a certainty he certainly did not feel.

"What we have here, folks, is hot air—pure, unadulterated hot air. Since these . . . gentlemen traced you here, they obviously knew you were freelancing; they knew—hell, everyone knew—you've been cut off from the world, which means you were very vulnerable to a scam like this."

"You mean, they're not government agents?" Dorothy said.

"Oh, I'm sure they are; but what would you like to bet they don't have anything remotely resembling real legal authority to take you under some kind of custody. Right?" he said to the shorter, stockier one, who sat on the bed, grim faced.

"It's just your bad luck, gentlemen, that this is Professor Leonard Griese, one of the leading . . . legal . . . scholars in the United States. What's your take on this, Professor?"

For God's sake, don't say the wrong thing.

"I couldn't agree more," Griese said flatly. "In all my years of study, I have never seen a more blatant constitutional outrage."

Attaboy.

DeRossa pushed aside the venetian blinds and pointed out the window to the parking lot.

"Here's another detail you geniuses didn't factor in. You see that station wagon, friends? That's a crew truck: complete with video cameras and parabolic microphones. My hunch is that every word we've spoken here is already on tape; and, gentlemen, if you think for one minute that this half-assed, phony-as-a-three-dollar-bill mumbo jumbo would stand up for one second in a court of law, you're crazier than I think."

DeRossa walked to the nightstand and dialed a number.

"Butler? DeRossa here? You getting all this?"

DeRossa heard a cell phone being dropped several times before the croaking voice of Alan Butler responded.

"Huzzats?" Al Butler, DeRossa knew, was famed throughout the news division for his ability to fall asleep within ninety seconds of settling in behind the wheel of his crew car.

"Good," DeRossa said into the phone, nodding and smiling broadly. "Just keep shooting. And make sure you get the two feds on camera; you can't miss 'em. Nobody else will be wearing suits and button-down collars at midnight."

"Whhuzzat?"

"Great going, Alan." DeRossa hung up, then wheeled to face the two marshals.

"In your court, fellas. You can get out, go away, and let Dorothy alone; or you can be starring coast to coast on *The Morning Show, Evening News, Nightside . . ."*

"What happens if we leave right now?" the shorter, stockier one asked.

Good question.

"We forget this ever happened—unless one of your friends tries to get in Ms. Ledger's face again."

"I don't believe you," the taller, thinner one said. "You sons of bitches would throw your mother off a cliff for a great story."

"You'll just have to believe me," DeRossa said. *Especially if you knew that we haven't got a goddamn thing on tape.* "Go on—get the hell out of here now, throw those bogus papers in the trash, and go arrest someone for ripping the tags off a mattress or something. And leave these people the hell alone, or I promise you, you will be leading the evening newscasts, the morning newscasts, the . . ."

"Okay, right," said the shorter, stockier one. The two marshals looked at each other, shrugged, and walked out. A moment later, they heard a car speed away.

"I can't believe you did that for me," Dorothy said. "I can't *believe* you gave up a story like that."

Griese nodded.

"You realize that there isn't a single academic who'd believe it."

"Yeah, well, do me a very big favor—do not mention this to anyone back at the network—ever, ever, *ever.* And now, Professor," DeRossa said, "I need to press you into service."

"Which is?"

"Which is to stay here with Dorothy until the morning—and then go with her to wherever we figure out she can go without being stopped."

"But I have to get in touch with—"

"I know," DeRossa said. "But it's obvious that your cover's been blown. Somebody very powerful knows where you are, and what you've been doing. Anyway, I think we've put the fear of God into those jokers. I think you'll be free to let your . . . friends know what you want them to do."

"But that's the point," said Dorothy. "I don't know what to tell them."

"Ms. Ledger," DeRossa said, pointing to Griese, "you will be trapped in a room with one of the foremost authorities in the field. And you have the entire night to figure it out. Now, I've got to get out of here and figure out how to look like we know what we're doing when we go on the air in . . . thirty-one hours." He got up to leave.

"What I'd still like to know," Ben Weinstock said, "is how in God's name they did it."

"I'll tell you a much more interesting question," DeRossa said. "Considering that this kind of surveillance is about as illegal as it gets, I'd like to know *who* in God's name got them to do it."

FORTY-ONE

★ ★ ★

"Hey, Marsh, Ms. Kramer, don't you have enough sense to come on in outta the cold?"

Jack Petitcon beckoned them out of the late-night chill and into the center hall of a home whose exterior modesty was spectacularly contradicted by what was inside. A marble staircase ascended upward from the rear of the hall; a rich burgundy fabric covered the walls; early American portraits lined the hallway, at least two of which Sharon Kramer could have sworn were Gilbert Charles Stuart originals she had seen some years ago hanging in the Corcoran Gallery. From the center hall, Petitcon gestured them into a study that edged close to parody: floor-to-ceiling bookcases, with two ladders that slid along brass rails anchored just below the molding; leather-bound books everywhere; a massive desk with broad planks of polished wood, bare except for one feature: a simple black telephone.

"Please, please, have a seat, get comfortable. Can I fix you two a drink?"

"No, I'm fine," Marsh said.

"Nothing for me, thanks," Sharon Kramer said.

"Ah 'pologize for the short notice an' the skulkin' around, but these are parlous times, parlous times. I jes' figured, hell, if anybody knew that this ol' yellah-dog Democrat was sittin' down with a couple a' rock-ribbed Republicans, there'd be hell to pay in the morning. Jes' thought it was better this way, right?"

"It *did* seem a touch melodramatic," Sharon said. *More like an old movie. Drive to a parking lot at Fifteenth and K; wait for a man driving a black Lincoln Town Car; I'm surprised he didn't make us use a password.*

"Well, you kin call me an old fool if you like, but I'm gonna lay it on the line with you—this is one of those conversations you jes' don't want anybody knowin' about—maybe not ever."

Petitcon walked over to the love seat across the coffee table from Marsh and Kramer. He took a long sip from his drink, then leaned forward until he was barely six inches from their faces.

"Folks, we are at what Dick Nixon used to call 'nut-cuttin' time.' I intend to talk to you right now with the bark off; 'nother words, if you put a bullshit detector on me right now, it would register a big, fat zero. And I hope you will return the favor. So tell me," he said, his words coming out slow and deliberate. *"Do—you—have—the—votes?"*

Marsh and Sharon looked at each other, then at Petitcon.

"Oh, Christ almighty, do you think I'm talkin' to you as some kind of Democrat spy? You think I'm tryin' to finger out how to shaft you people? For God's sake, don't you folks watch the news? Don't you read the papers?"

Petitcon leaned in even closer; Sharon thought for a moment that he'd pitch forward out of his chair and crash his head on the Chippendale.

"Do you have the vaguest idea who I've been holdin' hands with on the phone for the last four days? 'Course you don't. I am talking about sultans and emirs; I am talkin' about bankers and moguls; I am talkin' about people who haven't drawn a fearful breath in this world since you folks were in trainin' pants, and they are scared out of their goddamn *minds.* We are not talkin' about some little chicken-shit question like whether the donkeys or the elephants get the White House. We are talkin' about all these people with all their money watchin' us stagger our way through a process none of them ever imagined they'd be seein'—all these people meetin' in towns with names they never heard of, seein' if they can get us a President. And if you don't have the votes, and that damn electoral college deadlocks, then they get to sit aroun' and wait for the Congress to come back into session. And what happens then?"

"Well," Marsh said, clearing his throat. "I think it's clear—"

"Nothing is clear, Marsh, not *one* damn *thing.* If the House votes along party lines, you know who wins the presidency? *Nobody!* There's eighteen states where the Democrats have a majority of the members; sixteen states where you do; and 'nother sixteen where it's dead even, which means if they vote along straight party lines, nobody gets a majority. But of course, it won't happen that way. You'll have people jumpin' party lines, so maybe—jes' maybe—your Mr. Block gets his majority, only we won't know that for weeks. Only by then, it won't matter a tinker's damn. Because you are gonna have all these folks all over the world, decidin' that if we can't figure out how to choose a leader, maybe they got the wrong idea about what a safe, secure country we got. An' then, you know what you'll see? It'll be like a great big faucet bein' turned on, and hundreds and hundreds of billions of dollars drainin' out of the U.S.A. like *that."*

He got up and began walking around the room.

"Now, indulge me in the world's shortest history lesson. If that happens, it won't just be this country that'll wind up on its butt. If we go bust, how long do you think before Europe and Japan and the whole damn world finds itself right smack in the middle of a depression? Now, I'm the only one old enough to have a dim memory of what that meant, so pardon me if I state the obvious: but the last time that happened, we ended up with a gentleman named Adolf Hitler runnin' things, and fifty million corpses later, we got some dim understandin' of the real cost.

"Now *this* time, we got a slightly different scenario. *This* time we got, I dunno, six, eight, ten countries with nukular weapons. Would you like to see them in the hands of one of those crackpot Russians who thinks that their country by rights stretches from Alaska to Berlin? How about an Iranian, tellin' his people they're starvin' 'cause of the Great Satan? Have I spelled this out enough? Now tell me dammit: *Do—you—have—the—votes?"*

"We don't know," Marsh said.

"I think we do, but we don't know," Sharon Kramer said.

Petitcon nodded.

"Well, shoot, I guess nobody can blame you," he said, in a tone that indicated he sure as hell did. "Which is why I may have some good news—"

The black phone rang. Petitcon looked at it so sharply, it was remarkable that the phone had the aplomb to keep ringing.

"Yes," Petitcon said. He listened for a long time, his face showing the faintest trace of disapproval.

"Yes . . . yes . . . no, you really didn't have a choice . . . yes . . . you had to, yes . . . all right, all right."

"Well," Petitcon said, "that good news wasn't so good after all." He picked up the phone again, spoke for a short moment in a voice far too low to be overheard, then turned back to them again with a friendly smile.

"Well, now, if it's not a violation of the two-party system, I'd very much appreciate you takin' me through your vote count. I used to be pretty good at it myself; you won't find it in the history books, but I'm the guy who told Jack Kennedy that Wyoming would put him over the top out in Los Angeles. So, since I've done all the talkin' here, lemme sit back and let you take me through your count."

For fifteen minutes, Marsh meandered through a state-by-state estimate of the electoral vote count. Petitcon nodded sagely as Marsh explained the unknowns: whether, for example, the hard-Right conservatives in California and the West would unite behind someone like Senator Billy Doggs, giving the most conservative members of Congress a powerful negotiating club if the election were thrown into the House.

"Good Lord, can you imagine how that'll play in Europe—they'll think we've gone completely off our rockers."

Then there were the moderate-liberal Republicans, or what was left of them. Would Walter York pull any of them into the camp of Mueller? Would they vote for Walter York—and could he become a symbol of bipartisanship, a compromise candidate if the House in fact deadlocked?

"No, no," Petitcon shook his head. "Can't be. Your party would tear the Capitol down; he's a renegade, a Judas; it can't happen."

"Well, then there's the possibility of votes for Foyle—how they'd be counted, whether they'd be counted, we don't know, but—"

"Enough," said Petitcon, who had been checking his watch so frequently that Sharon wondered whether he was somehow bored by the vote count.

"See, here's the point," Petitcon said. "There's only one thing that can possibly happen day after tomorrow. Your boy Block has got to win a majority. Every other possibility is absolutely unacceptable."

The doorbell chimes sounded faintly through the closed doors. Petitcon's face relaxed in a smile of reassurance.

"Excuse me for just a minute, folks," he said.

"Do you have a clue?" Sharon asked when Petitcon left the room.

"No," Marsh said, "but I'm a little relieved. All night I've had the feeling he was going to propose himself as a compromise candidate for President."

"Are you kidding?" said Sharon. "Give up all that power?"

Petitcon threw open the study door with a wide sweep of one arm; the other was draped around the broad shoulders of a tall, stunning black man.

"I'll be damned," said Marsh.

"Hardly," said the Reverend W. Dixon Mason.

FORTY-TWO

★ ★ ★

"All right, let's try it again! When you get the cue you walk—*quick*ly, *purpose*fully—to your assigned positions. If you are holding a piece of paper, *stop*—put the paper *down*—count to seven, you're all in college, I'm sure you know how to count that high—then pick *up* the piece of paper, wait *'one, two, three,'* then go back to your original positions. Do not *laugh,* do not *talk*. If you are assigned to a phone, pick *up* the phone, listen for *ten* seconds, then say, 'Yes, I understand,' hang *up* the phone, then type into the computer for at *least* fifteen seconds. For God's sake, don't say *any*thing else, we've got half a million lip-readers out there. And don't type anything into the computer except what's written on the paper in front of you. Now, do you all understand?"

A dozen stunned journalism majors from Georgetown University nodded. They had been rounded up and bused to the network's Washington studio, giddy with the prospect of working for the next twenty-four hours on the special-events coverage of the electoral college—or, as the network logos were now calling it, "The Winner Is . . ." ("Sounds like the Academy Awards," the senior vice-president said. "I know," the president said with a big smile. "I know.") When the earnest young men and women arrived, thrilled to be eyewitnesses to history in the making, they were each given a box lunch, fifty dollars in cash, and a set of written instructions directing them to sit, stand, move, and talk into the telephone.

"You mean, like we're . . . *extras?*" one of the students asked.

"I wouldn't think of it that way at all," said Patricia Rollin, associate producer of special events. "Look at the size of this studio. You could play a basketball game on this floor. We've got forty desks, a hundred telephones, eighty-five computers, fifty video monitors, not counting that thirty-square-foot high-definition monster on the far wall, and sixty news people—and when we go on the air in . . . less than an hour, it'll *still* look half-empty. So what's going to happen when people tune in, thinking they're going to be watching the biggest political story of their lives? If they see a half-empty news set, what does that tell them? It tells them the story isn't really that big after all. It mis*leads* them, right? So what you're doing is helping us communicate the real *drama,* the historical significance, of what they're watching."

"Total bullshit," the student whispered to her friend.

"Hey, it's fifty bucks, free food, and a backstage pass," the friend said.

As the young men and women practiced their walks, pivots, and turns, Al DeRossa sat at a desk in the middle of the chaos, oblivious to the hammering, the hollering, the walls going up all around him, fielding a steady stream of telephone calls. He kept one eye on the dozens of monitors built into the walls, each of them trained on an exterior shot of a state capitol, or the interior of a legislative chamber, where the electors would soon gather.

The phone calls were more ritual than reporting: feverish exchanges of inaccurate information, rumors of defections, breathless queries about alliances and intrigues.

Had he heard that the Speaker of the House and Connor Doyle were behind closed doors on Capitol Hill—no staff, no press availability, not even an announcement on the public schedule? Was there anything to the story that Governor Block had tried to place a telephone call to Bill Mueller to propose that Mueller be named Vice President in a coalition government? What about the story that eighty-five House members and twenty senators were calling for an emergency congressional resolution declaring that Foyle's death had created a vacancy in the office of President, and calling for a special presidential election to be held at the end of January?

It was the sort of heady, intoxicating nonsense that made Election Days fun. Today, DeRossa wanted no part of it. On normal Election

Days, this breathless gossip was the cocktail hour; the main course would arrive when the first exit-poll numbers came pouring out of the computers, when those on the inside began to sense the pattern of colors that would fill in the map of the United States. Today, that huge map once again dominated the far wall, with each state lit up in red or blue, indicating how it had voted in November. To the right of the map was a bright blue elephant, under which was the number 305—the electoral vote that Foyle and Block had won. To the left, a bright red donkey and the number 233—the total for Mueller and Vincent.

And that was all they knew.

At noon, Eastern time, the first group of electors would begin filing into the state senate chambers, or the old supreme court conference rooms, or the rotundas of the state capitol buildings, each one more ornate, more gilded than the next, many of them tributes to the joys of government building contracts in an age before auditors and IRS agents. It was possible that nothing was going to happen, that except for a few mavericks, Ted Block would be chosen as President, with Sherwood Phelps at his side.

It was also possible that at the end of the day, the United States still would not know who its President would be.

"Forty-five minutes to air, people, forty-five minutes to air," Ken Crenshaw's voice boomed out across the immense set. There was an unsettling edge to Crenshaw's voice, a tone worrisome enough to propel DeRossa out of his chair and up the flight of stairs to the control room. He found Crenshaw sitting in his command chair, scanning a bank of four dozen monitors.

"You okay?" DeRossa asked.

"Sure, sure, why wouldn't I be? You know, this is probably a good thing, good for us, I mean, if you take the long view, you know, Al? I mean, we've all gotten stale, everything is cut and dried, you know? We're at a convention, we have the guy's acceptance speech, what do we do? He talks about old people, we got a guy eighty years old with a straw hat dozing into his newspaper. He talks about poor people, we find a black guy, maybe it's Bill Cosby, doesn't matter, if he's black, he's gotta be poor."

Crenshaw began to shred a dinner roll, sending little puffs of dough cascading into the air.

"And the inaugurals, you know what I mean, Al? The new President says Washington, Jefferson, Lincoln, Kennedy, we go *boom! boom! boom! boom!,* the monument, the memorial, the memorial, the eternal flame. I mean, where's the excitement, where's the tension, you know?

"Well, here it is, Al. Right here. Maybe there'll be fistfights; maybe the National Guard in Georgia will shoot an elector. Maybe three incredible things will happen at the same time, and I'll have to get *every one of them* on the air! Is that great or what?"

Crenshaw slammed his fist down, punching through a glass panel built into the console. A stream of blood began to trickle down his right hand.

"Good Luck, Ken."

"Mr. Roses?"

Al looked up into the face of one of the student interns.

"You mean, 'DeRossa'?"

"Yes? Right? There's a phone call for you? Like, I'm supposed to pick up the phone and pretend to talk and hang up? Only the phone, like, it keeps ringing? And there's someone who says they need to talk to Mr. Roses? So, like, I'm thinking, this is a mistake? Like they want a florist or something? But then some guy says, maybe it's for you? On line eight?"

"Thank you," DeRossa said, reaching for a phone. "By the way, what's your major?"

"Communications?"

"Of *course* it is . . . yes?"

"Al, it's Len Griese."

"Len? Where are you? You're okay? Dorothy? . . ."

"We're more than okay. But you're not gonna believe where we are, or what's going to happen."

"Are you kidding? After the other night, I'll believe anything."

"All right. After you got those goons off our backs, we stayed up 'til dawn talking: Dorothy, me, Ben, and she got two other people—a guy in New Jersey named Walter and a woman in Texas, Faith, I think it is—on the phone. By five A.M. or so, they figured out what they were going to do. See, once they ruled out defecting to Mueller, since they didn't want the loser to win, and once they figured they had to do what they could to keep Block out of the White House, then what are your options as a good Republican elector?"

DeRossa rubbed his forehead.

Once a professor, always a professor.

"I don't really think it—"

"Here, let me put Dorothy on. It was her idea, let her tell you."

A moment later, Dorothy Ledger came on the line, sounding as if she'd been named valedictorian and homecoming queen on the same day.

"Al, do you believe it?"

"Believe *what?*"

"Connor Doyle. We're going to vote for *Doyle.* It's so . . . logical, I can't believe it took us so long to get it. He's the Republican leader of the House, right? Sixteen votes short of being Speaker of the House. Right now, Doyle's the highest-ranking Republican in the government. If enough of us vote for him so that he finishes in the top three, maybe the House Democrats will go for him for President."

"That's impossible, Dorothy, the Democrats hate Connor. He's done nothing but make their lives miserable."

"So what's their choice?" she said. "Are they going to vote for Ted Block? They spent the whole campaign telling America that he was Bozo the Clown in a blazer. They also know they're not going to get more than one or two House Republicans to vote for Mueller, no matter what Walter York says. Besides," she added, dropping her voice to a whisper, "you haven't heard who we're going to vote for for *Vice* President."

"Okay," Al said, checking the clock. "I give up."

"Theodore Pinckney Block," Dorothy said.

And I thought it couldn't get weirder.

"It's beautiful," Leonard Griese chuckled into an extension. "Dorothy and every other Republican elector pledged to cast a vice-presidential vote for Block—and that's exactly what she's going to do."

"Wait, wait," Al said. "How does it make any sense to put a guy a heartbeat away from a job you say he's unfit for? And anyway, the regular Republicans are going to vote for Sherwood Phelps for veep. If the Senate decides the vice presidency, and they get to pick from the top two, that'll be Phelps and Vincent. Block won't even make the runoff. . . . Oh, oh, my, that's really neat."

"Exactly," Griese said. "Dorothy and her allies do their constitutional duty. And if it should happen that Governor Block is denied an opportunity for further public service, so be it."

"And that's good enough for me," said Dorothy. "Do I think Connor Doyle will make a good President? Maybe. I hope so, I think so. But right now, he's the one way I can help keep the big boys from cramming Ted Block down our throats. For all I know, it won't make a damn bit of difference if it *does* go into the House; maybe Block'll win there. But if they have to sweat enough, maybe they'll remember the next time they try one of their stupid little power games. I'm pretty sure," she added grimly, "they'll remember *this* time."

DeRossa looked through the windows of the control room down to the election set, and saw several hands frantically motioning for him. He held up a cautionary finger, then pointed to the phone and gave a thumbs-up gesture.

"How many have you got to go along with you?" Al asked. "You got the thirty-six you need?"

"I don't think we need that many," Dorothy said. "If Ben's computer friends are right, we think there'll be a dozen votes at least for Foyle. They may not count, but they'll keep Block's total down, and that's all that counts if we're trying to deny him a majority. Then we figure maybe eight or ten votes in the South and West for Senator Billy Doggs, and then maybe one or two really off-the-wall votes, the kind nobody can even guess right now. But we think with fifteen or twenty votes, we throw it into the House."

Jesus. How could I have forgotten?

"Dorothy? Where are you guys?"

"I'm in Lansing, Michigan. We drove all day and—I'm so stiff I don't know if I'll be able to make it up the capitol steps. I'm in an apartment five blocks from there; my friend Faith has a friend at Michigan State who's lending me her apartment. Isn't it great? In twenty minutes, I walk up the steps of the capitol with a federal court order. Maybe they'll try to arrest me, but you know what? I think then they've got a martyr on their hands. That could even be worth another defector or two out West when it hits the TV—okay, okay. Al, I gotta go. And please, Al, please. Don't use this. It's *got* to be kept quiet. 'Bye."

After he hung up the phone, Al thought it over: the rules of the game were clear. If somebody told you something, and didn't tell you it was off the record at the beginning, then what was said was on the record—you could use it without losing a minute's sleep. Then he thought about this perfectly ordinary woman who had spent a lifetime working for her party, and who had one day stood up and said one word to every blue suit with a VIP parking place, every fixer with a midwinter tan and a first-class upgrade, every smug insider with a private line to playoff tickets and rock concerts and the college waiting lists.

She had said, "No."

Screw it, DeRossa thought. *It'll make a great footnote to the history books.*

He gave Crenshaw one final pat on the back, and hustled down the stairs to his position on the election set: a hollowed-out bunker three feet behind and four feet below the Anchor desk. As he looked up at Ed Steele's backside, DeRossa silently prayed that Steele had not eaten a rich Mexican breakfast.

"Okay, folks," Crenshaw's voice boomed out. "Two minutes to air! Cue the kids!"

And as a waiting nation held its breath, as a two-hundred-year-old piece of fragile political machinery creaked into action, a dozen bright-eyed journalism students began marching around the set, trying very hard not to laugh out loud.

FORTY-THREE

★ ★ ★

It was a tasteful, elegant, solemn beginning.

As the recording blared the familiar notes of "Ruffles and Flourishes," aerial shots of half a dozen state capitols filled the split screen, each dissolving into another at two-and-a-half-second intervals. Anchor Ed Steele welcomed viewers by saying, "This is a day for the history books. By sunset tonight, we will know whether the most serious test of our constitutional system is over or whether we're just beginning a new and more dangerous chapter. Will we have a President; could the candidate defeated at the polls last month wind up in the White House? Will the choice be thrown into the House of Representatives, under rules that could paralyze the federal government for weeks, even months? The stakes . . . could not be higher."

"This—is a special report," the unseen announcer with the Voice of Doom intoned. " 'The Winner Is . . .' Brought to you by Heath and McFadden, protecting your family's future since 1926; and by Denta-Free, with a gleam in every glass."

"Would it have killed them to knock off the voice-over plugs just this once?" Kathy Conicki said. She was jammed in next to Al DeRossa in the subsurface workstation just beneath the Anchor desk, trying to keep her pencils, pens, research cards, and tabulation sheets in some form of order.

"Would you like to tell the advertisers they don't get an opening pitch to twenty million viewers?" DeRossa asked. "Or would you like to convince Corporate that it's worth a giveback of, oh, a quarter million or so? Besides, it's time to look smart."

Kathy handed DeRossa the first batch of cards, which recounted every marginally interesting fact about the electoral college's history. DeRossa fanned through them, then handed up the first half dozen to the Anchor's research assistant, who in turn subtly fanned them out in front of Steele. Without ever breaking eye contact with the camera, Steele somehow glanced at the cards and wove the information into his unscripted comments.

". . . The debate goes back to the earliest of our political campaigns. When a Federalist elector from Massachusetts threatened to bolt the ticket in 1800 to vote for Jefferson, one irate citizen said, 'Do I choose Samuel Miles to think? No! I choose him to act!' This is exactly what the Republican Party hopes their electors will do today. For more background on this, we bring in our Distinguished Commentator—actually, I'm told that something is happening at the state capitol in Richmond, so let's go there."

The network's millions of listeners could hear the distinct crack of a pencil being snapped in two an instant before the craggy planes of Ed Steele's face disappeared, replaced instantly by flailing arms; faces contorted in excitement, fear, and pain; and the barely controlled voice of Petra Feschin, a local reporter for the network's Richmond affiliate.

"Yes, Ed, we . . . we have a . . ."

("—don't get that fuckin' *camera* out of my shot, I'll deck ya!")

". . . Ed, we have a situation developing here, and I'm—"

("Aaagh!")

"—I'm not exactly sure what is happening, but—"

"Petra." Ed Steele's voice was ominously calm. "Petra Feschin. This is Ed Steele. What is happening down in Richmond?"

"He wants to know what's happening!" Petra's sound man could be heard yelling over the disjointed jabber of the mob.

"What the hell does he think I'm trying to find out!" Petra yelled back, forgetting that her mike was live. Ken Crenshaw quickly switched to an overhead shot from a NewsScene "Eye in the Sky" helicopter, circling a few hundred feet over the capitol building. Outside the Virginia State

Capitol, a cluster of men and woman nearly one hundred strong, armed with microphones, cameras, pads, and pens, had coalesced, listing first one way, then the other, like a huge mass of organic flotsam waiting for any wave to hurtle them in one direction or another. In an instant, the wave hit; the mass moved. The mob surged toward a twelve-year-old Plymouth Escort parked just outside the capitol building, in which William Black had driven Helen Tharp, his eighty-one-year-old mother-in-law and a longtime Virginia elector, to the vote. Mrs. Tharp, a woman of fragile physical and emotional health, took one look at what she saw as an armed mob of thugs, and collapsed with severe intestinal pains. William Black swept his mother-in-law up in his arms, deposited her in the back of his Plymouth Escort, and drove his car at full speed into the pack of reporters and camera crews, injuring five. (He was later charged with attempted vehicular homicide; after his attorney screened the tape for the court, the jury acquitted Black, following deliberations that lasted twelve minutes.)

"An unfortunate scene of disorder that can only mar the sense of gravity that surrounds today's proceedings. I wonder now, if our Distinguished Commentator . . . no, we go to Concord, New Hampshire, now, where an apparent change in the schedule is taking place."

"Don't think I don't know what you're up to, Crenshaw," the Distinguished Commentator growled. "You're jealous of my *contract;* you're jealous of my position here, you're—"

"May I remind you," said the senior vice-president through the closed-circuit microphone, "that there are a dozen media critics in the Green Room, doing pieces on how we're covering this story? They can't hear me, but they sure as hell heard you. Now I'll start trying to convince them it's all an inside joke, so why don't you try to control yourself, okay?"

At the state capitol in Concord, the four New Hampshire electors were hurriedly making their way into the state senate chamber, as the governor mounted the rostrum.

"Take 'im now!" Crenshaw yelled.

"Fellow citizens," the governor said, pretending he did not know that he was live from coast to coast, "one of the great traditions in American political life is that New Hampshire is first—first to cast their primary votes for President, and first in November, when the townspeople of

Dixville Notch gather at midnight to cast the first Election Day votes. We count it as one of our state's many great traditions."

"What's the other one?" Kathy Conicki whispered.

"We thought it only appropriate," the governor continued, "to be first in the nation to cast our electoral votes. So let us proceed."

The four electors, three men and a woman, strode to the well of the state senate. Three of them were off a New England picture postcard; their weathered faces and gnarled hands spoke of a lifetime of honest toil. The fourth was a twenty-six-year-old systems analyst who worked at a computer graphics design firm on Route 128 outside of Manchester, who appeared uncommonly nervous as he gazed repeatedly at his ballot before dropping it into an ancient oak box, which was handed up to the governor.

"I will now count the ballots," he said. "One vote for Theodore Block for President, Sherwood Phelps for Vice President. Another vote for Theodore Block for President, Sherwood Phelps for Vice President . . ." He paused for a moment, and looked up angrily.

"There is a vote here for . . . Connor Doyle for President, and Theodore Block for *Vice* President."

Oh, my God, DeRossa thought. *That's one of Dorothy's.*

In the press gallery of the New Hampshire State Senate, one of the veteran members of the press corps bolted to his feet, raced to his phone in the press room, and punched up the number of his metro desk.

"There's been a defection! There's a vote for Connor Doyle for President!"

The snicker at the other end of the phone was clear.

"We know, Dave," said the dayside metro editor. "It's on the TV live, remember? Now go back and get us some local color. And, Dave? In case you pick up another scoop, we heard that Lindbergh made it."

"The chair is at something of a . . . loss to determine the proper method of counting this ballot," the governor said, gazing over to a wizened midget of a man who sat on a ceremonial thronelike chair to the governor's right. John Greene, for forty-seven years the senate parliamentarian, slowly turned his head to the governor, realized he was actually being asked a critical point of procedure, and gave his head a slow, steady back-and-forth shake.

Knowing he had to make some decision or be branded a dithering fool in the eyes of the nation, the governor slammed down the gavel.

"Since it is the task of the Congress to decide whether electoral votes have been 'regularly given,' it is the decision of the chair to count these ballots as marked, and transmit them to the Congress with a formal notice recognizing that one of these ballots has been cast in a manner not in accordance with the recommendation of the national party."

"Well," Ed Steele said to his audience, "a dramatic beginning to the day. Based on our count," he said, turning back toward the huge map on the far wall, "the Republican ticket of Ted Block and Sherwood Phelps has already lost one vote."

The electronic number under the elephant flashed and changed from 305 to 304. "We do not know, of course, whether this defection represents an isolated incident, or in fact means that we may, indeed, end the day without anyone achieving the two hundred seventy votes needed for a majority. I'm sure our Distinguished Commentator has some words about this."

"Indeed I do, Ed," said the Distinguished Commentator, barely concealing his impatience at the long delay. He had no idea what this vote meant, and not even that much curiosity. It had been years since he had last done any original reporting, preferring to gather his opinions by reading the pages of four newspapers and two magazines, and shaping them into an easily digestible consensus. For the Distinguished Commentator, a successful day was measured solely in the amount of time he had been featured on the airwaves.

"This vote represents a potentially major, major event," he began. "We can't know, of course, whether any other elector will follow this example, and of course, unless thirty-five other Republican electors decide not to vote for Governor Block, why, of course, then he becomes the President—actually, I suppose, the President-elect, until Inauguration Day. But I wonder, Ed, I wonder whether we shouldn't see this early vote as a portent of some kind, a signal, maybe not conclusive, maybe misleading, but a clear signal, nonetheless, of a potential for some very, very interesting developments in the hours, and perhaps days ahead. Ed?"

"Nobody listens, Al, right?" Kathy Conicki asked. "That's the only explanation, right?"

DeRossa shrugged.

"Could be worse," he said. "He could be on PBS teaching people how to wire their kitchens. He'd kill *thousands.*"

"We go now to Augusta, Maine, where four Democratic electors, pledged to William Mueller, are gathering to vote. We suspect that there will be a steady stream of such votes for the next three hours—after which we will know whether this American melodrama is ending—or just beginning."

- Maine's four electors, including the Esperanto lady, held firm. Under the donkey, the 233 light flashed.
- In Montpelier, Vermont's three Democrats held firm.
- In Providence, one of the six Democratic electors bolted, and voted for Dr. Gerald Baker for President; Baker had spent the last twenty years crisscrossing America on a bicycle, urging an end to all artificially powered machinery. The defecting elector, wearing a brown, one-piece, hand-stitched garment made from a hand-driven loom, refused to appear before the press after casting his vote, claiming that he wanted to be no part of any enterprise that encouraged the massive misuse of electrical power created by fossilized fuel.

On the network's tote board, the number under the donkey flashed and changed to 232. Under a now-illuminated question mark, the number 1 began to flash.

- The image quickly shifted to Hartford; there, one of Connecticut's eight Republican electors voted for former Senator Walter York, as a sign of respect for his "inspiring example of personal and political rectitude," causing Jack Petitcon, watching the returns alone at home, to burst out in an appreciative chuckle. He grew instantly somber when another elector cast her vote for Connor Doyle for President and Theodore Block for Vice President.

So that's what the bitch had in mind, he thought. *Nice try, Dorothy.*

- The big news came from Trenton, where three of the fifteen Republican electors, led by a rangy senior citizen named Walter Ames,

Jr., stood up as a group, strode to the ballot boxes in the state senate, and cast their votes for Doyle for President, and Block for Vice President. Under the elephant, the number 300 flashed.

"If that goddamn number starts blinking with a two in front of it, we've got ourselves a serious problem," said one of the Young Blue Suits to the group assembled in Marsh's office.

"Yeah," Alan Veigle said with a chuckle. "I'm shakin', I'm shakin.' "

"Why don't you try being quiet—just this once, okay?" Marsh snapped. "Just—be—quiet."

"You're awfully confident," said the Young Blue Suit.

"That's because I'm at peace with myself," said Alan Veigle. "You know, like Mark Twain said? I feel like a Christian with four aces."

DeRossa's phone rang as the image began to focus on the New York electors, gathering in the senate chamber in Albany.

"Al, it's Dorothy. I'm on a cell phone. We're leaving the apartment now."

"We?"

"Me and the lawyer. We'll be at the capitol in about ten minutes. I think the bad guys'll be waiting for me at the steps."

"Right," Al said. "Thanks." He punched up the direct line to Crenshaw.

"Thank God it's you, Al," Ken said. "Since it's you, I know this is really important, and not some asshole executive telling me he didn't like the framing on the beauty shot from Hartford."

"Gotcha. Ken, we've got a big one coming in from Lansing—Michigan. Dorothy Ledger's going to be walking up the capitol steps in about ten minutes. I think we can expect a confrontation outside."

"No shit? Like George Wallace at the schoolhouse door back in '63? Boy, that's great stuff. She's not wearing an RF mike or anything, is she?"

"I doubt it, Ken, but trust me, there'll be enough press there to pick it up."

"All right!"

Okay, now you can be a real journalist, DeRossa told himself, and pointed an urgent finger toward himself. Ed Steele, in the midst of introducing the thirty-three New York electors pledged to William Mueller, didn't miss a beat.

"Al DeRossa, our intrepid political director, may have picked up some political intelligence. It's been pretty hard to come by, hasn't it, Al?"

"Yes, Ed, but we've just learned [*Just? Try an hour ago!*] that the much-in-demand Dorothy Ledger, the Michigan Republican who began this revolt at the National Committee meeting, is about to try and make her way into the capitol at Lansing, where she intends to cast her vote for Connor Doyle for President, and Theodore Block for Vice President. In fact, Ed, those defecting votes that we are seeing appear to be the product of a strategy developed by Ms. Ledger and an unidentified group of her political allies. Their clear intention is to deny Ted Block a majority, and to force this vote into the House of Representatives."

"I knew it," said the Distinguished Commentator, triumphantly. "That's what I was trying to explain earlier, when I—"

Ed Steele interrupted.

"We go now to Lansing, Michigan, to the steps of the capitol, where a potentially historic standoff may be about to begin."

"What about New York?" Kathy asked.

"Last time we checked, it's solid for Mueller," DeRossa said. "Maybe one of the whackos will try and vote for Fidel or somebody, but that's about it."

As the overhead helicopter shot from Lansing moved in on the state capitol, the chatter and clatter on the vast news set began to lessen; when the camera panned down to a lone woman walking swiftly, purposefully, down the street leading to the capitol, the set was still. On the monitors bordering the set, the image of Dorothy Ledger filled every screen. (Her lawyer, no stranger to the media world, had deliberately dropped back half a dozen paces.)

"Je-sus," Alan Veigle whispered reverently. "It's fucking *High Noon.*"

The shot switched to the ground-level camera mounted on the capitol steps as Dorothy approached a narrow pathway to the building marked by police barricades. Two men in gray suits began to step forward toward her.

"Good afternoon, gentlemen," Dorothy said. "My name is Dorothy

Ledger, duly appointed presidential elector, here to cast my vote. Do we have a problem of some sort here?"

Suddenly, Ken Crenshaw's voice cut into the live feed.

"Go to New York! Go to New York, goddamnit! Something's happening in New York right now!"

The floor of the New York State Senate had suddenly erupted into chaos. In the well of the Senate, six African-Americans surrounded a corpulent figure clad in a mauve suede jumpsuit, a well-known political figure known as Pastor Bill Gendron, universally dubbed "activist" by the people who captioned news photos. Each of the black electors was holding up the formal embossed ballot that had been handed to them. On either side of them, clusters of electors stood screaming, shouting, waving fists, pointing accusatory fingers.

"What is this?" Steele barked into the closed-circuit connection to the local reporter standing outside the chamber.

"I don't *know,*" he whined. "They sent me up here at the last minute. I cover consumer stuff, you know? Back-dated milk, appliance rip-offs. I don't *know* what's happening!"

It became clear soon enough. The six black electors ceremoniously ripped the ballots in two, tossed them onto the floor of the state senate, removed from their breast pockets their own ballots, and dropped them one by one into the ballot box. The secretary of state, a career political hack whose biggest previous challenge had been the redesign of state drivers' licenses, paled visibly as he received the written tabulation from an equally flustered clerk, and read the totals.

"On the balloting for President and Vice President of the United States," he began, then looked over at the clerk, who nodded vigorously, and resumed.

"There are twenty-seven votes for William Mueller for President and James Vincent for Vice President . . . ," he intoned.

"Twenty-seven?" DeRossa exploded. "New York has *thirty-three* votes. What is this?"

". . . and six votes for Theodore Block for President and Sherwood Phelps for Vice President."

The chamber dissolved into chaos. A dozen Mueller loyalists, including three blacks, rushed Pastor Gendron and his flock of a half dozen, and pummeled them to the carpeted floor of the state senate before shocked security guards rushed in to pull them apart. Other electors were demanding a recount, demanding a recess, shouting out points of order that the ballots be impounded, invalidated, nullified.

"This is another utterly unexpected, utterly breathtaking political shock," anchor Ed Steele reported, his voice barely hinting at the turmoil. "In New York State, six Democratic electors pledged to the Mueller-Vincent ticket have bolted, throwing their electoral votes to the Republican ticket of Governor Block and Congressman Phelps. We simply do not know what the fate of these votes will be, but at the moment"—he turned to the map behind him—"at the moment, the ticket of Block and Phelps is up again to three hundred six electoral votes."

• At Block's headquarters, one of the Young Blue Suits looked admiringly at Marsh, Veigle, and Sharon Kramer.

"Wow," he said. "You guys are *good.*"

• Before the news media could get its teeth into the New York story, the Pennsylvania electors convened in Harrisburg; five black electors, four from Philadelphia, one from Pittsburgh, stood in the well, tore up their ballots, and dropped in hand-lettered, signed ballots of their own for the Republican ticket of Block and Phelps.

• Almost simultaneously, three black Democratic electors from Massachusetts staged precisely the same ritual in the statehouse in Boston.

• And that is when the Very Reverend W. Dixon Mason walked out onto the steps of the nation's Capitol in Washington, D.C., and read a brief statement.

"My fellow Americans, let me explain to you what is happening right now in people's houses all across this scarred yet magnificent land. Over the last few days," Mason said, "I have been engaged in prayerful conversation, in person and by telephone, with some forty-seven presidential electors of African-American descent, forty-four of whom were elected as Democrats. It may have been true that they were placed on these slates as a symbol of power, a token of power, if you will, but fate has decreed that they now hold authentic power, to decide who shall lead this wounded land."

"Get to the point," hissed the Distinguished Commentator, with that special scorn reserved for those who stood between him and a live camera.

"Many of us still bear the scars of the battles for our fundamental rights—none more sacred than the right to vote, and to have those votes counted freely and fairly. No group of Americans more deeply feels the pain of being denied the full scope of those rights.

"We did not walk the streets of Montgomery, we did not feel the pain of the police dogs and fire hoses of Birmingham, to deny those rights to others. We believe that in America, the majority rules. In the past, members of the white majority have stood up and spoken for the minority. So today, we return the favor; we ensure that the will of the majority shall prevail, by ensuring that the Republican Party, which won the majority of votes on Election Day, shall in fact have the power it has earned. Thank you."

With that, Reverend Mason turned and, for the first time in his public life, walked away from the dozens of cameras pointed at him.

• "Holy shitski," said Kathy Conicki. "Ho-ly shitski."

"My sentiments exactly," said Al DeRossa.

"Is that it?" Kathy said.

"Oh, yes," said Al. "Game, set, and match. "Mason would never have gone public if he didn't have the votes to give Block a majority. I just hope they're ready to put the boys at the federal mint on overtime, 'cause this one is gonna *cost."*

• At the Mueller campaign offices, Joe Featherstone sat blinking at the television set, like a jungle beast felled by a falling tree trunk. All around him, the volunteers who a moment ago had been cheering each defection from the Block total sat mute.

"Joe?" one of them finally asked. "What does it mean?"

"It means that you should seriously begin exploring the joys of graduate school."

• Less than a mile away, Jack Petitcon smiled broadly, poured himself two fingers of Chivas, settled back in his chair, and gazed off into the middle distance, contemplating the vagaries of politics and the immensity of his accounts receivable.

• As he folded his six and a half feet into the back of a waiting car, the Very Reverend W. Dixon Mason kept a solemn mien on his face, knowing that the cameras would keep rolling until the car pulled out of view.

That's right, you bastards. Keep your cameras going, so you can catch the face of a man who put patriotism over party, fairness over fratricide. Make sure that Joe Featherstone gets to see this on the news, so he can think about how much fun it was to keep Dixon Mason in the kitchen, instead of inviting him into the parlor. Do you get it now, Mr. Featherstone? Have I made myself perfectly clear?

• A thousand miles away, Dorothy Ledger still stood at the barrier to the state capitol, where she, a phalanx of reporters, security guards, state police, and lawyers, had watched Reverend Mason on a tiny portable TV monitor. When it was over, the lawyer for the Michigan Republican Party looked at her.

"Dorothy? I still have to serve you with this subpoena ordering you not to—"

She took it, smiled weakly, stuffed it in her purse, and turned away.

"Thank you," she said, "but I don't think it really matters much right now."

She turned and walked back down the street; not a single camera followed her retreat.

FORTY-FOUR

★ ★ ★

When it was over, eleven Republican electors had cast their votes for the late President-Who-Never-Was, MacArthur Foyle. Nine more had voted for Senator Billy Doggs, from Tennessee. Five Republicans had voted for "others," including ex-senator Walter York, radio talk-show host Avi DuPoir, and onetime radio crooner Glenn Glade.

And twenty-three electors had voted for House minority leader Connor Doyle for President, and Governor Theodore Block for Vice President. That would have been more than enough to throw the Presidential election into the House of Representatives—except that thirty-nine black Democratic electors had cast *their* votes for Ted Block and Sherwood Phelps, giving the Republican ticket 296 electoral votes, a clear majority.

The defections had triggered angry denunciations throughout the Democratic Party; a rump group of liberal Democrats in the House had threatened to challenge the ballots. But Joe Featherstone had put it well in his last phone call to Bill Mueller, just before fleeing the country for six months on Bali.

"It's a terrific argument, isn't it? We argue that *our* electors can't vote for *their* guy, so that when *their* electors don't vote for *their* guy, or maybe if they vote for *our* guy, we can claim *their* guy doesn't have enough votes to be President. I'm sorry, sir, but we're hoist with our own petard, caught in our own trap; we're screwed."

There were still some unexploded bombs littering the landscape: for one thing, seventeen Republican electors had voted for Block for *Vice* President, on the theory that this was what they had pledged to do. There was already a nasty fight brewing among the senators about what to do with those votes. And the wise-guy pop culture was already declaring a national day of celebration over the prospect of Ted Block as America's President.

And two weeks later, as shoppers packed the department stores for the post-Christmas sales, as the New Year's Dread settled on single men and women across the continent, as workmen hammered the inaugural platform into place on the west front of the Capitol, Al DeRossa sat across a quiet table in the corner of the Tabard Inn on a late afternoon, and raised his glass at a weary, haggard, still uncommonly attractive Sharon Kramer.

"Your health," he said with a smile.

"What's left of it," she said, and knocked back her glass of wine in three quick gulps.

"Another, please?"

DeRossa signaled to the waiter in the nearly deserted bar.

"I thought you'd be heady with power, with no assistance from alcohol."

"Well, funny you should say that," Sharon said with a small smile. "You know my dear friends Marsh and Veigle, right? The minute the vote was over, they pretty much took up full-time residence at headquarters. They're in there nineteen hours a day, fighting over the White House staff, the Cabinet . . ." She reached for the fresh glass of wine and drank half of it.

"Maybe we should get something to eat," DeRossa said.

"Not to worry, Al," Sharon said. "I took a cab over here, and I'll take a cab back—unless you've got a better idea," she said with a wink.

"Not if you keep putting away that wine," DeRossa said, laughing. "If I ever *do* get my hands on you, it's not going to be with you half in the bag. But it's a little odd hearing *you* talk about somebody else's love of power. I don't mean this unkindly, love, but you haven't exactly been lacking in that department."

Sharon nodded.

"Fair enough, fair enough. But not like this, Al. Not with the Reverend Mr. Mason on the other end of the telephone a dozen times a day. It's nothing blatant, you understand; more like fifteen minutes of the latest on his causes, the striking cannery workers in Galveston, the homeless shelter that collapsed in Chicago, wouldn't it be a good idea if the new President would stand shoulder to shoulder with the least among us . . ."

"So far so good," DeRossa said.

"Yeah, but sooner or later, before you realize it, we're talking about Job Opportunity Zones, and Community Training Partnership contracts, and isn't it amazing how the Reverend Mr. Mason and his Live the Dream Foundation have just the right people to organize and run these worthy enterprises."

Sharon signaled the waiter for another glass of wine, then looked sharply at DeRossa.

"Don't, Al. Honest, say one word and I'm out of here. I'm not going to get shitfaced, I'm not going to blow lunch on the table, I'm not going to rip your clothes off. I need a little bit of time with an old friend who's not going to give me grief if I get just the least little bit buzzed.

"Now where was I? Oh, yes, the Reverend Mr. Mason. A fascinating fellow, Al; you just never know where the ward-heeling, pocket-lining sonofabitch leaves off and the great crusader begins. I'll give you a little scoop, DeRo—isn't that what some of your buddies call you, DeRo?—President Block is going to have *three* blacks in his Cabinet. First time ever for the Republican Party. *Three.* And I'm not talking Harvard Law School colored people. You know Winnie Carr?"

"The Hospital Workers' Union in Detroit?"

"The very same. What do you think of Ms. Carr for Health and Human Services?"

"I think Senator Billy Doggs is going to fall down and die on the floor of the United States Senate," DeRossa said.

"Right; but see, the next minute the Reverend Mason is bending Marsh's ear about minorities in overseas investing, and tax abatements for black entrepreneurs, and all of a sudden I'm hearing the rustle of Swiss bank account applications in my sleep."

"And how is Mr. More-or-Less President Block handling all this?"

Sharon paused for a moment, and leaned toward DeRossa, who strained to hear her voice while not staring down her blouse.

"This is the weird part, Al, and this is so off-the-record I can't *begin* to tell you."

"Come on, this is me."

"Yeah, you—a guy who works for a network news operation. Okay, I'm sorry. He almost seems . . . depressed. Teddy Block. Mr. Chipper."

"Burden of the office?"

"Are you kidding? Block? I spent four months with him. He really, truly possesses the inner calm of the not terribly bright. It's something else. I think . . . it's like he just hates how it all happened. If Mack Foyle had died in office, fine. If Block had walked into the White House as the heir apparent, fine. I think he could even have handled all the crap being thrown at him. You know, remind himself about Truman; 'to err is Truman,' that sort of thing. . . . But I think he feels like he won a fixed fight. And he *hates* that. His whole life is about playing by the rules his parents taught him, especially his mother."

"Um, yezzzzz, it all starts viz ze muzzah . . ."

She swatted his hand.

"Damn you, I'm serious. A little bit high, maybe, but serious. Mr. Block may be a bit of a dim bulb—hell, okay, no 'maybe' about it—but he's got this sense of how you're supposed to play the game, and that's what got him through all the crap during the campaign. And now he wants to be this . . . *healing* figure, and he sees himself in the cartoons as a puppet on Dixon Mason's hand, and he hears the snickers. . . . He even feels bad about Dorothy Ledger—hates the fact that this 'decent gal,' he calls her, this 'decent gal' stood up and said he shouldn't be President. I think he minded her more than all the wise guys on the tube. What ever did happen to her, Al?"

"Beats me," he said, hoping that she and Leonard Griese were enjoying their two weeks in the Caribbean he'd squeezed out of his budget.

"Your Ted Block's not completely dumb, you know," Al said, smiling at her. "Dorothy really is a remarkable woman. To stand up to all of that garbage the way she did, the press banging, the spooks—"

"Spooks?" Sharon said sharply. "What spooks?"

Ah, shit.

"Forget it, forget it, I guess you're not the only one who had too much wine."

Sharon grinned wickedly.

"Not a chance, asshole. You're not leaving this table 'til I get the full story."

"Okay, okay, if I don't tell you, you'll just get the IRS after me once you take over." Al briefly explained about the abortive visit Dorothy had received from the two gentlemen callers. When he'd finished, Sharon looked at him for a long moment.

"Let me get this straight. You got those guys off her back—and you didn't go with the story? What the hell kind of journalist are you?"

"What was I supposed to do?" DeRossa said with a touch of exasperation. "After everything Dorothy had been through, was I supposed to put her through another circle of hell? Forget it."

Sharon reached out and touched his face.

"No, Al, I don't want to forget it. I want to remember that not every man I meet is a first-class putz." She pulled him to his feet. "C'mon," she said.

"What are we doing?"

"I'm glad you asked," she said. "You're going to call your office; tell 'em you've got a sudden case of the flu. Then we're going back to my place, turn off the telephones, and tend to some unfinished business we started in a hotel room in Manchester, New Hampshire. Say no and I'll leak that story of the scoop you buried all over town."

DeRossa threw a bill on the table and hurried after her.

"All right, Sharon," he said with exaggerated grimness. "But when I get you home, you're going to pay for this."

"I certainly hope so," she said.

DeRossa shook himself into a vague approximation of consciousness, looked out over the Washington night, and rolled over, nestling into a very fit, very warm body.

"Mmmmfff," Sharon Kramer said. "To think we waited eight years."

"I know, I know. I'm sorry if I got a little carried away there. . . ."

"Please," Sharon said. "When I think of all the guys I went out with who begged off a cozy nightcap because they had to run home and catch *Nightline* . . . besides, Al, I'm a conservative. We approve of politically incorrect sex; bite marks and all."

"Maybe we could make a deal," Al said. "You tell me what stories you don't want us to run, in return for—"

She swatted him on the head with a pillow.

"It was really nice, Al. Really nice. Even if I wasn't carrying the weight of the world . . . and you know what the worst part is?"

"Sure—in less than a month. Ted Block's going to be the President of the United States."

"No, the worst part is that the one thing he's feeling good about is that he *thinks* he's coming in with a free hand; he *thinks* that he and Phelps and the Reverend Mason will form a triumvirate of national reconciliation. I tell you, it is positively Lincolnesque."

DeRossa burst out laughing.

"You haven't lost all your instincts, I'll give you that. Even with nothing but a sweaty sheet wrapped around you, you still haven't forgotten how to spin."

"I don't mean *that* part of Lincoln. I'm talking about what happened when he sent his supporters to the Republican Convention in 1860. The last thing he said was: 'Make no deals!' And they all said, 'Right, Abe!' 'You bet, Abe!' And they went off and cut every deal they could make to make sure he got the nomination. Of course," she added, "we have to remember that his biggest supporter was a newspaperman."

Sharon took Al's hand and kissed it.

"I really do thank you for being here," she said, and DeRossa saw the faint gleam of mist in her eyes. "I don't just mean here"—she pointed to the bed—"it's just very, very hard to keep this all in: knowing that after all of this, we're winding up with a not very good man—actually, he probably *is* a good man, but not for this job, God knows. . . . The only thing I keep thinking of is that at least we got it settled. If this election had gone into the House, I don't know what would have happened. Petitcon was right, it would have—"

"What?"

"What 'what'? Ouch, Al, you're hurting my hand."

DeRossa lessened his grip, but didn't let go.

"What do you mean, 'Petitcon was right'? What does *he* have to do with all this?" Sharon looked at him with alarm.

"Forget it, Al, please just forget it. It's the wine, and the sex, and . . ."

"Not a chance, friend. I leveled with you back there at the table. Now you level with me. Just . . . *level* with me."

Sharon talked without stopping for ten minutes. When she'd finished, sitting up on the bed, shaking her head, DeRossa jumped up and began pulling on his clothes.

"And Block doesn't have a clue, does he?"

Sharon shook her head.

"What do you think would happen if he found out?"

"He can't, Al. He just can't." Then Sharon looked at him for a long moment.

"Unless . . ."

DeRossa nodded, gave Sharon a long, lingering kiss, and hustled out of the room. He hoped the sunspot season was over; they could play hell with phone connections to the Caribbean.

FORTY-FIVE

★ ★ ★

From the rear porch of Theodore Block's home in the hills of Litchfield County, the lawn sloped past the slate gray terraced slabs of the shrub-bordered pool, still decorated now with the Christmas lights that were strung, as they had been for a hundred Christmases past, on the trees and shrubs of the grounds near the main house, over to the fifty acres of woods that sloped gently down to a broad valley of pines and evergreens. At the bottom of the valley was a wide lake, its still surface broken only by the glide of a lone sailboat. From the far shore, the land rose up again to a small mountain range. A screened-in gazebo sat midway between the pool and the tennis courts; inside the structure, six Adirondack chairs circled a wrought-iron table. The porch itself had a stone-and-marble floor and walls color-coordinated with the pool patio. The wall-mounted lamps were of highly polished brass; groups of chairs, love seats, and couches were placed evenly along the porch's 110-foot length. The cluster of half a dozen men stood around the built-in wet bar, craning their necks to take in everything.

"It's what God would have done, if He'd had the money," Alan Veigle said. "I know, I know, Alexander Woollcott said it sixty years ago, but I couldn't help myself."

"Mighty fine place," the Speaker of the House said, for perhaps the twentieth time since they'd arrived a half hour ago. "Mighty fine place." He shook his head. "Hate to see what the Secret Service's gonna do with it."

"They've already started," Connor Doyle said, pointing to the gazebo. "Take a look."

Outside the gazebo, six men in dark suits and white shirts were unloading corrugated steel cases from a golfcart; thick black cables snaked from the gazebo across the lawn to a dark van studded with antennae and with a small satellite dish on the roof. Down by the pool, two more figures in dark suits and white shirts were leading a huge German shepherd slowly around the perimeter of the terrace. Every so often, they stopped to mutter a few words into their wrists.

Their presence was the one tangible sign of Theodore Pinckney Block's impending presidency. They had been waiting earlier that day, when the Marine I helicopter had come to rest on the temporary helipad installed on a flat stretch of land on Block's family estate. They had been at the two separate checkpoints between the pad and the stone fence that surrounded the Block manor house. ("You know," Alan Veigle had said as they drove up the quarter-mile gravel road to the house, "we never did find out where the President stands on land reform.") Now they were grouped in clusters of two and three at either end of the porch, watching as the small group nibbled at the nuts and crudités and sipped at their drinks. They knew full well that the men they were watching comprised the top rank of President-elect Block's transition team, as well as the leadership of the United States Congress, thus substantially lessening the likelihood of a violent assault on the person of President-elect Block. But they watched, just the same.

"So," Connor Doyle said to Marsh, "where is the fair Ms. Kramer?"

"Can't say, really," Marsh said. The protracted struggle for the presidency had left him drained; even now, three days before the New Year, six days before the new Congress convened to formally declare Theodore Block President-elect, there was a vaguely haunted look to Marsh's visage. Only occasionally did the prospect of great vats of virtually unchecked power bring a bounce to his step, a sparkle to his eye. "I gather the President's tasked her with some regulatory reform stuff."

Alan Veigle barely suppressed a chuckle.

"Right—and she may be asked to help Sherwood with the vice presidency. You know what Ted—you know what the President said about 'a real first-mate on the bridge.' Anyway, she's been out of pocket for a while. Guess she went home for Christmas."

"I was hoping," the Speaker said, "that she—that *somebody*—was working on the Cabinet. I know it's been . . . well, 'strange' is hardly the word, but there *is* a government to put together. And the sooner the better, as far as I'm concerned."

"Couldn't agree more," the Senate majority leader said. "The last thing anybody wants—my side of the aisle just as much as yours—is any confirmation fight. You give us halfway decent nominees, you can have 'em as fast as we can make it happen."

"I'm sure the President appreciates that very much, sir," Marsh said, wondering how many colon spasms he would have to undergo when Senator Billy Doggs and some of the other Republicans got a load of the Reverend W. Dixon Mason's friends.

"So, Mr. Marsh," the Speaker said, "is that why we've been called up here on four hours' notice?"

"Well, Mr. Speaker," Marsh said with a smile, "I'm sure that's something the President would rather present on his own."

He damn well better, Marsh thought angrily. *'Cause I'm damned if I know. Putz calls me on three hours' notice in the middle of Christmas, tells me to get up to that goddamn estate up there in Connecticut, where everybody wears pants that look like they got caught in a sherbet factory explosion. Says it's "kinda vital." Won't give me anything else. Probably wants to talk about federal aid to homeless yachtsmen.*

A moment later, Ted Block came striding onto the porch, accompanied by a handsome, sweaty golden retriever and three wet, winded Secret Service agents. He had been out running, although only a thin sheen of sweat covered his lean chest and bright blue running shorts. Block shook hands all around, accepted a tall glass of iced tea from a retainer, and sat down in a wicker rocker, extending his long legs and reaching his right arm back to massage his neck.

"Good of you to come, fellas, sorry to bust into your holidays."

"Not a problem, Mr. President," the Speaker said. "There's lots of work to be done. But the first thing we want you to know is that you're going to have no problem about the vote count; Connor and I have been talking, and I've given him my word of honor that we're going to accept the votes the Democrats cast for you. Oh, some of my friends on the Left will challenge, but even that's going to be a rump faction. There's a general feeling that we've all been through enough already. And, uh, then there's uh . . ."

"What Topper's trying to say," Connor interjected, "is that the last thing the Speaker's liberal buddies want to do is to stand up on the floor of the Congress and argue that all these black folks were too damn dumb to know what they're doing, or that they all got together and agreed to break the law."

"I don't think I'd exactly—"

"Oh, come on, Topper," Connor said. "I'm just razzing you a little. Besides, I think everyone here understands what a nightmare we get into if those votes for Block are challenged; then we challenge all those Republican electors who voted for me, and I kind of like the idea of coming in third place for the presidency without even campaigning."

"Good," Ted Block said. "Then I think you're going to like my idea even better."

"Yes, Mr. President," the Senate majority leader said. "I was hoping we could talk a little bit about what you have in mind for your administration. You've heard all the talk about Sherwood stepping down, and maybe your appointing a Democrat as Vice President. I've even heard my name thrown around. I just want you to know that the Speaker and myself are ready to publicly back you right to your own Vice President. We need to show the world that the man we chose can actually govern. Now, the Cabinet, there's someplace where I think a few respected Democrats could be very helpful. . . ."

"That's not where I'm going with this," Block said. "Marsh, Alan, I'd like you two to leave the room, if you don't mind."

Marsh looked at Block as if he had just announced he was about to fly around the room.

"With all due respect, Mr. President, I think that would not be the wisest—"

"If you'll *excuse* us," Block said, in the tone of voice he would use to dismiss the upstairs maid from a family council, "you fellas can wait in the south study. Ed here'll show you the way."

One of the Secret Service agents stood waiting by the entrance, until Marsh and Alan Veigle slowly got up from their chairs and followed the agent down the hall.

"Christ, how many rooms has he got in this place?" Marsh said.

"I don't know, but if they ever want to remake *Citizen Kane* and set it in New England, I think I know where they can shoot the Xanadu scenes."

"Have I ever told you how much I *hate* this movie crap of yours?" Marsh said, as they trooped down to the south study.

After the two operatives had gone, the four congressional leaders sat, waiting anxiously for Block to speak. For a long moment, the President-elect sat and rocked, back and forth, back and forth.

"Mr. President?" Connor Doyle said after a while. "Are you okay?"

"Hmmn? Oh, yes, fine, fine. Gotta tell ya, though, I've been thinking . . ."

Block stopped speaking.

"Yes, Mr. President?" the Speaker said after an uncomfortable silence.

"Yup, been thinking . . . it's not good."

"What's not good, Mr. President?" Connor said patiently. *He's the next President, keep telling yourself that, he's the next President, he's going to have nuclear weapons, learn how this guy thinks and talks if you know what's good for you.*

"This . . . this . . . ," Block said, waving his hand in the air. He seemed to be suggesting dissatisfaction with the design of the house or perhaps the color of the walls. The Senate minority leader wondered for a dreadful moment whether Ted Block had had a silent stroke.

"It's not right," Block finally added. "I didn't earn this. Don't you see?" Block was leaning forward, elbows on the rocker arms, hands open and extended, almost beseeching. "It's not my turn."

"I'm afraid you've lost me, Mr. President," Connor Doyle said. "You won the vice presidency; Mack Foyle died; the National Committee picked you in his place; the electors voted for you; the Congress will confirm those votes next week. What more do you need?"

"That's bulldip," Block said. It was the strongest oath he had uttered since his undergraduate days. "The *country* doesn't think I should be President. I wouldn't even have the votes if it wasn't for . . ." He paused.

"If it wasn't for Dixon Mason and his allies?" the Senate minority leader said. "So what? They're entitled to vote; to be honest, it isn't the worst thing in the world for a Republican to come into the White House on the shoulders of black votes. I'd like somebody to tell me the last time that happened."

Block shook his head.

"That's not it," he said. He lowered his voice to a conspiratorial whisper.

"It was . . . a *setup*. You understand what I'm telling you? It was a *setup*. That Petitcon fellow . . . my campaign guys . . . it was a *setup*." Block was almost spitting out the words. "They played me for a sucker, only I'm not going to play."

"Ted," the Speaker said. "Let's cut the crap. What are you telling us?"

Block rocked back and forth.

"When you come back into session on Tuesday, I want you to let me speak to a joint session of Congress. I'm gonna tell them what I'm telling you right now: I'm not going to take the presidency."

"Oh, Christ, Mr. President, stop it, just stop it," Connor Doyle said. "This is insane, it's just insane."

"Hear me out, Connor," Block said. "I'm not asking you; I'm telling you. I'll tell 'em whatever you think best. I can either tell the truth—and that means talkin' about Jack Petitcon, and Dixon Mason, and all of . . . that. Or," he added with a smile, "I can tell them that my doctor found a heart problem, and that I refuse to put the country through another crisis."

"What heart problem?" the Speaker said. "You're a goddamn machine, you run five miles before anyone else has rolled over in bed."

"I know," Block said. "But that's the beauty of Dr. Morris Hirsch. He's a very well known specialist among some of my friends. Know what he specializes in? Well, you know how every once in a while, a banker or a broker finds himself in a legal fix? Maybe he mentioned a stock when he wasn't supposed to, maybe he gave a loan he shouldn't have, and took something in return he shouldn't have? Ever notice how often when these folks go to trial, there's a doctor telling the judge about a weak mitral valve, or an arterial wall that's ready to pop right inside the head?" He nodded to himself. "That's Dr. Hirsch."

"You're joking, aren't you, Mr. President?" said the Senate majority leader. "This is all a put-on, one of those pranks you guys play up at Yale or Princeton, right?"

"Couldn't be more serious," Block said. "The minute I get up to speak, the doc'll be distributing copies of my medical report. There isn't one doctor in a million who could possibly contradict him."

"Just so I understand this," Connor Doyle said. "You're going to save the country from some underhanded political deal by lying about a phony health problem—and you're going to leave us with Sherwood Phelps as President of the United States? I don't think that's much of a noble step for America."

"Course not," Block said. "Woody knows he can't be President under these circumstances. He's authorized me to announce he'll refuse the job."

"This will be a nightmare," the Speaker said. "The House will meet to count the votes for President; the Senate will meet to count the votes for Vice President; and none of it will mean a damn thing. After what we've all just been through, you might as well turn the whole damn country over to repo men. You're talking chaos, Ted."

Block shook his head with that same affable expression that had driven staff workers insane for years.

"No, it won't," Block said. "Because as soon as I finish speaking, the House will elect the Speaker." He pointed at Connor Doyle. "They'll elect you, Connor."

Doyle leapt to his feet.

"I'm calling a taxi back to Planet Earth. Mr. President—Ted—for God's sake, I'm a *Republican*. Remember? The *Democrats* control the House. Topper's the Speaker; and he's going to be the Speaker."

"No, wait a minute, wait a minute, Connor," Topper Huggins said. "I think I get what he's getting at. We vote for you for Speaker. When Block and Phelps step down, there's a double vacancy. On January twentieth, you become President; then the House votes again, and the Democrats take over again; with me as Speaker." Topper looked at Block. "Is that what you have in mind, Ted?"

"You got it, Topper."

"Boy, I don't know. My people aren't exactly crazy about Connor; he's been working us over with a flamethrower ever since he showed up."

"He's right, Ted," Connor nodded. "I do not show up well in the 'Mr. Congeniality' portion of the competition."

"Well, I just don't think there's any choice here," Block said flatly. "The Republicans won in November, so it has to be a Republican. I'm not going to take it, because the way I got these votes just wasn't right. If I'm out, so's Phelps. And that leaves you, and you, Mr. Leader," he said, pointing to the Senate minority leader. "And the way I read the Constitution—I really can read, contrary to some of our late-night geniuses—the line of succession runs through the House. And frankly, I think we've screwed around enough with the Constitution. We might as well try to get back to it as close as we can."

"You got any ideas for Vice President?" Connor asked wryly.

"Why, no, Connor," Block replied evenly. "I assume that'd be up to you. Soon as you get the job, you nominate a v.p., and the Twenty-fifth Amendment kicks in. I do have one suggestion, though; in fact, I'm gonna put it in my speech to the Congress. We got to fix this electoral college system. Let's get an amendment through fast: maybe pick the President by direct popular vote; at the least, get rid of the electors, make the votes automatic. Just make sure we never have to go through that again."

"It'll be a caretaker presidency," Connor Doyle said, half to himself. "There'll have to be a bunch of Democrats in the Cabinet."

"That's not so bad," said the Senate majority leader. "You might even get some decent stuff done in the next four years. Might make you tough to beat next time, though."

"No, God, no," said Connor. "I'll have to govern without a shred of a mandate. Well, hell," he added, "maybe that's fair enough, after all we've put the country through. You know, Ted," Doyle said to Block, "if the country could see you this way, I think they'd decide you might make a decent President yourself."

"Too late for that," Block said. "But thanks. And, Connor, there is a favor I want from you—actually, it'll be a favor for yourself as well."

"Which is?"

"Have your IRS run a full field audit on Jack Petitcon. I think you'll find enough there to keep your Justice Department busy for quite some time. You'll get points from the good-government types, and you'll save yourself a whole lot of headaches."

"Thanks, Ted. You hand me the White House, and now you want me to hit myself in the head with a hammer?"

"Connor, just think about it—think about it very hard."

Block eased up out of the rocking chair.

"I hope you'll excuse me now. Gotta get ready for New Year's. Old family tradition that we write a poem about what's happened to us this year. Mine's gonna be a little longer than the others, think. The boys will see you out; Connor, Mr. Speaker, leaders. Oh—do me a favor? Would one of you break the news to Marsh and Alan?"

Block walked quickly out of the porch, up the stairs, and into a small library off the hall, where Al DeRossa, Leonard Griese, Dorothy Ledger, and Sharon Kramer were waiting.

"How did it go, Mr. President?" Sharon asked.

"I think it went fine," Block said. "And if I were you, I'd get ready for some very tough days. Connor would be a fool not to bring you with him. I also want to thank—"

A bloodcurdling scream came from the south end of the house.

"What was that?" Dorothy asked.

"I think Marsh has just learned that his occupational prospects have been severely altered," Block said. "As I was saying, Sharon, I want to thank you and Mr. DeRossa here for the intelligence report. Geez, I can't believe I didn't have a clue."

Be nice, Sharon, be nice. He's trying to do the right thing.

"And, Professor Griese, I appreciate your flying up on such short notice to help me figure out how we might resolve this dilemma."

"My pleasure, Governor. I don't know how many other politicians would listen to a man who tried to help keep him from becoming President."

"As for you, Ms. Ledger, I can't say I appreciate everything you said about me—"

"I'm sorry if I hurt your feelings," she said simply.

Block smiled.

"That's what I admire, Ms. Ledger. Anyone else would have said they didn't mean it. Well, I know you meant it. I know what it cost you, too."

"Well, other than missing out on the thirty-year service pin, I can't say I'll miss the bank that much."

"Are you going to need some help?" Block asked solicitously. "I can't imagine that Sharon here can't find you something with the government, if that's what you need."

Jesus, Sharon thought. *Is this guy for real, or is he going to climb to the top of a tower someday with four Uzis and a thousand rounds of ammunition and start spraying everything in his path?*

"Thanks, Governor," Dorothy said, "but something tells me I've had enough contact with the government to last me a very long time. Besides"—she cast a conspiratorial smile at Leonard Griese—"I've got more options than you might think. And I've decided to do a book about what happened. The advance should tide me over okay."

Griese laughed out loud.

"Tide you *over?*" What would it take for you to earn that kind of money at the bank? Fifteen years?"

Theodore Block motioned DeRossa out of the room.

"Al, I don't know what your understanding is about the ground rules for covering all this . . ."

"Haven't figured it out myself, Governor."

All I know, DeRossa thought, *is that sometime between tomorrow and the end of my life, I've got a reasonably decent story to tell.*

"I know you'll do the right thing, Al," Block said.

And I hope to God he never learns about Dr. Morris Hirsch.

"I'll do my best, Governor." He reached over to shake hands with Dorothy and Professor Griese.

"I've got to be on my way now," DeRossa said. "You two take care of yourselves."

"Give me a lift, Al?" Sharon Kramer said.

"You got it."

As they left the grounds of Block's family estate, Sharon leaned over and nibbled at his ear.

"Wouldn't it be great to check into one of those country inns they have around here; with the huge feather beds?"

Al patted her knee.

"Right; you call me the first time Connor Doyle gives you the weekend off, and we'll do it."

"Great," Sharon said. They sat in silence for the next ten minutes, each wondering how long it would be before that long, lubricious New England weekend would get out of the fantasy stage.

"Where are we going?" Sharon asked as Al swung the car through a massive set of stone gates. "I thought we were headed back to New York so we could grab a shuttle home."

"We will," Al promised, "but there's a quick stop I have to make."

Al parked the car in a small gravel lot outside an imposing Tudor structure. It was uncommonly quiet; only an occasional worker trimming the hedges broke the stillness. A discreet plaque mounted outside the door identified the building as the home of Glenn Springs Residential Home.

"I'll just be a minute or two."

DeRossa entered the building, identified himself to the nurse behind the desk at the door, and was quickly escorted up the stairs to a sunlit corner room. In a chair facing the window, rocking slowly back and forth, sat Ken Crenshaw, producer of special events.

"Hello, Ken," DeRossa said softly, having been told not to make any sudden noises. "It's Al."

"Hi, Al," said Crenshaw, still staring out the window.

"How are you doing?"

"Okay, okay; doctor says I'll be out of here in a day or two, and I can head back to work on Monday."

"Fine, fine. Ken, I have to tell you something."

"Sure, Al. Sure."

"It's about what's going to happen next week, when you come back to work."

"Yes, Al, go ahead."

DeRossa turned Crenshaw's chair toward him and began to speak, very slowly, very softly. A nurse walking by peered in, and saw Crenshaw nodding again and again as DeRossa spoke, nodding over and over and over, as a trickle of tears ran down his cheeks.